SONG FOR AN APPROACHING STORM

PETER FRÖBERG IDLING

SONG FOR AN APPROACHING STORM

a fantasy

Translated from the Swedish by
Peter Graves

PUSHKIN PRESS
LONDON

Pushkin Press
71–75 Shelton Street, London WC2H 9JQ

Original text © Peter Fröberg Idling and Natur & Kultur, Stockholm 2012

English translation © Peter Graves 2014

Song for an Approaching Storm first published in Swedish
as *Sång till den storm som ska komma* in 2012

This translation first published by Pushkin Press in 2014
This edition first published in 2015

The cost of this translation was defrayed by a subsidy from
the Swedish Arts Council, gratefully acknowledged.

0 0 1

ISBN 978 1 782270 61 4

Set in Monotype Baskerville
by Tetragon, London

Printed and bound by CPI Group (UK) Ltd, Croydon CRO 4YY

www.pushkinpress.com

Later the real war was unleashed, to be conducted in secret by radio through the U.S. Embassy in Pnom Penh. South Vietnam was already a wasteland, deluged by high-explosives, poisons and fire. Mr. Kissinger had said that the dominoes were falling, so now it was the turn of Cambodia and Laos, delivered to the greatest holocaust ever to be visited on the East. It consumed not only the present, but the past; an obliteration of cultures and values as much as physical things. From the ashes that remained no phoenix would ever rise. Not enough survived even to recreate the memory of what the world had lost.

Norman Lewis, *A Dragon Apparent*

I. SAR

Now we are sitting here in our weightless waiting
With far too many wristwatches in a ticking little living room
[…]
—while silence lets its wasted croquet ball
roll against the wall

SVEN ALFONS
Rear-view Mirror Towards Dawn

MONDAY, 22 AUGUST 1955

You put the heavy matt-black bakelite handset back on its cradle. Your thoughts are already elsewhere, not at the other end of the wire.

TUESDAY, 23 AUGUST 1955

You're standing in front of a car. It's a black car and it belongs to you. You inherited it. You inherited it from a sister who got it from her lover. It's not a new car, but twenty years ago it was a car for kings and prime ministers and its chrome and paintwork are gleaming. The headlamps are two big yellow eyes high up on the curve of the mudguards. There are two inverted Vs on top of the slim flutings of the radiator grill. The steering wheel is white.

You're holding the car keys in your hand.

Presently you are going to get into the car and drive through the city, which has already been emptied by darkness. But stay a little while, stay for the few minutes of honey-coloured light that precede sunset.

The evening is close and still. You can if you wish take your wallet from your portfolio case and take out the photograph. Let her smile at you, her head inclined slightly to the left. The well-manicured fingertips of her left hand are lying against her collarbone. Her dark hair has been curled and let down so that it frames her pale smooth face. Looking out beneath eyebrows that are just a shade too thick, her eyes meet yours. She is laughing her bright laugh, lips closing in a smile over even teeth, eyes holding yours for a moment before moving on. Then she stretches her back and the shot silk of her blouse shifts from chalk white to greyish pink. The waiter pours more wine but she moves her hand over her half-full glass to forestall him. And finally you succeed in dragging your eyes away from her and, still with the hint of a smile, look down at the white china in front of you. You cut a piece of duck breast, draw it through the gravy and slice a potato. Then you see one of her hands gently grasp her wine glass and involuntarily you follow the curving movement the glass makes on its way back up to her mouth.

You're standing in front of a car. Go and sit in the car. Start the engine, listen to its even rhythm. Then engage first gear and begin the journey as planned. Don't take any detours apart from avoiding the district around Marché Abbatoir where the streets are muddy and potholed. Drive to the river smoothly, staying in the higher gears. The eye of the lighthouse will be drawing circles in the darkness of the bank where the Mekong and the Sap meet, and you will drive on along Quai Sisowath and Quai Norodom and Quai Lagrandière until you can park under the big trees outside the cathedral. You will have to wait there for a little while again, until the big silent shadow of a cyclo comes gliding up. After you've exchanged passwords, take a seat in the cyclo.

Take a seat in the cyclo.

He will take you somewhere quite different, somewhere far from starched linen napkins and dresses with high necks and gold embroidery.

Y

Y   Y

You are somewhere different. You are standing outside a simple house built on tall stilts. A glow in the windows suggests that there is a paraffin lamp alight inside. A pig can be heard grunting away in its pen. The dense banana palms are a darkness darker than the surrounding darkness. Behind you the cyclo departs after you have a momentary glimpse of its driver's face, as he lights a fat cigarette rolled from green tobacco leaves. An elderly man, whose face seems to you almost frightening in the fluttering flame.

Walk towards the house. Even though it may be a trap, walk towards the house with its steep steps. It could always be a trap. Push your hat back so you can look up without bending backwards. Tuck your handkerchief down into the breast pocket of your jacket so it won't offer a white target for a marksman to aim at.

You climb a steep concrete staircase. The night is full of all the animal sounds of night, but no other sounds. You're carrying a portfolio case in your hand and in the portfolio there's an elegant wallet and in the wallet is a photograph of a young woman who lies in your heart behind that white handkerchief.

You have climbed a steep staircase and now you are standing on a veranda. The heels of your shoes have left a mark for every step you took across the check pattern of ceramic tiles on the veranda. Place the palm of your hand on the polished wood of the door and stand there for a moment. Consider your choices yet again. What might happen now? Anything at all might happen, but just think what will happen if a security policeman opens the door. It will be a tall slim man with sinewy hands and a scar on his left forearm. Or, perhaps, a thickset man with a low centre of gravity and with short hair like pig's bristle on the back of his neck. Irrespective of what kind of man opens the door he will be the same sort of age as you, and he will be moving very quickly to catch hold of the sleeve of your jacket or to aim a kick at your crotch. There is also the possibility that he will strike the side of your head with a bamboo baton or will even be holding a loaded revolver in a two-handed grip.

You think about what will happen after that, about how the story develops, branching and splitting time after time. Some of the lines it takes always lead to the men listening being impressed by your unsentimental and pleasant smile. How, against all odds, they let themselves be convinced by your explanation of why you are at this very place at this very time with a portfolio crammed with compromising material. And then they let you go with a stern warning and a wink. Or, at a later stage, you are granted a meeting with the prison governor, who believes the righteous indignation you feel at being lumped together with communists and assassins when you are innocent.

But you know that this is just wishful thinking on the part of a mind under extreme tension, that the real story is the one in which the bamboo baton strikes the side of your head, in which you are confused by pain and tripped up before you can reach the staircase. The one in which the thickset man ties you in a chair with your hands behind your back and then without warning smashes your molars with a kick that knocks over both you and the chair. The one in which the bones in your fingers are broken one by one, even though you have betrayed your friends one by one.

You stand there with the palm of your hand against the wooden door and those behind the door are waiting for you.

Knock on the door.

Knock once, twice, three times and wait for the whisper from inside. Answer the whisper.

Y

Y   Y

You are sitting by a paraffin lamp. You are sitting in a room that loses itself in darkness beyond the circle of yellow light from the lamp. Two illuminated faces are suspended in front of you, one thin, the other

14

wide across the jaw. The table is covered with sheets of paper with French words and long lines in your own language. A mosquito net is hanging furled up over a low bed. Like you, your companions are dressed in short-sleeved shirts and dark trousers. Their jackets are hanging over the backs of the chairs.

You know the two men in front of you. You have known them for a long time. You met them at the discussion club at Vannsak's place in Paris. Together you have fantasized about the life you are now leading, you have discussed it in cafés, after lectures, over cheap meals at cheap restaurants. The face with the wide jaw is called Yan. The thin face is Sok. You used to meet regularly on rue Lacepède at what, with time, came to be called a party cell. That is what you are doing now, too, even though the name of the street outside is unknown to you.

You talk in low voices. If anyone were to be standing quietly beneath the window and listening, he would hear no more than a mumble. Your talk is concentrated, you exchange thoughtful glances and, with your fountain pens, scratch down words on sheets of paper the wet season has caused to swell.

The meeting is marked by the feeling that there is a great deal at stake and that there is no time to lose. You listen attentively to the others but always with an ear open for noises that are not the normal noises of the night—dogs that begin to bark and the direction the barks are coming from, a car door closing, a shout of command, the pounding of running feet on the stairs.

The day's agenda lies in front of you. It was written in haste and there are many items—they form a blue-ink column that slopes inwards towards the centre of the page. There is less than three weeks left to the parliamentary election and even though you are not letting on about it, you have a feeling that the ground is shifting. That things are moving, moving almost imperceptibly, but moving in the wrong direction. But on an evening like this, with Yan and Sok on the other side of the table, it is not the right thing to say. Perhaps they too can sense the inexorable slide, but the three of you are here to plan for something different. You are here to plan for victory. It is a night to be serious and to be enthusiastic.

There are tall drinks glasses on the table. Five of them, in spite of the fact that there are only three of you. Anything to confuse uninvited guests. The glasses contain dark jasmine tea and it glows the colour of amber in the weak light. A small round coaster sits on top of each glass to prevent it filling with drowning insects.

You deal with point after point, passing documents to one another and drinking the lukewarm tea. Outside there is night, darkness and a blessed silence. Yan asks the American question. You have nothing new to say about it and you say so: in the current precarious situation Vannsak thinks you should leave it aside—and you agree with him.

Yan asks the Chinese question, and then the French one, before returning to the American question. But you stick to your view.

How to relate to the new imperialism, the new colonialist, can be addressed or not be addressed in the election campaign. The fact that the prince has signed a cooperation agreement with Washington is a weak point. It can be used. But your intuition tells you to steer clear of it. The prince has some hidden reason for the agreement. What it is, you don't know.

It is difficult to argue for something as personal as a feeling with men such as those sitting opposite you. So you remain silent behind your unwillingness to record the question on the order paper.

Yan and Sok look at you but you stay silent, and in the end Sok makes a note and says, let's proceed. Let's proceed, he says, and although you cannot decipher his writing there is no need to. You know that your silence will be reported back to the centre. But you count on them understanding. It is not your job to push through the policies of the Organization. You are to be pragmatic. From your prominent but hidden position within the Democratic Party, your primary task is to keep Yan and Sok informed about that party's internal affairs. Only secondarily to influence policy. The former is risky, the second directly dangerous.

It is Sok's responsibility to report those who fail to subordinate themselves to collective decisions. With his illegible writing he is putting his loyalty to the Organization above his friendship with you. The cause is more important than the individual. That is absolutely right and proper and you approve of his discipline and lack of sentimentality. It also means it is easier to read him. You recognize that Sok is a comrade the Organization can rely on, even if you can't rely on him.

You continue. Quicker now. The risk of discovery grows with every minute the three of you spend in the same room. The tension is infectious.

You give an account of the strategies of Vannsak and the Democrats. Vannsak seems to you to have boundless energy and you tell that to your companions. Each of them runs an index finger down all the entries in his diary, which you have copied. You all feel it's a pity he is no longer one of you. It is a long time since he—as a self-proclaimed proletarian—cut his ties with his well-off family.

There was a time when he was red. Now he is more like pink.

You mix dry cigarette smoke and tea and Yan reports the latest information about losses suffered by the People's Party, the part of the Organization that does not work in secret. There have been disappearances and hospitalizations. The authorities dismiss any violence aimed at you as *the settling of private grievances* and it does not even merit a mention in the newspapers. It is hardly a sophisticated tactic, but it's an effective one. Yan states that things are close to collapse.

You read the names on a list in Yan's handwriting but you cannot put a face to any of them. All of them are Meas's men. Meas himself has managed to evade both batons and handcuffs. Acting as the official leader of the People's Party as he does is a risky business. He is completely exposed to the state's machinery of violence. But if he survives the election he will probably become the next chairman of the Organization. That will correspond to his perception of his own importance. Meas is a man to be watched. And to learn from. You work in secret, he in the open. Which is the more effective strategy is something you will soon be able to demonstrate empirically.

Yan then gives a summary of the latest developments abroad. Your own country may be the target of your work but oppression is global, as is the struggle. In Paris you had friends from the whole French-speaking world, from countries you had not even known existed. The sense of being part of a worldwide context, of being one with a brotherhood that will force history to turn in a new and previously unforeseen direction, that sense is a constant source of comfort and inspiration. That is why you all carefully follow developments not just in the countries bordering your own but also in distant states. There are lessons to be learnt, for even if the preconditions are different, the resistance is the same. Yan reports on the French terror bombing that wiped out whole villages in Morocco, with hundreds of deaths. And you remember your Moroccan friends who joined the liberation movement. Yan tells of various attacks in Algeria, of French mobilization and of the mass arrests of Arabs in Paris. Of the disturbances in Tunisia. He moves on to the hard fighting in Gaza and you think of a Lebanese acquaintance, a friendly lanky fellow who was one of the founders of the Arab nationalist movement.

A really motley collection, but nevertheless inextricably involved in a common vision of the future.

Was that a noise or wasn't it?

Your eyes meet Yan's. They meet Sok's. Their faces remain utterly expressionless, only their eyes move. You all sit absolutely still and silence reigns outside. If there was a someone who revealed his presence a moment ago, that someone is now as motionless as the three of you. You and Yan quickly begin to gather up your papers. You lay one sheet carefully on top of another and place them silently in the portfolio case.

Sok raises his hand and you all freeze again. You wish you could stop the dull thumping of the pulse in your ear but, you think, a heart is not like a knee that can be bent at will.

You are sitting in a room with two revolutionary university teachers and a paraffin lamp that is burning with a steady flame. Outside there is silence and in that silence you imagine there are crouching men, their eyes gleaming in the moonlight as they approach.

There was a time when you would have felt ill. You would have felt your limbs paralysed by panic. But that was then. You get used to things, even to things like this. Now you feel heavy and solid and prepared. In the sense that you have accepted what may happen.

Yan gets up slowly, nods to you and to Sok. You see his face by the light of the paraffin lamp, the shape his mouth makes and then it all disappears. Nothing is left but sounds.

You hear his footsteps moving towards the door.

A grey panel opens in the blackness and his silhouette is outlined against it. The door closes on noiseless hinges and you wonder whether that is luck or a sign of careful preparation.

You sit in the darkness with Sok and listen to him breathing slowly on the other side of the table. The sweat makes the palms of your hands prickle and you wait for Yan to take a look around, and then come and knock gently on one of the stilts supporting the house. You are waiting for the two small dry knocks that will free you from this situation.

WEDNESDAY, 24 AUGUST 1955

Your black Citroën is parked round the corner, its lights off and its engine cooling. It is standing on a street that until quite recently was still called rue Van Vollenhoven. You can't remember what the street has been rechristened. They all have new names now. An independent country should have streets with independent names. But it does take a little time for people to change the habit of eighty years. So people apologize, say things like you know how it is, what's it called again, and then they smile and use the old name.

Your car is parked on what used to be rue Van Vollenhoven, right by the only newspaper stand on the street, Les nouvelletés françaises, and before going to sit in the open-air restaurant of the Hôtel International on rue Angkor, which has remained rue Angkor, you bought today's edition of *Cambodia*. The printing costs of the newspaper are paid with French money, and as a result of that it is a paper a schoolteacher with conservative values could well be seen reading.

If the scene is viewed from the other side of the street: an open-air restaurant in shadow. The hotel stands on a street corner and the sun has sunk down behind the frontage. The rays of the sun have moved on past the painted sign and the windows, which now look grey. They are now only shining on the dome up on the hotel roof and on the thin sharp spire. A waiter dressed in black and white has closed the parasols. Spread out among the tables are a young couple, two men on their own and a small group. The traffic at the crossroads is light and you are one of the men on his own.

Short-sleeved white shirt, dark trousers and an immaculate side parting.

You are sitting drinking a cup of coffee from the hotel's French coffee set, the moss-green one with gold rims. A cigarette is slowly burning to ash in the ashtray and you are reading a respectable conservative newspaper.

You are apparently reading a respectable conservative newspaper, but if anyone were to sit behind you, he or she would see that what you are actually leafing through is a different paper. A newspaper in a smaller format with worse print and with opinions of a substantially more radical kind. It is called *Solidarity* and your older brother is the editor. But no one can see it because the only thing behind the back of your chair is the ochre-coloured wall of the Hôtel International.

You are waiting for company to join you and while you wait you look over the top of the newspaper every so often and watch the people going through the crossing. The street is the busiest street in the city, with cafés and dirty shoeshine boys. It runs through the swarming centre of the Chinese quarter but ends at the square in the French Premier Quartier, surrounded by ponderous official buildings in the French style. The Post Office, the Banque de l'Indochine, the Hôtel Manolis, the police station, the Café de la Poste, the Restaurant La Tavèrne. In other words, a street *between two worlds*.

You let your gaze follow first one person, then another. People of Chinese origin are common in districts such as this. But there are even more foreigners here than other places. Various kinds of Westerner for the most part, but also bearded men in turbans.

And apart from them you can also see your own countrymen. They are like you, but you are not like them. There is a sort of tenderness in the way you think that thought.

You are one of the few people here who has seen the world beyond the horizon. Who has had the benefit of being educated at the world's leading seat of learning. You are not, however, referring to the lectures on wireless technology you missed at the Ecole Violet in Paris. No, the actual process of leaving your home country as one of the twenty-two scholarship holders of 1949 is—in your view—the most important examination anyone can take. You have lived at the heart of the empire and met people from its every corner. It was more than just a shared experience: you all shared the same longing for freedom and independence for your native countries. Together with young people from all over the world, you worked as a volunteer road-builder in Yugoslavia. You have seen what people can achieve if there is just one goal and everyone is working towards it.

Unlike your countrymen, you have seen things like that. You know the kind of things they can't know.

It is because of experiences of that sort that comrades such as Samouth and Van Ba have chosen you. The men who are the leaders of the movement that is going to liberate the people you can see in front of you; the men who are going to take them on beyond national independence; the men who are going to give them real justice.

You can admit it to yourself: you are a man with possibilities. Compared to your fellow-countrymen you have the qualifications to achieve something of real importance. Through Somaly, your fiancée, you have contacts at court and you know both the revolutionaries in the jungle and the politicians in the capital. You have a background few others can match, a position that no one can.

But though the future may well be yours, it has not arrived yet. That is something you learned during your months with the partisans. They thought you were more use to them emptying the latrines than as an ideologist. You resigned yourself to that fact. All work is of equal importance. Someone has to dig shit into the fields if soldiers are to have food on their plates.

When you went to join the partisan movement, you thought you would be able to say later that you took part in *the armed struggle*. You steer clear of that these days. That sort of claim could rebound on you if anyone in your circle happened to talk to the people who actually filled the latrine buckets.

But at least the march to the front turned out to be the short cut you had thought it might be. It has given you an advantage over better educated people who have been involved longer than you but who are still in Paris. They are undoubtedly superior to you when it comes to theory, but not any longer when it comes to practice.

You are drinking your coffee from a moss-green cup with a gold rim and you are waiting for someone to join you, someone who is arriving in a cyclo at this very moment. He is a man the same age as you, with a receding hairline and restless movements. His name is Vannsak and he pays the driver more than he is asked. As usual. His black tie-knot is crooked and you get up to shake hands with him, as has become the habit in the city among modern men like you.

Vannsak, who lived across the street from you in Paris. Vannsak, the poet, and now the politician too. He was the one you new arrivals could always turn to with questions and problems. You had nowhere to live. He fixed a flat for you. You didn't have any pots and pans. He lent you his. Your Paris years would have been quite different without him.

And you, too, would have been quite different. This man, who is now squeezing your right hand with his right hand and placing his bulging briefcase on the table with his left, is the man who took you to discussion clubs with him. It was in his living room that you met most of those who now make up the Organization. You have sometimes described your personal development as dependent on certain key figures, people able to open the doors that you yourself cannot. There have been several key figures of that kind, people you've had electrifying conversations with. Who have enabled you to see completely new connections when your thoughts were wearing thin.

There have been a number of them, like Mumm, Samouth and Meas. But none of them has been as important as Vannsak, for he was the first.

But that was then. Now you think he lacks the courage to remain a true visionary. You feel that his arguments have become more and more muddled, when you compare them with the spellbinding clarity they had when you first met. Instead of summoning all his strength in order to raise reality to the vision, he takes the easy way out and drags the vision down to reality.

But you are not sitting here at the Hôtel International outdoor café in order to confront Vannsak with his ideological compromises. There is another reason. Or, to be more precise, reasons, since your role is a double rather than a single one. And neither of those roles involves being his secretary, which is your actual official function. On the contrary, the two of you have equal status in the discussion. In a couple of weeks' time this independent country's first independent parliamentary election will take place, and both you and Vannsak have belonged to the Democrats for the last decade. Even as a teenager you used to distribute their flyers as part of the well-orchestrated make-believe democracy of the colonial period. From a political point of view things hadn't really been properly thought through, but then, in a political sense, you hadn't thought things through for yourself at that time. In those days, moreover, the item at the top of the party agenda was something as straightforward as *national liberation*.

Vannsak has manoeuvred his way into the party leadership since then. You have followed. Now the two of you meet on working days and holidays to discuss strategies, produce statements and formulate responses. Unlike your opponents the two of you stick to the issues. You don't accuse your adversaries of drunkenness and bigamy. You put forward concrete proposals for concrete improvements to real schools and real health care and real administration. You name names, you add up figures. You talk about what is achievable and what is not achievable. And it seems to work. Your audiences grow in number with every meeting—in spite of the fact that you avoid bandying insults or wooing the public in the crudest manner possible. The voters seem prepared to shoulder the responsibility which, as you are constantly telling them, is theirs and theirs alone.

Both of you don't tell them, however. It is Vannsak who shouts this mantra into the microphones. You stay at a proper distance from any platform. That's a necessary precondition of your other role. The role that considerably fewer people know about. What Vannsak and the others do not know is that you also carry a very different party card. Back in your modest house on the southern outskirts of the city. It's a little book with thin paper covers on which the words *Parti communiste français* are printed, and you have hidden it well. Consequently, Vannsak has no idea that the conversation you are about to begin once he's ordered his coffee will be reported back to the centre of the Organization. To people whose names even you don't know, whose faces could pass along the street in front of both of you without either of you reacting.

But what you do know is that somewhere in that dark centre your loyalty is being recorded, along with every small radical formulation you manage to place in Vannsak's speech. It is not a case of rewriting a whole party programme. But every slight shift can be of service to the Organization. If not now, then later. And that is why you must never be seen in the company of representatives of the People's Party.

There are presumably people who knew you in France and now wonder why you only associated with revolutionaries in Paris whereas here you have joined the Democrats. Why you seem to have completely changed your social circle. On the other hand, no one is more radical than when a student and you are now over thirty. And, of course, the man whose portfolio case you carry is your old mentor Vannsak, a man who had moved from red to pink.

So their thoughts remain just that—thoughts, not suspicions.

Outwardly you are a Democrat and nothing but a Democrat, the respectable secretary to one of the leading figures in the opposition party. Inwardly you are the Organization's indispensable link-man.

And then there is yet another role, one that no one but you knows that you are playing. It is confusingly like your first role.

It involves a twenty-three-year-old woman whose photograph you have in your wallet. A woman whose significance you deny to the Organization. Like a man devoted to the cause, you sometimes think. Like the disciple Peter, you think rather more often. Because the door the Organization believes you have closed is still wide open.

If events take their proper course Vannsak and the Democrats are going to win the election. The two of you have definitely not discussed what will happen after that. But the work you are currently doing at his side is hardly going to come to an end once the voting papers have been counted. You can't really hope to be a minister, but permanent secretary is a possibility. Your organizational talents are respected, as is your ability to win the trust of the humble as well as of the elevated. That portfolio case on the table may already contain a draft proposal whereby you are entrusted with a coordinating function in a future government.

A well-paid and well-respected office of that kind is what your fiancée Somaly expects you to get. Her family even more so. You do, of course, come from a good background back in your home district, but oxen and day-labourers are hardly a match for the royal blood that—slightly diluted—runs through the veins of your beloved.

In other words: no state office, no wedding.

You remember that remarkably cool day, the year the rains stopped earlier than anyone could remember, when you stood at the edge of the royal pavilion while the rowing races were taking place down on the brown river. An island of calm in the chaotic sea of people gathered to celebrate the festival. You remember how you saw her among all the other reserved and haughty figures who were slowly circulating in the shade of the gilded roof. In terms of external appearance—dress, hair, jewellery—she blended in with the other young women who had reached an age when they could be introduced into society. But unlike all of the others, who seemed so anxious to please that all their individuality was masked by a kind of blank and nervous smile, she stood out as being consciously unapproachable. As if there were a kind of darkness around her, in contrast to all the gold and the glitter that characterized the context. You yourself had felt uncomfortable in your white court dress, having been invited there by your sister, who was still welcome in the pavilion even though the old king had been dead for a decade.

You remember the way your eyes, with a will of their own, returned time after time to that sulky-looking girl, who could not have been more than sixteen or seventeen years old. You remember how, to your surprise, you saw an acquaintance of yours conversing with her as if they were old friends. How, even though you didn't really know each other well enough for such confidences, you eventually asked him in a quiet voice: Who is she?

And how he had sighed and answered: Not you too.

You had become flustered and asked what he meant.

All the men ask that, he explained.

Then he said: She is called Somaly, the daughter of Princess Rasmi. And no, she is not promised in marriage. Her father, however, is a reprobate.

You remember what a put-down it felt to be nothing more than one of *all the men*. No better nor different from all the rest of them. You against all of them—the competition seemed hopeless.

Later, however, she was to become yours.

And the future for the two of you will be decided by a free general election in which only a handful of those with the right to vote know that there is anything at stake for you and her apart from the distribution of seats in the National Assembly.

You are sitting with your back to the wall of the Hôtel International watching Vannsak put sugar into his coffee. The two of you have still not said more than a few words of greeting. It's as if you have so many important things to discuss that you no longer waste words on idle chat.

Everything seemed so simple during your last year in Paris and your first months back at home. You were completely taken up with the worldwide movement you were part of. You loved the conversations at the discussion club which, after a while, became secret meetings in even more secret cells. With the utmost secrecy you became a member of the French Communist Party.

And then you returned home as a man with a mission. The countryside was totally dominated by liberation movements that were slowly starving the towns of necessities. It seemed to you that the revolution was on the point of happening.

But the conflict did not break out. The colonial power simply packed its bags and left. One by one the posh villas in the Premier Quartier emptied. Their defeat in Vietnam turned out to be a victory for your country too. That meant that the freedom struggle came to a rather inglorious conclusion and the result was that the touchpaper that could have ignited the revolution was snuffed out.

There is no doubt that the unjust system still exists, but the possibility of overthrowing it by violent means has become no more than a hypothetical proposition.

Which is why—without the Organization knowing—you have introduced new factors into your calculation. Might it not be possible to achieve change by parliamentary means? It is not for nothing that the countries around the Mekong River were the diamonds in the French colonial crown. There are resources here that many other undeveloped countries cannot even dream of. It ought to be possible to build a new Uruguay here, surely? By means of a very, very slow revolution, one cloaked in reforms? Because you are well aware of the fact that however unjust the distribution of welfare may be, a number of the important preconditions of revolution are absent. For example: (1) a politically conscious proletariat. Or: (2) serfdom among the agricultural workers. It was possible to mobilize the poor peasant proprietors for national liberation, but they are unwilling to take up arms to solve more complex problems.

The road to revolution seems to be a long and winding one. It may be easier to achieve your aims by democratic means. So which to choose?

Indeed, which to choose? If only it was just a question of politics. But it isn't. Your fiancée Somaly, whom you almost forgot during your endless discussions with Mumm in Paris or when you were listening to Samouth explain Hegel's dialectic in the partisan camp, is ever present in your thoughts these days.

That is not the way it was meant to be. When you went to meet her for the first time after four years apart, you intended to break off your engagement. Falling in love is no more than a sentimental and egotistical weakness, something one can free oneself from through dedication and practice. And that is what you had done. How could you ever hope to dedicate your life to the struggle if you had a spoilt bourgeois woman at your side?

With Parisian self-confidence and unimpeachable ideological rectitude, you were going to put an end to what you had promised the Organization to put an end to.

But just the way she entered the room, just the way she walked over to you from the door. Everything that had attracted you so strongly when you first saw her at the rowing races had deepened and matured into something even more beautiful. It drove every rational intention out of your mind. And that was before—without any sign of shyness—she took your hands in hers and said your name.

But it is you after all. You really did come back.

Being in love is one thing, but this is something quite different. Something that lies beyond your control. It's as if everything else shrinks into insignificance when the two of you are in the same place. You don't turn up for work and you arrive late at important meetings.

You really did come back.

In the beginning you hated yourself for acquiescing so easily. It was months before you made peace with yourself. Even then it was only on conditions that were dictated by her mere existence.

You are sitting in an open-air restaurant on rue Angkor and you know you have to come to a decision. It is not a matter of both, it is either/or. But your usual decisiveness is not sufficient in this case. And your three-sided game is becoming more and more complicated all the time.

Even though her absence torments you, the situation is simpler when she doesn't get in touch. Two days have passed since you heard from her and you have already managed to get a good deal more done.

There is nothing unusual about her silence. You have learnt that her unpredictable behaviour is quite predictable. One week she is present at every event, filling the days with her ideas and her apparently unstoppable creativity. She writes, draws and deluges the tailor with new sketches and suggestions. She is always on the way somewhere, always with at least one girlfriend on each side. And the following week, or even two, she stays at home. And then you seldom hear from her. But you have got used to it. You bide your time and devote it to other things.

If these empty days stretch out and become three or four, a couple of pretty words in a letter, or the odd, small, well-chosen present left at her gate are quite sufficient. In return you may receive a slip of paper with a lipstick imprint on which the words *je t'aime* have been written in tiny letters between the lips. You have saved all of them and keep them in an envelope in one of the drawers of your desk. Under your party membership book, the one with the paper covers.

It is only two days since she last telephoned and there is no need to do anything yet. Her silence is open to many explanations. So you can concentrate on what Vannsak is saying to you.

Being seen out among ordinary voters like this is part of the strategy the two of you have adopted. You show yourselves in places where your opponents do not. Word spreads across the country. You are young, well-educated, privileged people, but you have renounced your privileges in order to be with the people.

It is not completely true, but the two of you understand the value of setting a good example.

In your view, the people who walk behind the plough and the oxen, the people who tap the sap from rubber trees, the people who empty their nets in the light of dawn, are not fit to govern a country. Not yet, anyway. The colonial power intentionally saw to it that the majority remained in ignorance. Only a few were picked out and enabled to become obedient public servants in the lower levels of the machinery of state. The population numbers many millions and the country has no more than perhaps a hundred schools. It is going to take years to educate the electorate to understand the principles of democracy.

So the two of you are very conscious of your responsibility. You are the advance guard sent to mould the people. Your task is to take the lead and draw up plans for the new society that the next generation will build. If you desert the cause there are no others to take your places. In which case new foreign rulers are waiting in the wings. The Vietnamese. The Thais. The Americans. The British. Perhaps even the French again. One as bad as the other.

Which is why you order more coffee and take out your fountain pens and clean sheets of paper. Folders of documents pass from one briefcase to the other. The sun has sunk even lower and the waiters are lighting the lamps. High above the lamps the glow of the stars is beginning to show in the night sky. Inappropriate things have been written in *La Liberté*. There was a speech in which someone accused you of taking bribes. And some election workers have been roughed up.

The two of you set to work.

THURSDAY, 25 AUGUST 1955

In front of you lie the dark, heavy swirling waters of the river and the eye of the lighthouse. Not the river you grew up by, but a different one.

And behind you the city, with all its cars, its restaurants and its gleaming palace. But also with its darkness. You have taught yourself to see it. Not just to focus—as you used to—on the patches of light, but instead to calculate how much room for manoeuvre exists between those patches. And it is considerable.

Turn around and look at the people strolling along the quay. Elegant young couples arm in arm, in frocks, jackets slung over shoulders. Families, whose carefully combed and plaited children chase one another. Street vendors selling lotus seeds, roast fowl and candyfloss. Fortune tellers with their cards spread out. Bowed widows, hair clipped short, in black skirts and white blouses, rattling the small change in their begging bowls. A thin balloon seller walks past, a colourful cloud of balloons above his head. The glow of cigarettes shows up more as the colour fades quickly from the sky.

Your own countrymen in among delicate-limbed Vietnamese, round Chinese faces and Europeans with noses like the beaks of birds.

Clouds of insects swarm around the heavy lamp standards along the quay.

Electricity is the master here, and Saigon—that huge city—is a boat-trip downstream, after which comes the wide world. But the greater part of your city still relies on paraffin lamps and cooks its food over open fires. It is only the stone buildings here in the Quatrième Quartier that gleam with light.

But one day, or night rather, you think, all the towns and villages in the country will be lit up. One by one by one. The question then will be whether your need for the protective cover of darkness will be greater or smaller than it is now.

You recognize some of your pupils and they recognize you and put their hands together in greeting. In the evening light and freed from school uniform they look older.

Take the packet of Cigarettes du Globe from your breast pocket and allow yourself a cigarette. Let the moisture-laden river air mix with the harsh tobacco smoke. There is no wind and the smoke rises at right angles to the white paper.

High above the heads of the crowds the silhouette of the Wat Ounalom is slowly fading into the night sky. It is a long time since, barefoot and cloaked in orange, you passed in and out through the wheel of life of its iron gates.

Yet another home you have left behind.

Now there are new boys chanting the verses written in miniature script on palm-leaf paper, new boys cleaning the older monks' quarters. You still remember the words, and where the brooms are kept. The same rituals, the same discipline. But you know your history and you know there was another age, an age of temperamental Hindu gods. And another age even before that. The spirits, though, are constant throughout the centuries. They inhabited the trees and watercourses of your country even before the arrival of the gods.

The palace stands just beyond the pagoda. Religion and monarchy so close that the prince and the abbot could wave to one another from their bedroom windows.

You think: soft oppression and hard oppression respectively.

The prince's security police and the abbot's upholding of a regime in which individual freedom can be ignored. A human life always depends on lives that were lived in past times.

Poverty is the well-deserved punishment of the poor; the list of entries in a bank-book is the well-deserved reward of the rich.

Marx is wrong about this, you think. Religion is not the opium of your people. It does not offer the solace of eternal paradise after a life of poverty as Christianity does. There are no angelic wings deluding them into believing in a flight up and out of penury.

Instead, the words of the abbot are shackles that fetter thought and guarantee that the social order will remain as static as it is unjust. Any attempt to exchange one's lot for a better one is an attempt to effect a minute shift in the order of the cosmos. It is hardly any wonder that people resign themselves to their fate, however unjustly they are treated.

It has taken time for you to recognize this. Religion has many advantages. But you have let yourself to be convinced that the advantages are not so tightly tied to faith that they cannot be achieved in other ways. You kept your objections to yourself when you were first introduced to the discussion club through La Maison de l'Indochine in Paris. The others followed lines of reasoning that were absent from your own thinking. The way they drew apt and appropriate support from philosophers you only knew by name. If that.

But there are nevertheless aspects of the existence of barefoot monks that can serve as examples even in the radical political struggle. In this respect, you think, your people have an advantage over many other nations. The monks live in the very simplest of circumstances.

They play no part in the spiralling and stupefying cycle of material consumption. They submit to a higher goal and they strive indefatigably to attain it. It is a way of life that can be learnt from. Devotion worthy of admiration. It is, moreover, an experience which the majority of your countrymen share, so the groundwork is already in place. That will be important when the day comes—as it surely will—when people will have to accept suffering and privation in order to make the reform of society possible. The day when resources and opportunities will be redistributed: from each according to his ability, to each according to his needs.

You learnt the importance of discipline during your time with Prince Chantharangsy, if not before. His forces could have played a decisive role in your country's fight for freedom, and you went straight to them once the boat from Marseilles had docked in the harbour you can see below you now. But when you were with them you realized that the revolution was not going to be their work. Chantharangsy made a great commotion, demanding first one thing and then another, while he himself lived comfortably in Chbar Morn with his concubines. The preconditions were certainly present, but not the ability.

Consequently, his soldiers refused to sacrifice their lives when they went on the offensive. Instead, they killed civilians, burnt houses indiscriminately and thus brought the wrath of the poor peasants down upon their own heads. The same poor peasants who had silently supported them and voluntarily joined their ranks. You did not stay in that company for long before moving on to the more revolutionary partisan phalanx.

Humility and a preparedness to make sacrifices, along with the importance of setting a good example. Those were some of the experiences you made a note of and later reported to the Organization.

The monks, of course, even have a wheel as their central symbol. You could not avoid noticing the connection when you first encountered

35

Marx's wheel. But the similarity is one of form alone. The wheel of history is rolling towards a more just future. If anyone sticks a foot in to try to stop it, his leg will be snapped off. The wheel of life, on the other hand, merely stands and spins on the same unjust spot through the decades and the centuries and the millennia.

Y

Y   Y

You are sitting at your desk and in front of you there are piles of pupils' work waiting to be marked, party reports to read and secret documents for the Organization to prepare.

The paraffin lamp is smelling of smoke because you bought the fuel from a stall on the street. A sooty smell for you and money for the poor woman instead of for the multinational petroleum companies, you think—she was sitting there among her bottles of petrol and paraffin, her eyes glazed by the fumes. In this respect, however, as in many others, you are less than consistent. The petrol that drives your car, for instance, was bought from the pump on Avenue de Verdun.

It is a good evening. You are working in a disciplined way. One thing at a time. You mark mistakes and write figures with your red pen, write cramped lines that are difficult to read with your blue pen. The piles of paper shrink and grow. In the darkness outside the noodle seller can be heard drumming his usual low call-sign with a chopstick on half a coconut. Wood against wood in a lonely and intricate rhythm that slowly comes nearer, reaches a climax and then fades away. But you do not rush out and stop him; you pour more tea into your glass instead.

There is simplicity in this. An escape into a purely mechanical activity. You can put your other concerns aside and work on indefatigably into the silence of the night.

FRIDAY, 26 AUGUST 1955

You are sitting in a dark and empty classroom preparing a lesson on classics of French literature. Strips of light filter through the closed shutters, and a little while ago you saw him. You think of the truth of what your grandmother used to say, that people should be careful what they say. That talk can bring trouble down on your head.

A short time ago you had a quick lunch. Another overcrowded open-air restaurant. Vannsak was sitting beside you, his shirt collar unbuttoned, his tie loose. You watched how he carried on talking without a pause, not even pausing when he shovelled noodles into his mouth.

The conversation between you was a serious one. Not many smiles. You tell him what you were told when you rang party headquarters during the morning. That another two candidates had been reported missing. A thirty-four-year-old in Kompong Speu, a forty-three-year-old in Kompong Thom. You also told him that several more politicians from rural areas have turned up in the capital, hoping to take advantage of its relative safety. And Vannsak stated the obvious—that it is impossible to run a nationwide election campaign when all the candidates are campaigning in one and the same area.

The two of you ate your noodles, supped up the juice and discussed Sam Sary, the deputy prime minister. It looked as if there were no limitations being put on him any longer.

The government used to be satisfied with drowning out the loudspeakers at election meetings by using even bigger speakers. Then there came a stage when they used megaphones and yelling crowds. Recently, however, Sam Sary has taken to emptying the prisons of criminal elements, and that lot are not satisfied just to chant obscenities. Now there are these disappearances, which are becoming more and more common. Some candidates are found in work camps; some are

37

found face down in their own brain matter, hands tied behind their backs; some are not found at all.

The terror, which up to this point has been aimed at the Organization and the People's Party, has spread to include the Democrats. That is not surprising, perhaps, but you really did not expect it of the prince. Did not expect him to resort to the kind of thing that is quite alien to the European democracies he claims to admire.

The two of you discussed Sam Sary, the prince's favourite minister. The strange thing is that during his years in France he seems to have adopted the colonialists' view of his own people. He uses the same methods against his fellow-countrymen as the French are currently using against the freedom fighters in Morocco. Batons and brutality. But—you remind Vannsak—even when Sary was an examining magistrate he used to *interrogate* suspects to death with his own hands. Yes, Vannsak remembers your telling him, and he says he has since had it confirmed by others.

It was afterwards, when you had finished eating and gone your separate ways after arranging to meet later in the evening, that you saw him. You were taking your usual route. But your usual route was different this time because there was a gleaming black car parked on the rue du Palais in front of the yellow palace wall with its leaf-shaped battlements. And he and his driver and a young newspaper seller were standing between the car and the wall. You passed them, your eyes fixed on Sam Sary and his driver. He was wearing a suit as black as the car; the driver was in a driver's uniform, complete with epaulettes. The newspaper seller seemed to be crouched between them, smiling uncertainly. You watched this incomprehensible scene as long as you could, until the street curved and a wall blocked the view.

He was shorter than you had thought. Or perhaps his driver was unusually tall? But standing there on the pavement he exuded a kind of pondus, and you don't know whether it was natural to him or whether it came from the power he enjoys or whether you and your fear simply projected it onto him.

You are sitting in a dark classroom and in a short while you will be teaching a lesson on Rousseau's *Emile*. It's an important lesson. Not because *Emile* is one of your favourite books but because it is very well suited to the political discussion that will follow. The kind of political discussion that you as a teacher are not allowed to hold but which can easily be concealed behind the book.

Just now, however, you have turned your head towards the window and in your mind's eye you can see the gleaming black car and the three men in the far distance. You brush away a mosquito, imagine yourself pressing the accelerator to the floor and, when you are about ten metres from them, forcing your car up onto the pavement. The car lurches and bounces on its suspension and the three of them turn towards you, their faces horror-stricken. Then you continue south at high speed, mudguards buckled and the front of the car spattered with blood. Newspaper pages drift slowly to the ground in your wake.

Up to this point the fantasy has been a pleasant one. The fact that two innocent lives have been lost merely serves to underline your decisiveness, your preparedness to commit an unforgivable injustice in order to achieve a more just world, your readiness to relinquish your place in the community of the blameless for their sakes. But then, when you have to dispose of the car and explain why and provide yourself with a convincing alibi, things quickly become complicated. The fantasy loses all its attraction when the prince declares a state of emergency and Sam Sary is given a state funeral and Vannsak and the whole party leadership are executed by firing squad. So you rewind back to where you see the three of them by the palace wall and cut the bit about accelerating away south, engine roaring.

You are sitting at a desk made of dark heavy wood, the whole of its flat surface covered with your books and notes. There are twenty-five minutes to go before the classroom fills with thirteen-year-olds whom you, in turn, will fill with potentially subversive knowledge.

The photograph stands alongside the sheets of words written in pencil. The black and white one in its scalloped white frame. You angle her eyes towards you and think Tuesday, Wednesday, Thursday, and today is Friday.

You have devoted five years to the struggle. In Paris it was initially a matter of company, of filling lonely evenings with discussion clubs that turned out to be dynamic and entertaining. And the conversations and the pamphlets that passed round led you from clarity to clarity, from one insight to the next. How everything fits together, how there is a coherent answer to all the difficult questions with all their contradictions. The fact that history has a direction and that, as a consequence of that, every individual action is a significant part of forward development. And all these individual actions of yours soon began to take over from your studies. They led you to miss lectures and eventually there wasn't even time for the exams. You felt yourself being absorbed into the *body of the revolution*, and you enjoy being part of the fist that is going to smash the oppression of imperialism and capitalism, the worldwide realm of injustice.

And yet.

You are even afraid to put it into words to yourself, an irrational fear that it might *leak out*. That the secret might be revealed. But you really do want Vannsak to win the election. You want him to put you in a beautifully furnished office in the chancellery and give you an influential mandate. For not even a dreamer like you can imagine there is any other way to a life with Somaly. And since the two of you were reunited after your years in France, you know that you want to see the world through her eyes. You want to be embraced by her enthusiasm and you want to hear her calm breath beside you when you wake in the night.

A future of that kind would compel you to compromise with the lie, but, you think, there are revolutionaries much more committed than you who have climbed down from the barricades for similar reasons.

And anyway, the struggle can continue in many other ways.

You look at her black and white smile and think of the past year and all those times in Vannsak's living room, which is empty during the day and at your disposal. How the two of you talked about everything and, when you finished talking about everything, sat there silently—in a silence that seems to you to contain everything that hasn't yet been said. You with her hands between yours, struggling to overcome your desire to hurl her back on the sofa and unbutton all the buttons on whatever garment she is wearing—whether it was an import or one designed by her, it was equally frustrating.

But merely leaning over her and inhaling the scent from the neck of her dress has often been sufficient to induce a haze of intoxication light as a butterfly's wings.

You believe you have convinced the Organization that your continued engagement to Somaly provides sophisticated cover for your *purposeful infiltration* of the political establishment. Secretly, however, the situation is quite the reverse: the *infiltration* is what provides cover for the real ambitions of your heart.

In the past you never understood traitors. Never understood how they could sacrifice the struggle for petty egotistical reasons. But in that respect, too, you have now been forced to move from clarity to insight.

You put the photograph to one side and return to the dog-eared book with all the underlinings. Concentrate, you think, concentrate, concentrate: but it's more of a mantra than anything else.

Y

Y   Y

You have given up waiting for Vannsak and you are looking out over the sparse traffic on the Boulevard Norodom. The lights of the cars are yellow and red in the twilight and the cyclos haven't yet lighted their paraffin lamps. You are standing leaning against the wall that surrounds the school behind you. Vannsak's house stands on one corner of the block that is occupied by the ochre-coloured barrack-style buildings of the school. His house is yellow too, its window arches red and its shutters grey. You had arranged to meet each other on his veranda and you have been waiting in vain.

Not even Vannsak's French wife was there to open the door to your knock. But the door had not been broken down and through the window you could see that there were no papers, clothes and books scattered all over the floor. That calmed your concerns.

You have any number of things to be getting on with. Reports to write, statistics to be broken down, tactical thoughts to be thought. The meeting that has failed to occur has given you a gift of a couple of hours that you really don't have. Your sense of duty demands that you get into your black car and drive home to the piles of papers.

But you stay, your back resting against the school wall that is still holding the warmth of the sun, and you smoke yet another Cigarette du Globe.

The lights of Ciné Lux a couple of blocks away can be picked out between the dark tree-trunks along the boulevard. Your wristwatch tells you that it is a few minutes before six and the pale street lamps come on along the middle of the narrow boulevard.

You think of the cinema adverts in Parisian newspapers. They filled several pages and there seemed to be a film for every occasion, for every mood. You often chose a film without knowing where the cinema was. You would go down into the Métro with just an address and your well-worn map. The one that eventually split where the folds met. Whole districts disappeared into those holes.

You would walk along unfamiliar streets between unfamiliar buildings looking for a neon sign and a brightly lit entrance. You particularly recall the cold half of the year, remembering what it was like to let your body sink into the warmth of a new auditorium.

And you can remember the feeling of shoving your hand into your jacket pocket looking for matches or for a couple of centimes and feeling all the stiff little tickets from your visits to the cinema.

But you have to go further back in time to reach your most fantastic film experiences. They were preceded by the anticipation sparked by the arrival of a lorry driven by tall, pale, lightly dressed Frenchmen. Its wheels had wooden spokes and it carried a projector and screen on the back. They always arrived unannounced. Or perhaps it was just that you were too small to understand the rhythm of the visits.

Your older brothers and their friends helped to put up the screen and tension it. They ran errands for the Frenchmen. Then hundreds of you sat down under the stars and watched their films. You can remember the dull hum of the generator, the explosive bursts of laughter in unison, the insects crawling across the black and white movements of Charlot. You can remember watching the alien milieux through which he was being chased. Even the dogs looked different. Then you all walked home through the night, full of the film, whose twists and turns would be talked about for days afterwards.

You light a cigarette from the glowing butt of the one before and stroll across the boulevard. The spire of Wat Phnom can just be picked out far along the boulevard and you take the pavement on the other side.

There are cars and cyclos waiting outside Ciné Lux. People are silhouetted against the foyer and the performance will be starting in just a few minutes. Big hand-painted signs above the entrance

43

advertise *Les Affameurs*. There are pictures of threatening-looking men in cowboy hats. James Stewart. Rock Hudson. And a woman, beautiful in a Western way.

The soundtrack of the film comes booming out of loudspeakers facing the boulevard. Dialogue, the sound of horses' hooves, grand music.

You buy a ticket and for one quick moment you are back in Paris where you also used to go to the pictures on your own. It is several years since you last did so and the empty seat beside you is different now. It is no longer an empty space filled with freedom. Rather the opposite. Now it is the sort of emptiness that takes you by the arm and accompanies you into the darkened auditorium.

And you think how it might have been, how you and Somaly might have squeezed into a cyclo as you usually do. She would sit on your lap and you would feel her soft weight on your thighs. You would have discussed the film and she would have seen connections that neither you nor anyone else you know would have noticed. The two of you would be trundling through the night towards her mother's house, and you would have that fragile sense of happiness that comes from never knowing whether you will accidentally let slip something that will cause her high spirits to turn into irritation or a sullen silence. But that is precisely the reason why your feeling of being the *chosen one* is constantly being renewed.

You sit down to watch a film with James Stewart and Rock Hudson and Julia Adams.

Y

Y   Y

You have been watching a film with James Stewart and Rock Hudson and Julia Adams.

You think of James Stewart and the way he is betrayed by his greedy friends. The moment of pain on his face when he realizes their deceit. But what really makes an impression is that he does not allow himself to despair, he re-establishes his honour by taking revenge. Tight-lipped, purposeful. However confused and uncertain he may be, he still dares to trust that what he is doing is the right thing.

And you remember how, when he is with the wagon train, he says that his country has been destroyed by incomers. That the purity it had in the beginning has been lost.

JEREMY: *Good country, Glyn.*
GLYN: *Yeah, real good country.*
JEREMY: *Let's hope we can keep it this way. Missouri and Kansas was like this when we first saw 'em… good, clean. It was the men who came in to steal and kill that changed things. We mustn't let it happen here.*

Your feelings are still coloured by that film and you know that it affects your judgement. And you cannot avoid drawing a parallel between James Stewart's *Oregon* and your own country. Now just a fragment of what it once was. Under constant attack from all points of the compass. Everyone wants the fertile soil of the lowlands and the timber and precious stones of the mountains. You think about the way the prince's grandfather was forced to ask for help from the French to prevent his kingdom being swallowed by the Vietnamese and the Thais. And how the monarch in his time of need put his faith in the assurances of *the Europeans.*

In the film James Stewart saves his friend Arthur Kennedy from the gallows. His reward is yet another act of betrayal.

It is a good land, Glyn.

In the case of your own country almost a century of slavery followed, during which convoy after convoy of your natural resources disappeared down the Mekong River.

We mustn't let it happen here.

It has already happened here. And, you think, it must never be allowed to happen again.

Y

Y Y

The rain is lashing down in the night and you are sitting with your back against a discoloured wall covered with mould. The plaster is bulging and pocked. You have stopped thinking about the film with James Stewart and a couple other white Americans.

You have just finished the second bowl of long white noodles of the day. It's standing on a rickety folding table in front of you, the chopsticks lying neatly alongside it.

The neon light from the food stall reaches a metre or so out into the darkness. The torrential rain makes the street look as if the surface is coming to the boil. The light from the second noodle stall can scarcely be seen through the wall of water. Brown rapids are foaming along the deep gutters that line the pavements. The air is saturated with the fine mist formed by the rain beating down on roofs and streets.

You drink weak and watery tea, smoke your cigarettes and wait for the rain to ease off.

You remember the light sunny showers of your first summer months in Yugoslavia. The rainbows that arched over the mountains. The cool that those welcome showers brought to the heat of the day.

You were all working together to widen the old road. You did not just double its width, you quadrupled it. And the crumbling verge was buried deep beneath the smooth new carriageway.

Together you shovelled gravel while heavy yellow steamrollers rolled out the black tarmac that refused to set in the heat. It stayed hot enough to burn the soles of your feet far into the night.

The whole country resembled an enormous building site. New dams drove new hydro plants and the new electricity from them powered new factories. New locomotives pulled new carriages on new rails. You were working alongside Americans and Armenians, Bulgarians and Britons, Swedes and Slovaks. But also Albanians and Croats and Slovenes and Serbs and all the rest, whatever they were called, who had previously been fighting one another but were now united behind one leader and one vision. They had put religion and history behind them. Every project completed was proclaimed to be a step forward in the victorious struggle for national self-determination.

Is it possible to envisage a functioning federation between your country and its neighbours? A Federal People's Republic of Indochina? Would it be possible to create a structure that prevented one country dominating the others? Or would that be impossible given that one of the countries is three times the size of the other two together?

You remember how you used to sing the songs of your homelands to each other. And dance the dances of your homelands as the nights grew dark. You remember how the languages got mixed into something everyone could understand. You can remember scrubbing yourself in the dawn light—it is difficult to imagine now how cold water can be. Pumped straight from the mountains. You can remember your reluctance, which grew greater every morning. How you used to fill the palms of your hands with lather before beginning a shivering dance under the ice-cold jets.

Then you would all sit there, skin rough with gooseflesh, drinking sugary coffee until the sun warmed the mountainsides and your bodies, and then the machines would roar into life in clouds of diesel smoke.

Now you are sitting alone in an outdoor restaurant and the rain is pouring down in front of you with undiminished force.

You are attracted by the assembly of nations you were part of for a few summer weeks. But how could something like that be achieved here? Do you have to have a devastating war first in order to make it possible to unite different peoples? A horrifying but necessary baptism by fire to clear the ground totally?

And what do you do with people like the prince and Sam Sary? You find it difficult to imagine them anywhere other than in a prison cell. And it is doubtful whether even that would be secure enough.

It would take an exceptionally powerful unifying force, one capable of compelling people to unite behind it—even people who have their own ambitions and different agendas. Otherwise everything would disintegrate into ever more fragmented factions. Political consciousness, discipline and a better future within reach—that is what will be necessary to bring about something that resembles your Yugoslav summer.

And there was another journey. You think about it now. You went by train and it took several hours. There were four of you in the compartment and you recall that the journey felt like coming to some kind of decision. For the four of you, the journey marked a move from words to actions. The French autumn landscape outside the carriage window provided the backdrop.

None of you could afford to eat in the restaurant car, so you had taken your own food with you.

The train eventually stopped in Poitiers and with the help of a map and some enquiries you managed to find your way to the small house. Son Ngoc Than opened the door himself when you rang the bell. The legendary freedom fighter and former prime minister whom the prince had driven into exile. You assumed he was waiting for a new and more favourable situation to arise. The sort of situation you had come to offer.

You sat down in his living room, described the Organization you represented and suggested he should lead it. It was not large but its members were well educated and well organized and, above all, dedicated. You all offered to return to your homeland with him during the coming year and to form the nucleus of the struggle for independence. Many, very many, people would be prepared to fall in behind his name. Ideologically speaking, you stand quite close to him. That is the conclusion you have drawn from his articles and speeches.

He was smaller and slimmer and younger than you had imagined. None of you really succeeded in getting over your initial awkwardness, and he kept his thoughts to himself. When you had finished putting your case he remained silent. Then he shook his head and said that he did not believe in an armed struggle. The preconditions were not present.

He was interrupted by the telephone ringing and he went to answer it. He was away for some time and Mumm spent the wait in front of the well-filled bookcase. He ran his finger along the spines and found volumes by Marx as well as Lenin. When he took them off the shelf, however, the pages proved to be uncut.

By the time you were on the way back to the railway station you were already beginning to draw up new plans—ones that excluded your former hero.

And now, with his credit used up, he is occupying a shrinking base in the jungle, far away at the foot of the Cardamom Mountains. Sure enough, he did return. And, sure enough, he did take up the struggle, weapon in hand. But far too late and without the support of any of you. Having offered to ally himself unconditionally with the prince—without receiving as much as an answer—he is now a marginalized force.

A good example that will later serve as a useful lesson in the Organization's basic political education, you think. It shows what happens when someone doesn't know how to keep up with the way society is developing—which is in great leaps forward. And while conflict and struggle are undoubtedly necessary to move mankind forward, it is vital to choose the right time and the right terrain.

SATURDAY, 27 AUGUST 1955

You are lying in bed, the mosquito net a large transparent cube over and around you. You are lying on your back and through the open windows you can hear the splashing of innumerable drops of rain dripping from leaves, roofs and branches. You can hear the clatter from a neighbour's kitchen and there is the murmur of a radio.

The light in your room is still the grey light of dawn and the hands on the clock point to five.

Your house is a simple one. There is no ceiling and, lying on your back in bed, you stare up at roof tiles and spiders' webs. You will get up soon and set about the business of the day.

You lie there in your bed and count Tuesday and Wednesday. Thursday and Friday. And now it is Saturday.

Almost a week and not a word. You used to get restless after two days of silence. Then it became three. But every time you wait for Somaly's silences to end you become less concerned. The pattern repeats itself—she will suddenly get in contact, apologize and brush away the silent days with a joke. And when she does that, she teases a laugh out of you and you realize that all the things you have saved up to say just seem so petty.

It is a Saturday at the end of August and you will soon be getting up and setting off for the morning classes at the school. You are going to meet your brother in the evening, but at the moment you are counting the number of silent days and every time you count them your irritation grows. And your irritation itself irritates you. You ought to be able to rise above it. You ought to be able to focus on other more important and more constructive things. But you lie there in your bed stuck in a cycle of counting.

You wish things were simple and you could just go to her house and ask what is going on. But if she is withdrawing, as she is now, she is hardly likely to want to meet you. To make an uninvited visit would simply be to risk lengthening your waiting time. You have made that mistake many times before and you don't intend to make it again. So the only thing to do is to cultivate patience and devote your time to waiting—that occupation of the powerless.

You lie in your bed watching the light get lighter and you think that there must have been at least one occasion on the Tuesday or the Wednesday or the Thursday or the Friday when she could have found time to send you a card.

These are not new thoughts. You should be used to them. But these days in particular, in the run-up to the election, you need her presence more than ever, because now, in exchange for a life with her, you are prepared to sacrifice everything you believe in. Her unexplained absence is the last thing you need: at first you enjoyed the peace to get on with your work, but that has been replaced by a stubborn and nagging anxiety. What is she doing, you ask yourself angrily, that is so much more important than getting in touch?

Your sudden flare of anger is immediately replaced by shame. You know that she is not doing this to be unpleasant but because she cannot do otherwise. What you should do instead is count all the small slips of paper bearing the outline of her lips in various shades of red. The ones you have collected and keep in the drawer of your desk. The ones she has sent you over the years. There are considerably more of them than the days that have just passed.

You decide to think constructively during the minutes that remain before you throw back the sheet and step out onto the creaking floorboards.

You think that every day of waiting means one day less.

Good.

It is a Saturday at the end of August and the postman will do three rounds of your district in the course of the day. Three real possibilities.

Good.

Your various tasks will take you back and forth through the city many times, so—perhaps—luck will allow you to bump into her. Luck has been generous to the two of you in the past. And, after all, you are a man with luck on his side, you think.

Good.

Now you can get on with your day. It is a cool morning and the air is fresh after the rain in the night. And if a card with a lipstick kiss should arrive, you can suggest something for tomorrow. It will be a Sunday and you have few fixed tasks. Just the day for a trip to the hammocks by the lake at Tonlé Bati or for going to the pictures hand in hand.

Y

Y   Y

You are standing in front of a blackboard. You have a piece of white chalk in your hand. There is a moment of stillness.

You have just written out Hugo's "Demain dès l'aube" by heart, and behind your back you can hear the sound of pencils scratching away on notebooks. A chair makes a short, sharp scraping noise as one of your pupils changes position.

The light is falling into the room from the left, your gaze goes out through the light. As so often when you read poetry, the beauty of the poem has given you a sense of the great immensity of space beyond the world around you, of there being a greater context into which everything fits together in harmony.

It has also caused your early morning peevishness to fade. All you feel now is a quiet devotion to Somaly. That is how she is, you think. That is how you both are, you think.

The chalk feels smooth in your hand and you think that she needs someone like you. Someone who can indulge her whims and fancies. Someone who can see beyond her self-willed independence and is prepared to forgive her.

No other couple is like you. You make the most handsome couple in the city when you sweep into restaurants and dances. You have seen it in people's eyes, seen how their warm glances cling to the two of you, as you walk past on your way to the table at which her friends are sitting with glasses of champagne and smiling faces. Long ago your friends began to tease you by referring to her as the *beauty queen*. That has now gone from being a nickname to being a fact since her election as *Miss Cambodia*. And you with your gleaming car and your French manners make an almost perfect partner for her.

She needs someone like you, someone who can see beyond the surface and recognize the restless, truly kind and talented individual that lies behind the pleasing surface.

People meeting her for the first time may be tempted to believe that all her qualities are pleasing qualities. But you know her, and you know that the positive things are counterbalanced by what others might consider to be negative. You, however, are above that. It is her wilfulness and destructiveness and touchiness that creates the dizzying depths that lie concealed behind her attractive exterior. You know that her inner beauty—because of the imperfection that you believe very few men would tolerate—makes her even more beautiful. There is a darkness there that you, with your bright disposition, will be able to dissipate.

You can, perhaps, sense a kind of *stiffness* in her personality now compared with the receptive and wholly unresisting girl you left when you went to France. There are times when she looks at you with a distance in her eyes that you don't remember being there before. It was not there before, you know that for sure. But it is of little importance. Your role remains the same, to be the one who enables her good sides, her talent, to overcome the destructiveness that is constantly giving rise to new difficulties.

Even when you are arguing and she loses her self-control and tells you to go and never return, even then you think that what she is saying is *you must never give up on me*.

You do not know whether she was made for you but there is no doubt that you were made for her.

You catch yourself nodding gently at that last thought. And you realize that there is now complete silence behind you.

The words in chalk on the board in front of you come into focus again.

Take the first white sentence into your mouth and turn round.

You are lost in memories. The swollen rivers are flowing beneath you. Their brown waters meet here at the quay. The enormous mass of water in one of them has reversed the flow of the other, so that while the Mekong rolls on southwards, the Sap is now being pushed north. You watch the torrents of water tugging at the hulls of the boats, constantly pushing them off course.

Quai Sisowath lies behind you, the red-tiled roof of the Club Nautique to your right. But that is not where you really are. You are back among the swarms of people in Prey Nokor and you are walking up the gangway of SS *Jamaïque*, a vessel well past its prime, its French ensign hanging slack.

Then came those weeks when the thin line of the sea surrounded you on every side. You remember how strange it was to come home on the same ship four years later. Strange because it was just the same. Because the sea was the same and because, by degrees, your skin remembered the climate as you sailed south. Because everything was just the same, but time had passed through your body, and the friends of your outward voyage, bored but full of expectations, were not even present as ghosts on your homeward voyage. The future and the past were one and the same on the deck of that ship, just as the two rivers in front of you share their waters.

But the years in Paris lay between. The city in which you got lost and at the same time desired so passionately to learn.

At first you took the Métro wherever you were going. Straight lines, in clear colours, underground, easy to deal with compared to the confusion of crowded streets. And you can remember the sense of surprise you felt when making your way down into the Mabillon Métro station to go to Odéon where the Americans and Scandinavians tended to hang out. At the far end of the street you could just see another circular sign with an M on it. For a moment it felt as if there were two quite separate Métro systems, one on the map and the other—the one down the street—a secret one. You stopped on the staircase and let curiosity take the upper hand, even though you were already late. You turned back and walked along to the mysterious station. And you discovered that it was Odéon and that far from being kilometres apart there was no more than a couple of hundred metres between your intended *départ* and your *destination*. You stood there feeling rather foolish and you felt the city shrinking around you. After that you devoted every afternoon and every free day to taking extended walks in order to master the city, and so the islands around the Métro stations you had become familiar with slowly joined up to form a continent.

You are sitting in the shadow of a tree watching the meeting of two rivers and remembering a time when the traffic was held up by a red light and for the first time you walked over to the railings in order to look at the Seine. Jacket in hand, you felt a moment's disappointment. Was the most important river in France no wider than this? When everything else was big enough to defy scrutiny?

The Mekong, you think, is so much mightier.

You don't usually wallow in nostalgia. Your memories are usually pale and anaemic unless, like now, you permit them to become parasites on the present. If you allow them to do that, they flare up in warm colours and you can smell scents and hear responses that you didn't remember you remembered.

But afterwards you are left with a vague sense of distaste. Not unlike the feeling you had after the self-abuse you could not avoid performing in your poky room on the rue Létellier. A stale feeling of transience.

Now you are sitting under a tree in the slow capital city of your slow country and you are remembering.

You run through memories of education, of New Year parties at La Maison de l'Indochine. People you met, your gradual entry into a more sophisticated circle. Those who did not simply live on their good contacts and privileged upbringing. Those who even enjoyed the respect of French intellectuals and were invited to seminars and to visit other countries. All those young people from all those oppressed countries that were on the point of taking the future into their own hands. The Vietnamese, the many different faces from French Equatorial Africa and the Polynesian islands. The many accents, which eventually became a language in their own right with French French as no more than one of the variants.

Think for a while about the summer after the one you spent road-building in Yugoslavia, when you went back to camp in the same area. Remember how your skin darkened again in the sun, how you looked out over the Road of Brotherhood you had built. The humble pride you felt watching the traffic roll along the smooth tarmac. Your tarmac. Remember your feeling that it is possible to change everything, that roads can be built and landscape changed. The mountains that tumbled down into the strangely salty sea.

Y

Y   Y

It is a different evening again and the rains come earlier and earlier. You are sitting on a blue veranda, a paraffin lamp on the table that separates your chair from your brother's. The neglected garden in front of you has disappeared in the darkness and the downpour. Only the two of you are here, with your cigarettes and the little lamp.

The door number on the right-hand side of the street door below you is Forty-four. Four plus four equals a lucky number. You aren't bothered about rubbish of that kind but the landlord is and, conse-quently, the rent is higher than that paid by the neighbours.

You're not bothered, but it is a lucky number anyway.

The two of you are sitting there in silence and you can see your brother's face emerging and fading in the glow of his cigarette as he breathes in and out. A face that over the years has become more and more like yours. Or perhaps it's the other way round.

You are both careful about visiting one another. You prefer late evening, like today. The rain is making most people stay at home. The absence of moonlight makes the streets dark in districts like this.

Your brother's newspaper is still being allowed to appear. But you know that the security police are monitoring its editions and several other publications have been forced to close. A whole string of editors are now raking salt in Kampot or breaking up rocks to build roads.

A moment ago the two of you were joking about having two such different circles of readers. One of them radical republicans, the other the secret police of a reactionary monarchy.

As a matter of fact the two of you really should not be seen together at all. It is not in your interest and not in his. Or, to be more precise, not in the interest of the interests of either of you. But among your siblings you two are the closest to one another. Not just in age, but also in opinions. And on an evening like this when your eldest brother has let the two of you have the use of his house while he is visiting your parents, you have assessed the risk to be acceptable.

As does your eldest brother. As a courtier in the king's entourage for many years he has built up a significant capital of trust. But it is a currency that could quickly be devalued if the young prince's suspicions were to be aroused. It is a small city and your relationship is no secret. The less you two irritants are seen together, the less likely the risk of the prince's agents suggesting you are sent to the salt fields.

So you are sitting with your brother on your big brother's blue veranda and the rain is pounding down in the night. You have been discussing the politics of the day for the last hour. You don't agree with one another though you share a great deal of common ground. You have warned him against continuing his agitation.

You are two of a family of nine children. You were the lucky number four plus four. You don't know what Marx's theories say about luck but you do know that it has considerable importance. It is, after all is said and done, what separates you from those of your partisan comrades who were torn to pieces by French mines.

You were number eight, one of the little ones who grew up in the corners of the house, silently watching your parents and your older brothers and sisters. One of those the others could hardly keep count of. Now you are sitting here with the somewhat less lucky number seven and you are surprised that he does not understand the need to be more careful. It's a character trait you recognize from childhood. He would stick to his guns and argue his case until your father gave him a thrashing—or delegated the job to one of your older brothers.

Now the two of you are sitting in silence in the rain. The paraffin lamp between you is burning with a yellow flame, and you are allowing your thoughts to be drawn towards Somaly's silence. Another morning, another day and another evening have been added to the days of silence. Their number is now approaching the point when you will be forced to act. For one moment you wonder whether to confide in your brother. To tell him and only him how she has made it impossible to meet her and how much that torments you. With him you ought to be able to give in to the strain, stop being the inscrutable one for a while and just be his despairing little brother.

But it is impossible to gauge the risk. He might say something to someone else who might in turn hint something to a third someone, and finally some story about your vacillating position will reach the Organization. So pull yourself together. Light a cigarette with steady hands, overcome this weakness.

You light a cigarette, shielding the flame with both hands. The smoke gets in your eyes a little, making you blink two or three times.

You more than anyone know the value of keeping things hidden. How many times have you seen people act on assumptions you have known to be false? With no more than a couple of sentences you could have made them aware of their error and then everything would have happened differently. But you kept quiet and watched them carry on.

Just as your silence in the dark of this night conceals many things.

The unsaid does not exist.

You more than anyone know the value of being economical with information. It should be served in small portions, to the right people. You must, moreover, always remember who knows what and who is likely to pass the information on. Think where it will be collated and who might draw independent conclusions from it. That's why it is impossible to tell your brother about Somaly's silence, to tell him that she sometimes disappears and that you are desperate. It would be impossible to gauge the risk of such an action. Who, in turn, might he confide in? What does he already know about the two of you? About her?

You tap the ash off your cigarette and feel vaguely grateful that you resisted the impulse to tell your brother. It would doubtless have been a relief, but you are stronger than that. And you will learn from this, become more close knit. To put it simply, you are no longer the sort of person who allows himself to be defeated.

SUNDAY, 28 AUGUST 1955

You are standing on a pavement. The sun is beating down mercilessly between the buildings and people are silhouettes among the shadows. You are standing in front of a cyclo and the man is leaning forward waiting to be paid. So dig in your pockets among old piastres and new riels. Pay him in a casual way so that your face will blend in with those of all his other customers.

It is against your principles to travel in this way, to let yourself be transported by men who own nothing, who hire their vehicles from very rich Chinese and who are only allowed to keep enough money for a handful of rice, a couple of cigarettes and the right to carry on pedalling. You and your comrades normally refuse to be part of *capitalist oppression*, of your brothers in misfortune *being exploited by foreigners*. And that is precisely why it is your *moyen de transport de préférence*, because it is common knowledge that Organization men do their own pedalling. The fact that the personal secretary of one of the leaders of the Democrats chooses a cyclo rather than a car brings respect: had you chosen something even simpler, it would have made you a suspect.

You have paid off the cyclo and you are now walking nonchalantly down an alleyway. You have already walked through the same kind of alleyway in a different part of the city. And in between you've changed cyclos twice. Now you are only two or three blocks away from the street corner where you started your circuitous route.

It is unusual and risky behaviour. You don't usually bother about being so obviously careful and you don't understand what the point of it is. But it was an order and you welcome the possibility that chance might lead Somaly to appear somewhere along your circuit. That you might see her in another cyclo, on the pavement, in a shop or out for a walk with her girlfriends.

Just seeing her would mean a lot.

Don't bother counting the days again. It just puts you in an even worse mood. Concentrate instead on the task in hand. Something of considerable significance is about to happen. Or has happened. Otherwise the information would have been passed along the usual line from mouth to mouth, but now it's going to be given to you directly.

You cross the street and enter the lane on the other side. There are children chasing one another, a man with two blocks of ice on the ends of a yoke, women hanging out washing, a seller of Vietnamese pancakes squatting on his haunches. Many people see you but there are many other passers-by just like you. You hope that their passage will erase yours.

You turn a corner and see that you are the first. Take a seat on one of the low stools of the street restaurant, order a misted glass of iced tea and open your paper. Let the news of the brutal way the French broke up the protests in Morocco harness your thoughts. A thousand dead. According to French military sources. The question then is, how many times does that figure have to be multiplied before it accords with the truth?

You are sitting at this restaurant waiting for someone and you don't know who that someone will be. You are taking a considerable risk by coming here. But there is nothing about your appearance to reveal your mission. You are just a well-dressed young teacher reading his paper.

A man takes a seat, not at your table but on a stool at the neighbouring table. Cautious procedures of this kind seem almost ridiculous to you. But it points to discipline. There are two cyclos standing twenty or thirty metres away, and you recognize one of the drivers as the man who took you to your meeting with Yan and Sok last Tuesday. They are smoking and it's impossible to tell whether they know one another, but each of them has an identical bamboo cane tied on parallel to the frame of the cycle.

You turn your head slightly towards the other table. Mumm is sitting there.

You are sitting at one table and waiting for your neighbour at the next table to say what he is here to say. He comes from an unbelievably wealthy family and is the only man in your country to have been to the Ecole Polytechnique in Paris. Under no circumstances should the two of you be seen together, for your respective tasks are so similar. Like you, Mumm is one of the Organization's trusted men and he too has infiltrated the Democrats' election campaign. But while you are a secretary in the background, he has been elected to the committee of the party. You manipulate while he acts.

The security police would merely make a note of it if a member of the party leadership was seen in the company of an unremarkable bag-carrier from lower down the hierarchy. But if these two were already filed under "Paris" and "Communist Party Core Troops", the police would not be satisfied with merely noting the fact. And the leadership of the Democrats, too, would almost certainly consider the hitherto unknown socialization between two party members worthy of investigation, particularly since those members had a questionable past in common.

You are in danger and at last you are able to drag your thoughts away from Somaly's silence. Your thoughts are all on the here and now, while you wait for the man at the neighbouring table to address you. You are in danger, but you feel safe in his presence. It is an irrational feeling. Mumm brings Paris with him, and everything in Paris consisted of words and non-dangerous theory, whereas here and now it is a matter of potentially life-threatening practice. You watch him out of the corner of your eye. His suit, his high forehead, his heavy eyelids.

A waiter in ordinary clothes serves Mumm and Mumm turns to you and asks the time in the way anyone would ask a stranger for the time.

Stretch out your arm and look at your watch. Tell Mumm the time and hear him say thank you.

Start a conversation before he returns to his paper and say something about the price of rice—the biggest headline on the page he has open. Listen to Mumm complaining on behalf of the poor and hear him add that he, at least, is lucky enough to be able to leave the country in these expensive times. That he will be flying to Paris tonight. And then as an explanatory statement: that it is all the more welcome since you *never* can tell when distant visitors from a poor country district might come knocking on the door *uninvited*, force their way in and turn the whole house *upside down*.

You nod and smile and try to take in the information. Mumm is fleeing the country. A raid is imminent. Vannsak was right that there are no longer any restrictions on what Sam Sary can do. Not even the party leadership is exempt.

You hear Mumm saying goodbye. You say safe journey to his departing back.

You see him take a seat in one of the cyclos at the corner and once his cyclo has gone twenty metres, the other one rolls off slowly in the same direction. Your eyes follow them and you see the two cyclos turn left and disappear. All that's left is a busy crossroads.

Stay where you are on your stool and keep your eyes fixed on the news and the notices. Things are serious now. They were before, but now there is no room for anything else. Danger is a permanent condition from now on. None of you is safe.

You try to sort through all these new questions. What does it mean that the security police are intending to arrest Mumm? What does it mean that he is fleeing? For the Democrats? For the election? For your mission? For you? Is your name the next one on the chief of police's list?

And in addition to that:

What does this mean for the other young radicals in the party leadership? For Vannsak? You think you must warn him, but you ought not to. How would you explain that you know about Mumm's flight? An official explanation of his sudden disappearance will come soon enough.

You are sitting in an open-air restaurant and in a rather convoluted way you are glad that these new problems are forcing you to give your attention to them rather than to Somaly's damned absence.

Y

Y Y

You are sitting by a paraffin lamp. You are sitting in a room that is lost in darkness beyond the circle of yellow light made by the lamp. Two faces are lit up in front of you, one wide jawed and one thin.

The table is covered with sheets of paper with writing in French and with long lines in your own language. A rolled-up mosquito net is hanging over a low bed.

Sok and Yan look more tired than they did last Tuesday. So do you. Sok offers his cigarettes around—Red Club. Take a Red Club. It makes a welcome change from your perpetual Globes.

Your folders contain important information. Pass the folders across to Yan and Sok. Give them one each to look through. Explain to them how the information should be interpreted. Then give them an account of the developments of the last week and describe the deliberations that are going on within the left wing of the Democratic Party. You have the reputation of being a good analyst. Analyse the situation. Justify your reputation. Clarify the reports and fit them into a context that can be understood.

Then tell them about your meeting with Mumm and that the friendship between his mother and the old queen is probably what saved him. Tell them about Mumm and watch the relief spread over their faces. You could perhaps add something ironic about the advantages of the upper class in comparison to the masses waiting to be liberated. Or rather, in your opinion, to liberate themselves.

After that it is Yan's turn, followed by Sok. Listen to what they say in their quiet musical voices. Make a note of keywords to help your memory, but not so many of them that they could be understood if the document fell into the wrong hands.

Take one of the five glasses of tea. Lift the lid and drink. You have drunk too little in the course of the day and your thirst does not begin to ease until the fourth mouthful.

Yan reports from memory on the new people who want to join you. What a memory he has—everything in it seems immediately accessible. Everything is structured and archived in a simple way. Now he plucks two or three candidates from his memory. You can refer to them as one, two and three. Three and two are students, number one moved in from Svay Rieng. From memory Yan gives an account of their family backgrounds, how they approached the Organization, what they have said about the ways in which they could possibly make a contribution.

Think about what has been said about one, two and three. They aren't unsuitable nor, however, are they particularly suitable. There are circumstances that need further clarification, follow-up questions to be asked, simple tests of loyalty and ideological receptiveness to be gone through. The very fact that someone wants to join you given the current situation suggests that they are either infiltrators or lacking in judgement. But what can be done about it? Your ranks have thinned out in recent months. The Organization has to be ready for every eventuality.

Which way will you vote? Recommend acceptance or rejection? What do your instincts tell you?

A picture comes to mind. Manicured fingertips resting on a collarbone, dark hair, curled and let down. A smile, red-painted lips, a smooth neck in a high collar.

Cut there.

A loud unabashed laugh after a reply given with long Chinese vowels.

Cut there. Hurry up and cut there.

So.

Scrub the picture from your mind. You have no use for it there. Quite the opposite.

Scrub it.

Now you are scrubbing a picture from your mind.

Now.

Now you are in a house with the lights off. It's on stilts, in a street you don't know, in a part of the city you seldom visit. You are sitting facing two men, both dressed like you. They are waiting for you to answer a question.

Answer it.

Ask them to postpone the question of membership. Argue that you should wait and see, that you should think of the times. Say all that stuff about infiltrators and lack of judgement; it sounds good. There is a risk of the election turning everything upside down. It is only a few more days and waiting is something that every soldier must learn, isn't that so, especially those who are fighting for the revolution with fliers and good arguments as their weapons. Let the Organization say nothing. Let them understand the absolute precondition of their future involvement: *that they will never get to know more than they need to know.* That preparedness is the quality that ranks highest, after their loyalty. That they must always be prepared simply to get up from the dinner table and go straight out into the jungle without any baggage other than their sense of duty and their burning conviction.

Argue for the question to be postponed. You will get your own way, just as you almost always do when the number of people around the table can be counted on your fingers. You are not a mass orator who can spellbind an audience from the rostrum. You strength reveals itself in thoughtful, low-key conversations.

Yan nods and says, let's move on to the next point.

Now you should all practise self-criticism.

Practise self-criticism.

Give an account of your shortcomings, because you have not succeeded in completing all the things you promised to complete. Give an account of the priorities you have privately set yourself. Be open with your comrades, accept your guilt face to face. Tell them how you have neglected your studies, that you chose to turn off the light and go to bed even though there was still work to be done.

Ask forgiveness for your shortcomings. Dig deep into yourself and promise to redouble your efforts in order to measure up to the expectations of the Organization. Promise to be stricter with yourself, to discipline your indolent will and make it one with the Organization.

Ask your comrades honestly for their forgiveness.

But make no mention of what really matters. Say nothing about the picture that was occupying your thoughts earlier. Don't tell them why it made you stare off into the shadows for several seconds, while they thought you were turning things over in your mind. Keep quiet about your urge to miss this meeting and go looking for her instead.

Drink your tea. Listen to your friends' confessions with benevolent attention. Be understanding and constructive in your comments. Say that all of you are human. That you do as well as you can.

We all do as well as we can.

The meeting is drawing to an end. An understandable weariness has replaced the earlier tension. Everything has gone as intended. The security police haven't come pounding on the door. Sam Sary's mob of liberated jailbirds hasn't called you out into the gleam of their torches, while working themselves up by pummelling the stilts of the house with bamboo clubs.

One more step towards justice has been taken. There are many left, but with each step that is taken, there is one fewer left to take. *There is more suffering on earth than stars in the sky*, but the country as you know it is not static. It is possible to change it, history will be your witness on that point. There are great resources and no one will need to go to bed hungry if those resources are shared out better. Everyone can learn to read as long as someone teaches them.

Everything belongs to all of us.

Y
Y   Y

You have just left a secret meeting with your revolutionary comrades and you are walking through dark streets that are still waiting for tarmac and lamp-posts. It was a rewarding meeting. You agreed on a date for the next meeting and you are already looking forward to it.

But you do not feel the degree of commitment you usually feel.

The sound of your footsteps beneath a moon that is somewhere between half and full sets off the usual series of excited barks. There was a time when you, like most other people, believed that dogs that bark at night were barking at a passing ghost.

That has been a fair enough description of you for some little time now. Things should be different.

With every step you take you feel yourself swelling up with unusual bitterness. You, one of the chosen ones. You, a man with the right contacts, the right experiences, the right knowledge. This is your great challenge. You are now being put to the test. And it is a test you have all the qualifications to pass, as long as you can concentrate on it to the exclusion of everything else. But what do we find? We find *the struggle between petit bourgeois private interests and the just liberation struggle of the people* materializing within you of all people. And while this is going on Meas is consolidating his position.

You think about silence as a means of power. The pressure it is capable of exerting. In another part of yourself, one that is capable of cold and clear thinking, you note the thought that *it is silence that produces speech*. It is, at least, a useful experience.

But what is the value of speech if no one is listening? Or, to be more precise, what sort of statement is needed in order to make her respond?

How long will it be before you drive your car through the closed gate of her house? Before you visit her and call her to account for what she is doing to you?

Slow down, your annoyance is making you walk faster.

Stand still for a moment and take a deep breath. Inhale the scent of damp earth, the odour from the simple kitchens outside the houses that surround you. Meat being grilled on skewers, jasmine rice, fish oil.

Tear your thoughts away from her.

You know the importance of avoiding open confrontation, of retaining control. That all significant actions in a schism between two sides gain by being postponed. That is the basic principle of your political dealings, and there is no reason to believe it would not be the right method now. Victory goes to the man who is patient, the one who can wait for the right opportunity. Who can mask his rage with a friendly smile and then strike with all his strength when his opponent thinks the battle is over.

The ancient custom of your people, which is to ensure that when vengeance is taken it is many times greater than the original injustice, is not something you see any reason to break with. Quite the reverse—it is a very effective arrangement.

Listen to the barking of the dogs, which cannot be directed at you any longer and must be following a dynamic of its own, a contagion moving from one farm to the next. You have just attended an important meeting. Try to concentrate on that.

You are standing in pale moonlight and taking long deep breaths. Put her to one side.

Free yourself.

And move on. Move on with calmer steps. A bat flutters noiselessly past your head. Follow its shadow and see it disappear into the night.

You pass a man urinating against a wall. It reminds you that tea is the only dinner you have had up to this point.

You walk along slowly and recognize the district you are in. You are approaching the racecourse, which lies there silent and huge under the stars. You have your thoughts under control now and there is a knot of hunger in your stomach.

It has been a long day, full of suppressed disquiet. Mumm's hasty departure, your meeting with the party cell. But you are still free. You should have been arrested many times over in recent months, but you are still walking free, and you are finding it more and more difficult to resist the smell of food.

Think about it. It could have been worse. It could have been significantly worse.

You go round a corner and now you have tarmac under your feet. You can see white fluorescent lights hanging over a modest open-air restaurant a block farther on.

Go there. Take a seat on one of the low wooden benches and wave for a waiter.

Y

Y   Y

You are sitting on a low wooden bench on a dusty pavement in the Troisième Quartier. You have just finished a plate of fried noodles and pork. There is a small upturned Vietnamese coffee glass on a plate on the low table in front of you. Bright light and French pop music are streaming out of a gramophone shop. At the other tables there are groups of men with loud voices, their eyes dulled by alcohol.

Their eyes sometimes settle on you, before moving unsteadily on and fixing instead on the mouths of their companions or on glasses of palm wine.

Take out the cigarettes you bought from the cigarette seller on the way here. Study his handiwork. In one single movement he took paper and tobacco and rolled it into what is now a perfect cigarette. And in exchange for that skill you paid him a trifling sum, hardly enough for him and his fellows to afford anything to eat other than rice porridge with no meat in it. In spite of the fact that society needs his services just as much as it needs yours. In the name of justice, you think, every function, every variety of work, should be given the same value and therefore receive the same remuneration.

Politely ask the man beside you whether you may take a match from the box he has tossed down on the table in front of him. Wait for his flushed face to turn towards you and for him to wave his hand rather aimlessly in a gesture that could be taken for a yes. Strike the match and light your perfect cigarette.

You are sitting there full of thought on a low wooden bench on a pavement at the other end of the city. You chin is resting in your hands and white smoke curls up from them into the still night air. The food and coffee have calmed the earlier surge of emotion.

The men at the neighbouring table are arguing about which brothel to go to. You imagine pink fluorescent lights and big rooms in which young women are sitting in a line waiting to be chosen. You play with the possibility of asking the party to let you accompany them.

For the same reason as you and your comrades will not use cyclos, you also refuse to use the poor girls enslaved in *bordellos*. The sessions of self-criticism, however, reveal that this is an edict that few are capable of sticking to. And you are no exception. But there was even less choice in Paris. There were fewer brothels than here and you were so poor that you could rarely choose your company. The thought of bedding the women of the colonizing race had undoubtedly been a tantalizing one, but in reality they were too big to be attractive and their pale skin felt coarse in comparison with what you were used to.

Since coming home you have controlled yourself, stayed away from the brothels, apart from a few lapses that weigh on your conscience. You do it for Somaly, because you assume that she disapproves of that kind of thing. And that, of course, is why you are tempted to go along with the drunks at the neighbouring table.

Not as revenge, for what is there to avenge? No, more as a way—as you see it—to re-establish the *balance* between you and your fiancée.

You know you would be deceiving yourself. But the feeling that the possibility exists is worth more than the imagined redress. Because the heat of redress would immediately be replaced by the chill of deception. Which would mean that the balance regained is overdone, so becoming an act drained of its content.

Stay where you are. Watch them leave.

Think instead, rather distractedly perhaps, of Mao, of Stalin, of the late lamented Lenin. How they succeeded in spite of the pre-conditions, because they had history on their side. As you do. The question is, when should the opportunity be grasped? You watch the drunken labourers depart. Are they ready? Will they follow you and your cautious friends? Are the signs there but you are incapable of interpreting them? Or is it all still too soon?

Mao marched through China. Ho Chi Minh conquered Vietnam. Everything was against them but they were victorious, thanks to their dedication and their patience.

Patience and dedication. Just as in love.

If only you could have been there. Just imagine yourself among the audience for Lenin's speeches, imagine him catching your eye as you stand there in the crush of all those men wrapped against the cold. Imagine yourself as the adjutant who was with Stalin when he heard of Hitler's suicide. Walk a few steps behind Mao across the endless plains.

Learn from them. Even though Somaly is moulding your thinking more than Marx at present.

Dedication. Patience.

So. Finish your coffee. Get up and say goodnight to the waiter. You are full up and you are tired and you are unsure whether to take the street or the alleyway.

Give a thought to luck. And give another to the importance of being careful.

Then take the alleyway. Put out your cigarette and disappear into the soft darkness.

MONDAY, 29 AUGUST 1955

You close your eyes and step back into memory. You are alone by the river. The mud is grey and oozy. Your bare feet and legs sink down into its soft depths. You have just been picking at a cut on your toe in order to check again whether it hurts or not. That is something new and you feel some degree of pride at this sign of growing up, but also a little unsure. The cut is covered with mud at the moment, but it shows every time you pull your foot free from the grip of the ooze and swill it off in the current. The sun makes glittering reflections in the swirling brown water of the river. Your job is to water the oxen, but they aren't thirsty and are lying in the shade of a large tamarind tree.

That is all that's left. You are not even sure it was really like that. Perhaps the glitter of the sun belongs to a different occasion or, indeed, perhaps the oxen do.

You are sitting on a veranda that overlooks a small well-kept garden. Vannsak is sitting beside you. He is talking to you, but when he is speaking in that particular tone he does not expect an answer. You just have to look interested and mumble an... mm... of agreement every so often.

A fan on the floor is buzzing away behind your rattan armchairs. Raindrops are falling from the leaves but the morning sun is already turning the moisture to steam.

The two of you are drinking coffee with fresh milk. You moved on from tins of unsophisticated condensed milk ages ago. You are men of the people, but your coffee habits come from Paris.

Look around you. What evoked the memory of being by the river? You can neither trace it to anything that has been said recently, nor to any taste, nor to anything visual. Perhaps there was something out in the garden that evoked it, two colours beside one another, perhaps? You haven't thought of that cut close to your toenail for years. But just for a moment it broke into the cycle of your thoughts, which keep returning time after time to her silence.

Go back into your memory. Stand once again with your feet deep in the cool mud. See the wet black bodies of the oxen in the shade, see them go grey, patch by patch as they dry.

Permit yourself to slide forward in time to your first visit to your home village after France. Remember your uncle meeting you at the station with a cyclo—not sitting in it but as its driver. The man who had owned many oxen and employed whole families.

Do you remember how taken aback you were when you saw him in the saddle—he was pleased as punch that you had returned but also deeply ashamed of his own poverty. How he ran his hand through his cropped white hair time after time and laughed as he praised your suit, your pale skin, your shining pomaded hair.

And how he then wiped the passenger seat of the cyclo with his scarf even though it was already clean, not once but three times before you managed to stop him.

You are sitting in a cyclo pedalled by your father's younger brother. You watch a familiar landscape rolling slowly past and you smell the sour smell of your uncle's unwashed clothes. You have noticed that he has lost several teeth and they have not been replaced with gold ones. Your uncle has the mouth of a poor man, his sunburnt skin is that of a manual labourer.

The road is a strip of red sand through the grass and your body sways in time with the swaying of the cyclo.

The oxen lying in the shade of the tamarind probably belonged to your uncle. He was the one you went to, anyway, to show the cut, which had stopped bleeding by that point. He examined your foot carefully—the little flap of skin had stuck down slightly crooked on the cut. He asked you if it was sore and you shook your head, showing off. He looked at you and said, now you've really become a man. Then he fetched a ladle of water from the rainwater pitcher to wash off the mud. You can remember the way both his tone of voice and his body language changed after he'd said you'd really become a man. And while your uncle was washing your foot, you started to cry anyway. When he saw that, he lifted you up onto his lap. The skin over his muscles warm and soft, the stubble on his chin coarse.

You were sitting in a cyclo and even then, twenty-five years later, tears ran down your cheeks. You were careful not to let your uncle see them as he chattered away happily behind you. Even going uphill his chatter showed virtually no sign of slowing down. You swallowed hard and shouted polite questions whenever he took a breath. He told you of events in the family and what had happened to neighbours and friends. Through the blinked back tears, you caught glimpses of the landscape you were trundling through, with people dressed in rags and abandoned rice fields.

You are sitting on the veranda in front of the elegant teachers' residence attached to the city's elite school. Your uncle's cheerfulness gives way again to Vannsak's impassioned earnestness. Listen to your friend. Listen to him talking about the conditions in which the rural population lives—they are very close to what was the norm a century ago. Two centuries ago.

Listen to him contrasting it to the way people in the cities live. The question is, how are you going to be able to bring this deep injustice alive to the people you talk to? How to make them capable of recognizing the obvious? Listen to him echoing your own thoughts of a few evenings ago when he asks how it will be possible to break through the rigid and intellectually stifling weight of religion. A religion that says that the disadvantaged are disadvantaged because they lived badly in their earlier lives, whereas the favoured are favoured because of their good deeds in some distant past. How can you slice religion so that the comforting element remains but the oppression vanishes? It is like trying to slice a coin, you think: however many times you slice it it will always have two sides.

Remember how you rode in a cyclo, its seat springs worn out, pedalled by the sinewy body of your uncle? Remember, too, how just a month or so before that you rode the Métro under the massed buildings of Paris. The cars flowed like cataracts of steel along the streets, the aeroplanes glinted in the sky. Remember the burning neon nights, the laughing food-filled mouths in restaurants, the stifling odour of the thousands upon thousands of perfumes pouring out through the doors of the Galeries Lafayette.

Remember how everything became clear to you as you sat there in the cyclo. How the whole world came together before your eyes—the world with all its fields and great forests and the minerals that gleam in the depths of the mountains. How human beings were not so numerous that it was impossible to count them; and how every single one of them had exactly the same birthright to whatever the fields and the forests and the mountains had to give.

And how the good things in this world were so unfairly distributed that it was shameful.

The thought was far from new, but it was there in that cyclo on that dusty potholed road that the emotion struck home.

You saw that it is possible to take stock of all the riches of the world and you saw that they are not limitless. You saw the world's resources as a great vessel with many connecting chambers. For one person to become rich, someone else must become poor. For Europeans and Americans to be able to enjoy abundance, millions and thousands of millions of others must be left in poverty.

That is why they, like your uncle, are poverty-stricken. People like him, with their bare hands and aching bodies, lay the foundations of the affluence on the other side of the world. And he does not even understand how poor he is in comparison with people of his own age with French or British or American names.

Remember how painful it was when you realized that everything that you rejoiced in in Paris depended on the deplorable state of things here. That it was impossible for you to love the cinemas there at the same time as hating the hovels here.

And Vannsak's voice breaks into your memories and says that everyone has a right to justice.

He is talking about the city you are in and the countryside that surrounds it. About this minor counterpart to the great system. About the fruit that is grown by the poor peasants but eaten by the *nouveaux riches* in the cities.

Look at him. At his earnestness and at the power in what he is saying. The suppressed rage, even now when all he is doing is practising his next speech. Like you, a man in his best years. It is people like him who will put a stop to the injustice.

People like him, and like you.

Y

Y   Y

You are standing in front of a blackboard. You are holding a piece of white chalk in your hand. There is a moment of stillness when you stop moving your hand. The silence of the schoolyard fills the classroom, that and the chattering of the birds in the trees that shade the dusty yard. Thirty-eight students are sitting in straight rows behind you, transferring your words from the blackboard to their notebooks.

Carry on moving the chalk across the board. Write *les maîtres d'école sont des jardiniers en intelligences humaines*, followed by *Victor HUGO*.

Turn around to the class with a smile.

Ask them the meaning of the sentence.

Continue to smile encouragingly when they hesitate. Note which of them is pretending to be still busy copying down the words. Wait until they, too, have raised their eyes to you as if silently signalling their readiness to answer.

Repeat the question and then pass it over to Punthea.

Punthea's round features light up with quiet pride when he becomes the centre of attention. You recognize the feeling of being picked out. Of being the one recognized as having the ability to see the grandeur in a brief quotation.

You feel a certain pride yourself in taking the role of the master gardener. And here, with the light slanting in from the left through the open windows and being reflected up from the floor onto thirty-eight concentrating faces, you can keep all your thoughts focused. They are no longer disturbed by the demand for strategic deliberation or by the silence that is drowning everything else. Here there is nothing but the beauty of pages waiting to be written on and of the coil and loop of words.

Listen to Punthea. Listen to him giving a literal interpretation of the words. Thank Punthea and ask the class whether anyone has anything to add. But don't let the pause last so long that someone feels compelled to put up his hand. Connect back to the introductory lecture you heard in Paris instead.

Shut your eyes for a moment. Put yourself in the mood.

Imagine the low wooden benches that climbed the sides of the auditorium towards the enormous cut-glass chandeliers with their weak yellow bulbs. Remember the huge painting that formed the backdrop—a churning sea and an open boat in which white men in old-fashioned clothes are struggling against the waves.

Remember the short and corpulent professor far below and the way his dull voice carried all the way up to you and your fellows. The way he began by saying that there is one question that is more beautiful than any other. A question that captures the very essence not just of scholarship but of life itself. Do you remember how curiosity drew his listeners out of the sleepy torpor they had sunk into upon entering that warm, dark lecture hall after an unusually chilly morning walk?

Do you remember how you thought that the question would give you the answer to something of decisive significance?

Now do what the corpulent professor did. Raise their expectations. Stress the importance of the question. Refer to Montaigne and other names you have taught them to respect.

Now do what that professor did no more than a decade ago.

Pause for effect.

Then say: *Que sais-je?*

Notice the way your pupils hesitate slightly before leaning forward over their notepads as one man and writing down your three words and the two punctuation marks.

You can remember how confused you were in that massive hall with the maritime motifs on the wall. So much excitement that it becomes a tremor. Is this supposed to be the question of questions?

But don't mention your own confusion, nor that of the others in the lecture hall at the time. Instead, borrow the authoritative self-evident attitude of the corpulent professor. The question will stick in your pupils' minds just as it has stuck in yours. They will come back to those three syllables, they will ponder them. Dismiss them as being far too simple, like the emperor's clothes. But they will come back to them. And the question will come to glow with a mysterious light all of its own.

What do I know?

Indeed, what do you know?

Let the silence last a few moments more. Let it make the words even weightier. Then bring things to an elegant conclusion—that, my friends, that is all for today—before beginning to put your papers in order even though they don't need ordering.

You hear your pupils gathering up their bits and pieces. You hear pencils being put in pencil cases, notepads rustling as they go into folders, books thudding as they go into cases. No one says anything because everything they now want to say must be said out of earshot.

As they leave the room they say goodbye in a friendly and spontaneous way. You are well liked. You know you are well liked. The quiet way you discuss things makes them respect you, as does your willingness to go back and explain things to those who haven't understood.

You don't lecture—you explain. That is how they would describe you.

Answer their greetings with a friendly nod.

Now turn your head to the right, to the door that is swallowing your pupils. There is a man standing in the doorway. He is a young man and you recognize him but you don't know his name. He is one of the older pupils at the school. You recognize him because you know he belongs to the Organization, although you know neither his name nor his role.

Let him see that you have noticed him.

When Punthea and Prasith have gone at last and the room is silent and empty, you tell the man to come in and close the door behind him. The closed door is of little practical significance since the windows are open, but closed doors lend meetings a certain formal dignity.

Respond to the man's brief greeting and adopt a friendly listening expression.

The man steps up to your desk, leans forward confidentially and, in a subdued voice, passes on a message. He says that the house of one of *Monsieur*'s brothers is surrounded by the police because *Monsieur*'s other brother is thought to be hiding there.

Receive the message without showing any emotion. You may, however, assume that the man notices the tightening around your eyes, the way your presence becomes absolute.

Look out through the window at the groups of young people in short-sleeved white shirts, navy blue trousers, identical haircuts and bags crossing the open ground outside. See how some of them are walking slowly and discussing things whereas others are chasing after one another. Hear their loud voices and laughter while your own mind is running at a gallop. It is amazing how everything can be normal and all of a sudden it no longer is. Or how everything has seemed normal in spite of the fact that the change probably occurred a couple of hours ago.

Ask the young man if anyone has been hurt and hear him answer that he does not know. Then ask him if he has any more to say. When he answers that he hasn't, turn to him with an expression full of goodwill and determination and thank him. He in turn bows quickly and leaves the room, leaving the door open.

Slow down and get a grip on your flustered thoughts.

For a long time now you have been ready to be tested. How or where or when has been uncertain but one thing has always been certain and that is that the time would come. Not once, not twice, but more times than it was worth speculating. You have been prepared for a long time and the most important thing now is not to do anything too hastily.

Sit down at your desk and think through the situation that has arisen. See what cards you are holding, assess your chances of acting—and the risks of not doing so.

The disturbing thing is not that the younger of your older brothers is going to have to spend the coming weeks or months raking salt under a baking sun out on the dirty-white flats at Kampot. The disturbing thing is that the police have not simply gone into the house and taken him out.

So the question to which there is no answer: what are they waiting for?

Two possible scenarios come to mind. The first is that the purpose is to teach your brother a lesson and the whole business has nothing to do with you. The second is that the fact they have not arrested him is actually some sort of act of provocation. To which you are expected to react.

You turn your head towards the line of windows, almost as if you were expecting Sam Sary to be standing out there watching you.

How you choose to use or not to use your limited political influence on your brother's behalf will be noted. And irrespective of what you do or don't do, it could still provide the security police with an excuse to remove you. The man closest to Vannsak. A suitable target now that Mumm is safely in France.

If that happens you will never see Somaly again.

If that happens it will be the end of both your public political career and your nocturnal revolutionary conspiracy. There is, moreover, a risk hanging over your head—the risk that if the first of those possibilities is their motive, they are bound to uncover the second. In which case you will drag a significant part of the Organization down with you. Assuming—and this is the unpleasant part—that it hasn't already been uncovered. In which case the current deadlock has probably been engineered so that the security police can chart your activities.

If it is just about your brother, you are in no danger. If it is about you as Vannsak's secretary, it will mean the salt fields. If it is about your role in the Organization, you can expect an unmarked grave on a rubbish tip.

So think slow thoughts. Don't do anything hasty.

Should you behave like a loyal brother and hurry to join your brothers? Should you behave like a loyal brother with certain political contacts and hurry to speak to influential friends and acquaintances? Should you behave like a member of a secret revolutionary movement and hurry to give your comrades a discreet warning? Plans undoubtedly exist for dealing with this kind of dangerous change in the balance of things, but to activate them would mean *movement in the Organization* and movement brings with it the risk of discovery.

Or should you simply gather up your papers and prepare your next lesson?

TUESDAY, 30 AUGUST 1955

You are standing in front of your modest bookshelf. It holds a couple dozen volumes and you have read all but two or three. Despite all the many times you found yourself wandering past the dark-green book boxes of the *bouquinistes* along the Seine, you can still remember without any difficulty when you bought each and every one of them. You remember how you used to pick through all the old books, printed papers and picture postcards that had ended up in their boxes. How the seasons came and went, how sunshine turned to rain and then back to sunshine.

You still have several of the postcards, which now serve as bookmarks in the volumes in front of you. They are fragments of a correspondence in which an unknown French man is courting an unknown French woman. You came across them quite by chance in different book boxes. What connected them was the extremely fine and elegant handwriting, and you bought them with a vague sense of being on the track of something. You carried on looking for more on later occasions but never found any. And you only have his side of the story, since you never knew what her handwriting looked like and the postcards in the boxes ran into tens of thousands.

Five picture postcards from a man who was becoming more and more unhappy. To a woman who became more and more silent. It is remarkable how the world around you is filling with more and more signs and reminders, all of which point to your own situation.

You have taken off your shirt and you are standing barefoot in your ready-made trousers. On an evening like tonight you are utterly sick of the magnetic attraction her silence exerts on your mental state.

Your body is covered with a thin layer of sweat. The city outside is falling silent.

You think Tuesday and Wednesday and Thursday and Friday and Saturday and Sunday and Monday. And now it is Tuesday evening.

You have tests to mark. You have the drafts of two speeches to write for tomorrow. You need to report to the Organization. You have to come up with some response to the house arrest of your brothers.

You should not be counting the days of the week. Counting the days of the week was what you were doing.

A week now. It's humiliating.

Take one of the unread books from the shelf of books you have read. It's a novel in French by a French author. Its publication date was over twenty years ago but you feel it could not be more apposite and current. In spite of its lack of theoretical correctness it still matches the Organization's demand for instructive literature. You turn the book over and read what is on the dust jacket, which bears the fingermarks of previous owners: *The time is the end of the 1920s. The place is Shanghai, "a paradise garden of suffering", where the motto is kill or be killed. The giant that is China is writhing in the grip of fever. The white masters are cold-bloodedly investing their capital in whichever one of the Chinese factions currently has the upper hand. The author focuses on a handful of men in order to bring alive the whole of the confusing and bloody epoch that saw the birth of the new China. It would be hard to improve on the author's snapshots in terms of laconic authenticity and embittered commitment.* It's a book you have been meaning to read for a long time and you have been waiting for a suitable opportunity. This is not the right opportunity, which is perhaps why you are now about to read this novel about Chinese revolutionaries, all of whom are doomed. Perhaps the unsuitable opportunity is actually the only suitable one. You can still remember the conversation you had with the Algerian comrade who first mentioned the novel to you. How he—bespectacled, sharp, well read, dark-skinned—emphasized that the real subject of the story is man's absolute responsibility to choose his own road. Not to duck that responsibility even when the consequences are the worst imaginable, even when the choice necessitates the ultimate sacrifices. If there is anything you need at this moment, it is the strength to come to a decision and to stick to it. So turn the book over, open it, inhale the odour of the dry pages, read the text in a rather old-fashioned font and allow yourself to be transported back to a half hour after midnight on 21 March 1927.

Lift your eyes from the book you are reading. Not because there is anything to see but because there is something to hear. It is half an hour after midnight and there are voices approaching along the alley. They come closer, but before they come so close that you are compelled to act, they come to a halt, remain at that distance and are then muffled by a door closing behind them.

Feel your pulse calming down to its normal rate while you look at the paraffin lamp, which can only just cast its light as far as the last line on the left-hand page before the letters begin to merge into shadow. The night sounds have now returned to normal. Crickets, sporadic and desultory barks. The engine of a moped splits the auditory backcloth and then disappears.

You know how things are. What those with power can do to people, what violence can achieve. You were told about a comrade who was careless/unlucky/the right man in the wrong place/the wrong man in the right place/found wanting in some negligent but decisive sense. You were told about the interrogation sessions in a bare room where the windows were sealed and the lamps always lit. *The interrogations*: brutal, going nowhere. So after a couple of days or a couple of weeks—the report had trouble deciding which—the chief interrogator said he needed to urinate.

Your comrade was sitting in front of him tied to a chair, arms fastened behind his back. The interrogator opened his fly and ordered him to open his mouth. He refused. The chair was kicked over backwards and a guard locked your comrade's head between his knees. Then he held the prisoner's nose and forced his jaws open by pushing his fingers hard into his cheeks. And the chief interrogator urinated a strong clear stream into your comrade's mouth as he coughed, choked and thrashed about.

The interrogations continued for days and weeks, the report is quite certain about that, and every day the interrogator passed water in the same way.

After some months the questioning came to an end. But the inter-rogator rose from his desk every day, walked past the toilet door down to the room where your comrade was incarcerated, gently raised the scarred face and met the prisoner's broken gaze before filling the unresisting mouth which, of its own accord, had opened just the right amount.

The voices in the alleyway have fallen silent. What noises there are now are just the usual ones. So go back to your book. It's been a long time since you allowed yourself to read a novel. The floor and the table are covered with folders of material waiting to be edited and commented on and analysed. But you are sitting there with a fat little volume with yellowed pages and grease stains on the dust cover.

In the novel you meet men who are how you would like to be. Indomitable, unsentimental, at a turning point in history when everything is clear-cut in a way that makes decisions possible. At first sight their uncompromising attitude might seem to be the result of an uncomplicated intellectual life, one in which simple answers have been given to difficult questions of right and wrong. But that is not the case. Their radical conclusions have been reached as a result of long and hard thinking, they have had doubts but have gone on to overcome any objections. You have underlined with a blunt pencil one of the statements made in a conversation: *Marxism is not doctrine, it is will. For the proletariat and its supporters—for you—it is the will to learn to know themselves as proletarians, and to be victorious as such. You should not be Marxists in order to be right but in order to be victorious without betraying yourselves.*

A moth, grey and dazzled, is fluttering against the glass of the lamp. It drops onto the page in the book but then crawls back towards the flame.

You can only wish you had more men of that sort in the Organization. But as you make progress bit by bit, adding experience to experience, you and those around you will also become more single-minded, more unified. Disciplined. Like clockwork, you think, and look at the watch you are wearing on the inside of your left wrist. Complex but nevertheless reliable.

You think again about the sacrifices the great revolutions have demanded. Of the importance of holding a steady course even when it proves costly in the short term. That it demands a will that has been tempered to steel and an ability to listen to history rather than to the pleading of individuals. For if there is to be any possibility of giving back to your uncle and all the other poor and oppressed people in the country the basic *respectability* they have been deprived of, sacrifices will be demanded of them too. They will have to pass through a harsh ordeal if all of you, collectively, are to be able to move the world on its axis. And you feel a paradoxical sense of *tenderness* for the people, for they will sacrifice themselves for the future in the same way as you stand ready to sacrifice yourself for them. The people: there is no doubt that they will suffer great privations, but in the end, purified and clear, they will be able to look the world in the eye with a steady gaze.

Return to the bustle of Shanghai, to the men who do not betray themselves even in defeat. Return there, for now the story has come to a section which drags you down into the slough of unhappiness you had hoped it would lift you clear of. A woman enters the story, a woman your thoughts will return to time after time after time. She joins in the struggle on the same conditions as the men, is described as *intelligent and brave*. Not outstandingly beautiful, but no more masculine than her revolutionary work compels her to be. The sort of woman that, deep in your heart, you wish you had at your side.

In the novel the woman is German but you can't help seeing a woman from your own country, a woman you have met at political meetings both here and in Paris. She is called Ponnary and is a few years older than you. Short, pockmarked, she wears *practical* clothes, quite without finesse. No one would call her beautiful. But she has read the theoretical works the rest of you merely refer to. She sits in the front row at political seminars and she risked her life as a secret courier during the liberation struggle. She is utterly dedicated to the *cause* and is the sort of person you love in your mind but not in your heart.

And now your heart beats out Tuesday, Wednesday, Thursday, Friday, Saturday, Sunday, Monday, Tuesday. Nothing. All this empty time. You break it down into hours. You break it down into minutes. And all that remains then is rage and self-pity.

You remember yet again that when you were about to finish your most recent telephone conversation she reminded you, quite out of the blue, how she had waited for you during your years in France.

What was she trying to tell you?

And with a sudden attack of bitterness, you think: as if you, too, hadn't been waiting during those years! As if the whole long period hadn't been one long "soon" for you too! She is incapable of seeing beyond herself.

Calm down. Stick with your train of thought instead, for France is not a suitable analogy. There was a concrete explanation for that absence, there were oceans and continents between you. And geographical distances are something you know all about. They can be managed. Now there are only two thousand paces between you. Even if it were twenty thousand paces you wouldn't hesitate to put one foot in front of another twenty thousand times. But the kind of distance that lies between you cannot be overcome by stubborn feet. So what is it? Has she been seriously ill? Has her brother had an accident? Has she given you up or left you for another? Is it some kind of childish test of your loyalty?

Resist the idea that is breaking over you like a wave in whose wake you are being sucked into action. You should, you shouldn't, drive your car over to her house and see if her window is lit up or dark.

Avoid the abyss that opens up when you think that this time, this time she will not come back.

For the implication of that thought is that you will never again listen to your undisciplined heart, that you will have nothing but the struggle to devote your life to. And you know what that would imply. A permanent double life in which everything that really matters happens beyond and behind ordinary everyday existence. It might even be necessary to go underground. It might even be necessary for you to leave the city and rejoin the armed struggle in the most distant and disease-ridden jungles. There can be no doubt that you are ready to make that sort of sacrifice, but the fact that your numbers have become fewer and fewer recently, that support for and recruitment to the Organization has shrunk, means that a decision of that kind would have to be taken as *a result* of positions adopted in the past rather than as *a self-evident and glorious step* on the long road left before final victory is achieved.

Don't think about it anymore just now. Escape back to the novel instead. The hour is late, but sharing a bed with these stubborn thoughts would be insufferable. Nothing is decided yet and you still have a variety of futures in front of you.

You start to read and another half hour has been added to the new day. You pause and read the last sentence again. *To respect the freedom of another is to give it precedence over one's own suffering.*

You read the sentence again and feel astonished at the way it seems to have been written especially for you, especially at this time.

You wonder if this is the beginning of madness. Is it? Or is it just your imagination? Or were those discreet hints always present and you failed to notice them until now? But isn't it the case that heightened sensitivity of this kind is in itself an indication of madness?

Calm down. Feel the way the sentence is seeping down through your consciousness, the way your anxiety and agitation ease and are replaced by something that in this context might be called peace. And the way that in its turn is followed by the almost exalted notion that you must share this insightful sentence with her. As a sort of magnanimous act of forgiveness.

Open the drawer of your desk, take out your bundle of postcards. Untie the ribbon holding the thick white cards together. Unscrew the top of your fountain pen and hold its shining gold nib a fraction of a centimetre above the paper. Let the seconds pass, let them grow into minutes. Think out all the words before you place the nib on the white paper and form the blue curves of *Chérie*.

You come to a pause at the end of the incomplete circle of the *e*. Now you should place a punctuation mark to separate off what follows, but how can you bring yourself to make such a mark? You are stuck, confused by the thought that what you want to do is to unite, not to separate. That *is* what you want, isn't it? Indeed, what do you really want?

A blue ink-blot spreads out. The paper slowly absorbs the letters you intended for her eyes.

The moth is hurling itself against the glass with muffled thuds.

Put the top back on your pen and tie a new bow in the silk ribbon. Place the card on top of the glass chimney of the oil lamp and watch how a dark circle quickly takes shape before it bursts into a hungry yellow flame. Throw the flame into the small tin bucket you keep on the floor to burn compromising notes in. Within a few seconds the paper turns to ash and the shadows of night have taken up their old positions in the room.

Go back to the novel. There is still half of it left to read and perhaps somewhere in it you will find a different sort of answer to the uninvited questions that persist in arising.

WEDNESDAY, 31 AUGUST 1955

You put aside the photograph of a young woman. There is real presence in the look she is giving the photographer, and in her smile. You don't know who was standing on the other side of the camera, nor do you want to know.

You have begun to wonder at her ability to make someone who is no more than an observer of her portrait feel chosen. Is it because there is something about her that has nothing to do with a specific individual? The fact that, with all her charm, the object of her attention is herself? That her charisma and her charm are actually internal but she holds them up for the men around to mirror themselves in?

You remember how there seemed to be an almost shimmering quality about her in that beauty contest. The contest she had dismissed as a joke between friends when you wondered about it. Fifteen women on a stage, all them young, all of them beautiful. You remember their bare brown shoulders and the sheen of the silk as it shifted through every nuance of colour.

As you sat in the audience below the stage you saw her with the eyes of a stranger for the first time in a long time. The initial pride you felt in your fiancée turned into a sort of embarrassment you could not understand then and do not understand now. As if you weren't her equal in that hall of cut-glass chandeliers and discreet red-coated waiters. You saw how easily she moved among the other women as they tried to arrange themselves into the formation they had practised. She seemed made of different stuff from them. And you could see that it wasn't the admiration of the guests in evening dress that made her shimmer in that way. And it certainly wasn't your admiration.

You pick up the photograph again and look at the black and white smile she is aiming at the photographer, the fingertips of her left hand resting on her collarbone. Her hair is dark and curly and you place that charming smile face down on the dark surface of the desk.

You count the easily counted weeks that have passed since the moment the mayor placed the coronet on her head and crowned her the Septième Quartier's candidate for the title of *Miss Cambodia*. Then came her victory in the national contest. Confined to bed with a fever, you missed that. But you would have found some excuse not to be present anyway. Given the difficulty you had dealing with the distance between the two of you at the amateurish first-round, you would have found it quite impossible at the grand event, where you would have been relegated to a marginal position.

And now this long series of days of silence that makes it impossible for you not to assume some connection between the one thing and the other. You should have forbidden her to take part, shouldn't you?

Is it really appropriate for an engaged woman to put herself on show like that?

Shouldn't your fiancée, your future wife, remain at your side? Well, at your side, but one step behind, perhaps, as is customary?

Shut your eyes and open them again. Continue:

You take out a sheet of paper and sharpen a pencil. Keep going, you think, everything else is pain. And the pencil quickly fills the paper with handwriting.

You set out points, making them adhere to the rules you have worked out for the Organization. Your aim is to come up with something that can be both a moral and a practical guide. So the points must not be so visionary and abstract that they will be incomprehensible to illiterates out in the countryside. But nor should they be so simplistic that they could be dismissed by the well-educated café revolutionaries in the cities.

In short, you have set yourself the task of capturing the very soul of the struggle.

You have secretly sneaked a look at the Ten Commandments of the Christians. They are commendably comprehensible at the same time as being rather more than just an ordinary set of rules. You have even gone so far as to permit yourself a touch of irony in that the sixth commandment of the Organization forbids *inappropriate behaviour* towards women. You have twice as many commandments, however, in order to stress the superiority of the Organization.

What you have almost managed to forget is that your starting point was a model provided by North Vietnamese comrades. It had, of course, to be adapted to suit local circumstances and to the fact that your struggle is *more honest and superior to theirs*. That's what you say. That's what you think. But in reality your changes represent yet another stubborn attempt to deny the influence of the Vietnamese.

It is simpler than saying no to their money, their weapons and the school of revolution they offer.

You consider the first point, with its command to *love, honour and serve the working class*. You have added: *and the peasants*.

You consider the points that follow: they demand correct behaviour, solidarity, humility and respect for those you are going to liberate, a readiness to support them in their work without any recompense, the prohibition of games of chance and so on through to the final one—*You must be prepared to offer your life for the Organization without hesitation*.

It is a fine set of rules. Everything is covered. By following them new recruits will get along well enough while waiting to be given further and more thorough instruction in matters of doctrine.

But it is not so good that it couldn't be improved on. So you go through it once more, moving words back and forth. Adding bits here and erasing bits there.

If only, you think, if only you had cadres capable of investing local conditions with a sense of the overarching context of events. Cadres familiar with both the fine workings of successful revolutions through-out history and with the particular mentality of your nation. But now it is usually either/or. And those who do possess both tend to have their good qualities outweighed by enthusiasm for the Vietnamese, or for palm wine, or for brothels.

And the closer the future approaches, the more difficult it is to distinguish which elements are the decisive ones. Chance creeps into the machinery and existing assumptions are pushed aside. Carefully considered strategies don't last long when new situations are constantly arising. You stick loyally to the Organization's *line*, but it becomes more and more difficult to get an overview of the consequences.

Take, for instance, the urgency of your own situation. Your brothers have been under siege in your older brother's house for some days. And you, their little brother, have still not gone to them.

Y

Y   Y

Night has fallen.

You and a night that seems to have nothing to do with the day that preceded it. As if it is quite detached from its calendrical context. Your throat is only letting through just the amount of oxygen your body demands, so there is no space left to exhale. Your heart is beating hard within its bony cage, but how regular is its beat? How regular is its beat? It's irregular, isn't it, as if your heart has gone astray and is beating haphazardly? More and more desperately?

As if it is going to burst?

Your breathing. You must get control of your breathing. Keep your breaths short so that the air can both enter and leave your body. You've never been so *unreally real* before, have you?

There is no possibility of your getting through all the hours between now and the morning. The night is going to grind you to dust.

Your heart misses beats and gallops to catch up. The darkness pressing down on your ribcage makes you gasp for breath. Your throat becomes more and more constricted. The stars in front of your eyes shrink to concentrated points before exploding.

There is a glass of water by your bed. Reach out under the mosquito net and grasp the glass with your right hand. Drink it in small regular sips. Bring the normality of water to your breathlessness, bring the normality of the glass to the arrhythmic beating of your heart.

Feel the water in your mouth.

Open your eyes. Open your eyes even though it makes no difference. The darkness is utterly impenetrable. But open your eyes anyway and look at the darkness. The fan hums as it spins and it wafts a weak draught of air back and forth across your body. It is the night between a Wednesday and a Thursday, the night between the last day of August and the first of September and you can't breathe.

The nightly cloudburst will come soon. The air will be saturated with moisture and the odour of moisture. There will be the deafening noise of rain pounding on tin roofs and tiled roofs and palm-leaf roofs. You will lie there, a thin sheet covering your legs, and through the mosquito net you will feel the fan passing back and forth over you. You will look into the darkness, enclosed in the sound of the rain.

That is how your month of August will end and your month of September begin. And you can, if you like, take it as an omen. You can, if you like, see it as a simple symbol of the life you have chosen to live in the age in which you are living. Or you can just lie there and compare the darkness behind your eyelids with the darkness that is all around you.

You lie there and keep watch on your heart. It seems to be back in phase.

You have never experienced anything like this before. You look for reasons, but your thoughts seem locked tight in her silence.

That is where everything is.

Try to break these trains of thought that twist and turn in upon themselves, becoming intolerable, intractable. Try to break them by recalling the person you were half a lifetime ago: the fifteen-year-old whose sister danced for the old king. How you used to go after school to the house behind the palace where the dancers lived. To the rooms that men were not permitted to enter. But you weren't a man then, were you? Or, at least, you weren't considered to be one. Slim, pale-skinned, with a child's round face. That did not stop the bored dancers.

Sink back into memories of the dancing girls. Remember how your initial embarrassment left you and you began to feel at home with the jargon and the annoying games. Remember how the strange smells of make-up and perfume became a private universe of scents that you entered at the end of the school day.

You could have shown off by telling all the stories to your school-mates. But this early experience taught you that keeping a secret brings many advantages.

Go into the rooms. Go into one and then on into another. Fill them with a mixture of ornamented dark wood, imported tubular steel furniture and the mild disorder created by twenty or so spoilt young women. Sit down with Vichea and try to stop her unbuttoning your shirt buttons. In the darkness of the room alongside you catch a glimpse of Mom's nakedness, as she stands there facing away from you. Unaware that anyone is watching, her stance is unguarded.

Are you sinking now? Do you recognize the odour of the spacious rooms of the dancing girls? Do you recognize your niggling worry that your sister might catch you in the middle of doing something twice forbidden? Can you hear their voices?

Move farther into this calmness, move on through the next door, move on to another pleasing memory. Walk along the narrow rain-soaked pavement and see the silhouette of the Paris Opera over to your right when you cross the street. Allow yourself to be tempted for a moment by the smells coming first from the crêpe stall and then from the bakery. You are hungry. You are almost always hungry in this city. Take a deep breath of the cold dry air. Carry on along the street with your frozen hands tightly clenched in your coat pockets. You know exactly which way to go here. You even know the three men sleeping rough squashed in the doorway you will soon be passing. You have a smile and a shake of your head ready to respond to their demanding croaks and outstretched crooked fingers. Do you remember what it feels like to walk along that narrow pavement and to be wearing so many clothes, their weight on your body, the cold on your skin and the clouds over the rooftops?

But it is the wrong street to be walking down. One block farther on lies the post office from which you send your letters to her. In a flash everything disappears and you return to the surface.

You are lying in the dark and you no longer know whether your eyes are open or closed, and her silence is a storm roaring through your soul, a storm which tears loose everything you value and carries it along before hurling it out into meaninglessness. You get a sense of a smooth pond with greenery crowding right down to the edge of the water. That smooth water is her silence. Strong hands are pushing your face down beneath the surface and until now you have managed with increasing desperation to hold your breath, but tonight will see the unavoidable violent intake of breath. But it will only mean agonizing pain, without bringing an end to the breathlessness.

Sit up. The rain hasn't arrived yet. There is still time to act. Sit up and feel your way out of the cube formed by the mosquito net. Feel the numbness reluctantly leaving your body and limbs. Let your fingers search the dusty surface of the bedside table. Strike a match. Put it to the wick of the oil lamp.

The darkness is banished in a flash, withdrawing into the corners as shadows.

You sit on the edge of your bed. You light the oil lamp. You see the way the yellow light shades over into shadow in the corners of the room.

There is a small altar in one corner, left behind by a previous tenant. You haven't got round to throwing it out yet.

Take a couple of barefoot steps over to the altar. There is an empty small brass cup in front of this little spirit house. Fill it with fresh water and take out two incense sticks.

Do something that no amount of self-criticism in front of the Organization will ever be able to make undone.

Light the incense sticks. Blow out the flames.

White smoke curls up from the glowing tips of both of them.

Hold the sticks between the palms of your hands. It feels both familiar and unfamiliar. Then bring your hands to your forehead three times.

Place the sticks in the altar and pray to the spirit of the house that it will watch over your heart even though you have devoted years to denying everything supernatural. In spite of your constant destructive criticism of all *superstitions*, pray to it to give you sleep. It is the last day of a month, the first day of a new one. And if there is one thing you need it is the refreshment brought by dreamless sleep.

THURSDAY, I SEPTEMBER 1955

You hear the sound of rain on a tiled roof. A short time ago you defied the rain and now you are sitting there as wet as if you had been swimming. Your shirt sticking to your skin, you are about to wring out your socks and hang them on the rail in front of you. But unlike French rain this is warm rain and you don't feel cold.

Beyond the railings and the curtains of rain you can just make out Vannsak's garden.

Vannsak is not here yet because this is not an arranged meeting.

You have still not done anything to support your brothers. That is going to arouse suspicion—if it hasn't done so already. It is also going to be held against you by your very extended family, which forms a network too wide to survey, with influence at different levels.

But the passing days have done nothing to loosen the knot, to solve the dilemma. You are still at a loss as to what to do. Passive in the face of a situation that demands immediate action.

Which is why you took that quick walk in the rain. You could have taken your car, you could have taken your rain-cape or your umbrella, but it was more a matter of rushing *away* from somewhere than moving *towards* somewhere else. A pointless attempt to force the outer world to gain mastery over the inner.

Initially you thought of consulting Sok and Yan at tomorrow's meeting. The situation is an urgent one with the potential to do a great deal of damage to the Organization. It would be sensible to seek guidance from the centre. But then you thought that if the Organization had wanted you to act in one way rather than another you would already have been informed of it. You can assume, then, that you enjoy their confidence, that you have permission to solve the problem on your own. Some sort of test of your judgement and your ability.

Or—you then thought, with the sweet warm rain streaming down your face—even the unknown men in the inner circle of the Organization don't have any idea what to do.

So you are waiting for Vannsak, who should be arriving at any moment. To some extent your problem with the detention of your brothers is also his problem. You will ask him what he thinks you should do, and then you will attempt to fit his answer into the hidden whole that is known only to you.

Vannsak's house is behind you. It is still empty and silent. Suzanne is probably teaching. And you think that this unwanted dilemma has at least brought one benefit, which is that you cannot think the thoughts you would otherwise be thinking.

You are standing in front of your small blotched mirror with a half-knotted tie in your hands. You have wrapped the shiny black material round your slim fingers and are holding it up to your throat while staring into your own eyes. The years are beginning to show there, around the eyes. The rest of your face is still a young man's face. But something about this utterly habitual movement has caused time to concertina—memories, after all, don't tend to index themselves in the same chronological order as the calendar.

You are standing in front of a mirror getting ready for a *soirée dansante*. It is the first for many weeks and had it not been for the fact that it is being organized by an ad hoc combination of the youth sections of progressive groups you would not have been going to it.

Outside the stars are already bright and the bullfrogs croaking their bass notes. The oil lamp is on the bedside table, diagonally to the left.

You are a good dancer but you have never felt less like dancing. The only person you want to dance with won't be there.

Get on with tying your tie. You don't have much time.

Don't think about the cardboard box at the bottom of your wardrobe. The one filled with letters that were sent from here to Paris and then came home with you. Letters you have read many times and ought to destroy. It is not right for a revolutionary to be carting around sentimental souvenirs of that sort.

But you haven't reached that point yet. For four years the two of you were held together by letters and letters alone. Four years of saved letters should be a souvenir of love worthy of display in a glass cabinet in your home. A letter with a lock of hair tied in a silk ribbon, another containing gold glitter that has dribbled out and stuck to everything else.

You see Somaly before you. Her long neck, high cheekbones, small ears. The dress she is wearing is black with sparkling silver details, it is pale yellow with red patterns, it is olive green with graphite-grey silk *crêpe de chine*, it is gold silk that shifts to lilac. The nails on her long fingers are deep red and rose pink and dark brown. She is sitting in armchairs, on chairs, on sofas. She is sitting on a rug on the grass with the river behind her. In your car. She is walking up and down stairs. On her left wrist she is wearing a slim gold watch you gave her.

One thing that is constant throughout is the way her hands work while her thoughts are elsewhere. Mechanically picking to pieces a rose you have given her, tearing up a bit of scrap paper, taking apart a decorative bow that came with a present from you.

You can also change the memory picture to one in which she is drawing as she listens to someone. She is not short of talent, particularly when it comes to designing exclusive clothes. But she never knows when to stop. Every sketch reaches a stage at which it could be considered finished. There is almost always one more line that could be added, shading that could be deepened, a detail that could be filled in. But it could also be left as it is. Beautiful. But you watch her adding more, always adding more. She doesn't stop even when, distractedly, she thickens up elegantly sweeping lines or gives coarse weight to something that began as a light suggestion. In the end the portrait or the landscape or the objects she was drawing have all but disappeared under pencil or ink.

You think of everything else you could think of and you are amazed that these particular scenes are the ones that return the whole time. Ones in which she is reduced to being a kind of absence, or that reveal the instinctive destructive will of her hands. She is actually quite the opposite. Everyone she turns to is made to feel they are the most remarkable person in the world.

You don't have time to look for clues in letters that contain no clues. They are too old and too well read too many times to be hiding an answer to the questions you are now asking. Nor do you have time to burn them, which seems a more and more sensible alternative.

Instead, straighten your tie-knot and turn down the collar of your shirt. You have a front to keep up, now more than ever. Turn off the oil lamp and let the darkness close around you. Walk the few steps to the door. Open the door and step out into the clear starry night, where the full moon is bathing the city in silver light.

Y

Y   Y

You pick up the scent of perfume. An expensive and leafy perfume that you know well. You have detected traces of it in the innermost folds of her letters, you have known it to fill cars and to wash over you when she is standing in front of you.

You have had it shown to you in the sort of boutique where the assistants wear white gloves. And the thought came to you that *she is here*.

She is not. But inhale the perfume as you execute elegant turns among the other dancing couples in the muted light from the stage and from the small lamps on the tables. You don't know from which couple the scent is coming. It swept past just as you were beginning to lose yourself in the movements, in the rhythms.

Dance on. Brace yourself in case you should dance through that perfumed air again. Dance on in the forbidden recognition that you will leave everything behind once the election is won. Everything, in exchange for that perfume and for dance evenings more exclusive than this one.

Most of the people dancing in couples are Europeans. You are one of three mixed couples. Your fellow-countrymen are dancing in an elliptical ring in front of the stage, making the traditional hand movements and smiling gaily at one another.

But you curve and swing expertly among the couples dancing in the same style as you.

It is hot to be wearing suits or tight-fitting silk dresses. All the men's ties are still properly knotted and the women's light gauzy shawls are draped over their shoulders.

You follow the discreet four-four rhythm, leading a French friend of Vannsak's wife. Without any affectation at all she

J'ai caché

introduced herself as Anne and she has green eyes. She is travelling through and she is a good dancer. You have been conversing

Mieux que partout ailleurs

politely about sights worth seeing and then about French lyric poetry. Verlaine, Hugo. Now the two of you are lost in the same dance but in different thoughts. Swing and turn, follow the beat with gliding steps. Sense the force-field of her body just a few centimetres away from yours.

Au grand jardin de mon coeur

You are seeking a perfume that is not hers. But you cannot find it. You want and you don't want to find

Une petite fleur

it again. Perhaps it was just your imagination. Perhaps it was the ghost of a scent from other dances.

So sink into the music. Close your eyes. Merge with the tones and the harmonies and the syncopation.

Cette fleur

Let them become colours to your inner eye. Breathe yourself into the beat. Turn around, turn in.

Plus jolie qu'un bouquet

Become the music.

You breathe in, you breathe out.

Elle garde en secret

Your heart drums a dull rhythmic beat through your body. Breathe in, then out. Calmly, regularly,

Tous mes rêves d'enfant

a bass passage hands over

L'amour de mes parents

to a solo on the theme, the bright green, drawn-out tone of the clarinet. The dish of the cymbal sways, shimmers. And you

Et tous ces clairs matins

breathe in. You breathe out.

Faits d'heureux souvenirs lointains

The muffled rhythms.

You breathe in.

Quand la vie
Par moments me trahit
Tu restes mon bonheur
Petite fleur

You breathe out.

You make a turn. You follow the gently lingering four-four of the music. There are five men on the stage. They are wearing

Sur mes vingt ans

crimson jackets, black bow-ties and shining patent leather shoes. Their shirt fronts seem to you

Je m'arrête un moment

to be giving off their own light in the weak light, and now the drummer has exchanged his sticks for brushes and is moving them

Pour respirer

in a slow and absent-minded way. They are all playing with their eyes half closed and the saxophonist moistens

Le parfum que j'ai tant aimé

his lips and then makes a solitary note swell until it begins to coil capriciously through what the others are playing.

Dans mon coeur
Tu fleuriras toujours

Turn, follow the beat. Lead your partner between the other couples. Feel the slight dampness of her hand in your left hand, the smooth silk of her back under the palm of your right hand. Let your steps glide across the floor.

Au grand jardin d'amour
Petite fleur

You are here now. Nothing has changed but it is good for you to be able to disappear into the perspiring darkness of the dance. To dance with someone you don't know, someone *attirante*. To concentrate your mind on an irrelevant conversation. And the quiet satisfaction—in spite of the state of emergency raging in your mind—of being able to carry on a witty conversation without for one moment revealing your inner turbulence. A real test of discipline.

Then the music comes to an abrupt stop and the circular movements of the dancing couples around the dance floor are replaced by straight lines, as they make their way to the tables where their parties are waiting for them. Take your partner back to the table where Vannsak and Suzanne are sitting. See, the two of them are talking, with deep shadows among the smiles. The little lamp on the table appears to be standing in a pool of light, reflected by glasses and carafes. Pull out the chair for your Anne but don't sit down yourself because you have seen a familiar back standing over by the door.

Excuse yourself and walk over to the back. It belongs to a friend, yours and Vannsak's. You were in France together and now you are in politics together even though the Organization directed you towards the Democrats and him to the People's Party.

Go up to your friend and the people he is with, and place your hand on his shoulder. There is relatively little danger in being seen with him, here anyway, and you can always point to your joint French past.

He is talking in a loud voice and registers your presence with his eyes but continues talking. His eyes are bright with wine and his cheeks are flushed, but you know that does not necessarily imply intoxication. You all always joke about the way his appearance changes after just the odd glass. He only has to pull the cork out of a bottle for his shirt to get crumpled.

When he has finished the point he is making one of the others takes over, at which he leans over and says in a low voice that he needs to talk to you. Not now, but very soon. He hasn't finished the discussion he is having here, and he breaks in to continue his argument for a strong and pluralist parliament. *Whatever that so-called king or prince or fellow citizen or whatever the bloody hell he calls himself, His High-Arsed Highness Norodom Sihanouk, may try to introduce.*

You feel the carefree charm of the dance leaving you, being replaced by something that calls for a very different edge of sharpness. Your friend's errand must be very urgent, otherwise he would have chosen a safer, less public occasion. Probably, you think, there are urgent instructions from the Organization about how to behave with regard to both of your brothers. The Organization has taken its time about it, but any concerns you have that your passivity might have been found irritating are outweighed by your relief at finally getting instructions.

Without concentrating you listen to your friend's well-known volubility and you recall how frightening you found his intensity when you first met him a decade ago. His wide frog-like mouth and superior banter. Now you know his value and tend to worry that he will talk too loudly and too dangerously. It is people like him you're going to need if you are ever to convince surly caretakers at the Ministry of Fisheries.

He eventually finishes underlining his point yet again and, taking a light grip on your arm, he leads you to an alcove behind the table of refreshments. It seems such an obvious place to go for confidential conversations that you would never have chosen it yourself. Particularly not at a politically pinkish dance like this one, which will undoubtedly have attracted all kinds of informers. But you can't bring yourself to wait any longer and so you don't raise any objections. The face in front of you is serious although his hair is a mess in spite of his hair oil. He says that the news he is bringing is not too good. It has still to be confirmed, but it is not too good.

You nod for him to go on and you think the police must have tired of blockading your brothers and smashed their way in. That the words *not too good* imply that violence has occurred. You get ready for one of those rapid scene changes in which the happy buzz and the music are replaced in a matter of minutes by the tight-lipped silence that rules at a hospital bedside. That you will find yourself standing in a room with tiled walls lit by the grey-white light of neon tubes and there will still be some residual sense of the dance left in your body. A sense that is as superfluous and alien in that location as a dance card clinging to the sole of your shoe. With a dry throat, you swallow and nod again, more impatiently this time.

He tells you that someone on the edge of his circle of acquaintances, but someone he trusts, has told him that yesterday he saw your Somaly having dinner alone with no less a figure than the Deputy Prime Minister Sam Sary, *of all the swine that this government has to show for itself.*

There is, of course, room for misunderstanding (he says), but a rumour is a rumour he's sorry to say.

Your friend falls silent and looks out over the dimly lit room where the band is making its way back onto the stage. The movements in the room look almost choreographed as new pairs of dancers form up.

He pats you on the chest two or three times in a rather preoccupied way before nodding and returning to his party.

And your anguish bursts out like the opening of an ice-cold burning flower, and it blooms, and it blooms.

II. SARY

Let us stick to the truth:
It can create beauty.
The light of its fire is wonderful in the darkness of night.

WISLAWA SZYMBORSKA
Close to the Eye

FRIDAY, 2 SEPTEMBER 1955

And look, there he comes, the steps flit past beneath his Italian shoes, his manicured hand rises in a quick greeting, long strides, a half-smoked cigarette left lying on the marble floor. (The echo of heels.) And he moves on. In and out of rooms, up and down staircases, a signature here, a couple of comments there, before he sinks nonchalantly into an armchair while the permanent secretary stands at attention behind the desk.

And up. And on.

SATURDAY, 3 SEPTEMBER 1955

He puts the document with the others he has signed. A hand movement not unlike that of a Catholic priest. Unlike the sign of the cross, however, which dissolves into the air, his movement leaves *a trace*. An unbroken ink line. Not wrapping around itself in ellipses and bows as is usually the case. No, no, no.

The mark of power. His name.

Seven small hard clear letters (now drying on the paper).

Where is he? In his office. What time is it? He does not know, but darkness fell hours (several) ago.

The day's newspapers are lying scattered on the floor. (7,000 DEAD IN ALGERIA   HARD BATTLES IN GAZA   THE OUTLOOK FOR A POLITICAL SOLUTION IN MOROCCO WORSENS   THE MAU MAU REBELLION IS WANING   STATE OF EMERGENCY IN ARGENTINA, etc., etc.)

The next document. With an accompanying map. He turns it the right way up, bends forward to look at the various districts. They have been drawn in such rudimentary detail that it is little more than a sketch. It depicts the area of the forthcoming EXPOSITION INTERNATIONALE DE PNOMH-PENH 1955. That is the southern part of the Troisième Quartier. Or *the European part* of the city. (The division is not quite that categorical but, on the whole, the ambitions of *the colonizers* have been realized. That is, one part of the city dominated by the whites (Power), one by the Chinese (Capital) and one by the Vietnamese (Bureaucracy). Many people (Sary, for instance) feel that the majority population of the country has been *passed over*. Disadvantaged, as in many other respects.)

Sary runs his finger along the thick black line that marks the enclosure around the exposition. On the north-western side of Wat Phnomh he finds what he is looking for: six ovals marked with the figure 8 (defined in the column alongside as "zoo").

He thinks: so our nation is supposed to regain its proper place in the world with the help of a zoo. A bloody zoo.

Give a big hand to the yellow niggers and their monkeys!

He thinks (it's late, his concentration is not what it should be, the pills have worn off) of another exhibition, at another time, in another country. To be more specific: the carnival in Graneville in Normandy in 1949 (the year before he came home from France). A long pier running out to sea. White-painted wood, stained by standing where wind and water meet. Seasons which—unlike here—came and went. Pennants fluttering colourfully in the wind and people walking around in their Sunday best. Their eyes lingered on the foreign faces—his and his friends'. But he had been smartly dressed (it was just after his annual stipend had been paid). And for the war-marked participants at that festival, money had been almost as important as origin.

(That *strange freedom* he had in the land of his colonial masters: there, but not here in his own colonized homeland, he could sit anywhere he wanted in the bus.)

He varies the scene. *Take out*: his friends Bith and Van. *Add in*: Somaly (dressed in a close-fitting red—no, cream—dress. Parasol in the same shade.) He imagines them walking together on the *boards* of the pier. The whites stare at them open-mouthed. They stroll (slowly) out towards the strip of the horizon. She has placed her gloved hand on his arm. (In his mind he has veiled the sky with thin white cloud.) Her voice through the wind, something that makes him smile (something like: He: "Why won't you take the diamond ring?" She: "Don't want it." He: "But it's a symbol of my love and you know that diamonds are forever." She: "But it's not me." He: "What is the right thing for someone like you, then?" She: "I don't know—cut flowers perhaps."). His eyes never leave her face. And there is something he notices in particular: even her ears are perfectly formed.

His eyes focus again on the map he is holding. Lines, figures, unbuilt structures fall into shape again.

He raises his eyes and sees his own reflection mirrored in the windowpanes: a bespectacled and slightly distorted oval, ghostlike, lit diagonally from below (his papers are reflecting the light from the table lamp). White shirt, collar unbuttoned. His thick unruly hair is partially swallowed by the darkness.

The air conditioning is humming softly over in the corner.

He thinks: the future is here, not there.

The future—what can be said about it? A great deal apparently, since no one seems to do anything but discuss it. (After having been fixated on the past—the golden age, injustices and so on—the nation is now suddenly ready to turn and face *what is to come*.) And Sary is more than ready, he can be heard arguing that the country has *unique possibilities*, a *mystique* that stirs the imagination (particularly of people from the West), excellent preconditions for *extravagant and expensive* tourism. In the vanguard of the young architects of the country, he can envisage a reallocation of national resources as simple as it is radical. Instead of allowing the country's riches to be transferred to the vaults of foreign banks, they will be used to sweep away the hovels and palm-leaf roofs out in the rural districts (images he is fond of using in his many electoral speeches). Rubber, pepper and rice will pay for new roads to new cities. (Details of all this are to be found in a bulging folder in the archives of the Minister of the Interior Leng.)

Sary, his eyes still on his own reflection, notes that one advantage of earlier stagnation is that there is less outdated garbage to be incinerated. A hundred lost years will be made up in a decade. I'll be damned if this isn't the new America. *Mon Amérique à moi.* The Mekong will become a glittering mirror for skyscrapers and, he thinks, it will be from the sixty-second floor that I shall view the world—a world that will look with respect and astonishment and envy at what has been achieved. *Just as once upon a time they respected and were amazed by our forefathers.*

This is the vision he has of her, at his side, electric lights burning below. (Her attire is the same, minus the parasol.)

And a zoo with a mangy tiger is not going to help to achieve that. Irritated, he closes the folder with the sketch map. Prints REJECTED on the cover and puts it back among the others.

Then he takes it back. Looks again at the faint lines of the exposition pavilions drawn over parks and pavements. He moves it over to the pile of documents for *further consideration*.

He takes the next folder in (dis)order. It contains a hundred or so sheets listing the customs revenues for the first half-year. He takes out the front flyleaf. Notes: that fatso Dara has written his name in cramped handwriting (wrapping around itself in ellipses and bows) below the heading, in spite of the fact that all the work was most probably done by some underling. (He rings for his adjutant: *Whisky and soda*. Lights another cigarette.) Leans back in his armchair, skims quickly/impatiently through the columns of typed figures.

SUNDAY, 4 SEPTEMBER 1955

He shuts his eyes, just for a moment. Opens them. Gets up. Walks briskly across the boards of the platform, gives the microphone a light tap. Hears the tap echo out over the faces turned towards him.

The sky is blue, the sun is scorching. Steam from the recent rain is rising from the foliage.

In a loud and clear voice he says: My dear fellow-countrymen!

He says: Kinsmen of our revered forefathers who built Angkor!

He says with a smile: Dear residents of Kompong Speu.

Then with a serious expression, an expression almost of concern, he continues.

The loudspeakers are good.

o

o   o

(*A couple of hours later*) Sam Sary is sitting in the back of his comfortable car (a modern car without a sliding window between the driver and the passengers). As usual, Phirun is his driver—a taciturn man. (Phirun is the same age as his boss as well as being the first cousin once removed of one of his wife Em's maternal aunts, and he has, in the usual order of these things, not been given the job on merit but in accordance with the *client system*, which has provided the real structure of this kingdom since time immemorial. It is a system that they all agree, rather touchingly, must be abolished if there is to be any chance of introducing genuine democracy. But everyone—apart from a handful of *idealists*—thinks it is up to the others to start the process of divesting themselves of the privileges they have acquired as a result of the well-oiled mechanisms of nepotism.)

The car brakes gently and stops. Sary steps out of the stuffy vehicle into the throbbing heat and takes a couple of quick steps across the pavement into the cool shade of the Hôtel Angkor. A smiling red-coated doorman is waiting to accompany him to the dining room, where a smiling white-coated head waiter shows him to a window table.

At the table Sam Nhean (his father, minister of culture, one of the leaders of the small and newly formed—but oh, so influential—Unity Party, and much more) is sitting reading the conservative Unity Party's own newspaper. Printed in an ugly blue. (The authoritarian, some might say *reactionary*, newspaper bears the motto: COUNTRY RELIGION KING.) There is a half-empty wine glass in front of his father.

After a brief greeting he takes the chair opposite. Then selects a dry cigarillo (Café Crème) from the tray of smokes. The dining room is almost empty and the head waiter himself brings his wine (Chateau Mont Redon) and strikes a match for him.

He looks out of the window. *Outside*: people are moving with afternoon slowness in sunlight that is almost white. Over beyond the quay heavily laden boats glide back and forth across the swollen brown river. *Inside*: a son becoming more and more impatient, as he waits for his father to put down the paper and pick up his wine glass.

He catches himself tapping his shoes on the stone floor and thinking that time is moving at a different speed for the two of them during the week that remains before the crucial day.

(His father's face over the top of the newspaper: heavy eyelids, the wart with long hairs on his cheek, certain lines and proportions he recognizes from his own face in the mirror.)

Then his father folds the paper and meets his gaze. Sam Sary and Sam Nhean, hair parted on the same side, suits that are stitched by the same tailor. (An informal node crackling with the sparks of naked power.) The son waits in a filial way for his father's opening remark.

For some years now Sam Nhean has been *his old self* again. That is to say, he is the Sam Nhean who made his way from province to palace, from nothing to everything. The man who was so (advantageously) close to the old king, whose services were sought by the French colonialists and then by the Japanese occupiers. And then, after the war, he made a number of uncharacteristic mistakes for a man on the make. (Officially it was all about trading in cotton thread without approved import licences. Unofficially it was about trading in goods of a very different sort.) After being out of favour for a few years he recovered with the support of the most gifted and energetic of his sons (Sary)—the launch pad being the founding of yet another new party (People's Party), which afterwards merged with the prince's Popular Socialist Community as final proof of the *unswerving loyalty* of the Sam family. In return he was rewarded with glittering but less than demanding posts: minister of culture, member of the Council of State, master of ceremonies at certain royal occasions and so on.

Is he satisfied? Yes, at this stage of his life (sixty-five), this is quite sufficient even for a man of such extraordinary ambition.

Does he want to see change? No, and that is what he makes clear (yet again) to his son. According to the patriarch Sam, ideologies are nothing but *figments of the European mind*, which will only lead people astray in this part of the world. His analysis? Power is a constant and its institutions only change form marginally over the centuries. Revolutions signify nothing more than changes in terms of the individuals who, for the moment, sleep in the palace and use its lavatories. *The foundation* on which the outer works rest *remains the same*. (And that is where all the elements of any importance are located.)

What does Sary do? He smokes another dry cigarillo, tries to look attentive. His father has now moved on to report what his conservative colleagues among the leaders of the Unity Party (Army Chief of Staff Lon Nol, old Nhiek Tioulung, Yem Sambur *et consortes*) have been up to recently. Cautious gentlemen all of them, who (rightly) consider they have a good deal to lose. But pragmatists, his father assures him, and explains: their *ambivalence* is increasing in the run-up to an expensive election—not least because the outcome of the election looks as if it will need to be fabricated. And his father asks rhetorically: Who are you and the prince actually trying to fool? The repression is already being reported in the international press, he says and points to the Unity Party newspaper (which will most certainly not contain a word about anything of the sort).

Sary:
That's not what I want, Father. Quite the opposite. If I had my way the election would be run properly.

Nhean:
And that monk Chung? The one you killed?

Sary:
As you know, Father, I'm not alone in this.

His father looks at him without any warmth and, after a moment's silence, says you're the one who's responsible anyway. That it would be better if we just went back to the traditional system, with none of these idiotic facades. That the colourful rags the prince has stitched together to form the patchwork coalition of his *Popular Socialist Community* do at least have *one thing in common*: they support the prince and don't give a damn as to what title the country is ruled under as long as their interests are preserved!

His father gives him to understand that he has carried out certain surveys. And this is what the results look like. Conclusion? Childishly simple—reduce the whole spectacle to a referendum. To a *yes* or *no* to the prince's policies (like the "election" of last spring). Or, and his father is not against the idea, off with the silk gloves! Give the police free rein, lock up the troublemakers, shoot those who refuse to play along.

(Nhean: *You are not a realist. The Democrats have 54 bloody seats out of the 78 in the current National Assembly. How are you going to be able not just to cut that majority but to overtake it in a week? Without resorting to force?*)

Sary objects. He says, with all due respect, that his father and his father's allies are underestimating the potential of the international non-aligned movement. India, the biggest democracy in the world, has taken the lead. Two thousand million people in total. All countries with a similar background, with the same problems and the same goals. (Sary took part in the Bandung Conference last April and is attracted, not to say impressed, by the visions and principles that were drawn up there. A road that is independent of the two Cold War superpowers (both of which insist on the express loyalty of all small states).)

He says: In the long term it seems to me to be a possible way to retain the freedom of the nation. *To put it more forcefully, our only possibility.*

He continues: If we take sides internationally, it will lead to a simultaneous polarization in terms of domestic politics. And that might lead to developments beyond our control, especially bearing in mind the *considerable support* which existed, in spite of everything, for the communist cause during the independence struggle. In order to win the respect of the Non-Aligned Movement and to gain influence with it, a free parliamentary election is absolutely essential—one that is approved of by electoral monitors from all the major powers and their satellites. The rest of the world was not impressed by last February's referendum, and that is putting it mildly. And, he adds with a shrug of his shoulders, *the prince is still enthusiastic about his election campaign.*

Is Nhean even listening to him?

Yes, he must be, because now he mutters: *What do you mean by free? Free to make completely crazy choices? The prince clearly doesn't know his own people.*

His father continues (eyes gazing out of the window): Well, you know where I stand on the question of suffrage. But ever since you and the prince were permitted to rub shoulders with the real *bong thom* (godfathers) in Geneva and Bandung, you seem to have lost all sense of proportion. Your *own* proportion. The *country's* proportion. You seem to me to be more and more some kind of *idealists without any sense of reality*, and this kingdom doesn't need any more of that sort. Lowering his voice even though the dining room is empty: This country is an insignificant little country, not a great power. And we should behave accordingly. Understood? Free elections? Where are you going to find them among the non-aligned nations? With Nasser? With Tito? Or Sukarno?

Sary does not answer. He has no desire to prolong this conversation, which is not so much a conversation as a confirmation of long held positions.

So the silence spreads, filling the dining room (apart from the whirring hum of the fan on the ceiling).

Sary opens his mouth to excuse himself but his father speaks before he has a chance to do so. Says, glossing things over (at the same time as making it obvious that this is the real purpose of the meeting): It would be best for us to see each other more regularly in future. We must act as one from now on. I may not always be properly informed about the very latest developments, but I do have a perspective (*based on my long experience*) that you will find useful.

Shall we say the same time tomorrow then?

The question strikes a spark that comes close to igniting his son's accumulated irritation. His days between now and the election are divided into half-hour slots, each of them already filled in. Why can't his father understand that? But he swallows hard and switches to his ministerial persona (thus making use of a formal structure that is actually the reverse of the real actual order of precedence). Says: *I'll ring you.*

His father looks at him with an inscrutable gaze, then answers (his mouth fixed in a scornful expression), *that will be good then*, before opening the newspaper.

And out. And on.

o

o   o

Madame Shum passes him a stiff photograph. (Shortsightedly, Sary holds it at an angle in the light of the oil lamp.) He remarks how time passes.

The shy young girl, who was introduced to him once (it couldn't have been very long ago, could it?) on the same veranda where he is presently sitting, looks out of the portrait with the self-confidence of a young woman. There is a hint of her mother's features. Though everything that is sweet and pretty in the daughter is only faintly discernible in the fat face that is hovering like a grotesque grinning mask in the shadows by the table.

Madame Shum:
Don't you think she became beautiful while she was in Saigon?

Sary:
Undoubtedly. How old is she now?

Madame Shum:
21.

The scene: A large bamboo building under a starry sky, framed by a garden with dense foliage. The window shutters are open, the light inside the room muted. The rattan furniture on the large veranda is unoccupied apart from two armchairs in which Sary and Madame Shum are sitting (he on the left, she on the right, seen from the entrance). There are small lighted oil lamps on each table. There is a sign over the door: SALON DE DÉSINTOXICATION. (Yes, well.) Dogs can be heard out in the darkness, a radio is playing hot jazz. Apart from that, a quiet September night between the rains.

The contents of the glass in front of him have separated out into lukewarm gin, lime juice and the water from the ice cubes. He leans back against the hard back of the chair, closes his eyes. And thinks some more about the girl in the photograph. (*Elle est pas mal la petite.*) 21, 21, 21. Even younger than Somaly, then. But what's the old woman Shum up to, showing off her daughter like this? Is it an offer? Or just boasting?

Whichever: one thing must be weighed against another (as always).

He thinks: what if we look at it another way? What if this woman is permitted to keep her establishment—would that be enough recompense? If she can first be convinced that closure is the alternative? Once the election is over the occasional trip to Saigon will certainly be on the cards. (Or exile, for that matter.)

On the other hand: wouldn't it be smarter to rely on the local talent *over there*? Rather than on someone who could simply pick up a phone and ring the gossipmongers back here?

He empties his drink, gets up. Madame Shum leads him through the double doors. The row of rooms is just as it was. The same Chinese furniture, now rather past its prime, the same dim lighting as when he was last here. The same glazed eyes glinting from the benches along the walls. The same sweet and sickly haze.

(And, as usual, reality corrects the remembered images. The young women in classically cut silk dresses, who are carrying trays to the men stretched out on the bamboo mats, look very dreary and ordinary.)

Low-voiced conversations, the bubbling of the pipes. Stifled coughs.

Madame Shum leads him to a room on the right. Screens separate the low tables. At one of them he catches a glimpse of the pale Western torsos. At another, Non is half-lying. She leaves them as she came, swaying, the glow of her cigarette in its holder like a firefly in the hazy darkness.

(*Condensed Biography*: Lon Non (d.o.b. 1930), number seven in the uncontrollably growing horde of children (ten so far) of the district chief Lon Hin; Lon is the little brother of Lon Nol, chief of staff of the army (whom he worships, with the result that some people scornfully refer to him as *petit frère*). All in all, a vain, energetic but *competent* 25-year-old. With the future (if short) in front of him.)

One of the serving girls gives him a sarong and a small, damp, cool terry towel. He changes, wipes his face and neck with the towel while the girl prepares his first pipe. She seems new to the work. He asks in a friendly way what she is called and she answers (without meeting his eyes).

He looks at her small soft hands, the shape of her breasts beneath the material of her dress. Perhaps, he thinks. Perhaps not, he thinks.

Turns to Non instead: *Well, Non? How are things going for us?*

Non gives a report. Low-voiced, efficient. (Perhaps it comes from being *little brother* six times over?) He tells him about posters torn down, local opposition politicians who have been visited, and one or two threats that have been turned into action.

Sary takes his first puff of the first pipe.

The French have not exactly left behind an experienced electorate. (God knows.) (According to Sary, who agrees with his father on this point) A degree of *bluntness* is necessary to make them understand what is good for them. In front of them lies an historic possibility and history teaches that such an *extraordinary process* (he shares his father's analysis on this point too) sometimes calls for *extraordinary powers of action*. But what does that mean in practice? (Possibilities worth considering: disruption of election meetings, rigged ballot boxes, rigged counting, assault, imprisonment, torture, permanent neutralization and so on.) We were perhaps naïve, he thinks, when the demand for free democratic elections was acceded to in the Geneva agreements. At that stage (not much more than a year ago) he had visualized a calm and *civilized* election of the kind he had witnessed during his years in France, minus the ridiculous parliamentary instability that occurred there, where ministers were scarcely given time to smoke in their offices before they were kicked out. We have quite sufficient here, thank you, with a prince who rearranges his governmental furniture so often that no outsider stands a chance of keeping up with it. Opinion formation is a hopelessly slow method, he notes, and what's more it does not offer any guarantees as to its results. (He assumes that more time would have been needed to do anything of that sort. And, without doubt, party functionaries who know what they are doing.) Consequently, he has (driven by circumstances, or so he says) *turned the screw* (that is to say, embarked on a number of the *possibilities* suggested). It's not me, he thinks, it's this bloody country. But, and now he turns to Non, *for the most part* things must be done by the book. I don't want the people you *win over* turning up in the mortuary. I've had quite enough of it with that monk Chung.

Non (with an obliging smile):
No, of course not, but…

Sary (irritably):
What do you mean but? No bloody
buts!

Non:
… the body count keeps on rising.
The chief of police's stunts…

Sary (cuts him off):
There's to be an end of that.

He makes himself comfortable, says, *we'll talk more about that presently*.
And he inhales deeply and slowly. Brown bubbles in the bowl of the
pipe. And pictures begin to unfold. Skies. Horses.

MONDAY, 5 SEPTEMBER 1955

A young face, beautiful, almost aristocratic. Spectacles with French
frames, the elegant cut of the grey suit.

He studies Ly Chinly (who is concentrating on leafing his way
through a blue folder). Watches his long slim fingers running down
columns and figures. Not even thirty yet.

The jangle of the telephone in the adjoining room is replaced by
the mumble of the secretary. The door stays shut. He lights another
cigarette.

Ly Chinly locates the information requested, lists the villages in
which the party's mobile electioneering film has been shown. (A
precise typed sheaf of papers gives the number of viewers. Then
an appendix of the number of gifts distributed. And then another
sheet with the number of registered voters in each electoral district.
Put them all alongside one another and pleasingly high percentages
can be extracted.)

New diagrams, new rows of figures. They are making gains in important areas. Making fewer gains in less important areas. In the former the fight is against the Democrats. In the latter they risk losing to the People's Party.

Ly Chinly only completed his studies in France last year. Since when the prince (with his usual feeling for usable ambition and talent) brought the young lawyer into the circles just outside the government. In the urgent work with the party programme of the Popular Socialist Community (which the prince with his habitual engaging nonchalance has entrusted to Sary), he has found Ly Chinly's meticulousness useful. He had telephoned him late at night and the young man had immediately come to his house to discuss any details that were difficult to grasp.

Consequently, Ly Chinly with his fine features was an obvious choice when he was setting up the working party for the election campaign.

But does he like him? He cannot decide. Usefulness versus self-sufficiency—which weighs heavier in the scales?

Sary interrupts the slightly monotonous murmuring. Asks: Is there anything in the new material that provides us with unambiguous information as to where the voters' sympathies lie? For the current week, that is? Or at least for the current month?

The answer is in the negative. Ly Chinly says in the same tone of voice as before (monotonous) that they would need to carry out a survey of the kind invented by the American George Gallup. And it might be possible to do that in the capital perhaps, but (he shakes his head sorrowfully) not elsewhere.

Sary looks out through the window. Out there is the same view as always (and all of a sudden it sort of *represents* his question. But not even there, among the massive trees in the garden, in the vault of a sky heavy with the threat of rain or in the angles of the buildings, is there an answer). And half-aloud, as if to himself, he remarks, *so we just don't know.*

Ly Chinly says, no, we don't.

Sary continues, admits that he has a feeling that public opinion is unstable. A feeling that enigmatic forces are at work. But he cannot determine either their direction or their goal for sure.

He asks: *What do you think?*

Ly Chinly does not seem to find his sudden frankness troubling. He thinks that there are two sorts of young men—those who are worried by honesty on the part of their superiors, and those who know their own value and consequently are not worried.

The young man answers that he can't claim to be very familiar with the mood out in the rural areas, but most things suggest that the prince's popularity has deep roots. They can let the free democratic process takes its course without concern.

(He considers what has been said—noting that it does not serve to allay any doubts.)

What separates a successful politician from one who fails, he says, is not the sharpness of his thinking. Nor is it his capacity for work or even necessarily the ability to convince others. (Ly Chinly raises his head and suddenly looks at him with interest.) The decisive thing, when all the other characteristics are equal, is *intuition*. So, he continues, I shall modify the question: What do you think? What does your *intuition* tell you?

Ly Chinly hesitates but then repeats (tone of voice the same—calm, low) that he's sure they can feel confident about the result of the election.

He fixes the young man with his gaze, asks: That's what your intuition tells you?

The answer is a yes.

He says, there you are, there, you see. Funny, isn't it? My intuition tells me *the exact opposite*.

He lights another cigarette (even though the one before is still burning in the ashtray). Blows out the smoke in a silence that lasts longer than a pause for effect and is filled with expectation of what will come when the silence is broken.

He breaks the silence.

And says that when we are finished here, I want you to take the initiative in setting up new surveys. Take Mau Say as your assistant. I want to know what the situation is. Understood? We can't allow the election to be reduced to a game of chance. The alternative, which I know you dislike even more than I do, is that we hold up two fingers to the law and win this election by any means available to us.

Ly Chinly nods slowly, says that he understands. And adds: Talking of games of chance. You know there is organized betting going on about the result of the election?

Sary: *Put a stop to it. Tell the chief of police and say hello to him from me.*

The young man gets up, puts his folders into his briefcase.

Then he is alone again. He glares at the closed door for a moment. And then up. And on.

O

O   O

(*Later the same morning*) His car drives on past the stables on rue Paul Bert at the back of the palace. The windscreen wipers in front beat out momentary bursts of visibility through the curtains of rain. Through the side window he glimpses (equally momentarily) the silhouettes of the royal elephants. Brown water is cascading along the gutters. Puddles link to form pools, their surface boiling beneath the thrashing rain.

He tries to make out the hands of his wristwatch beneath the cuff of his shirt. The storm has turned morning into dusk.

The shadows of people are standing under the shelter of the metal canopies over shopfronts, hurrying along the pavements with their wet clothes clinging to them. His driver (Phirun, who else?) turns into the palace zone. They glimpse a face in the window of the sentry box.

One guard (the slightly older one) hurries out, huddled under a black umbrella. Opens the door, says something (in French, as if everything *was just as it used to be*). The words are swallowed up by the noise of the rain. He gets out, briefcase in one hand, cigarette in the other.

The gusts of wind make the rain wash in waves across the concrete slabs of the approach.

A plumpish adjutant he hasn't seen before bows and takes over at the entrance. Leads the way through the rooms. He is asked to wait in the usual side room. (Soft, pale-grey, wall-to-wall carpet, *modern* furniture of dark wood and black leather. Everything in accordance with the prince's own ideas and design.)

He takes a cigarette from the silver box on the table. Smokes it slowly by the window and studies the garden inside the palace wall. The downpour shows no sign of easing. What a time for an election, he thinks, in the middle of the rainy season. What an idea! How is the rural electorate that is so loyal to the prince supposed to get to the polling stations when the roads are impassable? His thoughts move on to the public address he is due to give Wednesday evening (OWING TO CIRCUMSTANCES: CLARIFICATION OF THE GENEVA AGREEMENT). He chews on a flake of tobacco and the need for a better opening.

The adjutant opens the door behind him, and he has just time to turn round and bow his head as the prince makes his entry with a strained smile on his round face. A secretary at his heels. *Dear friend, dear friend,* the prince says and sits down in one of the armchairs. (Black pomaded hair, a black suit on the black leather furniture. A handkerchief white as chalk in his breast pocket.)

He sits down (following an impatient instruction from the prince) in the other armchair. The prince spears a cube of pineapple on a toothpick and says, *well then*. Chews it quickly and spears a cube of papaya.

He summarizes the reports that have come in from informants. (Successes and failures.) The prince listens, now and again echoing a headword for the secretary to note down. And, the prince interrupts, how are things going? With *La Miss*, Miss Cambodia?

He answers *yes* and continues.

The prince pouts his lips, strokes his nose with his finger, interrupts him again and says, *bring her with you tomorrow evening, why don't you?*

He gives a reluctant nod and passes on to his (short) list of suggestions for (civilized/legal) measures that can be taken.

And is interrupted by a knock at the door. The adjutant lets in another secretary (dressed in identical clothes to the one standing behind the armchairs). More documents are handed to the prince, who makes a gesture for him to continue with his report while he examines them.

Before Sary can remember the point at which he had stopped, the prince suddenly puts down his pen and says: As a starting point for this little *discussion*, let's recapitulate the larger context. (The prince continues:) We can expect China to regain its historical dominance in our part of the world, can't we? Not necessarily by military means but by *size alone*. As you know, I anticipate that our dear neighbours, the Annamites, will reunite within the foreseeable future. Very possibly, even probably in fact, under the red star. In which case our poorly armed little kingdom, with me—*le pauvre Monseigneur*—*a feudal relic* as the Reds call me, will have two overwhelmingly powerful communist states to deal with. At the same time we can be *confident* that old habits die hard. Peking is hardly going to tolerate regional competition. And is even less likely to diverge from the old imperial ambitions to act as policeman and ensure that peace reigns outside its borders. After that the Red River can run as red as it wants, can't it? And then there are these stubborn Americans who have got the domino theory on the brain and are concerned that the whole of the East is going to be transformed into a *castle haunted by the spectre of communism*. SEATO is consequently going to remain a headache for us and will undoubtedly continue demanding that we join. Now then, how should a little country like our dear kingdom behave when the elephants start dancing?

The prince fixes him with his gaze. (Eyebrows raised histrionically.)

He gives the reply expected of him and notes parenthetically (to himself) that that facial expression turns up in all the films His Royal Highness has acted in.

Correct! The prince exclaims. *By playing off any interests superior to our own against each other*. That is our only possibility. And as you know, the prince says (lowering his voice), it is a valid view even in domestic politics. But what is happening at the moment is not—how shall I put it—*balanced?* We may be able to rule the country the day after the election, and perhaps even the day after that. But taking the longer view, the current *excesses* endanger the necessary stability. We need discipline in the ranks. *Vous voyez bien, Monsieur le Ministre.*

Sary breaks off the glowing tip of his cigarette in the ashtray and says that of course he shares the prince's analysis. But, he goes on, we also need to *be aware of the people we are dealing with*. They are people who are out on the extreme fringes on both sides. The conservatives, among whom I count my father, are afraid of losing what they have. When we push them they retreat reluctantly, one step at a time. Keeping an eye on their own house, so to speak. The opposite end of the spectrum, on the other hand, is peopled by *idealists*. Confrontation with the apparatus of state merely reinforces the buggers' convictions, it radicalizes them and makes them take even greater risks.

Exactly, the prince interrupts him. In order to control *them*, metaphorically speaking we have to crush them. And the simplest way of doing that is… well… to do it *literally*.

Sary looks at the prince sceptically. Says: Is that what you really want? According to the opinion polls I've had done, that would mean that we'd have to break the necks of a frighteningly large part of the population. Doesn't that conflict with your worries about *excesses*?

The prince (with a mocking smile): Are you worrying about the gross national product, dear friend? There aren't that many of them, *les petits khmers rouges*.

But (the prince continues, serious again) you are right in principle. We risk creating unbridgeable gulfs if violence were to become—what should we call it—a *reflex response*. I want the whole country behind me. In spite of your efforts the current situation, if I understand it properly, is that an electoral victory with a desirable margin is far from guaranteed—am I right?

Sary says (intentionally provocative: there are times when he finds it impossible not to adopt *the big brother's role* he feels in relation to the monarch, who is five years younger than him): Are we going to do what they've done in South Vietnam then? Prime Minister Diem's success in the election can be explained by his heavy-handed methods. Emperor Bao Dai has been effectively outmanoeuvred there.

The prince, irritated, shakes his head and says that that doesn't hold water. Bao Dai gambled away his people's affection at the roulette tables of the Riviera without any help from anyone. Look at me, the prince says (raising his voice), unlike Bao Dai I know my people. *Mes petits enfants* respect me. And that is because I am *present in and a part of their lives*. All my journeys to the provinces. The schools, the roads, the bridges I open. The opportunity they have to come to me personally for justice. I am also *Citizen* Sihanouk, an absolutely ordinary citizen even though I have a greater burden of responsibility on my shoulders. Presence, says the prince, slapping the arm of the chair with the palm of his hand. Being there, that's what matters, isn't it?

And that jackass Diem (clenched fist, with the princely index finger raised) is guilty of reaching a *fundamentally false conclusion* in that he confuses fear and respect. He does, doesn't he? He has sown dragon's teeth and now he is carefully watering them. No, my dear minister, we won't have that. And it's your bloody responsibility to keep it all within the boundaries of the law.

(The prince firmly squeezes a few drops of lime over the next piece of papaya.)

My prince, are you including les khmers rouges in that?

(Silence.)

I am relying on you.

Sary (nods, satisfied) says, *of course.*

But, the prince goes on sharply, Thursday night. I want to see *concrete* results. That man has forfeited his rights. (The prince continues, muttering:) Less than five years ago his comrades in the party had to *scrape* up the remains of Ieu Koeus from the pavement outside their headquarters. And still there are *these senseless attacks* on such fundamental national values as the monarchy and, by extension, the constitution itself. Not criminal, perhaps, by the letter of the law, but nevertheless in a *criminal spirit*. They seem incapable of learning from their mistakes, don't they?

Sary mentions the danger of creating more martyrs. Especially this close to election day.

A couple more pieces of pineapple disappear into the prince. Chewing impatiently: No, Vannsak has to be neutralized without coming to any harm. Make an obvious example on Thursday and by Friday morning at the latest I want documents to show that the problem of *King* Vannsak has been solved. Understood? Are we finished?

Sary (chuckling): *King* Vannsak. That's good.

Sihanouk (brightening up): It is, isn't it?

And he nods once again. The prince stands up. They walk (noise-lessly) across the soft carpets, part at the door. And, the prince calls without turning round, *don't forget to invite your Miss Cambodia.*

o

o   o

(*Later*) The telephone rings. It's her. Why does the secretary connect it without checking with him? He says that this really is a surprise and then answers the question that follows: No, not at all unpleasant, I can assure you of that. Quite the contrary!

But then he says that unfortunately he doesn't have time just now, that he will get in contact soon. With a suggestion perhaps. A suggestion which he would in any case advise her to accept.

He rings off (and at once goes out to the secretary).

o

o   o

(*Later still*) He is sipping from a spoon, his mouth fills with French tastes. Moments from the past, light as gauze.

Just the odd word stands out from the hum around them. His wife (in the chair opposite) gently dips a piece of bread in her soup.

A quick glimpse of Monsieur Mignon himself in the kitchen is visible as the waiter passes through the serving door.

She says that she appreciates him making time even during a week like the present one. He looks at her but cannot detect a trace of irony and says that *even if war breaks out* their table at La Taverne will remain reserved for twelve o'clock every Monday. She smiles, turns her profile to him, chews a piece of bread. You shouldn't talk about it so flippantly, she says, slowly soaking another piece of bread in her soup. With her eyes on the bread: I hear what is said among my teachers and students.

He sucks his teeth. We don't have complete control, he admits, lowering his voice. He says that we have gone beyond the plan. The problem is that more people than we would wish *are improvising* off their own bat. It has irritated the prince, and rightly so.

The starched stiffness of the white linen napkin under his fingertips. She sips her wine. (Her lips leave a red shadow on the rim of the glass.)

He says that he and the prince are trying to regain control of the course of events, but there is far too much at stake for far too many people. And, he asks (rhetorically), how far can a branch be bent before it breaks?

She brushes a crumb off the cloth and says that she won't be worried as long as the table they are sitting at is reserved every Monday. He puts his hand over hers (smooth). And, she adds (roguishly), she is looking forward to a time when these moments can once again be *extended by an extra hour*.

And he feels a quick hot flush at the nape of his neck as he meets her smile.

She looks playfully into his eyes, draws her hand away. Touches the corners of her mouth with the napkin.

She passes on greetings from their children. They are getting on well both at home and at school and the fever the little one had has not come back. The soup plates are removed and he says he is sorry that he won't have time for them before the end of next week at the earliest. But perhaps they can take a trip to the seaside then?

It is an attempt to be artful. He thinks and hopes that that *little promise* might succeed in focusing her mind on the prospect of an excursion—her feelings of goodwill will distract her from the rest. There is no time for hesitation now, he must get it all said in the same tone and tempo, and so he says (as if it were an aside) that he will actually be going there himself the following evening. Yet another of these *soirées dansantes* the prince insists on. At the casino. And on the way there he can drop in by the house and let Kosal know that the whole family will be coming weekend after next.

She asks whether he will also be spending the night there, that would be the practical thing to do, and he answers, perhaps, we'll have to see: heavens above, there may be dancing but discussions will still be going on. And it may be that the prince will require them to stay up on the mountain. Or they may return to the city the same night. Everyone knows that the only thing you can be sure of with the prince is that you can't be sure.

A small-calibre lie. He daren't meet her eye to check whether she has seen through it. Hardly even a lie. But if he looks to see whether she has seen through it or not, she will certainly see through it then (if not before). She has an amazing talent in that respect, seems to sense every unconscious shift.

(Em (long ago): *I can read you like an open book, mon cher Sary.*)

Had it been possible, she ought really have become an examining magistrate rather than a college principal, he thinks and nods to the waiter, who is waiting attentively by the serving trolley with their *suprême de volaille*.

The conversation continues but now it feels as if a veil has been hung between them. He considers asking whether there is anything the matter. But if he is wrong, she will immediately start wondering why he is wondering. He decides to ignore the slight crackle he feels he can hear between the words. It might be the sleepless nights, the pills, the stresses that have put his nerves on edge. He takes a large mouthful of his wine.

Now, instead, she is the one to ask if there is something he isn't telling her (probably because of the hasty swig of wine). He shakes his head and mentions sleepless nights, pills, stresses, *exhaustion*. There are only a few days to go now, she says. Then it will be over.

He says, yes, then it will be over, but thinks that nothing will be over, everything will just continue.

o

o   o

He closes his eyes just for a moment. Opens them. Gets up. Walks briskly across the boards of the platform, taps the microphone lightly. Hears the tap echo out over the faces that are turned up to him.

The sky is grey, the sun a shadow. He will be forced to cut his presentation short in order to avoid the rain.

In a loud and clear voice he says: My dear countrymen!

He says: Kinsmen of our revered forefathers who built Angkor!

He says (with a smile): Dear residents of Pursat.

Then with a serious expression, an expression almost of concern, he continues.

The loudspeakers are bloody awful.

o

o   o

The secretary takes the envelope with both hands. Reads the address label hanging from it. All there is on the front of the simple white envelope are the words "Mlle Suong Somaly" written in black.

He explains, as if in passing, that the secretary should deliver it personally. That a car should then be booked to collect the individual in question at lunchtime tomorrow, and she should then be conveyed to the Hôtel Knai Bang Chatt in Kep-sur-Mer where a room for two should be arranged.

The secretary confirms that this is understood. (Yawns. Excuses himself.)

> Secretary:
> *Was there anything else?*

Sary:
No, that's everything.

> Secretary:
> *I'll be off to this address then.*

Sary:
What's the time?

> Secretary:
> *Almost eleven.*

Sary:
Make it the first thing you do in the morning.

> Secretary:
> *Very good.*

TUESDAY, 6 SEPTEMBER 1955

(*Pursat again*) He bites a hole in yet another longan. Presses the soft flesh of the fruit into his mouth. Throws the sand-coloured shell on the ground, chews and spits the seed the same way as the shell. Swallows. All of a sudden alone (at last) on the fringe of the chattering people.

Ill-fitting suits of synthetic fabric, traditional ankle-length skirts covering broad backsides. While he was making his speech he looked at every one of them. *Farmers' bodies.* Dark-skinned, bad teeth. Admittedly some of the women teachers were young—but that is all they were.

The governor with a hand-rolled cigarette in the corner of his mouth. Broad, loud and self-opinionated in the grey uniform of a civil servant. Gold rings on stubby fingers that end in coquettishly long nails. Talks about nothing but issues that lie on this side of the horizon.

The three elderly monks (they handled the spiritual side of the inauguration ceremony) have sat down under a tree and are watching the excited gathering of local dignitaries. The saffron-yellow of their robes has faded to a shade of beige. The oldest of them is chewing betel nuts, his toothless jaws red with the juice.

(Outside the organizers' programme) Sary leaves the vague shade of the awning and walks hesitantly towards the school building that has borne his name for the last hour. The plaster is hardly dry, the roof tiles are still an intense fiery yellow. People's footprints form a wide path through the dust—where not trampled, the red dust is still bobbled by the rain. He chooses to walk alongside the footprints. Slightly ridiculous, of course (as he is the first to admit), but it *feels better* that way.

He stops by one of the wings of the building. No wind: the flag is drooping on the flagpole in the middle of the schoolyard. As are the pennants that have been hung up for the day. The banner welcoming him is hanging loose between its two poles. Over by the other wing four children in school uniform have stopped whatever they were play-ing. (White shirts, navy blue trousers.) Probably some of the children ordered to come to the inauguration. Now they are standing there in silence and watching him intently. (At this distance they could be mistaken for his own boys.) And through their eyes he sees his own apartness in this context: his dark, well-fitting suit, his polished shoes, the pale skin of his cheeks and the backs of his hands. Sunglasses.

He squeezes another longan into his mouth. (An innocuous fruit.) He holds the seed (dark brown, smooth, shining) between his front teeth for a moment before letting it drop into the dust. Glancing to the side he catches sight of the headmaster's nervous face and discreet gesture calling him back.

But he turns his back on the crowd. He feels (with some surprise) unusually alert. As if the burden of work over the last few weeks had not existed. The muffled weariness that the pills leave behind has gone.

The hum, the smell of paint and damp earth. The milky-white sky. The rice fields with their grey wooden houses that take over where the concrete buildings stop. He breathes slowly. The pale pink lotus flowers reflected in the ponds. Through the back window of the car, he glimpses the silhouettes of his driver and his adjutant asleep in the front seats.

He thinks about the distribution of cloth and foodstuffs that followed the inauguration ceremony. The queue of paupers. The *gratitude* in their eyes for every gift he handed out. He understands why the prince devotes so much time to outings of this kind. (Even though the prince most often uses a helicopter. But the symbolism of that is just right for his simple subjects. The demigod who *descends* from the seraphic spheres in his shining steel bird.) The prince's endless electoral campaign, which continues whether there is an election or not. The prince, who can't get enough of that kind of feeble attention.

For his own part he senses a bitter aftertaste to the warm emotion. Every can handed out, every length of cloth, represents *a sort of corruption* of his self in relation to the world around. (His self-esteem is fuelled by his role as giver of good gifts.) But it would be a grave mistake to take political action based on that self-image. *The important thing is,* he thinks, *to keep a firm grip on one's sense of judgement.*

Moreover, the distribution of one day's bare necessities simply means that the recipient will survive until tomorrow (when there won't be anything). The reward is immediate, but the change it effects is very temporary. Something different is needed if a lasting improvement is to be achieved. Which is why the work to reform, say, the distribution of rice is very much more significant to these poor wretches in the provinces. That and changing from the old piastres the French used to a currency of our own. But abstract ideas of that kind don't win votes among illiterates. A bag of rice and a piece of cheap cloth are much more effective. If you promise them a new road and the tarmac is not there fresh and black by the time they wake up the following morning, they dismiss your promise as so much hot air. On the other hand, if the sun rises over a full saucepan your electoral victory is assured.

But he can, however, see that there is something wrong with that reasoning. Namely: the communists in the People's Party have nothing to distribute but promises, but they still… So?

According to one of Ly Chinly's many surveys, the said communists, *les khmers rouges*, might form an alliance with *les khmers roses* (the Democrats), a pretty incongruous alliance but nevertheless one that would amount to nothing short of a *coup d'état*. Hatred of the establishment (him, the prince, their network of protégés and lackeys) could undoubtedly drive them into a coalition for long enough for life as he knows it to be over. But the prince would never sit still and allow himself to be deposed and put in a display case in the National Museum. And what could we expect if that were to happen? A civil war? (With North Vietnam fanning the flames of the red fire, and South Vietnam and Thailand the white. So we would be back with the chaos that ruled before colonization by the French, back to a time when our neighbours used our country as a plaything/buffer zone/source of natural resources/battlefield? Back to the centuries when the only thing our enemies could not agree on was the exact lines along which they should slice us up?)

Sary remembers how the prince reacted when they hid incognito in the building next to the Democrats' party headquarters. They had listened together to attacks on the monarchy accompanied by the sound of rising jubilation. Beside himself with rage the prince had stared straight ahead, tears running down his plump cheeks. And he thinks of the return of Son Ngoc Than a couple of years ago and the way the people filled the streets. *Of their own free will,* not because the authorities had encouraged/commanded them to do so as, for instance, when the prince returns home from one of his visits abroad. The prince had shut himself away for days after seeing such crowds of people coming out voluntarily to greet the old rebel Than.

Than, however, is now sitting in the jungle outside Siem Reap, having outmanoeuvred himself. Out of step with developments, rejected by the prince, marginalized within his own party by Vannsak and the other smart young leftie bastards. Soon to be so peripheral, Sary thinks, that we'll be able to fetch him in and put him in front of a firing squad. Whether the Chinese are right (about Than being seriously courted by American intelligence) is less important. At the same time, however: Than may have proved to be his own worst enemy but he hasn't yet been rendered totally innocuous. So, CIA man or not, he needs to be written off once and for all. Well, he thinks (hearing the governor calling out his name behind him), the election will decide Than's fate too.

He turns round. They are all standing in silence watching him.

o

o   o

(*Next stop/Kep-sur-Mer*) The road through the landscape. Not wide enough to allow two vehicles to pass at high speed. He watches paddy fields flash past, and the occasional clusters of huts. Blue mountains in the distance. He ought to take the opportunity to get some sleep but his whole being feels like the car—a well-oiled engine running at high revs. His thoughts are running on smooth gleaming rails. (Below the surface, a buzz of expectancy about tonight.)

The first time he saw her. That clumsy beauty contest. *Why can nothing be organized with any degree of sophistication in this country?* But what did he see? A light-skinned, comparatively tall, young woman in a close-fitting dress (he can't remember the colour which, as he knows, says more about him than about the garment in question)? That remarkable aura that made the other girls pale into insignificance? Yes, yes, all that, but also something more.

He had let it be known that her presence was requested at his table. Then he had watched closely how she received the message, how she had leaned towards the waiter in his white jacket to listen to him, then turned her head towards the table he was sharing with colleagues/ acquaintances/others (only men). How she had asked the waiter something and how he had pointed in their direction as confirmation. Was that when it had happened? Or was it when she came over to them? (Rather warily, but more curious than shy. Her face beneath the diadem flushed, her long neck, her erect bearing.) Or was it the direct way she met his gaze? Not challengingly but *self-aware*. It had confused him, though he did not let it show.

This Somaly is very different from the usual flighty girls. (Alongside others of the same age, he thinks, she stands out as *being genuine.* He cannot think of any other way of putting it. But what does it mean?) He tries to find something to compare her with. Is she perhaps like his wife Em when Em was her age? No, Em may well be beautiful in her own way but she would not have won beauty contests. (Her beauty is revealed when she is picking a problem to pieces or coming up with a simple explanation of something that seems tangled to the point of incomprehensibility.)

Somaly had accepted his invitation to dinner by return (which did nothing to diminish his confusion). He did not know then how to take it (nor does he know now). Perhaps she lets anyone and everyone invite her? (But if that were the case he would surely have heard of it.) The dinner had been pleasant but *wary*. And, besides, he had had to hurry on to an evening meeting with the prince. But she had at least said *perhaps* when they were parting and he had asked her whether they could do the same again some time. A *perhaps* that undoubtedly meant *yes*. (The surprising telephone call the day before undoubtedly reinforced that interpretation.)

But: he wishes that he had been allowed to determine the pace himself. If it had not been for the prince's sudden whim, if the prince had not insisted, he wouldn't have invited her to join him this evening. (He likes to give very careful consideration to whom he will invite to the sort of *scene of speculation and gossip* that a *soirée dansante* represents.) In his view, it would have been better to meet *tête-à-tête* a few more times. Not just to work out what she expects of him (what ambitions she has). But also to come to a better understanding of what he himself feels. Because the way she intrudes into his thoughts in the most unexpected contexts is not something he is used to.

It's not absolutely certain that she will come. (There hasn't been an answer to the message his secretary delivered.) That implies a degree of uncertainty. Which deep down he disapproves of since he has an infinite number of other things to concentrate on. (A comforting thought: the hotel room is booked and if she fails to come there will almost certainly be someone else willing *to stand in* for her.) And should she get the idea that she can *treat him as she pleases*, none of her family's protectors would, he thinks, be in a position to prevent him destroying her.

O

o   o

Soft leather soles on the sun-warmed steps. Music from the open windows. Voices. A group already in conversation on the balcony above the entrance. He walks across the first terrace quickly.

The air is cooler here, a kilometre or so above the low country.

The hostesses are standing on each side of the open doors. They curtsey and greet him with heads bowed low. They are dressed in traditional costume, like a toned down version of the royal *corps de ballet*. (His gaze rests lightly on the nape of their necks, follows the fine hair down into their collars.)

He steps out of the blazing white afternoon light into darkness.

The sound of jazz and the hum of voices increase. He takes a glass from the tray held out to him and looks around.

Who is there? The usual contingent of dignitaries, diplomats and carefully selected businessmen. Their white suits contrast with the bright colours of the dresses worn by the young society ladies. The doors out to the large terrace are wide open (which lets in a slight but welcome draught). The sun is still too hot for the party to move outside.

Soft hands are proffered for shaking. There are polite phrases to respond to. He navigates his way around the rooms. *Who* is *where?*

Nouth, the president of the Council, comes over to him and puts an arm on his shoulder. He draws him towards the roulette wheel, suggests that he tries. He shakes his head.

Sary:
You'll have to excuse me. I'd rather save my luck for more important occasions.

Nouth:

As you like. I've got plenty of it. And remember this, my young friend, it is only in politics that you have to have luck all the time. Once is sufficient with the roulette ball.

Nouth was appointed to the Supreme Royal Council at the same time as he was (and the Minister for Internal Security Kim Tith). Both Tith and Nouth are considerably older and Nouth is one of those people who seem to be above the turbulence at the centre of power. (Compared, *for example*, to his father Nhean.) Nouth (who is actually a born courtier with ancient mandarin blood in his veins) was made a minister when the prince was crowned—that's all of fourteen years ago. And since then Nouth has held numerous portfolios (the prince uses him as a sort of universal panacea). It was Nouth who (encouraged by his father) first introduced Sary to the prince as *the hardworking, well-educated, efficient and combative patriot, who can assist in the struggle for independence* that the prince had always been looking for.

(He and the prince had immediately taken to one another. As if they were communicating on a wavelength all of their own, one on which all earlier calls had gone unanswered. Going home from the first meeting he had felt an unparalleled enthusiasm, as if all of a sudden everything was possible.)

He leaves the older man with the palms of his hands resting on the green felt of the roulette table. And goes impatiently back to the foyer.

Is this where she is? Is she here?

Cameras are flashing in the foyer (stucco, a feeble crystal chandelier, faded French murals portraying odalisques). It's not really surprising. The prince is there, after all, posing with the ambassador of Czechoslovakia. Smiles for the camera. Then a change of wall and a change of ambassador. New smiles, puffs of smoke from the flash bulbs. The photographs to be dispatched and published immediately in one of Sary and the prince's recently founded papers. (When they shake the prince's hand the ambassadors crouch a little to compensate for the difference in height.)

The prince makes a speech, jokes, his gaze constantly sweeping across the semicircle of guests/listeners. His thickset body never still. He sees Sary and his face lights up even more, calls his name in his falsetto voice. Sary bows slightly in return. Another ambassador is lined up by the photographers.

He puts down his glass. Picks up another. Takes a cigarette from one of the waiters, who also gives him a light.

Then she is standing there, her back to him. (Immediate recognition of the curve of her shoulders, the long line of her neck.) She is talking to two other young women he thinks he can remember from the beauty contest. She is wearing another close-fitting dress, new to him, in various shades of graphite grey, pistachio green and pale yellow. Sequins glitter on the yellow and on the high collar. (The other two girls are dressed more conventionally. Which, he thinks, some of the men present would no doubt find preferable.)

The acid taste of champagne in his mouth, his mild intoxication, her elegant (restrained) movements a few metres in front of him. (His quick flutter of breath, light as a butterfly wing.)

All of a sudden he becomes aware again of the people moving around him.

He turns on his heel, goes back into the big room. None of the eyes he meets shows any recognition of the fact that he had stood and stared at the young trio far too long.

Even though many people are inquisitive enough to ask which of the men arrived with Miss Cambodia, he doesn't think it would be impossible to make them believe she is present in her own right.

The music on the gramophone falls silent and the buzz of voices grows louder. Over by one wall the band is getting its instruments ready. The clarinettist is moistening a reed between his lips, the guitarist's fingers are hovering over untuned strings. *The Royal Jazz Band.* Five blue-blooded men from various lower ranks. He recognizes the prince's exclusive saxophone case, leaning in the window embrasure. It's covered with those ridiculous labels from different capital cities.

He surveys the room, which is framed by the gleaming rectangles of the windows. Dark reflections on the chandelier. Something touches his leg and to his astonishment he looks down and sees a black poodle (whose nose is now seeking his crotch). He shoos the animal away brusquely and it moves on to a group that (as far as he can see) consists of a permanent secretary from the defence ministry, a French journalist and an Indian diplomat. The men jump when the dog winds its way between their legs. (The Frenchman pushes it away roughly with the sole of his shoe.) And then, hardly a surprise, he hears Ambassador McClintock's thick American accent above the noise (even before he sees that the brawny figure has made his entrance). He notes that McClintock has at least shown enough judgement to leave his shorts and riding crop at home. But he has brought that awful dog with him.

He prepares to *withdraw* should the American approach. McClintock, however, makes no effort to circulate (he remains standing over in the doorway with the British chargé d'affaires Little Cook and some Australians). The poodle disappears out onto the terrace.

He hopes the prince will catch sight of the dog and, in a fit of rage, have it shot. Even though the diplomatic consequences would be *difficult to predict.*

A ripple runs through the gathering.

The prince is coming. (Like a sort of low-powered magnet that drags those in close proximity along for a few steps.)

The prince's shrill laugh, the guests smiling around him. Polite or beguiled or both.

Sary's eyes seek for something graphite grey, something pistachio green or pale yellow, seek the glitter of sequins.

The prince's progress proceeds at its usual slow pace. Each step offers the opportunity for princely repartee and showing off.

Young Mau Say detaches himself from the prince's magnetic field, stands discreetly alongside Sary. And in his low-key way asks about the manuscript. Sary answers that he is satisfied with the new section. Mau Say asks if it is all ready for publication and he answers, yes, by *Albert Portail* in Saigon. Mau Say smiles his quick timid smile, which Sary (always quick to judge) at first mistook for weakness. But behind the shyness the young economist has a hard edge that may take him far or be the ruin of him. (When they were fellow students in Paris both of them found themselves in conflict with the Reds in the student union. At the big meeting called to sort out their differences of opinion, Mau Say left the meeting, slamming the door behind him. Then he formed a new union.) Character and energy, he thinks. Mau Say asks: And the title? He answers that we'll keep the one we have. (*Bilan de l'oeuvre de Norodom Sihanouk pendant le mandat royal de 1952 à 1955.*)

They are interrupted: the loudspeakers are making unpleasant crackling noises.

He turns his face towards the improvised stage just as a couple of spotlights come on. The prince is holding a shiny square microphone. His eyes glide from listener to listener. (A broad smile, white uniform jacket embroidered with gold thread, black *sampot* trousers, a quick *boyish* wave to some special guests.) Dear Friends, the prince says, Dear, Dear Friends, thank you for your kindness in wanting to share this evening with me. This evening is an evening for dancing but also an evening for forgetting. Forgetting? You're wondering what I mean by that. Well, as you all know, on Sunday the future of our beloved kingdom will be decided at the ballot box. And who knows how it will turn out! But! (in a low seductive voice)… let us forget that for one night and, in the words of the worthy Señor Edmundo Ros, let us say *Si! Si! Si!* to the future, *Si!* to the wonderful night ahead of us.

(*Applause*)

And the prince turns to the band (which responds to him with the opening chord). With a pair of maracas in his hands, the prince (eyes closed) falls into the rhythm. Starts singing, almost in a whisper (*In Spain they say si, si / In France you'll hear oui, oui / Ev'ry little Dutch girl says ya, ya / Ev'ry little Russian says da, da / etc.*).

Sary turns his head, stretches to look over all the heads. And there she is. By the big fireplace at the far end of the room, partly hidden by the double doors. He watches her watching the band. A smile seems to be hovering on her face.

o

o   o

(*Outside, forty-five minutes later*) Far below them white pelicans are sailing on the rising currents of air.

Far below the pelicans: the dark green jungle with its screams, its chattering, its whistles.

After that (a thousand metres down): the sea. The thin line of the horizon shading over to dusk in the far, far distance. The smell of salt and endless water, filtering up through the scents of the rain forest.

And behind them: through the open doors and windows the *Royal Jazz Band* can be heard playing Django Reinhardt's drawling *Manoir de mes rêves*. Again. Probably at the prince's command.

Behind which *them?* Well, Sam Sary, Sim Var (newly appointed general secretary of the prince's Popular Socialist Community and one of the founders of the Democratic Party, who has recently changed sides—that is to say, a *vital recruit* who must not allow his loyalty come into question), guests, servants, a black poodle.

This Sim Var (who is now explaining, as he did to a larger audience a little earlier, that party districts should be organized on the French model) is not a man in whose company he wants to spend the rest of the night. But he still doesn't know *how to place* the older man, who is wearing his habitual light-grey suit and horn-rimmed glasses and who allows his dialect to colour his speech in a way that is easy to imitate (he has already—admittedly in Sim Var's absence—done so and reduced a whole government meeting to laughter). But there is something about the *goodwill* the prince shows to Sim Var that suggests a need to be careful. He doesn't understand what the goodwill depends on, since all he can see in the man is cold-blooded calculation concealed behind a rather wooden facade.

Then the prince joins them out on the terrace. (The sweat shining on his face shows that he has been dancing.) *So you two are out here conspiring*, he shouts in a shrill voice while he is still walking down the steps. Perhaps I ought to have you thrown over the edge, he continues, leaning over the balustrade and looking at the pelicans, the jungle, the sea. That light enervating laugh. His hands run through his thick hair, cufflinks sparkle.

Sim Var starts lecturing again but the prince interrupts him impatiently with *tomorrow, Monsieur, tomorrow*. There is a time for everything. Tonight we should be enjoying ourselves. As if there were no tomorrow. That's right, isn't it? *Say Si!*

The shrill laugh.

Sim Var smiles and looks inscrutably out towards the sea.

The band plays the *tutti* closing chord of the piece. In the silence before their next number a short dark roar can be heard from the jungle below them. It is repeated several times at regular intervals. The jungle is silent for a few moments before the chattering and whistling start again. The prince looks at Sam Sary in amazement and he looks at Sim Var in amazement and he in turn looks at the prince (and so on). *A tiger!* the prince exclaims and laughs once more. Did you hear that, my friends, *a tiger? I* am the tiger, aren't I, the tiger who rules over the wild jungle! Have you heard a tiger before? the prince continues, imitating the roar. More laughter. More imitations.

He looks at the excited prince who is leaning over the balustrade (as if there is any chance at all of seeing the tiger down there through the deep green canopy of the jungle), at Sim Var who is smiling in an almost paternal way, and he thinks, say what you like about superstition and omens but this is a good one. The lord of the jungle greeting his equal.

He notices that the first star is now twinkling in a sky growing paler out over the sea. Behind them the band has got back into the swing. He sees Monineth and some of her friends silhouetted in the doorway. He recognizes one of them—was it Nana? Nana, who also took part in the beauty contest. (The rest of them are new acquaintances whose names he has definitely forgotten.) But no Somaly. The young women are holding champagne glasses in their hands and every so often their inebriated giggles can be heard through the music. Monineth with her European features is wearing the same deep blue dress as on her nineteenth birthday (a few months earlier). The silver threads glisten when she moves.

The prince follows his gaze and says that *you could guess how beautiful Monineth was going to be even when she was just a baby*, and that *it doesn't show, does it, that she has already borne me two children*. He suspects there is a certain sharpness in the prince's words. So he looks out at the horizon instead, empties the lukewarm contents of his glass over the balustrade and gets a waiter to give him a new one.

The champagne and Monineth's close-fitting dress increase the tingle of desire he feels in his hands. But he can't leave the prince alone with Sim Var. He needs to be present during their conversation (even though it will probably turn out to be quite harmless). He asks the waiter for another cigarette.

The waiter (an immature adolescent who seems bowled over to be there—*in his imagination* he is already recounting everything he has seen to his peasant family and his easily impressed friends) gives him a light with obsequious fussiness, which (along with the stripling's conceited expression) annoys him, and after the first puff he asks the young man to wait for a moment. *Which party will you be voting for?* he asks and sees (with some satisfaction) a shiver run through the waiter's body. The man's eyes flit back and forth between him, the prince and Sim Var, both of whom are now waiting for his answer. His mouth hangs half open, questioningly. With a slight tremor in his voice he answers that he will obviously be giving his vote to His Majesty. The prince gives the young man a friendly nod and he bows and bows again before hurrying away pale-faced towards the steps of the casino.

The prince gives Sary an irritated look. Sim Var's eyes are hidden by the reflection on his spectacles.

Sary says (in a bantering tone) that we still have some way to go before the people vote with their hearts, don't we? The prince snorts and answers that one can't expect any more of *les petits enfants* than that they recognize what's best for them, can we?

It will come, Sim Var says, acting as mediator. A reform of the education system will not only create a more knowledgeable electorate, it will also create a more *grateful* one. It might, however, need to be given a *little help* at a first election such as the present one. But, Sim Var adds (without looking at Sary), the task has been made rather more difficult by the fact that we now have *twice as many* minds to convince.

Sary asks (more vehemently than he intends) whether Sim Var is referring to his wife Em's work for women's suffrage? In a modern democracy, surely, a *free* and *universal* election must *by definition* include all adult citizens?

The prince interrupts him:

Tomorrow, Messieurs. That's all for tomorrow.

He can feel the alcohol affecting his thinking. He shakes his head slightly. Thinks: I must sharpen up. The prince is totally capricious. And where is she?

The prince:
How many of the opposition are doing forced labour?

Sam Sary:
I don't have the exact number in my head but those bloody communists are constantly going on about their desire "to build the country" and that is precisely what they have now been given a golden opportunity to do—even if they are doing it in leg-irons!

Sim Var: (a short, dry laugh)

The prince (smiling):
You really must lend me those words for my biography.

He gives a slight smile. And hopes there are not going to be any questions about how the biography is progressing. He hasn't had time recently to do more than note down occasional princely quotations on slips of paper (which he has then proceeded to mislay here and there). But at least his and Mau Say's manuscript is finished. Almost finished.

The pale-red sky is becoming a cobalt blue firmament in which the stars are taking up their familiar formations. (Large shadows emerge from the top storey of the casino and join the growing yelping cloud of fruit bats. They swoop around the building before disappearing down towards the jungle.) Every time he shuts his eyes he feels a flutter of weariness come over him.

An adjutant comes down the steps, announces in a low voice that dinner is served and enquires considerately whether he should have a table set for them out on the terrace. The prince waves away the offer, invites him and Sim Var to join him for dinner. *It's very modest*, the prince explains, *just a taste of what the sea has to offer*. And he adds with a wink: *Take the chance while you have it. Come Monday you may be unemployed.*

The prince:
And where is La Miss, by the way?

Sary:
She's inside. I'll see that she joins us.

The prince:
And not a moment too soon. I'm looking forward to becoming better acquainted with this exquisite bloom on my family tree.

They mount the steps. A matt golden bowl has been placed at the door. It's full of big red apples, all the same size. The prince picks one up, carefully bites into its shiny peel. *His Excellency Zhou Enlai*, he explains, was kind enough to send me these apples from China. We got on to the topic of apples one evening in Bandung. He insists that nowhere else will you find apples as good as those that grow outside Yingkou in the north-east. I'm inclined to agree with him. *Help yourselves, Messieurs!*

Each of them takes an apple. The prince waits until they have taken a bite, peers at them and then continues: *Tell me, it's strange, isn't it, dear friends? Here we are standing on the very highest peak in Cambodia, but in the juice of this fruit we can taste the rain that fell on the rolling hills of Liaoning last year.*

WEDNESDAY, 7 SEPTEMBER 1955

A fine layer of invisible grains of sand on the brown surface of the bureau. He can feel them on his skin when he wipes the palm of his hand across the smooth surface. (And sand under his bare feet when he walks across the floor to the door they had obviously left ajar overnight.)

The sky outside is milky white. The sea is shading over to grey. The waves regular. The cool morning of a hot day. The shimmering flight of dragonflies in the trees down on the shoreline.

The head gardener and a helper pass under the branches. They are carrying a bucket and tools.

Sary leans on the doorpost. Lights a cigarette and smokes it restlessly. Returns into the darkness of the room, fetches a towel.

The surface of the pool is smooth. A couple round red leaves are drifting slowly on invisible currents. He sits down on the edge, slips into the water and pushes off with his feet. With powerful strokes he swims noiselessly to the short end, turns, feels the water streaming past his naked belly.

As he walks back across the tiled garden path, his wet footprints dry as fast as he passes. The heat is already building up.)

He pulls on his trousers, buttons his shirt. Looks at her, lying asleep on her front. The sheet is crumpled here, stretched taut there. Her shoulders are uncovered. Her face has a solemn look, the make-up around her eyes is smeared. He puts on his socks, stuffs his tie in his trouser pocket. Buckles his belt, his eyes resting on her skin and the black tangle of hair around her face. He notes: she looks (even) younger when asleep.

The contours of her body under the sheet. Breathing slowly through her mouth, open lips. He stops dressing, his hands come to rest.

But, he thinks, just finished washing. Stupid to undo it.

Instead, he quickly picks up his shoes and walks softly to the door. In the doorway he turns his head (she is still lying in the same position). He takes a few more steps, bends and ties his shoelaces, parts his damp hair with a steel comb and carries on.

o

o o

(*Provincial Route 33/31: return journey at 60 kph*) Is he satisfied now? Now that he has managed to bring her to this point? Can that question be answered with a yes? He feels (naturally) that he has crossed a boundary he has been longing to cross. But (naturally) the question could also be answered with a no. For what he wants, what he is trying to reach, is something different. (To put it bluntly: she won't allow herself to be reduced to a disposable item, which he hadn't really expected anyway, though he hadn't totally excluded the thought.)

But that is not what he is thinking just now. He has other things on his mind and he lights a fresh cigarette from the old one. (What is on his mind is not the fact that he has been unfaithful (again) to Em. The uneasiness he felt on the first few occasions has been blunted into a kind of *indifference* to adultery (his own, anyway). Not that he himself would call it "blunted". The feeling reminds him rather of *the clarity* he believes he has achieved in his work, the unsentimental *realpolitik* that he (jokingly, in close and trusted circles) calls his *sole ideological fixed star*. In the present case, then, the term *realerotik* might perhaps be a suitable designation.)

He has emptied his briefcase onto the seat. He opens a new folder, thumbs through the sheets. The blue stencils smell of spirits.

(The engine is purring under the bonnet. The road humming beneath the tyres.)

He finds what he is looking for. Reads it quickly, makes notes in the margin. Vibration makes his handwriting shaky to the point of becoming unreadable

The bends and the smell of the stencils make him keep his eyes on the road for a while. It's empty, no other motor vehicles. His driver (Phirun) drives fast but at a steady speed. The flat of his hand on the horn. Warning anyone who ventures out onto the tarmac. The car avoids ox-carts and the maize and peppers that have been spread out on the road surface to dry.

(Naked children wave. The bowed silhouettes in the rice fields look up as the shining black paintwork and gleaming silver chrome roars past.)

He lights another new cigarette from the old one and throws the butt out through the slightly open window (it bounces a couple of times, spluttering and glowing across the tarmac behind them).

Phirun drives in silence. A motionless broad-shouldered shadow enclosed in a grey uniform. His big hands slowly operating the steering wheel, the gear lever, the nasal-sounding horn. The only thing uncontrolled about the man are the drops of sweat. They burst out of the hair on the nape of his neck, find a way down inside his starched (itchy) collar.

Every now and then there are signs at the side of the road. Sary thinks: *It's peculiar to feel anything for road signs, but I really like the bloody things.*

What is there to like about them? Well, they have a sort of *civilizing feel*, don't they? (Place names printed in white letters on a deep blue background. The Double Dutch that fills the mouths of the peasantry is now firmly attached to the road. To be read through a windscreen while rushing along at high speed. By *the pioneers of the future.*) (Incidentally, the sign that just flashed past said Kampong Trach.)

Now that he has taken his eyes off his work he can return to Somaly (who, he assumes, is still lying in bed in Kep-sur-Mer). He thinks: of the way she walked down the staircase of the casino yesterday, out into the car he is now sitting in. Of the smoothness of her skin. Of her eyes tight shut in ecstasy. And in his mind he reverses the decision he made after his swim and takes her again. Half-asleep, a little surprised when he carefully draws her up onto her hands and knees. Spits on his hand for lubrication, the morning light on her back. (Goosebumps on the skin of her thighs.)

But it's better this way.

But next time he will stay. (*For there will surely be a next time?*)

Now to the ministry.

He looks at his wristwatch. He has won an extra quarter of an hour thanks to being abstemious. Perhaps as much as half an hour.

(The neon green rice fields slip past. Sugar palms. Pointed sandstone hills rising from the plain. On their summits, pagodas glimpsed through greenery. Pennants in many colours. Gilded details that look dull when it's cloudy. Occasional small red- and white-painted milestones at the roadside.)

He goes back to his papers. Approves a number of routine decisions taken by his staff. Thinks that you never think as clearly as you do in a car driving along a road through the countryside. He continues the thought: I'll be damned if government meetings shouldn't be held on the back seat of a Mercedes! But we'd need more tarmac. The present network of roads is more suited to water buffalo and elephants.

The next folder: the renovation of the electricity power station in Russey Keo. He reads: "Long since *underdimensioned* for the needs of the city. Built some decades ago by French engineers; machinery and other components of French manufacture. Not clear that an upgrade can be carried out without French involvement. Essential for the electrification of the new sectors of the city." *Etcetera, etcetera.*

New sectors of the city. New electricity works.

More of everything.

He scribbles: Investigate further. You have my permission to contact Saigon for possible non-French expertise.

He asks Phirun to stop where they can get a cup of coffee. A couple of minutes later they pull into the side of the road (at the next village). He opens the door out to the fresh air. Out to the contrast between them speeding onwards and the pleasing peace of the countryside. A gentle breeze is rustling the tops of the palm trees. Moisture-laden air, the smell of earth and of the smoke from a fire. In the distance metal striking metal in an irregular rhythm.

Phirun in his grey uniform looks enormous in front of one of the stalls that sell things to passers-by. The stallholder hurries from his hammock, bows (alarm written all over his face).

Sary gets out and leans on the car, keeps his trousers clear of the dirt on the mudguards. Takes out his sunglasses. He thinks: this utter submissiveness when faced with authority. So provoking, so simple, so *usable*. But it undermines every serious project. How few people there are who are prepared to weigh their own responsibility, their own competence, against respect for those of us who are their superiors. We ought to be leading development, not having to lever it with a crowbar. But given half a chance this fellow with the stall would lie in his hammock until death came and got him.

(Phirun shouts a question about sugar, about milk. He waves his hand in a negative gesture.)

The coffee arrives. A small glass on a plastic plate with faded floral decorations. Phirun passes it to him stressing the words *Your Excellency*. The stallholder, who had followed a few steps behind the uniform, looks even more frightened.

He sips the coffee. He nods to the little man. Looks at him benignly. *Really good, my good fellow!* (No one is going to be able to accuse him of being unable to make easy contact with *the electorate*.)

Chung, 47: I was nervous when a fine car like that stopped here. It was as if a snake were slithering its way through my intestines [*untranslatable wordplay*]. We're just ordinary people, after all. Nothing special. It must be at least a year since last time. Then it was whites wanting water for the engine. I don't know who it was this time, but he had fine clothes, black glasses and pale smooth skin. He wanted coffee. No milk and no sugar. He must be tough to drink his coffee like that! I got paid without any haggling about the price. Well paid. The notes were all clean and new, even better than the ones you get from the jeweller at the market. The fine gentleman liked my coffee. I've told everyone about that. I think more people will come to drink my coffee now. It's sort of become a bit special. He also asked who I was going to vote for. I'd been thinking of voting for the Democrats. I went to one of their election meetings and I thought they had a strong message. They had a clear and sensible plan. But I didn't dare say that to the fine gentleman, who was a friend of no less than the king, or prince as he now is. So when it came to voting, I voted for the king. It felt the right thing to do. It was as if we'd reached an agreement when they bought my coffee.

o

o   o

(*Early afternoon/somewhere in the kingdom*) He is talking about tarmac, about schools, about vaccine. He is talking about responsibility, justice and water. He is talking about the spark of electricity.

He is talking about canals and bridges. He is talking about concrete.

He is talking about the prince's courage and everyone else's lack of it. About the importance of the election.

He paraphrases the fable about the credulous monk and the monkeys.

He talks about the *fire carriage* on rails. How the rails will come all the way to their village. How the locomotive will come to a stop with a squeal of brakes at the station building that he constructs in a subordinate clause. (And the loco: *shining black, gleaming brass*.)

He talks about unity, about the difference between two clenched fists and ten spread fingers.

He looks out over his audience. Over to the right the sunshine on the gilded parts of the pagoda is dazzling. Straight rows of seats in the shade of the trees for the local dignitaries. Beyond them a tightly packed crowd of sunburnt peasant faces.

The loudspeaker is a good one.

He plucks out a headword from the notes he has on the lectern. He talks about schools and hospitals and then wipes his forehead with his handkerchief. He talks about the decisive role he played in Geneva when their country once more became their own.

The bright green rice fields and the horizon are shimmering in the heat. Swallows glide above the open space.

He talks about the colonial wars that are now raging (Morocco, Kenya, Cyprus, etc.), turning children into orphans and leaving parents childless. He says that a bloodless liberation such as theirs is a gift. That it is up to them, up to the people standing in front of him, to take charge of that gift at the election on Sunday.

Upright and earnest, he receives the applause that follows. His shirt is sticking to his back, sweat is making his forehead itch. He takes the lead himself in distributing packets of rice, gifts of cloth and tobacco. One by one his listeners accept the goods, their heads bowed, their eyes lowered. Gratitude lights up their weather-beaten faces.

o

o   o

(*An interior*) What kind of sacrifices are being demanded? In the present context the question may be taken in two ways: (1) In order to win the election? (2) Of him?

By the time Sary gets back his office is awash with survey responses. He is now sitting with the summary in one hand and reports from his many and widespread *trusted informants* in the other (the cigarette banished to the corner of his mouth). And he wishes he could turn the clock back a couple of hours to when his world was filled with the cheering of a jubilant audience. Back to *unequivocal clarity*. For what is it all really about (for fuck's sake)? Where is Ly Chinly hiding? And what has he done with the *walkover* election Sary and the prince reckoned on at the start? The opposite looks likely now—it could go *in any direction*.

So? Something must be done, but what? Is it time to follow his father's advice and to cancel the election?

Or to stand one or two opposition politicians in front of a firing squad in order *to send out a signal?*

He thinks of the family that took an interest in him in Paris. Of conversations with them and then later all the discussions he had with French students at the political science institute. (He had been older than most of the others because having been awarded a scholarship in 1939 he was forced to wait, wait and wait until the war was over and done with.) They had convinced him—indeed, more than convinced him—that a democracy in which every citizen has a vote is the only decent system. To measure the will of the people honestly and fairly by means of regular elections. Even in a country like his (where the majority of the population cannot even spell their own names).

But, Sary thinks, what ought to be done when the system turns against its own creator and runs the risk of destroying itself (and its creator—that is to say, him)?

He remembers what one of the chastened civil servants who had spent decades in *French Indochina* said to him in Geneva (at the end of the day's round of negotiations): *The biggest weakness of your countrymen, Monsieur, is that they lose every ounce of courage when faced with determined authority.*

The opinion of the bully, of course.

But nevertheless.

(*A different occasion*): Sary has just *witnessed* two *traitors* being blind-folded, tied to stakes and then, to the rattle of rifle fire, shot through their pale-grey shirt-backs by two four-man firing squads. (After which the officer in charge steps forward, grasps the hanging heads by the hair and blows away any remaining spirit of rebellion that might have been in their heads with a pistol shot.) Afterwards there is a recep-tion in the royal pavilion outside the palace—unlimited quantities of champagne and exclusive imported nibbles. The prince gives an improvised press conference to a handful of invited journalists. Sary, standing a couple of metres away, hears the prince say that *the bundles of dollars the traitors had received weighed light compared with the deaths they subsequently had to put on the other end of the scales.* But what he remembers most clearly is the look in the prince's eyes. They were the very eyes he encountered in the mirror when, as examining magistrate, he had lost control of himself while interrogating certain *criminal elements.* A kind of electric presence, coupled with a blackness that paradoxically made the eyes seem bottomless at the same time as lacking any depth at all.

Is that the true gaze of his people? he asks himself. (Is that the gaze he is meant to affirm?)

Perhaps his father is right when he says that a Western form of government does not suit *the soul of our people.* Perhaps our soul needs to be put face to face with *determined authority?*

That, perhaps, is actually the most sophisticated tool of oppression the colonialists possess. They have implanted their own values in *him,* thereby robbing him of his true identity. Convinced him that his inherited reactions are wrong.

So? If that is the case, what should the conclusion be? That the time has come to give free rein to quite different forces?

It's a possibility that fills him with emptiness. One that would imply the final betrayal of his *agreement* with his friends in France. Implying a return to a state he believes he has *transcended.* But (it has to be admitted) it also brings with it a sense of relief: the soothing relief that comes from familiarity.

There is no doubt that he fights best when his opponents appear to have the upper hand (as at Geneva), but it is not always possible to fight all of them. Then it is a case of quietly joining forces with one's friends and allies.

So the answer to the two questions, (1) and (2), is: that he should (for once) give way.

(*Primo / By telephone*) Meet me in an hour. I have some new instructions for you. *Which I know you will approve of,* little friend.

(*Segundo/At his desk*) A pristine sheet of white paper, a fountain pen with royal blue ink. He writes quickly, but is at pains to ensure it is legible. One name after another.

o

o   o

Place de la Poste. The heart of the city and, he thinks, the colonial ideology cast in stone. The massive post office, flanked by the police station (with its internal labyrinth of corridors, offices and interrogation rooms) and the bright yellow Banque de l'Indochine. Behind the back of his chair is the Hôtel Manolis. They together provide the framework of buildings that surround the dream square of a (medium-sized) French town. But built without any effort to adapt to the climate. Laid down *from above* according to some (false) perception of civilizing superiority. Dysfunctionally. (All the windows are wide open since the lack of natural ventilation in the building makes the rooms unbearably hot.)

Is that how *democracy* as a form of government is to be understood here? As something dysfunctional, alien, imposed?

(More importantly in a private sense: is he now well on the way to adopting his father's narrow world outlook? No, no, he defends himself. After all, he is not striving for that sort of traditional authoritarian state, is he? What he is contemplating at present is *an exception*.)

The capital city is not so big that you don't see familiar faces in a place like this: the wife (on the thin side, in a drab striped dress) of the restaurateur Mignon goes past in a cyclo laden with parcels. Right opposite, Van, the obese postmaster, is struggling up the steps, his uniform well pressed, his face shaded by the peak of his cap as he momentarily looks out over the square. And over there the chief of police's secretary is shaking his lighter in a failed attempt to get it to work.

He sees a wine-red Peugeot park alongside his own car.

He sees his driver salute the driver of the red car.

Who gets out and waves aside a pushy newspaper boy before crossing the square diagonally in the direction pointed out by Phirun. Horn-rimmed sunglasses, a silver-grey double-breasted suit, a dark blue silk tie, a hat that does not really match. He sees Lon Non's eyes scan the café and he catches his attention by raising his hand.

Then his sunglasses are on the café table. The hat has made a sweaty red line on his forehead. Lon Non holds out a packet of Grand Prix. He takes one, lights it with a match from the box lying in the ashtray. (The waiter puts out another glass.)

Sary:
Well, how are things looking?

Non:
We're proceeding according to the plan. But we had one hacked to death in Svay Rieng yesterday and another severely injured in Kompong Thom. (With a smile) Hit by an arrow.

Sary:
An arrow? From a bow?

Non:
I assume so.

Sary:
The foreign press are going to love that.

Non:
There's been shooting as well. In Takeo. With ordinary weapons. But no reports whether anyone was hit.

Sary:
See that the papers get the information.

Non:
Already have done.

Sary:
*The international agencies as well.
Especially AFP.*

Non:
Will do.

Sary:
Who is that fellow?

Non:
Which one?

Sary:
*The white fellow over there, talking
to the oddball in brown.*

Non:
With the briefcase? I don't know.

Sary:
*He looks familiar. Doesn't matter.
How are things looking for Thursday?*

Non:
*No problems. It's going according to
plan.*

Sary:
*That, among other things, is what I
wanted to talk about. We're going to
change strategy.*

Non:
Really?

Sary:

Up to now we've been at pains to be restrained. But developments suggest it is not working. The people are not mature enough, so to speak, to take responsibility. It's time to take off the kid gloves.

Non:

With all due respect, it's not a day too bloody soon.

Sary:

Indeed, I said you would approve. You are to make any necessary preparations. And everyone must get it into their heads that this does not, absolutely does not, imply that everyone is free to do what they like. I am the one who will decide who does what, where and when. Understood?

Non:

Of course.

Sary:

And as to Thursday, I'm thinking of being present myself. If there is nothing to prevent it?

Non:

Of course there isn't. But it's up to you to make the political judgement.

Sary:

That goes without saying. We'll see. I also want regular police to be stationed

close to the homes of leading figures.
Not right at the door, but certainly on
the block. And none at the party head-
quarters. Nor at the campaign offices.
It's important to keep individuals and
politics separate.

Non:
I'll arrange it.

Sary:
Have you got another ciggy? Mine's
finished.

Non:
No bother. Here you go.

Sary:
Thanks. (Taps the end of the
cigarette on the table.) *They're*
not up to much, these. (Lights it.)
Aren't you going to drink your wine?

Non:
Yes, I am. Of course.

Sary:
Do you have what you need? Is there
anything that's not clear?

Non:
No, there are no problems. I'll inform
you once all the preparations are
ready.

Sary:
That will be good, then.

Non:
(drinks his wine)

Sary:
One more thing. Here's a list of
some... specially selected... people
I'd like you to deal with. In a per-
manent sense, shall we say. (passes
over the folded sheet of paper)

Non's eyes skip through the list, then a quick nod.

And something else. (A hesitation?)

One of the names, Non says. An old school friend. Indeed, actually someone who was a *very close friend* in the past. They attended
upper school together in Kompong Cham. A certain *Saloth Sar.*
Admittedly he is now Keng Vannsak's private secretary but also—so
he has heard—a very popular schoolmaster. Wouldn't it be silly to
antagonize the students? Would it be in order to avoid *drawing attention*
to Sar at this point?

He drew deeply on his cigarette, unable to decide whether the flare
of irritation he felt was the result of (I) Non's objection or (II) his feeling
of being caught out. Yes, he was Keng Vannsak's secretary, yes, he
was an appropriate target, yes, yes—but yes, he was also—according
to what he had heard—Somaly's (ex-?) fiancé. And that latter point is
what led him to put this fellow Sar on the list. An *absolutely legitimate*
measure, however, in spite of that. But allowing the private to become
the political in this way does run counter to his principles. It was a
momentary weakness. Which might be misleading. And which has
now been pointed out by Non, without knowing.

Ah well. For your sake, Non, he says. For your sake. But let's bear
it in mind for the future.

Non thanks him, but already looks as if he regrets saying anything.

Another entry in the credit column, Sary notes. One thing must
be weighed against another.

And after a moment's thought. A hitherto unknown connection in this mishmash of relationships, friendships and hidden agendas. His sworn follower is obviously prepared to try to save Vannsak's bag-carrier. *Tiens, tiens*, is there more to it? Is there some hint of a secret alliance here? How unknowing is this man who doesn't know?

No, it's quite improbable. But suspicion intrudes deep into the territory of the improbable.

Non stands up, back to his usual self. Or more accurately, a manifestly keen and expectant version of his usual self.

Sary watches him back out and turn. Stops for a moment while trying to find the right gear. Then the car lurches, before slipping away (decorously, almost) and disappearing in the direction of the Quai Lagrandière.

It is not only the red Peugeot that is slipping away. The election campaign, too, he thinks, is slipping away in a direction he would have liked to avoid.

And, he continues (quite uncharacteristically), *for ten minutes, for ten minutes, I can sit here, just sit.*

To try to get to grips with what is coming.

And his wine is still cool.

And after that his lecture. After that the government meeting. After that a private discussion with Mau Say (who also has to be given new instructions). And after that? Sleep? No, there is all the rest of the work—which he certainly has not been neglecting but which accumulates faster than even he can manage it.

On the square in front of him: schoolboys in white shirts, neat haircuts and navy blue shorts. Rucksacks on their backs.

Em is the one who makes sure that their children work hard in school (they have nothing but good marks to show for it). The boys, who will step in and carry on the ascent his own father began—the ascent towards the very top *segment* of society. He has already got there, of course, but that is thanks to his own strength and without the lasting network of debts of gratitude, marriages and sworn loyalties that guarantee the status of future generations. It's his children's job to weave such a net (with their lives).

The Sam dynasty will be up there alongside those other families whose names run like red threads through the history of the kingdom.

He has no doubt that they will fulfil his expectations. There is nothing wrong with the characters they have inherited. When people praise his capacity for work he always points to Em. (*She is the one who is the real atomic power station.*) She is the one with the prestigious full-time job, with responsibility for five children, and she still finds time to be a driving force in the women's movement. (*And so on and so on.*) In addition to that: she possesses a will that matches his in terms of its hardness.

(He often talks of how difficult the negotiations in Geneva were. But only Em knows that the hardest thing was being away from her and the children. Their short visits gave him renewed strength at the negotiating table at the same time as the opposition was beginning to wilt with weariness.)

They are *a modern couple*. A *dynamic working partnership*.

In the new house (which they have designed themselves with the help of an architect who was in France on the same scholarship scheme as he was) the desks will be placed so that they can work face to face. Supporting each other; an active exchange of ideas and thoughts.

He lets his thoughts reach out to the future, to the office they will share. Air conditioned. Light. A pretty garden outside the windows. A telephone each. All-consuming work, *good work*.

o

o   o

And up. And on. Hurrying through a gallery now. He passes beneath lighted chandeliers, between antique statuettes, across a hardwood floor. The echo of his footsteps fills the vaulted ceiling.

Two years ago he could only have walked here by special invitation. At that stage it had been a building full of taller men with paler skins. Almost without exception men who *despised* him.

Not so now. Everything belongs to him now (well, to him and his fellow-countrymen).

But that's not what he is thinking about. (He is already used to the echo of his steps, to the placing of the statues.)

A doorman opens the double doors at the far end of the gallery. He walks on into the buzz of people, into the hall, without pausing.

Then he stands at the lectern. (Waits for the room to fall silent.)

He looks out over the straight rows of chairs. Over familiar faces, over unfamiliar faces. Those unable to find a seat are standing leaning against the walls. With the tips of his fingers he adjusts the papers already on the lectern, so they form an exact pile in front of him. Taps the microphone gently, hears the sound carried through the loudspeakers.

Cigarette and pipe smoke hangs over the hundred heads below the platform.

He takes a sip of water, clears his throat.

He says: "Your Highness, His Majesty the King's representative."

He says: "Monsieur the High Commissioner of the French Republic."

He continues: "Your Highnesses,

Your Excellencies,

Ladies and

(*a quick glance towards a noise in the darkness at the far end of the hall*)

Gentlemen,

(*a quick look down at his papers to catch the first line, then up again*)

For some time now events in the countries that border on Cambodia have once again brought the *Geneva Agreements* to the fore. We hear it being stated everywhere that these accords have not been respected."

(This is not the *exciting opening* he had hoped to come up with when he was waiting for the prince the other day, but he gave up trying to find one. In spite of everything, he is not in the *entertainment industry*.)

He talks about Laos and says: "Problems with the political framework there have degenerated into renewed armed conflict: Pathet Lao units, estimated as being several battalions in strength and supported by stormtroops from the Viet-minh, carried out massive attacks on 8 July and again two or three days ago in the mountainous region of Muong-Peun, some forty or so kilometres from the Socialist Republic of Vietnam."

Which naturally leads him on to the riots in Saigon and the uncertainty engendered by the announcement of an election next summer in both Vietnamese countries.

He says (in a tone of mild resignation, which suggests that this is still part of his introduction): "Since the start of the election campaign in this country, the parties of the left, the progressives, have been using the Geneva Agreements as the starting point for their propaganda. When they speak of the independence of Cambodia, they say it was *given as a gift* by the Geneva Conference. When they say they have studied the agreement dealing with direct American military support for Cambodia, they claim that it conflicts with the Geneva Agreements. When they want to explain the background to the election, they state that it was prescribed by the Geneva Agreements. In short, the Geneva Conference and the Geneva Agreements *explain everything*, they are the start of everything. This is what you hear everywhere and this is what appears in the local papers time and time again. As far as the Cambodian people are concerned—and they are for the most part baffled by these explanations—the agreements have taken on an *almost magical dimension*."

And (to round off the introduction): "Having been a member of the Cambodian delegation to the Geneva Conference, I should now like *to clarify* a number of the agreements that resulted from the conference and to correct some mistakes that are leading public opinion *astray*."

He moistens his lips with the water. (The fans flicker between the chandeliers.) By the doors at the far end of the room, among the people who have been unable to get a seat, he catches sight of two young women. A swanlike neck, a pretty profile.

What is she doing here?

He forces his eyes back to the sheet of paper in front of him and the words on it no longer seem to have anything to do with one another.

He reads the first three points word for word from the sheet, the tip of his index finger moving along the lines: "I shall first try to give an account of the *circumstances* that lie behind the most important paragraphs that concern Cambodia, then move on to the *implementation* of the agreements, and finally go on to the *consequences* of the implementation for the general election in Cambodia."

He looks up again. The two women have gone.

He takes a long drink of water, opens the polished lid of his cigarette case. Clears away his confusion, collects his thoughts sufficiently. Asks their forgiveness (with a smile as light as a feather). Brings the flame of the match to the cigarette (his hand shaking), while his eyes methodically scan every corner of the auditorium. Were the two figures an illusion? His introduction surely can't have bored her so thoroughly that she has left already? Perhaps she just wanted to show him off to her friend? Show that she has such a grand lover? But why is she out and about at this time of day?

He looks at the prominent guests. Tries again to focus his thoughts on his speech.

"What I should like to do is to make it easier for you to understand *the spirit* in which the Geneva Accords should be implemented, which is why I am now going to turn to the circumstances in which they arose."

He gives a detailed account of that chilly July evening in Geneva the year before. How he and his delegation insisted on further negotiations, which meant that the closing statement, which should have been delivered at nine in the evening, had to be postponed to the following day. How his driver got lost in the dark on the way to the supplementary discussions at the Villa des Ormeaux where Prime Minister Mendès-France and Foreign Ministers Molotov, Eden and Pham Van Dong were waiting. He describes the feeling of pressure in the room when he went in, how the clock passed the midnight hour and how Molotov leant forward, fixed him with his dark eyes and asked: *What exactly is it you want?*

He tells them how one o'clock came, and two o'clock. How, to everyone's surprise, Molotov changed his categorical "no" to Cambodia's demand to be permitted to enter military alliances to a shrug of the shoulders. How *he* (not anyone else) got Pham Van Dong to permit the import of military materiel via any border crossing the government might choose. He teases smiles from his listeners (he has them in the palm of his hand now) as he quotes the exchange of words that took place when Molotov dismissed Pham Van Dong's objections to the third demand (that the Cambodian communists should be disarmed).

That left the fourth demand. And he tells them how the Soviets were prepared to reach an accommodation with *him* on that point too, by accepting an international control commission for every single country in what had been French Indochina.

> Vyacheslav Molotov (with a touch of irony):
> *I hope that was everything you wanted.*

Sam Sary:
No.

> Anthony Eden, Pierre Mendès-France, the other delegates: (hold their breath)

> Vyacheslav Molotov: (looks taken aback)

Sam Sary:
I should like it made quite clear who will bear the costs of the International Control Commission in Cambodia.

> Vyacheslav Molotov (smiling (unusual), in a light-hearted tone
> (even more unusual)):
> *Given everything else you've achieved here, you can surely afford it.*

Sam Sary:
No, unfortunately it is beyond our economic capacity.

Playing his audience. But his portrayal of that dramatic nocturnal battle works. His listeners follow every twist and turn. He finishes the first part of his presentation (placing a subtle emphasis on *concessions* and *historic*): "I did not leave the Palais des Nations until about three o'clock in the morning. Our military delegates then spent a sleepless night revising the accords, so that they were in agreement with the concessions the communists had made at the last minute during a night that was so historic for the conference."

Almost in passing he points out that a multinational agreement as comprehensive and important as this, made as it was under such *special circumstances*, will undoubtedly *contain certain unclear elements*. Elements that do not only invite interpretation, they demand it.

Which, he says, leads them on to the second point of the evening: how should the agreements *be implemented*?

Her presence (real or imagined) has now been reduced to no more than background interference that can be ignored. He moves on to North Vietnam's obligations under international law. The demand made by the signatories of the agreement that there should be a withdrawal from Cambodian territory within ninety days has been respected. Indeed, the Vietnamese fulfilled that commitment with five days to spare. But, he says, and begs them to recall the doubts aired by His Excellency Penn Nouth, chairman of the Council of Ministers, in the October number of *Journal d'Extrême-Orient*:

I quote, he says and quotes: "According to figures provided by our general staff, only half of the Viet-minh troops have returned to Vietnam: *where are the rest?* A large number of them are probably still in the Cardamom Mountains, which face the Gulf of Thailand and are a traditional resort of smugglers, since they provide a route between Thailand and South Vietnam. As far as the Cambodian Viet-minh is concerned—that is to say the so-called *khmer rouge*, our own countrymen who either from malice or compulsion have become collaborators—many of them have now got organized, though it has to be said that they are still only poorly armed. Those responsible claim that 'all military equipment has been destroyed'. We dispute that *in the strongest terms possible*, because there are numerous bands of *khmer rouge* continuing to campaign secretly against the royal government."

He raps his forefinger on the dark wooden surface of the lectern as he reminds them of the hidden caches of weapons discovered along the border (a fact that *reinforces* the suspicions that he and Penn Nouth share):

"On our side, the royal government has fulfilled *everything that was prescribed for us*, legally as well as morally!"

And he continues (to deconstruct methodically all the myths and fallacies that surround the Geneva Accords. *His* accords).

o

o   o

(*Afterwards / on leaving the platform*) Sary is standing in the middle of a small group wearing light suits. He has given up hope that she may still be there, somewhere among the men talking together in the hall.

Quarter of an hour earlier. Thunderous applause. He was forced to quieten them before stepping down. (The account that reaches the royal chancellery will be one of anything but moderation. And be noted by the prince, that inscrutable mixture of brilliance, suspicion and whim.)

He has exchanged a few *friendly words* with Prince Monthana. The noise level has risen quickly since then. The double doors swing open, waiters in red jackets march in carrying trays of champagne. A *petite surprise* on the part of the organizers.

Now he is standing with Little Cook, the British chargé d'affaires, on his right and Prime Minister Leng Ngeth on his other side. (In formal terms Leng Ngeth is Sary's superior; informally, he does what Sary tells him.)

Among the dark clouds of night, pale shafts of light can be seen through the tall open windows.

Little Cook says obligingly (his French coloured by English) that it feels absolutely right that this speech, which has captured the Cambodian kingdom's struggle for freedom so well, should have been made in the locale which had earlier housed the French *Haut Commissariat*.

(Around them: conversations, glittering glassware, cigarette smoke.)

There are no French representatives near them, so he answers that such is the course of history. That there are many countries still waiting to come into their own. *The British Gold Coast and Nigeria*, for instance.

Little Cook nods. The fact that the French have lost Indochina, the jewel among French colonies, is undoubtedly (yet one more) proof that a different world order is knocking at the door. But, as we know, a great deal has been invested in the colonies. Politics is one thing, economics another. Both sides have legitimate economic claims, don't they? Of course it is your country that the railway runs through, but the iron in the rails comes from France.

And the hands that cleared the jungle and laid the track were Cambodian, Leng Ngeth points out in an amiable enough voice.

Quite, Little Cook hastens to say, but the engineers' *wages* were paid by the French state.

With the profit they made on our raw materials, Leng Ngeth interrupts him. Perhaps you British might have something to learn from our example in your... not entirely successful... *handling* of the Mau Mau. How many dead *terrorists* have you reached so far? I think ten thousand was the latest figure I saw, wasn't it?

(Sary, searching for a change of company, lets his eyes survey the suits in the hall.)

Little Cook pretends not to notice Leng Ngeth's acid tone. Instead, he leans forward confidentially and says that, irrespective of the economic background, it seems just a tad strange to an outside observer that, having taken fiscal power and all the economic interests away from Paris, you have allowed Paris to retain so much political influence.

Sary looks again into Little Cook's very blue eyes. A receding hairline even though he can hardly be forty, but indisputably an ambitious and intelligent fellow. He says that he assumes that what Cook is referring to in this case are the French military advisers?

> Little Cook:
> *Your Excellency, bearing in mind that it's your American friends who are generously sending you the equipment, it wouldn't be too much to assume that they were the people best suited to explaining how best to utilize the materiel.*

Sam Sary:
We are keen to have friends in every country. Even in Paris.

> Little Cook:
> *I think you understand what I'm getting at.*

> Leng Ngeth:
> *We understand what you mean.*

Sam Sary:
Politics is a rational discipline. A discipline of Deliberation. I'm sure

we agree on that. But, Your Excellency
Little Cook, the value of intuition
should not be underestimated, should
it? Without it no one would ever
become more than… shall we say…
a chargé d'affaires.

Little Cook: (laughs politely)

He smiles a smile that makes it clear that the conversation is over. But no sooner has he caught the eye of High Commissioner Gorce than Little Cook (that *lackey of the Americans*) holds him back: "I happened to notice that Your Excellency said nothing about the fallacious nature of the claim that the independence of your kingdom was negotiated in Geneva. His Royal Highness the Prince usually takes great pains to emphasize that de facto independence was actually achieved by him the year before. Now it sounds rather as if it was Your Excellency who…"

He interrupts him coldly: "*What do you mean?* Nowhere did I say that credit for our independence should go to those negotiations."

Little Cook smiles again and says, *no, of course not,* and: "But the prince takes the line, doesn't he, that the Geneva Accords are of secondary importance given that independence had already been achieved?"

He looks at the British diplomat again. (The conversation has definitely taken an unpleasant turn.) He says: "The title of this lecture was 'The Geneva Agreement', *n'est-ce pas Monsieur?* In which case it is hardly surprising that that is what I talked about. And, moreover, the prince's *line* is *my* line. Stop. End of story."

And off.

o

o   o

As the cabinet meeting is coming to a close there are a few moments of *spontaneous stillness*. The ministers raise their eyes from the table and look at one another in silence. The table in front of them is covered in documents. In the middle (like islands in the sea of paper) are the big black ashtrays with coils of smoke curling up slowly from them. Jackets are hanging over the backs of chairs, ties were loosened hours ago. Light is reflecting up from the white papers, spectacles gleam like polished disks.

(The odour of sweat, tobacco and hair tonic. A hand reaches out towards one of the ashtrays and taps the long grey column of ash off a cigarette.)

Where is Sary in all this? On one of the long sides of the table, near the middle. A cigarette in the fingers of his left hand, a pen in his right.

This is the kind of occasion that Sary would have looked forward to. Earlier. It would even have implied a certain amount of stress. The majority of the gentlemen present are older (and more experienced) than him and so he (and everyone else) has been brought up to respect them (*which in practice means*: to be subservient—without question—to their will).

But now he is, if only informally, an extension of the arm of the prince (and, moreover, from the moment that he *gave way*, he became *an iron fist* attached to that arm).

He is conscious that his rapid rise from (almost) nowhere has made those present envious. (That and the fact that he is so comfortable in his elevated role, that he seems to take it *for granted*.) (Which, in his own opinion, is perfectly sensible, given his education, his capacity for work and *his inborn qualities as a leader*. In other words, there is every reason why the prince should have such faith in him.)

But as things are, he feels no sense of satisfaction about what awaits them. It will take energy. And all his energy is focused elsewhere.

The silence and stillness last a few moments more, until Mau Say glances to the side and then leans over his notes again. His pen scratches, his fingertips are stained with ink.

Sary watches Mau Say fill yet another row with unclear symbols. And another.

Then he looks at Chuop Samloth, the justice minister, and at old Kim Tith, who has responsibility for internal security, at Lon Nol, the army chief of staff, at Sim Var in his horn-rimmed glasses and at all the others along the opposite long side of the table. For a second his eyes meet those of Pho Proeung, the minister of the interior.

He breaks eye contact and looks out into the night beyond the windows.

(The guard steps into the light of a street lamp, then out of it again in the direction from which he had emerged. Hands in pockets, rifle across his back. The glow of his cigarette moves along, gently undulating. Insects swarm around the lamp, their wings glittering.)

The meeting continues. Sim Var (clears his throat) draws attention to the last item but one on the agenda.

Pho Proeung confirms the arrangements at the polling stations. A couple of questions are raised and answered briefly. The time is after ten. (An infectious yawn spreads through the room.)

Sary seeks permission to speak but it is not given. Sim Var sees him raise his pen (of course he sees it) but moves on to the last item.

He keeps his face expressionless though his body tenses with annoyance. He can sense the purr of fellow feeling among the rest of them around the table—old loyalties are being confirmed.

He lays down his pen, interlaces his fingers in front of him and waits patiently.

Then it's his chance. And he says in a low calm voice that the prince wants to be able to look forward to election day with confidence. *Indeed, we all want that, don't we?* And that is why there must be an end to *private initiatives that do not promote the common goal.* (A slight shuffling can be heard in the room.) He says that *he* (no longer referring to the prince) will not tolerate any further *pieces of improvisation.*

As if dealing with a gathering of subordinates (which, in practice, is what they are at this point), he orders them to keep their people at a suitable distance when the polling stations have closed. That should be drilled into every level of their various organizations—emphatically.

Any questions that arise, you can bring to me; any objections must be taken to the prince.

Is that understood?

As I said, he says, public order. You must allow the representatives of the electoral commission to do their work.

They have all gone. He stays behind for a while, leafing through, but not concentrating on, a report the minister of justice gave him. Fatigue is making him feel slightly sick. He shuts his briefcase, struggles into his jacket and goes down to the foyer with its gilded suite of sofa and armchairs.

Mau Say (as arranged) is waiting in one of the armchairs. The young man's eyes are shut, his mouth closed, his hands resting on the papers in his lap.

He puts his bag down by the sleeping man, goes along the adjoining corridor to the gentlemen's toilet. Standing at the urinal his eyes move across the tiles to the left and there he sees it, raised on the sharp points of its thin legs on the filthy floor cloth in the corner. Shining plates on its black back; the strip lighting reflected in its many eyes; its jaws underneath.

(He feels his stream cut short involuntarily.)

Then it is gone.

He looks again. The floor cloth in the corner is still a floor cloth.

The large scorpion that was sitting on top of it a moment ago has gone.

(He looks again, all at once uncertain whether it is the floor cloth or the scorpion that was the illusion.)

Perhaps it was the creases in the rag that made the shape of the animal? But they aren't folded in the kind of way that might lead anyone to make that mistake.

He swills his wrists under cold water from the tap. Bathes his dry eyes. If it had been an ordinary scorpion he would simply have told the caretaker to deal with it. But the one he thought he saw was one of those poisonous tree-dwelling scorpions that he knows are only found in the most inaccessible jungle provinces. If one of that species were to turn up in the cabinet office *pissoir*, it really would be a zoological mystery. (And now it has become even more mysterious *since it has disappeared into thin air.*)

The hands of the clock over the door are approaching eleven. He studies the pale, washed-out version of himself.

He thinks that perhaps it is the spirit of the building trying to tell him something. But in that case what? If it was just a hallucination, it is even more disturbing because that would imply that his brain was overheating as a result of all the work, lack of sleep and pills.

He washes out his mouth. Returns to the room with the sofas and armchairs and puts his hand gently on the shoulder of the sleeping man. Mau Say's face slowly comes alive and he apologizes. Sary rattles his little red metal tube of pills. Mau Say nods. Without water they swallow one each and Sary says, now we'll continue.

o

o   o

(*Evening/cinematography*) The blonde woman sits down on the grass slope that runs down to the road. She picks up a small insect from the sand, puts it on the back of her hand and blows it away to freedom. Smiling she watches it disappear, after which the sad, sad and sorrowful, expression returns to her face.

Then music can be heard. She turns her head. There are three men in peaked caps coming over the brow of the slope behind her. They are walking merrily in a line, the first of them playing a flute, the second a clarinet and the last a French horn. They walk past her without a second glance. In the next scene she is walking behind them slowly, with an almost peaceful smile.

She makes a playful pirouette.

He sneaks a look at the prince's face beside him. In the light reflected from the screen, there is something timeless about the face. Soft, smooth, but with a sort of *paradoxical cruelty*. (On the other side of the prince he can see Monineth's pretty profile and then her friend, a girl whose name he has already forgotten.) Cigarette smoke drifts above them in the light of the projector.

The landscape shots in the film take him back to France. It's a year since he was last there. Fully a year. The children still talk about their months in Menton. While there his daughter became more of a tomboy than ever. Hardly to be wondered at given her four brothers and then the two sons in the Clement family. She has calmed down a little now that she has begun training with the Royal Ballet. She is, of course, too old and too big to be really good, but at least it provides a *suitable environment*. (The royal couple take a great interest in the ballet. The little dancers come from good families.)

The blonde woman in the film has arrived at a circus encampment. He hears the prince giggle when the fiddler the woman is watching takes a puff from a cigarette jammed between the tuning screws of his minute fiddle.

Suddenly the prince's face comes very close. The odour (heavy): eau-de-cologne, wine, a touch of sweat.

That's the director's wife, Gelsomina. Nothing to speak of, what?
(He answers in a whisper:) *Not exactly Hollywood.*
Rossellini did it better!
Undeniably.
(Their smiles melt together.)
The prince continues:

"Did you notice the simple way they changed scenes with just a tiny little alteration in the positioning of the camera? I'll borrow that for that… hmm… a little *divertissement* I've started filming. You probably didn't notice it, but it was very neatly done."

He puts on an appreciative expression and thinks that the one thing that is lacking among the prince's many talents is the ability to recognize where his talents end.

He is not a connoisseur of film. But since the prince doesn't lack *resources* (ultra-modern equipment, for instance), the reason for the *feebleness* and obvious *amateurism* that characterize the prince's melodramas has to be sought elsewhere.

How to explain it? Sary thinks that the prince is an example of *the mystery of genius*. To be more specific: what is the elusive artistic quality that explains why two painters of identical technical skill can paint the same person, and in one portrait the subject appears to come to life, whereas in the other (which is just as accurate a depiction) the subject remains flat and lifeless?

(Watching (as he is now) films/listening to speeches in the National Assembly/observing the ocean from the deck of a ship/etcetera often inspires Sary to this sort of *philosophizing*.)

Another example (of the same mystery): the fantastic photographs taken by his former driver Meta. Meta had never learnt photography professionally, his ability was obviously inborn. But the most banal situations looked like carefully constructed art in the pictures that Meta took. They became sort of *representative* rather than merely *representational.* (His own pictures, which had occasionally been taken on the same Duaflex film roll as Meta's photographs, completely lacked that superior quality.)

But, unlike the prince, he realizes that he lacks the talent, that he does not possess that elusive ability to perform *magic*.

The prince's lack of self-knowledge, his flagrant overestimate of his own abilities, is a daily (nightly in the present case) source of irritation. (The big brother syndrome again.) He has frequently considered explaining to the prince that filmmaking is an *utter waste of time*. But (the big brother syndrome again) it gives the prince so much pleasure, and his genuine, almost childish enthusiasm is touching. (And the prince does deserve some respite from all his many duties.)

So he has let the issue rest.

And (it has to be admitted) it is pleasant to be fetched to the palace in the evening, where there are comfortable armchairs in the private cinema and wine and very often female company. (*What did she say her name was, the one along there?*) It is, moreover, in the context of these film shows that the prince can be at his most visionary, and the two of them can draw up plans that don't just deal with the trivia of the day but which extend out to the decades to come. *According to the plans*: the 1960s will concentrate on the further modernization of society, the extension of the infrastructure, the education system and other basic essentials. This foundational work will begin to generate its own values in time for the '70s, and by the '80s we shall be moving into *the era of full bloom*. With just a little luck, both of them will survive into the new millennium, and he likes (really likes) the image of the two of them, both bent low by age, welcoming the new millennium on a roof terrace high above the international metropolis they created *together*. The flash of exploding fireworks as dim-eyed (and in silence) he and the prince clink their glasses to the conclusion of their (joint) life's work. The expression recently coined by the newspapers—*Le tandem Sihanouk–Sary*—will by that stage have become an informal institution. A concept that will be considered so self-evident that it will be the chapter heading in history books.

Unfortunately, however, the prince's self-belief does not restrict itself to the making of hopeless films. On the one hand, the prince is quite incomparable when it comes to seeing the talents of others and allowing them considerable freedom (Sary finds this impressive): it creates breathtaking dynamism in the powerful but informal circle with which the prince surrounds himself. On the other hand, individuals can be left with problems far beyond their power to solve. If they do succeed the prince is not slow to take the credit, but if they fail the failure is theirs and theirs alone. Sary, in fact, has no objection to that method as such. When all is said and done the prince is leader of the country. It is necessary to consolidate his legitimacy on a daily basis and, in the end, any progress is a result of the prince's overall policies. But—and on this point he feels at a complete loss—it seems to him that the prince has begun to believe in his own *corrected version of developments*. (A sort of sense of infallibility.) And (this is what makes the problem both personal and acute) *the absolute honesty* he has always shown to his friend and monarch and which the prince has expressly valued in a court full of yes-men, that honesty... well... has not been so welcome of late.

But, he tries to convince himself (with little hope of success), perhaps it's the parliamentary election? Uncertainty? But surely it's at times like these that honesty is most vital?

The honesty between him and Em offers a prime example. There are, of course, things he doesn't broach with her. (The most confidential affairs of state—and *ditto* those of sex.) But *if she asks*, he always answers honestly. A relationship illuminated by such an *unsentimental light of honesty*, he thinks, is not likely to start festering in the damp and darkness that surrounds things that are concealed, things that are hidden. And she in her turn is almost brutal in her honesty. He sometimes thinks that she carries it to extremes, using it as a weapon in the never-ending battle that is the relationship between two strong-willed people. Not that she needs to. But she finds the emotional and intellectual combat between them stimulating in itself. More often than not, as he is the first to admit, she has the upper hand.

He turns his mind back to the new house they are going to build to their own design. The planning of it may perhaps be said to provide him with the same kind of relaxation as filmmaking provides for the prince (with the difference that it doesn't burden the national budget). And, he thinks acidly, the result will be something that people will be able to talk about with *admiration*. She has already shown him her ideas for furnishing the various rooms. Tastefully. Ingeniously. Yet another of her many enviable talents. He looks forward one day to inviting the prince to their new home. He knows from Em's sketches that it will make an impression on the prince (who is himself devoted to *composing* the furnishing of the rooms in the palace). He can see how the prince will surreptitiously take note of the sensuously entwined initials *S* and *E* on the Limoges porcelain Em has commissioned. And how the different varieties of wood contrast subtly with one another. And the alternating lightness and weight of the furnishings against the background of the big windows.

A small *modernist palace* for and about their love.

The film cuts (abruptly). The screen fills with dazzling squares and the music is replaced by the rattling of the filmstrip, which soon stops. He sees the prince turn to Monineth and her friend. (In the background: a pendulum creaks and then strikes two weak strokes.) He lights another cigarette and smokes it slowly while waiting for the projectionist to change the reel.

THURSDAY, 8 SEPTEMBER 1955

Eight untidily franked stamps. How long has it been on its way? It's impossible to read the date. (But children are not fastidious collectors, anything pleases them.) Below the postmark the familiar French handwriting. Sary continues listening to Ly Chinly and Mau Say as he slides his paper knife through the envelope.

The letter is the usual length (three thin sheets) and dated a fortnight earlier. He quickly scans the black ink of the opening and closing passages. (There is no suggestion that there will be anything alarming between the two. He puts the sheets back in the envelope to read later.)

His correspondence with the family that took him in during his years in France provides him with a portal to something different. First and foremost to their joint past. Even more important, however, is the opportunity to *test ideas* without the consequences being more than a well-considered handwritten reply. With them (his French family) he can broach every dilemma he faces without holding anything back and receive an answer that will relate to their fundamentally shared values. They do not know his country but they do know him (and his intentions). And consequently, when they give advice, they can take the long-term view and don't have to take account of day-to-day political haggling.

But is that valid any longer? Immediately after his arrival in Paris, as a matter of practical necessity (nothing to eat), he chose to put an advert in *Le Figaro* seeking a French family who would support a *needy student* during those difficult days of rationing. But the underlying thought, which was to gain access to the everyday life of an affluent and truly French family, was rooted in his long fascination with the French bourgeoisie (planted in him as early as his elementary school—which was run by Frenchmen). Education, good taste, without inhibitions but nevertheless *controlled*. The sort of attitude towards the world that he had earlier envied in the members of the French colonial service he had come in contact with. He saw an opportunity to gain access to the *very heart* of this attitude.

It was in discussions with the other students in the informal dining club organized by the French family that he argued his way to the ideals and visions he later returned home with. (His conversations with the son of the family had been particularly rewarding. Partly because they were the same age, partly because he (Jean) had spent part of the war in a German internment camp and consequently felt he had been a *prisoner of an occupying power.*)

What should he write to them this time?

That they will have to forgive him for this temporary departure from the enlightened (*modern*) principles they share?

(Or simply let it sink into the abyss between their world and his world, into the expanse of silence that stretches between their letters? And hope that the big French papers do not focus on those particular aspects of the election campaign? And anyway, what do those bloody journalists know about what is *really* at stake here? They fly in and then they fly out with something half considered, half digested, which they present as the *truth.*)

He pushes back his cuff with the forefinger of the other hand. Sees how far the gold hands have travelled round the black face of his watch. (His calendar reads: "17.30 SOMALY", "19.00 VANNSAK". Taken together the two entries generate a mixture of anxiety and impatience that is difficult to channel.)

He turns his attention instead to the men in the armchairs on the other side of the low round table. Ly Chinly with his harmonious facial features, Mau Say with his low-key intensity. The former is wearing a pearl grey suit, the latter chocolate brown. (Sweat glistens at their hairlines; the light at the windows is a dazzling white.)

The two of them are talking about the price of rice in the city—which has gone up in recent days. A necessary increase (resulting from dwindling supplies). But the timing was unfortunate given that one of the planks of their electoral campaign is the notion that there is *increasing material abundance*. The question (more specifically) they are discussing is how to minimize the damage. To change course would come over as weak willed. There is no space on the radio or in the papers for a campaign to educate the public (no time to do so anyway). They could possibly lower the price of cooking oil and some other basic necessities on a temporary basis. But it isn't clear whether the slight rise in the price of rice is having any effect on opinion. The question is whether they would be better spending their energy on other issues.

He interrupts them and says that they certainly would. With an unlit cigarette hanging from his lips, he asks them for an assessment of their contacts with the electoral commission.

Ly Chinly says, yes and of course, and gives an account (unenthusiastically) of the hastily revised instructions that went out that morning to the personnel manning the polling stations. About the colour and format of the ballot papers. That certain *adjustments* in the number of names on the electoral registers have been ordered. That the electoral commission has been given the task of investigating the political background of the polling station supervisors and, where necessary, replacing unsuitable individuals with others (put forward by Mau Say).

Mau Say says that the latter point has to be understood with the usual reservation that there are insufficient competent people available. As they know, however, there is no reason for them to fear the fate that threatens some former colonies, which is that those who are well educated *allow themselves to be tempted by the superior standard of living* in France. (There is no one to tempt.) The only *necessary qualification* to occupy a lower-grade state office in this country at present is to have a backside of just the right malleability to fit the chair behind the desk.

Sary says (so quickly after Mau Say's last words that you could get the impression that he hasn't been listening or has been waiting with a pre-prepared sentence) that he no longer cares how they achieve what they have set out to achieve. Nor does he care whether it's done with any *notable degree of sophistication*. The main thing is that they get the right result (that is to say, the result the prince wants). So they must not permit a single voting statistic to reach the public sphere without having first passed before the eyes of those in this room. They are already fighting a war on several fronts with the foreign press, and they cannot expect any sympathy from that direction whatever happens. *We will do what we have to do, irrespective of what the so-called civilized world thinks about it.* Sary continues (after lighting a cigarette): Ly Chinly, my friend, you seem troubled by higher ideals—name me one country that has managed to introduce a democracy that functions fault-free during the first shaky year of independence!

Ly Chinly meets his gaze but remains silent.

He says: Well then. That's everything.

They gather up their papers (like three winners at a poker table). And up. And on.

o

o   o

He closes his eyes, just for a moment. Opens them. Stands up. Walks quickly across the boards of the platform, taps the microphone lightly. Hears his tap crackle out over all the faces that are turned his way.

The sun will soon be setting, deep red. The staccato notes of the insects in the trees.

In a loud clear voice he says: My dear fellow-countrymen!

He says: Kinsmen of our revered forefathers who built Angkor!
He says, with a smile: Dear people of Takmau.
Then, with an earnest, almost troubled, expression, he continues.
The loudspeakers are useless.

o

o   o

(Calendar entry 2: 19.00 VANNSAK, minus a minute or two) *The scene viewed through a windscreen*: the headlamps of the car sweep across them. The whites of their eyes light up. Men in everyday clothes. Young, middle-aged.

Sary *collects his thoughts* for a moment, climbs out and is met by silence (apart from the ticking of the engine after it's been switched off and the sounds of night—that is, barking dogs, wireless sets and so on).

In the distance: the buzz of many people.

Beyond that: stars impaled on the branches of the trees.

The outline of Non emerges from the general shadow and leads him out among the waiting people. He recognizes a couple of them. (Students, ordinary labourers. A civil servant from the customs office.) They greet him humbly, with gentle tentative handshakes. An odour of tension and alcohol. And the smoke from the kitchen fires in the nearby houses.

Cudgels in their hands, glowing cigarettes.

His mouth still tastes of lipstick, whisky and *canard à l'orange*. She was on time for once. Yet another new dress (this time dove blue, deep lilac, red). Her footsteps across the black and white squares of the floor. Pearl earrings (her mother's, she explained when he complimented her on them). The courteous smile as she stands up, which shifts to a more spontaneous one after a few steps. Her eyes fixed on his.

They ate in the hotel's dining room. The evening rain outside the window was whipping the water in the pool to a turquoise foam (lit from below). No talk of politics. She told him about a film she had seen.

(*A*—he would say—*dreamlike interlude* from the whirling course of events he has now returned to.)

When they were saying goodbye outside, she had kissed him quite shamelessly in the European manner, watched by the silent faces of the cyclo drivers. (The irregular drip, drip, drip from the leaves of the trees.) He had met her mouth.

In the car on the way here her scent still clung to the skin of his hands.

He had wiped his lips carefully with a handkerchief. Left it—with its pinkish red stain—on the floor of the car.

Then the last turn to the right. The men picked out by the head-lamps. All that was left when he stepped out of the car (into the silence of those gathered there) was the taste in his mouth.

He asks for and is given a bamboo cudgel. Non offers him a cigarette (the same useless brand as in the café). He looks at the pale phosphorescent hands of his watch. The distant hum turns into applause. There is the crackle of a loudspeaker.

They set off. (A man walks in front of Sary with a hand-cranked torch so that *His Excellency*'s Italian shoes won't get wet in the puddles of water.)

There is a seductive simplicity about this little walk, and the kiss earlier. And about what is going to happen soon. Being at the head of a group of men. Walking through the night. Stars up in the trees after rain.

(But this *simplicity* is at least as much a matter of *relief*. For what is it if it isn't the concrete result of *having given in*? Of just allowing the accumulation of irritation/aggression/antipathy to spill over all those who are vain enough to stand in his way? Making unreserved use of the force (one's own or that of others) that the (superior) power he represents ultimately rests on?)

The familiar voice in the loudspeaker. Soft, low-key, but inflammatory. Anti-royalist slogans. *The murder* of the monk Chung. The agreement with the Americans referred to as *putting our independence on sale*. Things that strike home, he thinks. (Shouts and applause.)

The street widens out into the open ground in front of Le Champ de Courses. An audience of a hundred or so are facing the improvised stage. (Which is more than Sary had been reckoning on, but not so many—in this context—as to constitute a critical mass.) The voice, lit by spotlights, is standing at the microphone. White shirt, sleeves rolled up. Sweat gleaming on his high forehead. Insects swarming around the lights.

A tirade about *the oppressor being replaced by the oppressor's lapdog.*

The people standing right at the back are now turning round to the new arrivals. The ripple of anxiety that runs through the gathering is almost visible. Listeners out on the fringes (it can be assumed that they are there out of curiosity rather than anything else) quickly slip away into the shadows.

Non comes up to him, informs him that their own loudspeaker system has been moved forward. He gives the go-ahead. A minute or so later the national anthem is booming out from diagonally behind him.

Up on the platform Keng Vannsak loses his thread. He puts his hand up to shade his eyes from the spotlights. Another handful of listeners drifts away. But there are still many left and they begin applauding the platform. Vannsak composes himself (he has, after all, been in this situation before) and continues at a very much louder volume.

Non passes Sary a microphone. Sary swallows and then breaks in. His words meet Vannsak's words (the latter unexpectedly ceding him the advantage).

He thinks their voices are like the thunder of gods in the night. One of them in the light, the other in the darkness. (Which, he thinks, is ironic, since *he* is the one who represents the true, the golden light, isn't he?) While the mere mortals listen, terrified. And Vannsak, standing small and alone up there, all eyes directed at him. On the defensive against an invisible adversary.

The listeners are silent at first. But they respond when Non and his men begin shouting sexual obscenities at the stage. Some of the listeners come closer. Hands waving. Lips shining with saliva.

That's how easy it is, he thinks. And continues jousting with Vannsak through the microphone.

Dear listeners, why did you come to listen to a liar?

> *Freedom of assembly is guaranteed in the constitution, Your Excellency Sam Sary. We have every right to hold this election meeting. That should come as no surprise to a man of the law like you.*

A freedom is only a freedom as long as it isn't abused, Mr Keng. Or should I perhaps call you Mr King instead? For those of our dear listeners who aren't familiar with the English language, "king" means ruler and that is what that liar on the platform wants to be.

> *You are in breach of the constitution, Your Excellency.*

How could you possibly trust KING Vannsak? He is lying now and he will continue feeding you with lies if you elect him. Just like the old primary-school teacher he is, he is now trying to teach basic law to a member of the Council of State!

Dear listeners, you can see for yourselves that the Mafia gang running the country has no respect for the rights of the people. It doesn't even respect its own laws!

King Vannsak talks rubbish. What does he care about you Cambodians? He calls himself a nationalist but Cambodian women aren't good enough for him. Not a single one of them is good enough for this fiery nationalist King Vannsak. His own people aren't good enough, so he has gone and married a foreigner instead.

His Excellency Sam Sary isn't satisfied with just one Cambodian woman, he uses them like handkerchiefs. Wipes himself a couple of times with each of them before quickly moving on to the next.

Another lie to add to King Vannsak's pack of lies. Listen now, Vannsak, are you married to a foreigner or aren't you? Well? I deal in facts while you wallow in gossip. Slander is punishable by law and I've got plenty of witnesses among our dear listeners.

A man's will to serve his country should be judged on what he does for that country, not on whom he is married to.

Oh, oh, oh, dear listeners, a true word at last from our self-appointed king. What was Monsieur King doing while I was in Geneva negotiating the independence of our dear country a year or so ago? I'll tell you what, I'll tell you. He was lazing around in Paris with his foreign wife!

Only snakes can talk snake language to snakes and only dogs can talk to dogs. We all know that independence would have been achieved weapon in hand if your establishment gang hadn't stolen our just struggle.

Weapon in hand, possibly, but not cock in hand in a luxury flat in Paris.

The pot calling the kettle black!

Statement

Response

Etcetera

Etcetera

Now?

Soon.

A shove. A couple of hands grab a shirt collar. Angry faces an centimetre or so apart. Bodies lurching around.

He cuts Vannsak off with a shout, followed by a stern command to the two fighters to let go of one another. Several people step between them, the yelling continues.

According to the script (I): Almost a riot. Calmly, slowly, in a carefully articulated way, he informs them that the meeting—*in the name of the law*—must *disperse. (By my authority as Deputy Prime Minister, I order all those present to go home.)*

For his part Vannsak exhorts the audience to stay. Not to let themselves be provoked.

(The dialogue between the gods, however, has ended and is beyond all redemption.)

Some of the men behind him throw stones and whatever they can find on the ground into the crowd by the stage. He repeats his command.

According to the script (II): Non is standing beside him and receives an affirmative answer to his question. He hands the microphone and his tie and jacket to Non. Non disappears in the direction of the loudspeaker set-up, which responds with a feedback howl.

He lights a cigarette. (His hands tremble slightly in the flare of the flame.)

Vannsak, still alone on the platform. Calling for calm. Then his voice is drowned out again by the crashing cymbals of the national anthem.

According to the script (III): He takes a last puff and throws away the half-smoked cigarette. Moves the bamboo club to his right hand. Turns round. His men are gathered there, clubs in hand. In a loud voice he asks whether they are ready *to give these bastards what they deserve.* As one voice they answer yes.

Then everything turns into flashes of tight concentration and disconnected sequences: people screaming and fleeing / blows falling on backs and skulls / oaths / bodies lying in the mud like bundles of rags with men beating them / Vannsak being quickly hurried away from the spotlit stage / a half-grown boy crying his eyes out / shouts / some young men in school uniforms fighting with their feet, their shirts soon stained with blood / an old man cowering / smells of sweat, wet earth, fear / the well-aimed blow above the ear he lands on a fleeing man, who crumples to the ground / the crowd beginning to thin out / blows raining down on fewer and fewer people.

And then the national anthem, sort of *fading in* again. Laughter, shouting, the elation of violence shining in the men's eyes. (It's that *look* again, the one he has seen on the prince's face—and on his own in the mirror.)

He takes a comb out of his back pocket and, hands still trembling, combs his hair. Then a cigarette. Calls to some of his men to stop beating a man on the ground (possibly the man he himself struck down).

In the light of the spotlights—still lit—the area in front of the stage is a wasteland. A hundred or more abandoned sandals (he finds the sight comical, as if they had broken up a *shoemakers' convention*). Several muddy and broken placards. (Someone abruptly lifts the needle from the record and the music cuts off in the middle of a crescendo.)

FRIDAY, 9 SEPTEMBER 1955

The short report from the security police lies on the table in front of Sary. Slap Soumlap is dead it seems. (*Who the hell is he?*) A neat sheet in a pale-blue folder. Stamped, signed by an unknown hand. (The superintendent of the hospital personally confirms it in an attached note.) According to the report this Slap Soumlap is—well, *had been*—Keng Vannsak's personal driver for a few days. Taken to the Calmette Hospital at midnight by his uncle, pronounced dead exactly one hour later. Cause of death not yet determined. But according to the duty doctor it seems "not unreasonable to assume that the cause of death was blows to the head with a blunt implement". The body is being held until further notice in spite of pressure from the family. Several family members are said to be sympathetic to the Democrats, although none of them is as active as the dead man had been.

He runs through (edited parts of) the evening before, more particularly the baton stroke with which he felled the fleeing man. Can it have landed *that* badly? Can he really have been *so bloody unlucky*?

Less than twenty-four hours ago young Mr Slap's existence was utterly insignificant (just like any other anonymous worm). Now his *non-existence* is a real problem, since he will provide the Democrats with another martyr (to place alongside the monk Chung). Another grainy photograph (derived from identity papers) to print on their placards. (We can assume he will have the same simple-minded stare as all the rest who have only had their photograph taken once in their lives, Sary thinks. And then he thinks: *The way the political game works is truly unjust. Here we are working hard to chart all the various relationships, who wields influence over what and whom and how. And then up pops a nobody—what's more, a dead nobody—from nowhere and becomes a factor in the power game.*)

The question now is this: what is the best way of dealing with this unfortunate situation? Denial? In which case, what tone should they adopt? And via which channels? Doing the usual thing and blaming it on a private quarrel, fuelled by palm wine and resulting from borrowed money / women / local loyalties / etcetera would be pretty insensitive in a situation as sensitive as this, wouldn't it? And there are likely to be a number of witnesses from the previous evening.

But (and he stretches unconsciously) why so defensive? He thinks:

I'll be damned if being careful has *ever got me anywhere*. Better to take the opposite strategy. And actually blame *this appalling murder* on that big bastard (Vannsak).

(Tried and tested tactic: if you say something loud enough and often enough it will eventually stick to the target. On the principle of *no smoke without fire*.)

He opens the next folder. A mint-green one. (His untouched cigarette is burning away in the ashtray.)

It is from the chief of police and the folder he thought he was opening when he opened the pale-blue one.

Keng Vannsak has been arrested at his house (without resistance) in accordance with *His Excellency Sam Sary's orders*. He has been taken to the prison at Prey Sar.

So that's clear then. The time for moderation is now definitely over.

He takes the top off his fountain pen. A clean sheet of paper on which he quickly writes an order to the director of the prison. The prisoner Keng Vannsak is to be held in solitary confinement. No (underlined) violence is to be done to him. Any objects that might be used *to take his own life* should be removed. But (underlined) the prisoner shall be deprived of sleep and adequate meals, including water. All daily routines are to be performed at irregular intervals. Prisoners are to be maltreated in the next cell, even at night. Everything to be done as you consider appropriate. Inform the prisoner that he is the subject of *a murder inquiry*. But (underlined) under no (underlined) circumstances should his life be put at risk (three exclamation marks).

His initials. Stamped. For immediate dispatch.

o

o   o

He closes his eyes, just for a moment. Opens them. Stands up. Walks quickly across the boards of the platform, taps the microphone lightly. Hears his tap crackle out over all the faces that are turned his way.

The sky is dark. No sun. Rain is pounding down on the roof, blocking out the world in the square of the windows.

In a loud clear voice he says: My dear fellow-countrymen!

He says: Kinsmen of our revered forefathers who built Angkor!

He says, with a smile: Dear people of Skuon.

Then, with an earnest, almost troubled, expression, he continues. Given the noise of the rain, the loudspeakers are too weak.

o

o o

He picks up the telephone, books (commands) a conversation. He can't pretend he hasn't thought it through. In spite of everything, however, he has hesitated by the telephone several times. It still comes as something of a surprise to hear Somaly's voice saying *Hello?* (But as if he was the one giving a surprise.)

o

o o

He raises his eyes from the sheet, hears the croaking of the frogs in the darkness outside. Two words, one following the other, have disturbed his concentration.

But the window has closed down again and he cannot remember which two words opened the door back to the year before last, to the house they no longer live in.

That is where his mind is now, at his old desk in his old study (one leg crossed over the other, elbows resting on the tabletop). The cool of the dry season through the open windows. He remembers the rooms clearly. Remembers how they are laid out, how the furniture was arranged in them.

What else does he remember? The way she moves through his study. Not much more than that actually. The way she finds a job to do in there when she *sees that he is watching her*. The way the whole course of events, in all its easy simplicity, is rather unexpected. What then follows, however, the actual *embrace* on the sofa, has (as always) become rather abstract.

(Somewhere at some point he has read: *physical pain and sexual pleasure are the two emotions that the human mind is incapable of recreating*.)

All that is left of that meaningless affair with the insipid governess / nanny / trollop is spiritual suffering, not physical. He prefers not to think about what happened afterwards. But now (because of some vague association in the text of the report) he finds himself once again sitting opposite Em at the dining table. (Her head bowed, face red with weeping. Her meal (fish soup) untouched in front of her.) Her eyes meet his all of a sudden and he can read that there is something irreparable in there. He can read what lies splintered beyond the tears and the rage.

He takes off his glasses and tells her to hit him. (In his heart he now shudders at that *pathetic* pose.) She does nothing, does not answer, just stares blankly and unseeing.

The quarrel about that idiotic episode on the sofa had been preceded over the years by other scenes of similar origin. Violent storms, all following the same dramaturgy (*quarrel-tears-promises-reconciliation-etcetera*). (It soon became familiar and, as a paradoxical consequence, provided a sense of security.) But it quickly became clear that this time was different. (He can't understand why. His best theory, though he has no evidence for it, is that it's because *this little slip* took place under their own roof.)

And an ice-cold recognition of the irrevocable nature of the change had seeped down through the layers of their emotions.

(A quick flash of indignation at the *injustice* of this. The change of fortune is not in any kind of proportion to what he felt for the girl; others (earlier / later) had been much more significant than that one.)

He had left the table, his dinner untouched, and not come back for several days.

He has two ways of returning after scenes like this. (I) To stride across the threshold combatively, his mouth full of what hadn't been said (or what bore repeating). (II) To open the door furtively, with overflowing bags rustling with sweets / silk scarves / perfumes.

But since everything was different this time, he had arrived home as if it were any other day. And Em greeted him as if it were any other day.

Nothing was said about what had led to his absence.

(Since then, he thinks, the glass through which she views him has been *crazed with fine cracks*. A slight distance that she makes impossible for him to bridge. And this business of the absence of any reconciliation. He cannot understand that: *your enemies* are the ones you don't reconcile with, aren't they?)

There are other lasting differences.

(*For example*) Em's anger when she hears news of something inappropriate, or *believes* she does, is wilder and more explosive these days. (As if the merest spark of suspicion is fanned into flame by the memory of that governess.)

(*For example*) He, for his part, has become more careless. (However hard he may try, what has been done cannot be undone.) Which is why he finds himself playing with the idea of suggesting to Em that they *employ* Somaly as the children's new governess (she could move into the room beyond his study—it is still unused).

Em must understand. Who else could? She is the most brilliant woman he has met. Her unique intelligence must understand his feelings. (He is a man, for God's sake, and still in the prime of his manhood.)

He remembers the French fable of the frog and the scorpion. He told it to Em once. (It was before they had children.) She had wondered why and he answered that *he found it hilarious*.

Hilarious? It is difficult to understand now what he meant by that. *That is my nature.*

He puts the bundle of papers down on his desk (and knocks over the untouched glass of tea as he reaches for the packet of cigarettes. He sweeps the spilt tea onto the floor with the palm of his hand).

Someone close to the prince ought to tell him that fable. (Someone who'll be allowed to collect his tongue from the cloakroom attendant afterwards.)

He returns to Em and in his mind he says to her: *Doing no wrong is not the same thing as doing right.*

And with his eyes already scanning the text to find the last sentence he read or the first one that is unread, he repeats (a thought he often thinks): *You have to be true to the circumstances you have been given. You must not allow considerations demanded by those around you to completely destroy your potential.*

He begins reading again. ("We consider it possible that diplomatic relations between Vietnam and Cambodia will finally be established once the governments in question have succeeded in regularizing the issues that remain unclear following the dissolution of the former *Cochinchina* and so on and so on.")

SATURDAY, 10 SEPTEMBER 1955

Her face emerges pencil stroke by pencil stroke on the white of the margin. He leans closer, moves the pencil with more precision. The

precise but intuitive movements of his hand emanate from a different part of him. A part which he realizes (now) has lain unused over
recent hectic months.

(The feeling is reminiscent of those occasions when, for no reason
at all, a barefoot walk along the shore turns into a short sprint. The
way the muscles do what is required without resisting, the naturalness
of the movements. A kind of sophisticated *capacity* just waiting for
its time to come.)

He hesitates about the distance between the curve of her jaw and
the contours of her lips. He tries to compare it with the nebulous
pictures in his memory.

Is it like her? In a certain sense it is, anyway.

He exchanges the pencil for the cigarette that has half burnt away
in the ashtray. Studies Somaly's features on the paper. And recalls
that it has been a long time since he spontaneously drew a *specific
person*. (These days it's nothing but vague and abstract doodles on the
telephone pad.) To be more accurate, a *specific woman*. And sudden
inspiration like this usually means that his feelings for the woman
run deeper than he has realized (or wants to acknowledge). Take
yesterday's sudden notion to ring her: when was the last time anything
like that happened?

In his mind he runs through their dinner at Le Royal the previous
Thursday evening and he becomes aware that his thoughts do not run
quite as casually as they usually do. (Another indication that there is
more than just lust involved in this case.) And his thoughts become
entwined with her account of her solitary morning in Kep-sur-Mer,
and his mind stumbles and trips over the smile that accompanied
the account.

(*The recurring question*:) What is it that she has that the others don't?
Apart from her indisputable beauty, youth and straightforward
manner? He doesn't understand it. The feeling is as elusive as his

inner image of her. (As if his thoughts can only observe her out of the corner of his eye.)

The pencil draws a straight vertical line, dividing her face in two. Then a horizontal one. Then a diagonal from top left to bottom right, crossing the other two. And then another diagonal from right to left. He continues doing this until all that is left is *a star of criss-cross lines.*

He exchanges the pencil for another cigarette. Flips open the top of his lighter and tries once more to concentrate on the words in the report.

o

o   o

He closes his eyes, just for a moment. Opens them. Closes them again. Opens them. Stands up. Walks across the creaking boards of the platform, taps the microphone lightly. Hears his tap echo out over all the faces that are turned his way.

The sky is blue, the sun scorching. It is the last day. He looks at those who are standing right at the front, then those in the row behind them, and he notes how row by row the individuals gradually become a crowd.

In a loud clear voice he says: My dear fellow-countrymen!

He says: Kinsmen of our revered forefathers who built Angkor!

He says, with a smile: Dear people of Prey Veng.

Then, with an earnest, almost troubled, expression, he continues. For once the loudspeakers are absolutely excellent.

o

o   o

Hello?

Is that Non?

Yes.

It's me.

I can hear that.

Are you alone?

Give me a moment.

OK.

(a pause)

Now then.

Good. It's time for us to strike a match! You know what I mean?

There you are. So it's got to that stage.

Yes. Get your brother to see to it that we don't have an audience.

Understood. When?

After dark, but before midnight. Do it properly.

As always.

As always.

Is that everything?

Yes. Thank you. (Rings off)

o

o   o

Her hand slides over the sleeve of his jacket. Fingertips on the cool smooth fabric. The darkness inside the car lightens and darkens in phase with the street lamps.

Figures are glimpsed in the dark of the streets.

On the pavement: fruits stalls, cigarette stalls, restaurant stalls (lit by the white light of strip lights).

The bright red of the occasional neon sign.

No sounds reach them from outside. In here there is nothing but the hum of the engine and the broad silent back of the driver. In her other hand she is still holding a slim glass of lukewarm champagne.

They are in the middle of a low-voiced conversation. (Flushed red faces, Sary's hand on her thigh.)

Behind them lies a reception on the lawn of the Bulgarian Embassy. (The anniversary of the country changing sides in the war.) She joined them when he had finished his most urgent duties (primarily castigating the bloody diplomats who had *expressed their concern* about the arrest of Keng Vannsak). She had stood by the illuminated pool, watching the turquoise reflections flickering on the guests closest to the edge. On their light suits, on their shimmering silk dresses.

And then he was at her side, taking her gently by her bare elbow. Leading her to a set of chairs, away from the crowd, under a flowering flame tree. (Out of most people's field of view, isolated, but not improperly so.) There were small coloured paper lanterns in the branches, hanging motionless in the windless night.

And now. The Hôtel de la Gare is their destination. (The car is following the filled-in canal towards the railway station at its far end.) They will soon be in the foyer, their heels tapping out different rhythms on the mosaic floor. The desk clerk will give them room number 17 without asking them to sign the register, and he won't show them to their room. Instead they will climb the creaking wooden staircase unaccompanied. First her, then him.

He won't give a thought to Em, not one. (Nor to Somaly.)

Nana:

Isn't it strange about insects at night?

Sary:

(his face in light or darkness depending on the street lamps)

Nana:

Swarming around the lights until they burn their wings.

Sary:

It's not strange. All animals are attracted by light.

Nana:

How do you mean?

Sary:

If you were shut in a dark cave or left out in the forest in the middle of the night and saw a light, you would go towards it, wouldn't you? Wouldn't you?

Nana:

Yes, I would, but I wouldn't burn myself on it.

Sary:

Same with fish in the sea. Which is why modern fishing boats use lamps at night. I was shown them when I was in Kampot, whenever it was. The lights attract all the creatures up from the depths.

Nana:

But when I'm in the forest, I walk towards the light in order to get out of the forest. Surely the fish don't want to leave the sea, do they?

Sary:

There are actually fish in the very deepest parts of the sea, down where it is pitch-black; they hunt with a little light they carry on an antenna.

Nana (giggles):

You're just making that up, darling.

Sary:

Near-death experiences are supposed to be like that. Like a light that attracts you. You walk into it et puis—c'est fini.

Nana (giggles):

Your antenna acts as an attraction, too, even though it doesn't have a light on it.

Sary:

That's something different. What you're talking about now is what's called a near little-death experience. And you can count on that once we get there.

O

O O

(*Intermezzo I*) The brakes go on gently, someone opens the door for him, he steps out into the bright starry insect-filled night, walks across the concrete drive and the front door swings open.

He still has that slight feeling of nausea that comes from being dragged from sleep, his muscles responding with a noticeable delay. But the inebriation has gone, his thoughts have a metallic clarity. He feels himself reconnecting with the day that preceded the night, *reclaiming himself.* (The urgent knocks and the confused conversation through the door at the Hôtel de la Gare fades back into the dreams they interrupted.)

He is taken to the lower reception room. The prince is standing at the telephone table, receiver to his ear. Swathes of heavy curtains hang in front of the windows. The prince's shrill laugh.

Dara, the court astrologer, is standing by the sofa, folding up the big leather volume with its yellowed and well-thumbed pages filled with tables. As always, the old man is wearing court dress (Sary finds it impossible to imagine him in everyday clothes), has three medals on the breast of his uniform and the Grand Cross around his neck. The lower part of his face is marked by a black burn, partially concealed by a small neat white beard.

They give one another a quick bow and it occurs to him that Dara's broad and bowed posture reminds him more and more of an *orang-utan.* (The astrologer backs out of the room with lowered eyes while the prince continues his conversation.)

The receiver is slammed down on its cradle, the prince spins on his heel. His face all smiles.

The prince is not wearing a jacket and his shirt sleeves are rolled up. He follows his example and takes a seat on the sofa. An adjutant emerges from the darkness and pours him a glass of wine.

Sihanouk:

Another nocturnal consultation. Your wife must be getting really sick of me.

Sary:

Of course she isn't, Monseigneur. In any case, I haven't managed to get home a single night this week. When we are finished here perhaps.

Sihanouk:

I imagine you must be wondering why I sent for you, aren't you? Would you like something to eat, by the way?

Sary:

No thanks, I'm not hungry.

Sihanouk:

Those tablets don't just keep you awake, they do wonders for your waistline, don't they.

Sary:

That's what they are marketed for in France, as you know.

Sihanouk:

How did it go with the Bulgarians?

Sary:

A bit of huffing about Vannsak, but nothing serious. How did the speech go?

Sihanouk:

Excellent, excellent. Crowds of people. A good day. Now then, I'll get straight to the point. I'm intending to present the new government on Tuesday, the fourth of next month. You will be named as minister of education, national planning and overseas economic relations. You will remain vice chairman of the Council of Ministers. I also think that before the end of the year you should take over as general secretary of our dear Popular Socialist Community. How do you feel about that?

Sary:

It's a great honour. A very great honour. A spur! And I can assure you that I shan't disappoint you.

Sihanouk:

No—if you did I'd have you shot.

(they both laugh)

Sary:

One thing though.

Sihanouk:

What's that?

Sary:

Give me finance as well. If national planning is to get anywhere, I need to have finance.

Sihanouk:

Not possible. It would be too much— even for you, dear friend.

Sary:

Who do you have in mind?

Sihanouk:
Not sure yet. Sim Var perhaps?

Sary:
No, that would never work. Make him the speaker instead. Which would also have the advantage of looking generous—more démocratique with an ex-Democrat.

Sihanouk:
(says nothing)

Sary:
Mau Say can be my deputy. We work well together. Unless we have overall control, we shan't be able to get things done with the necessary speed.

Sihanouk:
I'll think about it.

Sary:
Our aims are the same. Give me the means I need to achieve them.

Sihanouk:
I'll think about it.

Sary:
I shall look forward to your decision. Your new decision. What omens did Dara come up with, by the way?

Sihanouk:
Dara? He's no more reliable than a weather forecaster. And another thing— I've been told that fire has broken out.

Sary:
That's correct.

FORMER KING ASSAILS FOES ON CHARGE
HE SOLD OUT TO U.S. IN MILITARY PACT

—

PHNOMPENH, Cambodia, Sept 10 (Reuters)

Former King Norodom Sihanouk charged tonight that his opponents were using "dirty, slanderous methods" in accusing him of having sold Cambodia to the United States in a military pact.

Norodom heatedly told a crowd of 6,000 persons, gathered outside the gilt-roofed royal palace here: "The great Western powers, including Britain, have accepted American aid and have granted military bases in their territories in exchange. Only Cambodia and Yugoslavia have accepted American aid without granting any bases to the United States."

Norodom, who abdicated last March in favor of his father and then founded the Popular Socialist Community party, accused the Democratic Party of having lied to the peasants.

Polling takes place tomorrow to elect a ninety-one-member National Assembly. Some observers predict a victory for Norodom's party, but others favor the Democrats who have pledged to abolish the monarchy and set up a republic.

The Communist-led People's Party is appearing openly for the first time with thirty-five candidates. They have been backed by broadcasts from the Communist North Vietnam radio in Hanoi.

Norodom wants to reform the country's constitution because he fears it might eventually give power to corrupt politicians.

Meanwhile, French officers serving as instructors to the Khmer Royal Army will be kept indoors during tomorrow's polling. Many political observers feared armed clashes between supporters of the rival parties.

Some clashes, resulting in three deaths and six persons injured, have been reported this week in the provinces.

SUNDAY, 11 SEPTEMBER 1955

(*Intermezzo II*) During the few short hours of cool before the heat of the day, Sary is standing on the balcony. (Barefoot, suit trousers, shirt unbuttoned.)

He is listening to the barely audible pattering made by the big leaves of the umbrella tree dropping onto the concrete drive. Watching the fluttering flight of the white butterflies mirrored and doubled in the dark puddles.

A glass of lukewarm tea in one hand, the first cigarette of the day in the other. The *unusual* feeling he gets from being at home (it happens after spending too many nights in a row in unfamiliar beds with more or less unfamiliar bedfellows. As if returning from a journey with a sense of having changed a little, whereas time has stood still in these rooms).

Em is asleep in the house behind him. Beyond her the children are sleeping too.

The patter of a moped coming and going outside the gates.

And Sarun emerging from his gatekeeper's lodge with a short brush. Bending forward but with his legs straight under his sarong, he starts slowly sweeping up the dead leaves.

(His sons' pedal car in a corner by the wall, abandoned in the middle of a lap.)

The last day. Yesterday evening remains in his body as a moment of calm. But it hasn't eased the mental tension. Once again his thoughts seem to him *metallic*, but this time they are like the overheating components of a piece of thundering machinery that could be approaching breaking point.

He looks up at the sky, stretched taut like a sheet and far, endlessly far, above the crowns of the palm trees. He looks down at the little pond with its carp and its guppies. (Because of the rains it has been overflowing onto the lawn for weeks.) He looks over towards the frangipani tree with its big white and yellow flowers on branches that are otherwise bare.

He empties the glass, flicks the glowing cigarette end over the rail. And carries on.

o

o   o

Sary and Em walk towards one of the wings of the school. (Single storey, ochre rendering.) People seem to be hanging around (scattered in the shade of the trees). Those standing along the wall of the building take it in turns to peep in between the slats of the shutters. Alone, in couples, in groups. United by low-key curiosity; the event itself exerts an attraction. A provisional sense of expectancy (since the election results are not going to be published for several days).

Sary and Em walk towards the building. They pass beneath a bright blue banner with freshly printed white letters (ELECTORAL DISTRICT SVAY POPEY IV). A balloon seller on a bicycle is hawking his wares beneath a cloud of balloons.

The sun is already high in the sky, scorching and dazzling.

Faces turn towards them as they approach. Like the prince, he tries to exude *friendly authority*. The people nearest drop their eyes humbly and lower their heads.

There is a short queue at the entrance. Quiet, serious, identity papers at the ready. The queue is being supervised by an election officer (an official armband tied tightly around his right sleeve). The official sees them coming and loudly orders the queuing people *to make way there*. (The order makes a young man wearing a hat (but no tie) get to his feet. He has a camera hanging around his neck (Rolleicord), in his hatband there is a home-made press card, presumably inspired by hacks he has seen on the silver screen.)

The official disappears quickly through the dark doorway and returns with his double, who introduces himself as the local chairman of the electoral commission.

(Sary asks if the two of them are brothers, which they are happy to confirm.)

The chairman anticipates his next question and reports the number of votes that have been cast. Then hastens to assure him that *everything is proceeding excellently*. (The chairman's tone of voice is overfamiliar, as if they had something in common. He detests that.)

At the photographer's request he stands beside the entrance. Em on one side, her arm through his, the chairman on the other. The young man makes a long-winded and nervous job of taking three shots.

The Picture: all harsh contrasts; black and tired white. The wall of a building— bright, with a dark oblong opening to the left. In the middle of the picture: him and her (turning slightly towards each other). Smiling, eyes hidden in shadow. She is wearing elbow-length gloves, sunglasses instead of a hairband. Her skirt comes down to her ankles, as is traditional. He in a dark suit, as usual. White (?) handkerchief in his breast pocket. Beside them a young middle-aged man in a shirt is standing erect, smiling broadly with uneven teeth. Impossible to see his eyes too.

They go in. (The queue forms again behind them.)

Still dazzled, he feels as if the classroom has remained in twilight. (All the officials have risen to their feet and are only visible as bowing silhouettes.)

He asks the chairman where people's identities are being checked. The man laughs (heartily) and says, *of course* there's no need for that in his case. Yes, there is, he says abruptly (unconcerned that the man's subordinates will hear him being corrected). *We are no different from everyone else.*

They are directed to an elderly lady who nervously takes their identity cards, which are embossed with the arms of the government. Looks them up and down and quickly, hands them back without comparing them with the electoral list.

They move on to the next table and each of them takes a white voting paper with a portrait of the prince (Sary thinks that the monarch looks a touch too plump in the picture—a point that will doubtless be taken up later). They hand them to the chairman who has stationed himself by the ballot box. The two slips are ceremoniously dropped through the slit in the top of the metal box. The inkwell is pushed in front of him. He dips the top of his right index finger into it, blows gently on the finger.

(A glow (a vague mixture of pride and affection) spreads through him when he sees Em sticking her finger into the little bottle. This simple action, apparently unassuming, is the final confirmation of her long and indefatigable work.)

They find themselves standing there, each of them with a blue forefinger pointing at the ceiling. He sees that she can see the funny side of the situation, her eyes are twinkling with suppressed laughter.

But instead of giggling she suggests they stay a while and see how their new constitutional system is working in practice. He says why not (despite the fact that the chairman cannot hide his satisfaction).

The whole queue has squeezed into the doorway. (Everyone wants to see what they are doing.) The chairman's brother bellows at the onlookers/voters to get back in line. A thin elderly man with sticking-out ears ends up at the front. The woman with the electoral roll reads out his identity papers: a *tailor* (with a Vietnamese surname). Slowly and ceremoniously, as if to savour her moment of significance, she puts a tick in one column, draws a line (with the help of a ruler) through the tailor's name in another column. The man (following her instructions) then moves uncertainly on to the table with the voting papers.

The prince's white paper lies all alone in the middle of the table. (The other voting papers, all in different colours, are on a shelf behind the table.) The official stationed at the table offers the man a white paper, which he immediately accepts.

Right choice, the chairman announces loudly (winking at Em and Sary). The tailor's eyes shift evasively and a rather bashful smile forms on his face.

Sary himself takes the voting paper, which the man is holding out with trembling hands. Posts it into the silence of the ballot box. The man thanks him repeatedly while Em holds out the inkwell. (Cautiously, as if the ink is going to bite him, the tailor dips his fingertip.) Then he backs towards the door, bowing.

Next in line is a wholesaler in dry goods. Then a shop assistant. Then a teacher.

That will have to be enough. The chairman bemoans the fact that they have to leave so soon, but looks relieved all the same (as if it has all become a bit too much of a good thing).

The queue moves aside as they walk towards the exit.

They are out in the glare of the sun again. The dust in front of the step is white. The rumour of their presence has attracted even more people to the school. He raises his hand, forms a V for victory with his blue forefinger and his middle finger. His gesture is greeted with scattered cheers and applause.

They walk on through the shimmering heat haze. (He sees the driver coming to head them off on the way to the car.)

Then attention shifts. Heads turn to watch jerky movements under one of the trees. Irate voices, a raised baton and an angry scream when it comes down. He sees uniforms and something, someone *staggering* in the middle. Onlookers approach the scene cautiously.

He asks a woman going in the opposite direction. She answers bluntly that some poor so-and-so had been urging people to vote for the People's Party.

He tells Em to wait by the car. Strides briskly through the gathering crowd. He thinks this is an opportunity not to be missed. The opposition must not be given another martyr. In front of all those present, this will give him an opportunity to demonstrate *how fair* the government is. A chance to show that, in spite of everything that has been said and written, brutality and a lack of accountability are not things that have been ordered or will even be tolerated.

(He doesn't have to elbow his way forward. He just has to place his fingers lightly on the shoulder of a sun-warmed shirt or on a bare arm and they move aside as if burnt.)

But at the very moment he reaches the scene of the trouble, the man in the middle tears himself free. He is in time to see torn clothes and dark patches of sweat (or blood). Two soldiers give chase but the man is barefoot and they are running in heavy boots.

The three figures disappear in among the buildings beyond the school grounds, but the tension is still present like a concentrated force-field. He can feel the pulse in his neck throbbing. But there is still something that can be saved from this scene. *Who is in command here?* he asks sternly. A young sergeant answers (with the assertive pondus uniforms give young men).

He tells him who he is. He says that he demands an account of what is going on here.

Then he sees the soldiers returning without the man they were pursuing. He sees how the self-confidence in their stride deserts them when they catch sight of their sergeant cowering in the dust in front of him.

III. SOMALY

there is a short time when girls can do what they want.

therefore with a snap of their fingers they open the world, pull maps up from the ground, then go down on their knees and make plans. girls whose lungs are seething.

KARIN WIKLUND
What is love

MONDAY, 12 SEPTEMBER 1955

Strawberries from Saigon, oranges from Battambang. White orchids with pink tongues. She strokes the cellophane with her hand. The card is in French, in gold print: *Mon amourette*. No clue is given.

TUESDAY, 13 SEPTEMBER 1955

The soft dry noise of rubber tyres on tarmac.

The creaking of the cyclo's joints and springs.

The odour of sweat from the driver and his unwashed clothes, which settles around her every time he stops pedalling at traffic lights.

Where is she going? Nowhere in particular. She has him take her along the Avenue de Verdun. She has him take her along rue Sothéavong and Quai Sisowath. The river to her right, the other bank in the distance. The gilded spires of the royal palace to her left. People on the move everywhere, at the street stalls, on bicycles, in cars. Buses full, cyclos laden with groceries and with bundles of clothes the tailors have just finished. The only remaining signs of the election are the numerous posters bearing the prince's face.

The billboards outside the newspaper kiosks all have the same word: *VICTORY*.

She looks at the people she passes. The way some of them stare, others sneak a look. People who don't know her undoubtedly notice the slim cut of her dress in shades of grey and dark violet. The little French hat. The almond-shaped foreign sunglasses.

Then she tells the cyclo driver to turn left towards rue Pasteur. It's a whim. But then the whole of this excursion is a whim. She just wants to be on the move. Recent weeks have been spent at home predominantly. In that state of listless monotony that results from the rising and the setting of the sun, the coming and the passing of the rains. The reasons are many. In the first place it's all about avoiding meeting *une personne en particulier*. Or their mutual acquaintances. Vannsak, for instance. But she reckons that danger to be negligible today, particularly in the case of Vannsak who, from what she has heard, is under lock and key in Prey Sar prison. Apart from which the sky is cloudy and with the hood up, there is no risk of her skin being tanned by the sun.

She is now travelling through the leafy vault woven by the avenue of tall trees along rue Aimé Grand. The traffic here is less busy. The prince made his last election speech just a stone's throw away last Saturday. She went to it, briefly, driven by the hope of catching a glimpse of Sary. She had remained seated in the cyclo, her face half concealed by a scarf. Unlike today's light-hearted trip there was an unpleasant undercurrent of feverish expectation last Saturday. What was in store for them? A change of power? Riots? She had followed her mother's advice about being careful.

The prince had stood on the platform, which was draped with the colours of the flag. A white suit, black tie, soldiers in full battle kit down below. The audience must have numbered thousands, they filled the streets and the open parkland between the walls of the palace and the river. The cheering and clapping were deafening and, as far as she could judge, genuine. The prince was a good speaker, absolutely relaxed at the microphone. But it had been a long speech; she had heard him on her way there while still some distance off and he was still going at full strength when she left to go home. The whole thing had become rather disjointed, as a result of his spontaneous digressions.

She thought his visions of the future had been spoilt by the personal bitterness with which he settled accounts with the opposition. And Sary had not even been there.

The cyclo driver asks her for an address. She tells him where she wants to go and, allowing the cyclo to freewheel along, he tells her it's impossible because that whole district is sealed off.

And, he adds, the police might be everywhere today but they certainly kept out of sight last Saturday night. She can't decide if he is being sarcastic and twists round to look at him but the hood is in the way.

He lets the cyclo roll slowly to the side by the pavement, where it comes to a halt, waiting for further instructions.

You think the fire was started on purpose? she says, speaking into the curve of the hood. She does not get an answer. Perhaps he didn't hear. Or is his silence sufficient of an answer? Or is he pretending not to hear?

They remain where they are while several cyclos and one or two cars drive past them. She tries to remember what her cyclo driver looks like. Whether he is young or old.

Where should she go now? The shops and markets are unbearably overcrowded with people shopping before the holidays. And she doesn't want to go home.

She asks the cyclo driver whether he has seen the election result. He stays silent.

She asks him whether he likes the result.

No answer.

She raises her voice in an annoyed hello there (*what is the matter with him?*).

He says brusquely that he has never been to school and consequently doesn't know anything about these things.

Did you vote? she says, returning to her earlier friendly tone of voice.

He says that he did but it's no longer of any importance, and he wonders where they are going next.

She hesitates for a moment, then says Place de la Poste. Perhaps Mari, Nana or one of the others will turn up at the open-air café. But they have probably already left the city in advance of tomorrow's holiday. Sar will probably be on his way to his family in Kompong Thom. And Sary, she thinks, has probably also left for… where is it his wife comes from… Kandal? Somaly has contradictory feelings about the countryside. She considers it a blessing that both her father and her mother are natives of the capital city. To pack every suitcase in the house in order to undertake an uncomfortable and sweaty journey to the back of beyond strikes her as a punishment she has done nothing to deserve.

In spite of which she sometimes finds herself wondering whether she is missing a special relationship with something *authentic*. Several of her friends, actually the most travelled and worldly members of her circle (we might even say *cosmopolitan*), seem to feel a special sense of certainty when getting ready to visit their ancestral homes for national feast days. Links that initially seem painfully provincial but which clearly mean something to them. She doesn't understand this. When they come back afterwards they go on about the tedium and narrow-mindedness they encountered while away, about the dark-skinned peasants. But reading between the lines she senses there are other warmer feelings.

They are now trundling along rue Ohier, passing the untidy muddle of people, carts and trucks that is Kandal Market. Then on over what used to be the bridge linking the European quarter of the city with the Chinese quarter.

The cyclo driver is shouted at by a group of his colleagues parked on a street corner. He pedals even more slowly (*if that's possible*) in order to answer them. That gives her time to look at the canal that is no longer there. As new young lovers her parents used to meet here and walk along the bank. Watching the fishermen landing their catches. She can picture the gleaming sheatfish, carp, elephant fish, the men shouting. The different bridges. But then the French filled in the watercourse as part of their campaign against malaria and blood fever. It's grassed over now and there are some badly tended flower beds. The only things left from those days are the parapets of the bridges.

It is certainly better like this, she thinks. Healthier. But she still feels a vague sense of sorrow for an era she did not experience. As if her handsome, happy young parents had disappeared at the same time as the canal. And perhaps she herself would have been more at home in an earlier age? An age that was easier to understand than the complex age she inhabits.

Rather like the narrator played by Anton Walbrook in the film she saw recently: *We are in the past. I adore the past. It's so much more restful than the present. So much more reliable than the future.*

The film was beautiful. And Walbrook was attractive even though he must be almost three times her age. The people in the story were acting in their own small dramas, in which love arose in unexpected contexts. At the same time, though, she did not like the recurring image of love as a carousel with an autonomous mechanism that spins its riders in the same circles.

That is not how she sees herself.

They are now moving in among European buildings and she thinks that even though the time may be right the place is wrong. She needs to move to a metropolis. To her brother in Saigon first, perhaps. Then to Paris which—she imagines—is buzzing with the kind of sophisticated and interesting people who are very rarely born here or, for that matter, move here. (*People like me.*) Invitations to work abroad as a model would be coming soon enough. Miss World, Miss Riviera and Miss Elegance had been invited to her own pageant. She didn't have an opportunity to talk to them properly, but she understood that the occasion was just one of many similar ones they had taken part in.

Paris. She already knows the city from what Sar and Sary have told her, but even more because of the films she has seen. Endless. Enormous buildings. Trams. *Or perhaps they don't exist any longer?* People with big noses but oh, so enviably pale! People who always seem to be wearing too many clothes.

She tells the cyclo driver to stop outside the Café de la Poste. This gives her the chance to look at him. His face is immediately familiar to her, although she also knows that in ten minutes' time she will be quite unable to give a description of him. Neither young nor old. Something very everyday and vague about his features. The colour of his skin points to him being a farm labourer who has moved into the city. He accepts the coins without the kind of obsequiousness men usually show her. Was she wrong about the reasons for his lazy pedalling? She says goodbye and walks in among the tables. For one moment she thinks of turning round to see if he is looking at her. But she resists the urge and immediately dismisses him from her mind.

She looks around the few customers present but none of her friends is there.

The usual waiter is standing at her usual table. He takes her usual order but, as usual, pretends not to recognize her. On one hand, it makes a welcome change from most people's strutting and preening; on the other hand, she finds him *ridicule*.

He returns immediately carrying a *diabolo menthe*. She sucks up the icy chill, the bubbles and the mint through the straw, her eyes fixed on the post office over the road.

She thinks: think of all the times I have hurried impatiently up those steps.

Then she thinks: think of all the times I have come down those steps feeling happy.

And: all the times I have come down those steps feeling unhappy.

Sar had written to her often during the years he was in Paris, but not as often as she had visited the post office. He did not want to send his letters to her home address. To avoid gossip, he had explained. And she had let herself be convinced. As so often by him. She had accepted the arrangement even though it had struck her as unnecessary, incomprehensible and cumbersome. What sort of gossip? They were engaged, weren't they? Perhaps it was a way of exercising control over her from the other side of the globe? Forcing her to perform the frequently meaningless ritual of going to the post office for better or for worse?

What else does she remember from those years of love by letter? She had missed him dreadfully at first. She kept and cared for photographs and small souvenirs (shells, entrance tickets, picture postcards) from trips they had made together. And she had read his first letters (postmarked in Singapore, Colombo, Djibouti, Port Said, Marseille, Paris) so many times that she knew them by heart. For months after his departure she was still living in the single year they had had together up until then. Childish, she thinks now. But she had only been sixteen when they met, and he was twenty-four. He seemed so grown up, so *urbane*. Now she is almost as old as he had been then.

She thinks of an early excursion they made to the waterfalls at Kirirom together with some friends of her big brother. Sar was friendly with them too. There was that paradoxical feeling of strength and delicacy about him, like poetry she thinks now. How she had immediately felt she wanted to spend endless amounts of time in his kind, attentive company.

She had not waited for him to take the initiative. Patience of that sort is not in her nature. Then, as now, behind that charming and easy-going exterior he was very cautious. He never seems to do anything in too much of a hurry, he waits until it is *possible to survey* all the consequences. She can't imagine how long it would have taken him to make an approach. So instead she had asked him whether he would like to come to Kep-sur-Mer with her and her friends the following weekend.

He had said yes—after a moment's hesitation, if she remembers rightly. She wonders now what he had seen in her, in that self-confident precocious schoolgirl who had invited him so bluntly. On that occasion she had obviously forgotten any sense of what was proper, filled as she was with the feelings of closeness and intimacy she sensed had arisen *instantly* between them.

There had been no shortage of suitors before Sar. But they had courted her in one of two ways: either by being ingratiating, bowing and scraping; or by acting superior, as if generously offering to raise her to their level.

Sar on the other hand had talked to her as if she was just like him.

A little while after his departure, however, their past began to lose colour and as the months turned into years, he became a sort of abstract love. She had then begun to focus her desires on the future and on his return. But there were times when she felt destroyed by the seemingly never-ending present that consisted only of countless days without him.

But, she thinks, even while she clung on loyally to the thought of his return and the many forms of welcome she was planning for him, she was unconsciously settling into a different kind of existence. An existence that was undoubtedly dependent on Sar, since he was the one she always pointed to when her family (maternal grandfather, mother's two paternal aunts, all her many uncles, her many uncles' wives, the majority of her cousins) demanded that she should marry or at least accept a male guardian. But Sar was on the other side of the globe and that meant she was her own master. And it also meant that his absence, which she viewed at the time as an unbearably long ordeal, gave her a respite in which to contemplate the role that tradition had allotted her in the life she was expected to lead. It allowed her to come to a number of conclusions that even someone as *broad-minded* as Sar found difficult to accept.

It can be put even more bluntly: his absence was the precondition for her to become the person she became.

The person she is now.

And with time she got used to the loneliness, although she described it to others and to herself as a burden she had to bear. But that, too, eventually became a lie, though it was one she continued to believe in.

And she thinks, in what she thinks of as a moment of clarity, that *she misses the Sar that she missed when he was away*, not the one who stubbornly insists on being everywhere now that he has returned.

She is still very fond of his company, but their meetings leave her with a feeling that there is a gap, and it's a gap that's growing. She doesn't know how to deal with this expanding empty space.

She looks out over the square and suddenly remembers a visit she made to the cinema with two of her mother's younger friends when she was a fifteen-year-old. The friends had been visiting from France and she both envied and was fascinated by their self-confidence and elegant cynicism. She has forgotten the name of the film but she can remember that it was about two people in love whose relationship became more and more destructive. By the end of the film they hated each other as much as they had loved one another at the start. In spite of this they could not bring themselves to go their separate ways. After the film her mother's friends were ecstatic as they walked through the insect symphony in the clear starry night. Suddenly they turned to her and asked what she had thought of the film. It was so unexpected. That she had been allowed to go with them, that they had even asked her opinion, gave her the courage to be open-hearted. She answered that she had found the couple's relationship improbable. Why had the two of them come to hate one another? And why had they continued to let themselves suffer in the relationship when they were neither married nor engaged? Her mother's friends had exchanged glances and one of them asked whether she had ever experienced *passion*. She answered, a little uncertainly now, that she didn't know whether she had or not. They had laughed at her and said that if she didn't know she certainly had not. One of them had then added that you will understand one day, *my little one*.

She still does not understand that stupid film. But she is in no doubt that her mother's friends were right. She recognizes that her relationship with Sar is not like that, however carried away she has been at times.

And what about Sary? She thinks it unlikely that her relationship with him constitutes a passion in the sense of the film, though it is perhaps too soon to know for sure. But she is fascinated by his remarkable ability to attract. She has met many powerful men who have been used to *power in itself* being attractive to young women.

It has never had any effect on her. Indeed, it has usually had the opposite effect.

But in Sary's case power does not precede attraction, nor is it its precondition, so to speak: it is sort of secondary and sort of *entwined* with something else. And what is that something else? She knows it is not his appearance, nor the way he behaves, nor any great fortune, because none of those things are particularly remarkable. It is something else, something she did not even notice when she decided at the beauty pageant to accept his invitation and join him at his table. But since then she has been drawn into his *magic circle*, which she is absolutely sure she can leave whenever she wants, but she doesn't want to leave it since it both interests and entertains her.

She feels that it's rather like taking part in some sport or game at which she is proving to be very good even though she has never played it before.

Then she sees Chinnary standing with her bicycle outside La Tavèrne, feet down by the pedals as if she has been forced to stop unexpectedly. Standing there, sort of rigid, sort of at a loss. She assumes that Chinnary has come straight from teaching. She is wearing her dark-blue teacher's skirt and her white blouse, her bicycle basket full of books.

She lifts her hand, gives a little wave with her gloves. Her friend sees the movement and seems rather relieved.

Chinnary orders a Vichy Célestins, takes a seat and fans her round perspiring face with today's paper, which flickers back and forth between *VICTORY* and *Gitanes for the Real Connoisseur*.

And says (her voice has its usual sharp ironic tinge): Well, who would have thought it would be so *clear-cut*?

Somaly's initial impulse is to give in to the pressure caused by weeks of uncertain waiting (an uncertainty that has now been reduced to neat voting statistics and transformed into harmless percentages) to discuss the result of the election and the reasons for it for hours. Not in order to understand, because she certainly does understand, but in order to put into words something that is nagging at her because it is wordless.

But the *predictability* of a conversation of that sort only induces a feeling of jaded weariness. And she realizes that she wants to be alone with her disappointment. Disappointment about what? Not necessarily (or not at all) because the Democrats lost. Nor because of what Chinnary is actually saying, which is that what happened was inevitable but it's a pity it was done with such a complete lack of finesse. No, the feeling of loss has more to do with the end of an expectation—an expectation which, in itself, had been quite sufficient for her.

Perhaps, she thinks, it hadn't so much been a different world she wanted from the change, what she had been longing for was a change in herself.

Then, of course, there is Chinnary, who still thinks of Sar and Somaly as a unit and therefore presumes that Somaly shares her fiancé's outrage at the unfair defeat of the Democrats. And who will consequently talk to her in line with a series of assumptions that would reduce Somaly to something she isn't—and she is not in the mood to pretend.

How can Chinnary be so sure of her opinions? Somaly asks herself (without acknowledging that she herself has consistently supported the opposition until now). If the Democrats succeeded in overthrowing the kingdom with its many thousands of years of history, she would lose her title of princess, along with the modest privileges it brings. And quite apart from her own loss of rank, wasn't she more likely to be loyal to her family, her kin, her heritage, than to the upstart who was her fiancé? Was there any serious chance that she would completely distance herself from her upbringing, from where she really belonged?

So she sits there in silence while Chinnary chatters on: It's one thing to lose the election, but to do so in such a humiliating fashion! Who is going to believe statistics like that? My students are in a state of uproar. What will the outside world say? That the prince likes to make a fool of himself on the screen is one thing, but to produce *a farce* with the whole world as its audience is just excruciating.

She doesn't answer, waits for her friend to finish.

But she continues. As if the violence hadn't been bad enough? Murder, riots, arson. Brutality. The arrest of Vannsak and other party leaders. Do you have any news of them? Chinnary asks, her anger undisturbed by any signs of concern.

Somaly shakes her head.

Chinnary says that, at least, Sar is back at school, that he was teaching earlier today.

How does Somaly feel about receiving *that particular piece of information?* She had been unconcerned, convinced that he had left the city.

Her appearance gives nothing away. The same inscrutable expression behind the sunglasses, the drinking straw rolling back and forth between the fingertips of her left hand.

Inwardly, however, the impulse to flee, to get away, to go, is raging.

But, she thinks, trying to gain control of her panic, irrespective of when his working day finishes or finished, he must be (or must have been) in a hurry to catch the bus. It's difficult to get to Kompong Thom before dark, and he has even farther to go if he is to get to his parents' farm, on small roads that are not much more than ox tracks, if she remembers rightly. So it is very unlikely that he will turn up at the Café de la Poste.

But what does Chinnary mean when she says that Sar *is back*? She asks in a carefully modulated tone of concern, adding that so much has been going on recently, what with the election, that she had assumed he had been too busy to keep in touch—and so on.

Chinnary tells her that several of the politically active teachers had not been at work the week before. Some had been arrested and others stayed out of sight because of that. It was a relief to see that Sar was one of the latter. And: *The police wouldn't touch such a popular teacher unnecessarily*.

His cautiousness again, Somaly thinks.

Furthermore: so that's what his future looks like now. Not a minister, a *magister* more like. A respectable enough profession, you only have to think of her own father, and there is a certain amount of space for theoretical radicalism behind the desk. But it's a long way short of the major political circles he has been moving in over the last year. No sign of glittering prospects there, no sign of the *position* their marriage would demand. *Nothing*.

It's as if the future has finally arrived. The fact that the family allowed her mother to marry an ordinary schoolteacher has come to be seen over the years as *the big mistake*, even though he came from a good family. Sar doesn't even have ancestors (the goodwill he has been able to draw on at court, Somaly knows, arises simply from his sister having been the old king's favourite concubine for a while). And if Somaly insists on continuing the relationship they will all be against her. She would run the risk of being disowned. That's a risk she would have taken earlier—partly from love and partly to show them that she makes up her own mind. But now?

The complications are overwhelming. It's impossible to think a way to any sort of conclusion, she thinks. Only time can produce a clear answer out of all these conflicting emotions.

Chinnary takes a sip of her Vichy water, gives a little burp, carries on mulling things over, says that this business of the ballot boxes, this business of the election officials filling them with false ballot papers. It is all so... *so unsophisticated*.

She sits there in silence, testing her feelings. She shares Chinnary's relief that Sar has come to no harm. And feels a misplaced pride that he is popular with his students. But what she feels above all is that she does not want to be part of some tacit understanding with Chinnary. Why not? It's true that they have never been close friends but they have almost always seen eye to eye in politics. Now, however, what she is saying seems exaggerated, sleazy.

She asks: *How can you be so sure of it?*

Chinnary snorts that the litter bins outside the polling stations in Russey Keo were so full of voting papers that the lids wouldn't close. And they weren't the papers with the prince's portrait on them, whatever people say. And there are many similar cases.

Taking advantage of the inscrutability provided by sunglasses, she says in a tone of indifference: *The prince is very popular*.

She can't decide whether she has succeeded in confusing her friend, who is now leaning forward over her glass and appears to be watching the regular round bubbles rising to the surface. But she wants Chinnary to stop believing things about her, to stop assuming that her loyalty is a given.

The problem, of course, is that she herself is no longer certain where her loyalty lies.

She places some coins on the table, makes an excuse and says she has to go.

Chinnary shows no sign of getting up. Merely adds that the election result will soon be overturned, that the International Control Commission will never endorse it. Her friend looks up, her eyes just as defiant as before.

She forces a quick smile, says, see you soon and means the opposite.

*

* *

Where is Somaly's mother, her *Maman*?

She finds her mother in the garden behind the house. She is bending over the bed by the far wall. Sunglasses, an elegant cadmium yellow sun-hat and a stained apron in the same shade.

Completely unnecessary work, Somaly thinks, spoils your nails and your hands.

She dries the stone bench under the trees with a dirty towelling rag. From the weather-bleached pattern of roses she recognizes it as her own towel, one she had been looking for a month or so before.

Her mother is standing there straight-legged but bent double over the low bushes of white flowers. The secateurs snip through the thin grey branches with their dark thick leaves.

The garden is silent, resting in afternoon stillness.

Still perspiring from her walk home she would like something to drink, but the servants are taking their siesta. She lights a cigarette instead, watches the smoke rising slowly, unruffled by the wind.

Delicate pink lotus flowers are reflected in the pool in front of her. She can hear the sharp click of secateurs. They could employ a gardener if mother wanted one. But *Maman* enjoys doing that kind of work herself.

Not that any gardener would allow a garden to look like this one. It lacks both beauty and structure. Some parts of it seem to have been neglected on purpose, others utterly regimented. There is no position from which an observer can get a really good view without low trees and bushes obscuring it. The colours of the flowers rarely harmonize with one another and the placing of some of the plantings appears to be arbitrary.

It seems to her quite the opposite to mother's well-organized and productive rubber plantations. They are closer, she feels, to Sar's idea of what is beautiful. He has always sought perfection and has no understanding of the attraction of imperfection. Of things that are flawed. And this trait has become even more marked since he returned. Earlier on he did at least show some openness in the face of the incomplete, whereas now he seems to be constantly striving to achieve the *absolute*.

And her other man, how does he view perfection and imperfection? She doesn't know but she imagines that he sees them as *possibilities* rather than as static conditions. Something that can lead him and the country towards the goal that is always in view but always remains at a constant distance.

The reason for the endless hours Mother spends in the garden is something that evades her. Her first thought was that it might be the same *beauty of imperfection* that she herself is so fond of. But when she mentioned this, her mother replied that if Somaly didn't understand then there was no point in trying to explain.

In spite of all the work she does, Mother never makes any fuss about her *jardin* when they have guests. Aperitifs are sometimes served out on the veranda but no one ever mentions the asymmetric layout down below.

They are sitting together now on the stone bench. Mother wipes her hands on her apron and asks about the city. She answers that it seemed normal, that she has spent a while at the Café de la Poste and there was no one there apart from Chinnary, whom Mother only knows by name. But that was to be expected, wasn't it, since it's just before the feast days. She adds that the streets around the burnt-out party headquarters have obviously been cordoned off.

Mother says that that's what happens. That those *sans-culottes* had gone too far, hadn't understood the limits of what was achievable.

A week earlier Somaly would have contradicted her, quoted Sar and said that *everything is possible if people want it*, but a statement like that seems naïve and meaningless now.

She sees just a hint of a supercilious smile on her mother's lips, as if to say: *I know what you're thinking.*

Then her mother says: I've heard that your friend Vannsak has been offered safe conduct, as long as he gives the prince a public apology for the excesses of the election campaign. That's a generous gesture he would probably be wise to accept. And Mother continues in a mutter: This obstinacy, if they had kept their heads they could have achieved something. Filled certain posts. But not when they behaved like that. She then continues in a conversational tone: Take a look at our own plantations—look how many of the workers are communist sympathizers. It was obvious they were going to vote for a People's Party candidate. We can be certain that virtually all of them voted for that Red Sophal fellow. Officially, though, he didn't get *a single vote*. The prince's candidate got thousands but Red Sophal not a single one. That's what happens when you think you can overthrow the monarchy. It's over now, anyway, and just as well.

She sees the distorted reflection of her face in her mother's sunglasses and says, with unintended vehemence, that the combination of conservatism and cynicism is so *joyless*. Mother turns her head away and says indifferently that it may be so, but *that is what came out on top*, isn't that so? And: *now let's talk about something else.*

She shrugs her shoulders as a kind of confirmation even though her mother is not looking in her direction. It had sometimes been an enchanting dream to dream, but she always knew—silently, in her heart—that it was not actually her dream.

Now is now and a different time has already begun.

They talk about the following day, about practical matters. Which pagoda to visit first, and in what order to visit the rest. It's the start of the sort of conversation Somaly is constantly longing for, which shows how rarely it happens. What she and *Maman* actually talk about is unimportant, the important thing is that the distance her mother always seems to keep is diminished for a while. At least, it is no longer the distance between parent and daughter, nor that between older woman and younger. No, Somaly would describe it as the cool and reserved look that a sophisticated woman gives to someone who lacks sophistication. She can understand that. She is constantly aware of her shortcomings. But she has also come to recognize that outsiders see their relationship in a different light: in the eyes of the outside world they are *enviable*—an attractive princess and her attractive daughter.

In *Maman*'s defence, it has to be said that Somaly thinks she can sense a hint of underlying goodwill in that cool and reserved look, as if Somaly is some kind of natural resource, as yet unrefined. Or rather, perhaps, a domestic animal that can be trained. In any case, *someone something can be done with.*

Establishing distance when she needs to, behaving in a haughty way, being difficult to approach in company—all these come quite naturally to Somaly herself in most situations. But however distant she manages to be, she has never succeeded in turning the tables on her mother. It never leads to any compensatory approach on

Maman's part, just detachment and a lack of interest. *Maman*, with her poise and self-awareness, her life experience and her intellect, remains on top.

But there are occasions, such as the present one, when they are close. They discuss the coming evening as though they were bosom friends. They have no intention of making their entrance in the shadow of some self-important man. Two women arriving without a male protector (like some sort of *taxi girls*) will doubtless cause a general undercurrent of confusion and disapproval. But who could possibly say anything publicly? Mother is—formally speaking—still married. And she is engaged. Moreover, she is now the national beauty queen, a role that has made her a kind of institution sanctioned by royalty and thus above everyday convention. And, of course, escorted by her mother.

Why is Sar not providing them with male company? On a number of occasions during their first years together, he and Somaly attended *soirées* and dances together. He was as appreciated a dancer as he was a talker, able to slip pleasantly and effortlessly in and out of conversations. And then he went abroad.

The letters they exchanged during his years in Paris formed the basis of a new intimacy between them even though, in his last year abroad, Sar devoted more and more space to radical and critical interpretations of the prince's policies. It seemed to Somaly that these comments were directed at someone other than her. At some sort of imagined audience even. As far as possible she tried to view them as *confidences* of a sort.

But this room of their own, this room built of letters, proved impossible to enter when they were eventually reunited. It existed, no doubt about that, and they could both feel it, but the doors remained stubbornly locked.

During his long absence Somaly became dependent on her mother again in order to function in social life. And she reluctantly came to recognize that she no longer felt like a child being dragged along and that, unlike her girlfriends, she liked having her mother at her side.

To Somaly's disappointment, moreover, when Sar did return he immediately enlisted in a partisan unit fighting far away from the capital city.

Given this renewed loneliness, which even the postal service could not alleviate, she realized how much she valued the occasional closeness to her mother that feast days offered. She knows that he doesn't like the arrangement. Over the years she has learnt that in spite of his radical ideals, he is quite astoundingly *traditional* where she is concerned.

But in the end he gave her the freedom to go out with *Maman* without putting up any resistance. And she likes the idea that an anxious social world considers her to be *frightfully independent*.

Initially she found it hurtful that her mother made no comment about the unusual arrangement. She could not read anything into it other than that her mother was indifferent to the togetherness Somaly felt they shared. But she has overcome her resentment. As always, she has nothing to reproach her mother with. And *Maman* in her turn treats Sar with irreproachable amiability, even if there is a rather *distrait* quality to it.

They certainly aren't short of offers of company for Saturday's event. Several of Mother's so-called *gentleman acquaintances* have been in contact. These gentlemen have ambitions that are quite unambiguously more than *acquaintanceship*, and in the longer term they are hardly likely to be satisfied with escorting a married woman to sundry events or occasionally being granted the honour of taking her out for a meal. Somaly has no difficulty in seeing what it is they see in her: *Maman* is well-off again, and of good family. Above all, however, she is *different*, rather as if she has been imported from a much larger and more stylish context.

She has sometimes found these *gentleman acquaintances* unsettling, because she feels that her own relationship with her mother is cool and therefore weak. If *Maman* takes a new husband, who perhaps already has children, she is afraid that the distance between them will increase even more. What is more, several of *Maman*'s distinguished suitors have shown a discreet but inappropriate interest in Somaly herself, which means there is the risk of future family conflict of a kind she would rather not contemplate.

But in spite of her mother's lack of maternal closeness to her daughter, she has still not allowed anyone to come between them. In their public social lives they arrive and leave festivities together and more often than not they eat their meals at home together, spending the evenings together, even though each of them is occupied with her own business. The only one allowed into their fellowship is the son/big brother, but he left them several years ago to continue his studies at Chasseloup Laubat in Saigon, where he is now the agent for the raw rubber from the plantations owned by their mother and the rest of the family.

She tells *Maman* that her brother rang that morning to ask what she would like for her birthday. (Somaly is the one who has insisted that everyone in the close family should celebrate each other's birthdays, just like Europeans. She feels that there is a sense in which this implies that they belong to something wider than their own little country with its tradition of everyone having their birthday on New Year's Eve.) But she had not been in the mood to chat with him and had told him that she would like an empty mirror, a mirror that only reflected itself. Her brother, who, according to Somaly, is only concerned with things that are attainable or can be made attainable, told her (with a touch of annoyance, insofar as subtle nuances of that sort can be picked up over a crackling telephone line) to be serious. She then said she wanted a dark starry sky, one with only black stars. The line had hummed emptily for a minute, after which her brother answered, *d'accord*, just as long as he could find someone to wrap it.

That, she thought, was an unusually original answer to come from her brother, and her mother agrees with her, but makes no comment about the nonsense requests, which were Somaly's real reason for recounting the anecdote in the first place.

The conversation dies away, Mother lights a cigarette and walks back to the flower bed, secateurs in hand.

Somaly hangs on a little longer, pokes a patch of small feathery plants with her foot. They are growing wild at the foot of the bench—they quickly close up and then cautiously open again.

She decides to go inside and write the rest of her conversation with Chinnary in her notebook, which she keeps hidden—more or less—in a box in her bedroom. It is not a diary in any real sense. Her entries are not daily and rarely deal with things that have just happened, although this entry will. She has no shortage of girlfriends to confide in, but the conversation she carries on with herself in the pages of the book is a mixture of the trivial and things she cannot express anywhere else. Her handwriting is so untidy that it is virtually illegible even to her. But that doesn't matter. She seldom reads what she has written: she writes for the moment rather than for later. When she first began, in her early teen years, the entries tended to be accounts of what she had done since the last entry. In those days she sometimes flipped back and relived various episodes. But the focus has changed with the passing of time, becoming more and more a catharsis of her consciousness in which there is also space for contradictory thoughts or for things that are otherwise censored. The fact that her handwriting is so difficult to decipher is thus a conscious barrier to discourage anyone who might take it into their heads to read her *writing book* (as she calls it) in secret. She excludes the idea that her mother could be interested in what she has written but she doesn't trust the housemaid. That's always assuming that Kunthea is literate, of course. She buys her notebooks here and there from different stationers in the city, and in recent years, just to be on the safe side, she drops them into the river once they are full. She lets the book slide surreptitiously over the rail when crossing the broad brown river on one of the little ferry-boats. And since she always writes in blue ink, she can be certain that the swirling waters will have washed away the text within a few moments.

WEDNESDAY, 14 SEPTEMBER 1955

It is still dark when she wakes. The unchanging monotonous chanting of the monks can still be heard. It was there when she drifted close to the surface of consciousness earlier in the night. But time after time the peaceful voices lulled her back into her dreams—dreams that have been unusually *powerful* the last few nights.

It's a pity, she thinks, her thoughts still in the twilight zone, that they don't chant their verses all night every night.

It's a cool morning and she turns down the speed of the fan on the ceiling. The sheet, which had been sticking to her body in the close heat of the night, now feels too thin.

The new housekeeper is awake. *Maman*, too, perhaps. One of them has already lighted the incense on the altar below her window.

She stays in her bed and feels she can sense the spirits that are said to be still moving freely around this world before the impending closure of the portals of the realm of the dead. She senses them hugging the walls and wonders how many forefathers' forefathers there actually are. It's as if the spirits are a concentrate of the emotions they left behind them when they were living people, as if the room is full of their hatreds, their regrets and their worries. She imagines them poking around among the amulets she has inherited, which are lying covered in the ash on her dressing table. Imagines them bitterly asking themselves why she isn't wearing the necklace with *those wonderful wonderful tiger teeth, those wonderful wonderful crocodile claws*. She can certainly see herself wearing the small faceless ivory figurines, and she has thought of having the paper-thin gold charm with its small indistinct markings turned into a bracelet.

There is a knock at the door, it opens and Kunthea comes in without waiting for an answer: Somaly thinks that whatever amulets may protect you against they don't protect you against idiots. The maid is hopeless and only obeys rules that exist in her own head. The sort of person who doesn't know her place. That can, of course, be an admirable trait, but not in a pudgy clumsy body like this one. And by the time the girl's youth has withered, the trait will have turned into intolerable presumption.

She stays in bed and watches—without seeing—Kunthea opening the shutters out into the darkness and laying out the clothes she selected the evening before. On a day like today any room for personal taste is minimal. But, she thinks, even traditional clothing can hang well or hang badly and colours can harmonize more or less well.

What it actually all comes down to, according to Somaly, is a fundamental distinction between the small minority of people who understand what is beautiful and the great majority who do not. The latter think that everything they have been brought up to think of as beautiful is beautiful. And everything that the majority dismisses as ugly, they find ugly.

But if you really want to see what is beautiful, Somaly argues, everything else must be peeled away. The object must be seen in itself, in its own right. Without regard to anything else. Only then can its beauty be judged.

Wrapped in a sarong she goes out into the yard where the water butt stands. She pours scoop after scoop over her head. The cold water drives away the last of the sleep.

The stars are already fading in the morning light.

Then Kunthea helps her with her dress. It's rust-red silk with emerald green details. Not as classic as the *sampot pamuong* that most women will choose, but it couldn't be considered unsuitable. She tears off pieces of a croissant while Kunthea puts up her hair using long hairpins with coloured glass heads. Washes down the bread with fresh milk tinged pink with grenadine.

The film about the carousel of love comes back to her. She particularly liked the introduction. Why? Well, the raconteur ascends a short set of steps in the twilight, continues across a simple candlelit outdoor scene, carries on past some film cameras that brutally reveal that everything has been constructed inside a studio, moves out into the streets of Vienna where the sun is suddenly shining and where he stops by a hatstand, which has been placed on the street, to change into tails and a cape. In the sweep of this movement Somaly sees all the essentials of life, so to speak, although she couldn't express it any more clearly than that.

As a whole, however, she thinks that the film is contradictory. As if it doesn't really take itself seriously. She finds the six love stories rather banal, too, although every scene, when viewed as an image, is unarguably *beautiful*. At the same time she can't get away from the thought that even the simplest decisions made by the characters will have incalculable significance further on. That the passion of love makes such definitive claims on people that the future is changed as a result.

She thinks that if she ever has the chance to talk to the prince about the film she will take it. But then she hesitates. The prince has grand ideas about his own filmmaking, though he always claims the opposite. He might take it badly if she were to show more enthusiasm for Max Ophüls as a director than for him. Or she might fail to draw sufficiently interesting parallels between their respective *oeuvres*. If it is just a case of pleasing the prince it would be less risky to stick to talking about current models of sports cars.

For the whole of her life her relationship with the prince has been an effectively non-existent one. The number of princes and princesses is not far short of a hundred, and these days her family belongs on the wrong side of the family tree. All the descendants of the old king Ang Duong are invited to the royal palace a couple of times a year as a matter of course, but in a crowd like that meetings with the prince are limited to hello and goodbye. So it was unusual for the prince to be as charming and attentive as he was in Kep-sur-Mer the week before.

But as far as Somaly is concerned the prince's sudden interest in her is really just a belated correction of *an anomalous state of affairs* that resulted from the formal distinction between them. She understands, of course, that it has to be like that, but if you ignore everything around them (in the same way as when deciding what is beautiful and what is not), Somaly does not consider herself to be in any way inferior to the prince, whether in terms of artistic talent or in terms of qualities of leadership. Nor does she see the formal or informal *structures* as being barriers that are insurmountable. It's true that the country has never had a reigning queen but there are many examples overseas. She is especially fascinated by the young monarch of Great Britain, who is only a few years older than her. In reality, of course, she is not in the least attracted by taking over the prince's role, but it's fun to play with the idea.

So she hadn't been nervous when he asked her to dance under the crystal chandeliers at the casino. The man who bowed to her bowed as an equal. (The champagne may have had something to do with it.) He was a good dancer and he had even joked about being *the shorter of the two of them.*

But she doesn't let that deceive her. His geniality is based solely on the diadem lying by the mirror in front of her (with *Miss Cambodia 1955* engraved on the silver in among all the gemstones). And in spite of its apparent straightforwardness, the prince's game is quite artful, there's no doubt about that. He organizes a beauty contest, all international luxury and prestige, and then by dancing with her he ensures that the lustre of his own creation reflects on himself.

How did she come to be involved in such a cynical set-up, the only purpose of which was to make a ruler, who consistently puts the interests of his own branch of the family first, appear in a sympathetic light? She had not thought it through when she first saw the advertisement, merely fallen for the temptation to enter her girlfriends secretly for the contest as a little joke between themselves. (Nana and Voisanne had, however, taken their role as contestants seriously.) Then it had occurred to her that this might be a chance for her to display some of the dresses she had designed, so the element of competition became secondary. But while she was preparing to step onto the stage, she realized she was bound to win. Not only because there was no doubt she was more beautiful than the majority of the other contestants, nor because they lacked her experience of being at the centre of attention, of feeling themselves to be among the elect. (This was something that Sar later—and rather pedantically—explained to her as being *the privilege of the bourgeoisie*: the fact that the upper class always feels it has the right to be involved in every context, whereas the working class *stands cap in hand* praying for invisibility.) She had thought about this later, but at the time been struck by how uncomfortable, how ill at ease, he seemed, as if—in a contradictory way—he was unconsciously marking some sort of prescriptive right of ownership of her. No, the decisive factor in the contest had undoubtedly been the title of princess. It would have been impossible for any jury to bestow the crown on anyone else without it being perceived as an act of political provocation in the run-up to a parliamentary election. Once she realized this she understood that the beauty contest was part of the prince's electoral campaign, and she, as a member of the royal house, was guaranteeing the best possible result by being a participant.

Would she still have taken part if she had thought the opposite? Yes, she would, because she believes that, in spite of everything, there is more at stake for her personally than any benefit she may bring to the prince. When all is said and done, to the prince the beauty contest is merely an insignificantly small part of a big and complex game, but to her it could mean a ticket to Paris.

She wonders whether she is being too hard on the prince. The contest may well have been no more than a whim of the moment, not that that necessarily excludes ulterior motives. He does like enjoying himself and it's common knowledge that he made his initial approaches to Monineth when he was handing out the prizes at a local beauty contest she won. (According to Sary, however, that is just a cock-and-bull story the prince likes to put about. Sary insists that the prince had known Monineth's parents for years and that he first saw his wife—who is fourteen years younger than him—when she was just a baby.)

Kunthea has finished Somaly's hair and Somaly now starts on her face, while the maid makes the bed and sweeps the patterned parquet floor with a broom.

She strokes soft light cream into her forehead and cheeks, and moistens the black cake of mascara with a drop of saliva that still tastes of milk. And she experiences the familiar feeling of concentration and control that can hold her in its spell for hours. Facial features slowly change character in the mirror. Eyes can be made more prominent and then, with just a few strokes of the brush and powder puff, moved back to allow the mouth and cheekbones to take over. The shape of the lips can be changed with the lip pencil. The boldness of her face will depend on how dramatically she chooses to emphasize the arch of her eyebrows. The woman in the mirror can be changed slowly and methodically to an image of childish innocence and then into one who is brazenly seductive. Years can be added or subtracted.

At the same time, however, it is as if every line she draws, however different, serves to fill in *contours she otherwise feels herself to be lacking.*

Or, more concretely: *contours the world expects of her.*

Today, however, today is a day for subtle nuances and discreet colours. She makes her mouth a light cerise, her eyelids just a touch more golden than her skin. A thin line of kohl around each eye, a little rouge on each cheek. She works quickly, the endless number of times she has done these things compensating for her weariness.

Her body recognizes this morning. It has always been the same as far back as her memory goes. A day of waiting, of ceremonies and of familiar scents. A day on which everything happens in the same order, irrespective of the year, the decade or the century. When she was a child it had been a day that stirred the imagination, of being allowed to devote yourself entirely to showing kindness to the spirits of your forefathers. Later she had come to hate the predictability and the compulsory participation. Now, instead, she recognizes the way in which she is being made part of an ancient fellowship. How she is carrying forward an image of the world that has been shared by all the generations of young women who have lived by this river since it first came roaring down from the mountains of China.

*

*　*

Papa in front of the car. The black paintwork gleams even though it's an old model rarely seen any longer. Not so old then, perhaps, but still. A building of some sort in the background. A school?

It's a poor photograph. The sun is high in the sky and the strong light has blanked out some of the details and put his face in shadow under the brim of his hat. His white hat, his white suit. His tie, where it shows above the edge of his waistcoat, is perhaps grey. Dark leather shoes in the dust. But there is a sparkle in that smile in the shadow. A quality she senses in her own smile sometimes. Something that can ignite the animal look in the eyes of men. (If she leans forward a little, pressing her breasts together with her upper arms and smiling into their faces.)

He is impeccably dressed in the picture. As always. But his posture suggests something other than success. His back is straight, but there is nevertheless something broken about him. A weak spot in his composure. As if this frozen moment of time has partly captured someone other than the man who can make a whole roomful of superficial acquaintances feel at ease. Who can coax genuine smiles from the most cool and calculating members of society.

Or is that just something she is reading into the photograph?

She turns a page in the album. The next one is empty. She looks up at her mother who is sitting on the sofa but their eyes do not meet. And she thinks of what Vannsak told her about the time her father was his teacher at Pursat Provincial School before she was even born.

In his white suit, he lived in a tumbledown hovel by the river. Why? He must surely have had his appanage from *Maman*'s family, didn't he? He should have been able to live somewhere decent.

The schoolchildren used to bring coconuts there for him. He played cards through the night. With whom? He would be so tired during the day that he often fell asleep during lessons. Vannsak claimed that he had been given the job of keeping lookout at the door in case the rector came.

She can hear Vannsak laughing that loud laugh of his. *The born storyteller.*

"You know what boys are. They chased one another around between the rows of benches throwing paper pellets at each other. I was drawn into the riot and forgot to keep watch on the corridor. The door suddenly opened and there was the rector!"

She shuts her eyes. The blackboard is empty, her father is asleep with his head resting on his arms on his desk. Beside him his white hat. Pieces of chalk in half a coconut. The boys don't stop immediately. One by one, however, they notice the figure by the door and hurry back to their seats.

The shutters outside the barred windows are open. Silence falls. And her father is asleep.

Yes, well.

That was his time in Pursat. He had presumably been sent there to humiliate him. To teach him a lesson. To make him stop the nocturnal card sessions and the palm wine. But there can be little doubt that he seems to have walked straight into even deeper humiliation.

What a fool, she thinks.

What a good-natured, charming bloody fool. Not a bad word for anyone.

And then Vannsak's laughter.

"What a walloping he gave me afterwards. He was quite calm and collected as he kicked me with his elegant French shoes and punched me with his fists. I had bruises everywhere. One kick landed at the back of my head and that's probably why my hairline doesn't run where it ought to!"

The eyes of all the others rested on her when he had finished his story. How she had laughed with them, made a joke of it all. But the shame had made her cheeks burn and brought a knot to her throat.

She lights a cigarette. She doesn't bother with a cigarette holder and sees how her lipstick colours the thin white paper. A little redder with every puff.

THURSDAY, 15 SEPTEMBER 1955

She is taking clothes out of the wardrobe and is inspecting them. Looks at the big black patches that have spread on the silk, the rot that has got into the cotton. One by one they join the heap on the floor, at the bottom of which lies her beloved evening dress by Pierre Balmain. The high humidity and constant heat—there are times when they seem to be targeting her personally.

She feels as if she is moving in a mist of mould spores that the floral scent of perfume intensifies rather than disperses.

Once a week she gets Kunthea to burn rotting clothes behind the house. She sits on the veranda and watches the maid feeding the flames in an old tin drum. Thinks that this smoke must surely be one of the most exclusive scents in the world.

*

* *

EX-KING OF CAMBODIA ASKS FORGIVENESS FOR VICTORY

PHNOMH PENH, Cambodia, 14 September

(REUTERS) At a press conference on Wednesday Prince Norodom Sihanouk asked forgiveness for "an all too convincing victory" in Sunday's election. Norodom's party, the Popular Socialist Community, won all 91 seats in the National Assembly. The prince also used the conference to accuse the opposition of being guilty of serious violations during the election campaign, including murder and physical assault. The new government is expected to be announced shortly. Norodom repeated his earlier assurance that he himself will not be leading it.

A police spokesman confirmed that Keng Vannsak, the left-wing vice general secretary of the opposition Democratic Party, has been arrested in connection with Saturday's murder of a driver.

The murder suspect, an "ex-communist" policeman, stated during questioning that Keng Vannsak had also been planning to assassinate Deputy Prime Minister Sam Sary.

*

* *

The usual group is at the usual table. Sunglasses and cigarettes, clothes in the French fashion. All the same age, each with a Kir Royale. Small sweet pastries, salty fried insects.

They are talking about the evening before, about the reception at the American Embassy. Who had been there, what those who were there had said and not said, what they and the others had been wearing.

Somaly had not been there. She had started feeling out of sorts while still sitting at her dressing table. Or perhaps when she was looking at the photograph album and remembering her father in that hovel by the river. She had stayed there on the sofa with the photograph in front of her, and she didn't have the strength to get up and become her usual eye-catching self. All of a sudden the desire to be invisible was greater than her need to be seen.

And this strange debilitating weariness that comes over her more and more often these days.

Voisanne asks where she was yesterday and she answers, nowhere, it had just been *one of those evenings*.

They haven't all been together for a while and so Mari wants to hear all about the prince's dance at Kep-sur-Mer the week before. Mari had been forced to go away to a wedding in Battambang, and she gives them to understand that it was *very expensive* but *oh, so provincial*.

She stresses that the flight itself was the best feature, while her fingers pick and choose among the crickets with pork stuffing. Somaly thinks that her reference to the aeroplane is meant to compensate for the fact that she missed one of the most prestigious *soirées* of the season. She herself has never flown and she has no idea whether Voisanne and Nana have done so, but since they refrain from asking what things look like above the clouds she does so too.

Nana turns her sunglasses towards her and says that she hasn't seen Sar for a long time. It doesn't come as a surprise, Nana has always had an eye for Sar. Somaly has never known whether it is mutual, nor what to make of the friendliness and interest Sar shows towards her friends. And, not knowing, she has swung between jealousy on the one hand and pride on the other—pride that she has a fiancé so *modern* that he can mix with women so *naturally*. Nana says that yesterday's reception was the sort of function he might have been invited to, but in the following subordinate clause she notes that there had been no sign of any representatives of the Democratic Party. Voisanne jokes that it's probably difficult to convince the warders to let them out for a cocktail party. Then, turning to her, she covers herself by saying that it's dreadful, isn't it?

(An image: Vannsak hanging in an unnatural pose in front of a table on which there is a typewriter. His clothes stained with sweat and dirt, his face contorted.)

(Another image: Vannsak, eyes glazed, neck and cheeks flushed red by wine, hissing with a sort of strange satisfaction that Sary was the most brutal examining magistrate in the city before he went to France. That some interrogations ended with *what remained of the suspects* being buried in the rubbish tip.)

She hears Nana ask what Sar will do now that there won't be a post in the civil service for him. She answers that she doesn't know and after an audible hesitation Nana asks if they have split up.

At this point Somaly is in a good position to pre-empt the speculation that her friends will otherwise indulge in when she leaves. But
her instinct fails her and she is forced to say that she doesn't want to
talk about it, which is closer to the truth than she would have liked.
She picks a sugar-coated doughnut ring from the plate and says that
things haven't turned out as planned. *That they'll have to see.*

They know one another well enough for no one to press her, but
Voisanne says that it is about time Somaly did the same as the rest
of them. An older *but well-established* man is best. As a mistress it's all
benefits and very few duties. And the duties are not always unpleasant.
Quite the reverse. (General laughter.) As long as you take precautions
not to *end up in certain circumstances*, it is actually an ideal situation.
Nana and Mari smile in agreement and Somaly says, well yes, who
knows, and does her best to say it boldly and without any undertones
that might spark her friends' curiosity. If they suspect anything they
don't show it.

She remembers them as the schoolgirls they were just a few years
before. Sitting as they are sitting now but at one of the ice-cream bars
and wearing white blouses and dark blue skirts. Giggling about things
that at the time they could only guess at. They are the same but not
the same. Even though she has always been one of them, she has
never enjoyed that forced sense of excitement. It is better now, as if
she has finally grown into herself. She doesn't know how the others feel
and were she to ask she would not necessarily get an honest answer.

Suddenly she thinks she recognizes one of the cyclo drivers in the
shade of the palm trees by the police station, diagonally across the
sun-baked square. They are standing lined up side by side waiting
for customers. The man with the familiar face slowly sets his vehicle
in motion, as if he has noticed that she is watching him. He pedals
languidly into a side turning that leads to Wat Phnom. And then he
is gone.

Was it the same man who carried her the other day? Or is it just that he reminds her of someone else?

She turns back to her girlfriends' conversation about the next night's *soirée*. They are talking about the older men who pay for their dresses and earrings, who provide them with suppers and hats.

She feels no desire to tell them about Sary. Why should that be? It has nothing to do with keeping it secret because her girl-friends would not pass it on without her permission. No, Somaly's unwillingness is different. She realizes that part of the attraction she is experiencing lies in the fact that she and Sary exist, so far anyway, in parallel worlds which she can move between as she pleases. That makes it quite different from her public relationship with Sar. There is something attractive in the very exclusivity, in the fact that their meetings are not public goods to be chewed over by all and sundry.

In that sense he is hers, just hers.

*

*   *

When a transparent plastic bag like a misshapen jellyfish passes the hull of the boat, she suddenly remembers the dream she had in the night. In her dream she had seen herself floating above the floor in a room completely filled with water—a rather grand room in a palace, in fact. There had been nothing unusual apart from the water. It was a beautifully furnished room with light pouring in through tall open windows. She had been wearing a light cotton frock, one that did not resemble any of the dresses she owns in real life, and both the fabric and her hair were swaying with the slow sensuousness of seagrass. She had studied her own face, seen the closed eyes and the slightly parted lips, but it had all possessed the restfulness of someone sleeping rather than the dead look of a drowned woman. A blue-green shimmer is still lingering at the back of her mind, as she watches the opposite bank slowly drawing closer while the swallows swoop boldly above the brown whirls of the river. The ferryman standing behind her shouts a greeting to another boat. It is the same shamelessly staring and leering youth she had this morning, and in spite of his powerful strokes with the paddle he is having trouble holding course. She thinks that the most remarkable thing about her dream was not that she had been under the water, nor that she had been asleep and watching herself sleeping, but that she had dreamt what someone else would dream about her. That she had dreamt a man's dream about Somaly.

*
*   *

She slides a shiny black new record out of its stiff paper sleeve, lets the sleeve fall to the floor and turns the record the right way round between the palms of her hands. She puts it on the turntable, winds the handle and carefully places the needle in the groove.

First comes the obligatory prelude of crackles and clicks produced by a couple of flecks of dust as the record revolves. Then without warning the Glenn Miller Orchestra starts. As the opening fanfare leads into the seductive swing of the theme, she immediately feels the physical urge to dance along with it. *Je suis vraiment in the mood*, she thinks. The memory of Sary's body against hers, the mild euphoria induced by champagne, the shadows of the other couples gliding around them in the half light of the crystal chandeliers.

She sits down again with the pack of cards and lays spades, spades, diamonds, spades. Then she lays clubs, clubs, spades, diamonds, intentionally going against the rhythm of the music.

Her mother is sitting at her desk, spectacles on, doing the accounts. The air is still moisture-laden from the evening rain.

She lays spades, clubs, spades, diamonds and wonders whether the members of the orchestra ever think of their music being played at the very same moment in a quite different part of the world, on a clear starry night which is morning to them, or maybe afternoon. Or, it occurs to her, that their breath in their instruments will continue to sound long after they are dead.

Clubs.

One day it will be a dead orchestra led by a dead Glenn Miller that will strike up those first notes so clearly and self-confidently.

Spades.

The record on the gramophone turntable suddenly feels like a crime against the order of nature—an order determined by a mighty, merciless and incomprehensible creator whom it is best not to anger.

Clubs.

The dead should take their voices with them, let them disperse along with the smoke from their pyres.

Diamonds.

Not leave them as ghosts among those of us still alive.

She takes a breath and is about to share the thought with her mother, but closes her mouth again when she sees the concentration on the face over the books. Gathers up the cards from the unsuccessful game of patience and shuffles them more thoroughly than necessary.

She remembers the old belief that when a photograph is taken the soul of the subject is burnt into the negative for ever. She thinks that if that is true it means that there isn't a single film star either in heaven or in hell. Their souls are doomed to spend eternity consigned to a celluloid purgatory, constantly on call to replay their movements and dialogue. In which case even the lowliest extra will remain trapped on a few frames of film.

She used to feel sad when she looked at the props in a film. The fact that the furniture is in store, the set dismantled, the wonderful food long ago consumed, thrown out, disappeared.

But she hasn't found a way of including the actors in this awful transience.

She takes a card from the pack at random. Three of clubs.

What if one of them managed to flee from captivity and haunt the people who owned copies of the film? Then plead with them to destroy the reels of film so he could achieve peace at last?

Her gaze wanders and she sees the stubborn ghosts pass before her eyes.

Would the actor, who had fled to find freedom for himself and his comrades in distress, suddenly be absent from the scenes in which he had featured? Would the others move around as before even though he was gone?

She places the three of clubs in the patience and draws a seven of clubs.

That, more or less, is the way her family moved at first around the empty space left by father. But their film quickly took a different direction. A new script—one with no hopeless fathers.

She looks at the pack of cards she is holding. Did it once belong to him? Are these the cards that he fingered, are these the ones that were used by all the companions who came and went around the table? The cards that shaped victory and defeat? No, they look too new for that, though it does seem unlikely that *Maman* would have bought a pack of cards for the house. Perhaps they are her brother's? Or someone else left them behind?

She draws the queen of clubs, shuffles the cards again. She notices that her mother's foot is silently beating time to the music. As if her body has already moved on to tomorrow evening.

FRIDAY, 16 SEPTEMBER 1955

Kunthea tells her he has rung again. The message is the usual friendly one.

She goes into her room, shuts the door behind her. Walks across the twilit room, opens the shutters and fills the room with light. Puts a cigarette in her cigarette holder and then leans back in the armchair. The fan, forgotten since the morning, is still humming—another black mark in Kunthea's book.

She thinks: this impatience he has got himself locked into, she doesn't understand it. Or, she corrects herself, she does understand: he is used to me being the one doing the waiting, always, good little dog.

From his point of view, losing something is a more powerful emotion than the satisfaction of having something: is that how she should read him?

She thinks about what has happened, what hasn't happened and what ought to have happened. The fact that once upon a time she burnt herself on his beauty—the beauty of him seeing her in a way that no one else saw her. The fact that his gaze made her beautiful in the way she believes she was intended to be beautiful.

But what is that worth now? Now that their silences, once so full of everything, are full of nothing?

It's as if something has come uncoupled, as if everything has been left behind. Forgotten. And she didn't realize until it was too late.

She thinks: I was the one who carried us when he was away. It can't be up to me to carry us when he is here. I'm the one who's drowning in disappointment.

She continues: I don't have to answer him. I don't have to do anything. I'm the one who will decide. I'll make my decision when I'm sure of what I want.

But it is not lack of conviction that is Somaly's problem. Her problem is that she wants different things at the same time. And the feeling that no decision is ever reached is an exhausting one. When she woke up she knew she was going to leave Sar that day. But just a couple of hours later she was considering going through with the marriage, even though it would probably mean she would lose her inheritance and be removed from the family tree.

So she thinks: it must be allowed to take however long it takes—why should he find that so difficult to accept? To respect? A hurried answer would be worthless, wouldn't it? Just words thrown away. Like notes plinked on the piano.

Below the unfinished sketch of a dress on her drawing table she scribbles *you cannot force a flower to bloom.*

She puts down her pen and picks up the latest number of *Réalités Cambodgiennes.* As expected, it contains photographs of the Kep-sur-Mer *soirée.* Her blurred smile, among other blurred smiles, can be glimpsed over to the left in one of them. Sary is standing over among the white suits on the right of the picture, his head turned in her direction. His face almost completely broken up by the half-tone dots.

The picture is too small and there are too many people for it to be possible to be sure of anything. He could have been turning his head for any number of reasons.

And right in the middle is the beaming prince. Perhaps he is the one that Sary is looking at?

The Somaly now studying the photograph wonders if the Somaly in the photograph knew she was going to spend the night with him. Had she decided, or had she left it as a possible possibility? It is difficult to know at what stage a decision like that is made. A haze of alcohol, cigarettes and, not least, the fire of the blood coursing through her body lies between the smiling woman in the picture and the woman now looking at her.

And: what about the man standing over on the right—does he know?

She realizes (and for one moment the earth seems to tremble beneath her feet) that Sar might also look at the society pages in the paper. Someone might say something that would lead him to take an interest in them, mightn't they? She thinks that he often knows more about her and her acquaintances than seems likely. *Just something I heard*, he says. More often than not he doesn't let it show that he knows. Or, she thinks now, perhaps that's just a pose to give the impression of being omniscient?

Her sense of insecurity has been heightened by a car driving along the street the last few evenings. She assumes it's the same car because, judging from the sound of the engine, it slows down as it approaches and then speeds up once it has passed the house. She has resisted the temptation to look and see what kind of car it is because her silhouette would be visible in the window. In which case anyone in the car would be able to see more than she could. And how many nights had it driven past before she noticed it?

She is finding it hard to shake off the feeling of being watched by someone out there in the dark of the night. In broad daylight, as it is now, with the sun burning off all the shadows in the garden, it is easy to dismiss it as imagination. But, at night, the solitary lamp over the veranda can do no more than make the shadows recede a few steps.

Is it Sar in the car? Or one of his friends? Or is it Sary's men? Perhaps it's driving past purely by chance? Or someone who has discovered a short cut through this district?

Maybe. But chance does not explain all the times Sar has *happened to be* in the restaurants and cinemas or places she has visited in recent months. And even on those occasions when he has not *happened to be* there, it has felt as if he had been there or could suddenly turn up at any moment.

Somaly thinks that these intentional unintentional meetings are reminiscent of a bad farce. The more breathing space she needs the less he is prepared to give her. And the strange thing is this—no one has ever understood her as he does, so why doesn't he understand this, this fundamental issue?

She regrets the cigarette. It has made her mouth unbearably dry and the water in the carafe has long since reached room temperature, the chunks of ice melted. She rings for Kunthea to fetch her a glass of milk, fresh from the fridge and flavoured with grenadine. The girl then proceeds to make a great show of sorting the clean washing into the linen cupboard. As if cocooned in a world of her own.

She returns to her earlier thoughts, thinks about desire and the way it seems to consume all other emotions. Or at least to annul their significance. But it can also cloak them or muddle them so that it becomes impossible to decide what is what. What is the difference between the (addictive) glint in the eye of the man who says he loves her and the ugly rage that burns in the eyes of the same man when he accuses her of flirting with other men?

Are they expressions of the same passion?

To desire someone, she thinks, to want someone, doesn't that imply transgressing something in oneself, breaking one's own rules? It might even imply a crime against one's own morality, might it not? And when the eyes of that sort of criminal target me with his lust, they hold a promise that is both irresistibly attractive and simultaneously frightening. At times like that even a handsome man can reveal an ugly aspect and, conversely, an ugly man can suddenly seem appealing.

She asks herself: when I step out onto the floor and straight into the light of all men's eyes, is there hate in them too? Are those bright smiles simultaneously teeth bared in rage?

*

* *

She steps out onto the floor and straight into the dazzling glances. Her mother's cool soft arm is tucked under hers. Faces turn towards them, break into smiles.

Somaly feels (to her annoyance) her hand sliding up to her bosom. It's a reflex from early youth when she would try to cover herself from male eyes that were beginning to notice the changes in her body. She has long since learnt to control the movement, almost to the point of forgetting it. And so she lets her hand move on upwards, as if the intention had always been to check that her coiffure was faultless at the back.

She steps out onto the floor with a frisson of hope and a queasy sense of apprehension.

They are surrounded by shimmering silk dresses and suits as white as sugar icing. She sees ministers and officers, she sees diplomats and businessmen. She sees fellow-countrymen and foreigners and people who are neither the one thing nor the other.

The prince is not there, not yet anyway, but along with the minor royalty she can also see faces that are at home at court. She sees some of her friends and she says that everything looks truly splendid, doesn't it, and her mother answers that it does.

She thinks that it doesn't look to be the sort of occasion Sar will be at—fortunately. Before the election he would certainly have been invited. Or if he'd had the sense to change to the winning side. But not now. Not given the people who are here.

So she can forget her apprehension.

Mother is gathered up by Monsieur Hanin to join his conversation with a man of his own age, a Colonel Heng. She goes along too. Colonel Heng's broad white chest is covered with the colourful ribbons of orders and medals, the ends of his sleeves trimmed with gold galloons.

Over one of the colonel's epaulettes she suddenly sees Sary. He is standing together with his favourite colleague, Mau Say, both of them leaning on the rail of the balcony and framed by the doorway. The night forms their backdrop, they have cigarettes in their hands and their backs to the room.

So hope is fulfilled then.

Seeing him sends a white spark through her thoughts, just as it did at dinner in the hotel dining room the week before. She relives the choking feeling she'd had in her throat as he walked towards her. The urgency of the heartbeats through her body. The way her voice failed her as she uttered the first syllables of greeting. The sudden blush that came to her cheeks when she had to repeat them. The way the blush then became self-generating (she blushed because she thought she was blushing). The wanton physical reaction that added raging embarrassment to the whirlwind of emotions that overpowered her.

Now, as then, she feels slightly sick and childishly excited. Her thoughts become incoherent.

She pulls herself together, determined not to let her confusion show. It had been impossible to tell whether he had noticed it last time. Had he?

On the one hand, he has eyes that seem able to see right through people and to expose all their weaknesses.

On the other hand, the chaotic election campaign made him more and more *distrait* during the few meetings they had.

But then, thirdly, does it matter anyway?

Whichever it may be, she has no intention of letting him suspect that she does not know what to make of her own reactions.

She remembers an intimate conversation she had at the Café de la Poste with Mei, who appropriately enough is standing by the doorway out to the balcony. Mei has beautiful pale skin, a precociously mature face and a past in the Royal Ballet. And many suitors. But in their conversation in the café Mei had come up with a description of herself which, with a kind of triumphant resignation, she would use to cut off all attempts to make further progress: Mei (she said of herself) was *a hopeless beginner when it came to love*. But, Somaly thinks, it is not lack of experience that causes her friend's constant failure. Instead of being bold and using all the advantages nature has given her, Mei consistently withdraws into her own private insecurity. Mei quite simply fails to recognize that her suitors are attracted by their *understanding* of what she represents, not by her as an individual. That she is, in fact, superior to any of the men who approach her. Because she comes from a good family, because she is young, because she is beautiful, because she is a woman.

The beauty contest has only served to confirm this to Somaly. She no longer feels the need to assess her own worth by interpreting the opinions of admirers and then multiplying them by the number of men involved. She is, after all, now the owner of a tiara and a certificate in a gold frame, both of which attest to the fact that she is the most beautiful woman in the kingdom. Since then any suitor who attempts to make her feel insecure by hinting that there are other and better women is doomed to failure. (That, in turn, has made her suitors less subtle and more direct.) She knows—and this was what she said to Mei—that it is no longer her they are paying court to, no longer "the beautiful Somaly, daughter of Princess Rasmi", but Miss Cambodia. That is to say, *the woman that every other man also desires*. And, she thinks, in the final analysis, that last point is the decisive one.

Then, as if far off, she sees Sary's wife Em making her escape from the unimportant groups of conversing guests. Sees the dumpy but tastefully dressed woman go over and join Sary and Mau Say on the balcony. Sees them turn towards Em with open approving faces.

With an effort she drags her eyes away from the three figures in the doorway and fixes instead on the colonel's face with its open pores. The colonel is not slow to meet her eye.

Once the orchestra has finished the national anthem and struck up *Papa loves mambo*, she answers the colonel's smile and invitation to dance.

In spite of his bulk the colonel is one of those men who is light and lithe on his feet. As though there is a younger and slimmer man somewhere inside. And it is this slim young fellow who is reaching out to her, when the colonel proceeds to press her hard against his belly and chest.

He dances a predictable foxtrot. And he jokes about the gaudily painted temple coulisses that illustrate the theme of the *soirée*. For no apparent reason he mentions that he had not always thought of making his career as an officer. Rather the opposite, he continues, I am an artist. She responds, on cue, with a smile containing just the right degree of scepticism, and the colonel, pleased, explains that once upon a time he used to take singing lessons. *Tenor*, he says with unaffected pride. She wonders whether she should take this to be *a moment of honesty*? Or is it an attempt to impress her? Or is he just teasing her?

He is dancing so close that she can see the small beads of sweat in his sparse pencil moustache.

She sees that over by the balcony doors Sary has seen her and she therefore gives all her attention to the colonel.

And then the orchestra plays *La vie en rose*. The colonel doesn't even ask, just implies with a little squeeze of her hand and waist that they should continue.

Her partner tells her of his visits to Saigon and she forces herself to concentrate in order to take her mind off Sary and Em, but above all so that she will at least look unconcerned. He tells her the sort of thing that she thinks that he thinks she would like to hear. So he describes the Catinat-Ciné with its twelve-hour programme of films every day, the white linen tablecloths in La Pagode tea room, the shops with Chinese silk at any price you are prepared to pay. He then moves on to describe Saigon Cathedral as *the rust-coloured heart of the subversive infiltration of our beloved little kingdom by the French and the Vietnamese.* And by building that abomination of a sister cathedral in their own capital they have allowed their arrogance to betray their real intentions: the fact that its twin towers are taller than the spire of Wat Phnom is, according to the colonel and there are *many who agree with him,* final proof of what is afoot—*recolonization.*

The colonel keeps smiling his imperturbable smile while saying that it is very easy—for a military man—to see the strategy. They cannot conquer us face to face, weapon in hand, which is why they are relying on their alternative battle plan. He explains that it is important to have several choices, one for each eventuality and all of them equally well prepared. In other words, the result is more important than the road you take to get there. And given this kind of low-intensity offensive, society would eventually—and soon—fall under the control of foreign powers.

He says that he hopes that within the near future the prince will see to it that the cathedral is levelled to the ground it is currently desecrating. And will then expel all the foreigners. For the prince, he states emphatically, is *a patriot.*

Just take our language, he continues after a short pause during which his indignation grows even more intense. (It seems to her to be quite independent of his dancing, which continues to retain the same lingering seductiveness as before. And his smile is still in place.) But his ill-concealed agitation makes for a less than pleasing disjointedness in the colonel's paradoxical and unconscious charm, a charm that stems from combining a patina of sophistication with a lack of refinement. It's as if jigsaw pieces of the colonel's face have been placed on top of another face. (That particular image manages to hold her attention for a moment—a welcome chance to gather

her thoughts which had stubbornly insisted on straying over to the trio on the balcony.)

Just take our language, he says. For decades we have been captivated by everything French. We have adopted French vocabulary and expressions in spite of the fact that our own language has fully adequate equivalents. Advertisements are infested with them. It feels, he says, as if people believe there is some kind of unstated qualitative distinction, with French being a rather better language than ours!

We are under attack from every side at once, he states. But the majority of our people haven't even begun to understand it. And the elite of society, the people dancing here, they are incapable of recognizing the enemy within themselves.

She says that she attended the consecration of the cathedral. Not because she is a Catholic but because the nobility was invited. She says he's right to say it's very ugly. A sort of architectural mixture of factory and church. Remarkably dull and heavy, yet aggressive at the same time.

The colonel looks at her sceptically, but then his face softens again and he looks as he did before. Take a photograph of it, he jokes, because quite soon it's likely to be no more than a memory.

The melody comes to a long drawn-out close and she excuses herself. The orchestra takes up the next tune, *Mon amant de la Coloniale*.

It is not just the colonel who has been overcome by indignation during the dance. Somaly herself has ended up in an icy rage (or is it desperation she is feeling). As she leaves the colonel on the dance floor, she berates herself for not having been prepared for Sary to come with Em. Her mind had been preoccupied with how to behave if, in spite of everything, Sar risked turning up. And as for Sary, she had been happy simply to fantasize about the amusing possibilities of indiscreet glances and ambiguous exchanges. But the presence of *that cow* in the room has put paid to any such thought. The kind of game she'd had in mind, while remaining invisible, still demands the full attention of the other player.

The easiest thing for the two of them would be to pretend that he is the passing acquaintance everyone assumes him to be. But to be subject to a set of rules she hasn't been involved in drawing up (which is how she describes it at the moment) is impossible. Nor does she have it in her to cause a scene. That would quite simply be bad form.

She turns abruptly to a Chinese man standing on his own watching the dancers. She hasn't met him before but he stands out because he is wearing a close-fitting silver-grey suit instead of the appropriate white one. His hair is cut short and matches the shades of his suit. He gives the impression of being a man of the world, even if his shirt collar is too high to be the modern fashion. His delicate features are made for the round steel-rimmed glasses he is wearing. Despite his grey hair she judges him to be younger than Sary.

He accepts and offers her his arm. They glide out among the other dancers. (His light touch and neat figure in marked contrast to the colonel's obtrusive physique.) If he is confused by her taking the initiative he keeps it to himself.

She can't see if Sary is watching her.

The Chinese man says he is new to the city. Come from Singapore. *Business*, he pronounces it in English in the middle of the flow of French. His voice is soft and natural. She thinks that everything about this man seems to be well balanced. Well balanced and refined.

He tells her that he earns his living by arbitrage. And that now that the kingdom has its own currency, he will have reason to come here again. And he feels that the Chinese in the city—what do you call them, *la bourgeoisie*?—have been welcoming. Perhaps they view him more as a compatriot than as a competitor? Or maybe people here are so provincial that they still practise good old-fashioned hospitality? His line of business is still in its infancy here.

She listens. His voice, his attractive features and the nature of the dance compensate for the conventional content of the conversation. But her temper is quite unpredictable and, moreover, he subverts every statement he makes, so to speak. As if he is being ironic. Or is it just his accent, perhaps?

As the final notes die away he bows and thanks her without laying claim to the next dance.

Her eyes look for Sary, but she pulls herself together and goes to join *Maman*'s group.

Just a step away from the dance floor she is stopped by a Frenchman. He looks almost American to her with his prominent jaw and the quick smile that comes to his suntanned face. The white suit hints at an athletic body. He introduces himself as Monsieur Klein, cultural attaché at the embassy in New Delhi. Now on holiday and visiting the Angkor Wat temples and the *Côte d'Opale*. The temples, he assures her, are particularly interesting from an Indian perspective. But, he continues, we can talk about that another time. He explains that he would like to invite her out to dinner, or lunch if that is more appropriate, in order to tell her about a number of future events that ought to involve Miss Cambodia. He gives her his card, which has a telephone number written in large unambiguous figures in pencil on the back. My hotel, he says, slowly running his forefinger across the number while keeping his eyes on her.

She puts his card in her bag, thanks him and walks towards the row of papier-mâché pillars where she left her mother. The other guests are moving in the opposite direction, towards the dance floor where the orchestra is just introducing *Blue Velvet*, last year's hit. She can see Colonel Heng with a new partner. She can see Monsieur Hanin with Penn Nouth, the president of the council, a rather thin man. But she can't see her mother's sky-blue dress anywhere.

And then, suddenly, she finds herself just a few steps away from Sary. Despite the fact that her field of vision closes in, that she experiences the following sequence in slow motion as if underwater, she doesn't manage to notice the people he is talking to. As he passes he smiles at her, quickly, efficiently. And she thinks as she moves away through the people, the world having returned to normal speed, that his eyes and his smile did not match up.

She does not respond to the smile. And she wonders if there was anything in her face that gave her away.

Then she sees her mother, standing with her back to the seats occupied by Nana, Voisanne, Mari and several of her other friends.

*

*   *

Sweet, lukewarm pink milk. Cigarettes. Her face in the mirror, the way the make-up brings it all together. Immaculately. It would have lasted the whole evening and half the night. But she'd had to leave the *soirée*. She is surprised by how disappointed she is. By the strength of her feelings. But she feels that she is not like other people, that there is no reason why she should simply put up with things.

She runs through the course of events as if everything had happened simultaneously, and it is only now, in retrospect, that she can separate things and see the individual elements. She does not dwell too long on the moment she turned to the Chinese man and asked him to escort her from the *soirée*. Nor the hushed sensation it caused when the national beauty queen left an event early escorted by an unknown and inappropriately dressed foreigner. She did not notice whether Sary saw them, but he would undoubtedly have heard about it. No, the scene she replays in her mind is of her sitting in the car saying goodbye and the Chinese man about to close the car door. At the very moment of closing it he says: my name is *Monsieur Zhau*.

There is nothing improper about that, quite the reverse, and she should perhaps have introduced herself too. But there was a hint of eagerness in his voice, in contrast to the way he had done her bidding without any glint in his eyes behind his round spectacles when she asked him to escort her from the *soirée*. He was correct throughout, and politely distant. And then he tells her his name as if it is *important* for him to say it. What does he want me to do with it? Does he even know who I am?

Her first thought had been to leave discreetly, without anyone noticing. But then came the notion of *making something of it*. She is too tired and still rather too drunk to assess the consequences. (She starts the lengthy process of removing powder, eye shadow, lipstick.) She is, she thinks, possibly going to wake up with her body in the vice-like grip of anxiety, her head splitting from grinding her teeth. But then her anger flares up again. She is the one who is in the right. And she becomes even more angry, when she meets her eyes in the mirror and watches the lines drawn by the eye pencil begin to be dissolved by treacherous tears.

SATURDAY, 17 SEPTEMBER 1955

Kunthea knocks, comes in, says, *Good morning, Miss*.

She thinks she can smell the penetrating scent of lilies that have just come into flower.

Is it a real smell? The night was a jumble of very strange and utterly convincing dreams. There were times she thought she had woken up but quickly realized that she was still in a dream. And although noises from outside told her that the time was passing, she had been incapable of rousing herself into a state of wakefulness. Time after time she had slipped back into the soft darkness.

Through half-closed eyelids she sees Kunthea as a darker patch in the darkness of the room, a silhouette placing a vase of what she takes to be lilies on the table by the bed. A silhouette that is suddenly outlined by sharp white light when the shutters open to let the morning in.

Is she really awake?

There is an envelope poking out of the bouquet and she lifts the mosquito net to reach it. She breaks the seal and reads. *Pardonnez-moi. Sary.*

She sinks back in the bed, the stiff white card in her hand. If this is a dream it is a dream of victory.

*
* *

She carries on towards the river, in her hand the magazine she bought at the news-stand. She passes the small funfair that has been closed for some time. She finds an empty bench in the shade of the trees on the riverbank. She shares the shade with a fortune teller and a seller of swallows. The silent birds are crowded into a cage made of chicken wire; the fortune teller mixes chalk and betel nut in a leaf and folds it with practised fingers. Both women gawp at her. She, however, looks out over the brown swirling waters of the river. Heavily laden barges are fighting the current and the ferry makes its way back and forth, back and forth, between small open fishing boats.

Beyond the boats the other bank can be glimpsed through the haze. An untidy line of palms and trees.

Like an image of the future, she thinks. A vague goal in the distance with various ways of getting there.

Somaly's relationship with the future has changed with time. When it became clear there was no longer any money for schooling, the outlook had become limited to an advantageous marriage. She had been too young to question the actual assumption and had instead gathered all her strength to have the last word as to who the lucky man might be. Everything has changed now.

The two points of decisive importance are, first, her mother is solvent again and, secondly, the mayor with the sweaty hands placed that diamond tiara on her head. As a result of that she is no longer an economic burden to be transferred to someone else's shoulders. Nor does she lack real opportunities to make what she will of her life.

She may even be on the threshold of an international career that could eventually make her a fashion icon.

She thinks of the evening that followed the grand beauty contest. There was a show of the latest creations by Maggy Rouff and Hermès. She and the French girls walked slowly under the stars, slowly around the side of the illuminated swimming pool at the Hôtel Le Royal. They changed four times, from one magnificent dress to another. The audience applauded, there were even cheers as they made their last circuit together. She can see them now, all gathered on the lawn with reflections from the underwater lamps playing on their faces. Ministers, military men, courtiers, businessmen. All with their eyes and smiles on her.

Then an extended cloudburst had driven them all indoors.

She was allowed to choose a dress to keep. Her choice fell on a cocktail dress in champagne-coloured chiffon.

But even more important is that the French beauty queens were so friendly, that they said that she was *très chic*.

And now there is this cultural attaché Klein. What kind of event does he have in mind? Working at an embassy, working with culture, with the kind of winning appearance he has, he must be familiar with

Parisian society. Probably part of it. Which means he knows the people she wants to know. The question is, which would be more advantageous—lunch or dinner? How to balance advantage and propriety?

The coming years pass before her eyes. She sees life as a fashion model in Paris. She sees good earnings. Given a small amount of capital she should then be able to design a collection under her own name. Something up to date but also drawing on the traditions of her own people. Several of Maggy Rouff's creations had eye-catching *primitive details*: leopard patterns, a touch of Africa. But, as far as she could tell, nothing from Asia. That's where she would have her own niche. Given a couple of years as a model she ought to have made the necessary contacts. And her brother might even put some money into it once she has made a success of it. If things went really well he might even join her business. That really is a sweet prospect—the businessman of the family working *for her*.

The air suddenly fills with big shimmering dragonflies as she plans her own *maison de couture* in her mind. In the margin of the magazine she makes a new sketch for an evening dress, a playful variation on Christian Dior's *New Look*. Her own feeling is that the accentuated waistline patented by Dior looks particularly good on her figure.

And how would Sar fit into this French vision? He wouldn't. What part could a schoolteacher play in that sort of life? On the other hand, she was good enough to wait here while he was there. For the sake of fairness, it should be possible in reverse. But she knows that he would never accept his wife being exposed to all the dangers and temptations of being abroad on her own. Nor having people laugh at him and thinking him a fool for believing that the beauty queen who had *absconded* would ever come back.

She suddenly remembers the oblique kind of jealousy of the actual city of Paris she had felt when it took Sar from her. And she wonders if he would feel the same sort of thing if his wife went there.

And Sary? (Her heart pumps a warm wave of longing through every blood vessel in her body. This is a *phenomenon* that does not cease to amaze her.) He has friends there and he would certainly travel there quite regularly. Sends a telegram: MA CHÈRE STOP ARRIVE PARIS 4 DEC 17H STOP MEET ME AT PLACE DE HOTEL DE VILLE STOP IMPATIENT S STOP.

The distance and the absence of formal links would allow her world to remain open. She would be free to shape her own life, but in the certainty that Sary was there in the distance. *With* someone else, but *for* herself.

I am the one who will decide, she thinks. I am the one who will decide.

She looks at the clock, gets up and waves for a cyclo. The driver obviously recognizes her from the covers of magazines, his coarse suntanned face breaks into a smile—all bad teeth and masses of wrinkles. She describes an alley behind the Bamboo Market and the man pedals (slowly) up onto Avenue de Verdun.

The alley lies in shadow, the air still and heavy with the stink of rubbish coming from the market. Some dirty children recognize her and wave. The cyclo driver, his peace of mind now mixed with uncertainty in view of a destination that doesn't correspond to where a beauty queen ought to be going, offers to wait for her at no extra cost.

Somaly passes through the doorway and climbs the dirty and uneven steps in the dark stairwell. Political slogans and obscene scribbles on the walls.

The tailor himself opens the door on the top floor, at first just a crack but then, nervously, he lets her into the apartment, which also serves as a workshop. He opens the heavy curtains, banishing the darkness from the room, and she asks whether he has finished the job.

He hasn't. He rarely has.

She says nothing, just allows her anger to grow.

The tailor, a thin middle-aged Vietnamese with his untucked shirt hanging loose, who for inexplicable reasons has ended up in this hovel even though he trained with the finest craftsman in Saigon, says something about it being impossible to get hold of the right fabric. Also that Her Highness's creations are extremely complex and consequently take longer than estimated.

He changes in an instant from excuses to enthusiasm when he describes her designs (describing them to her, to the person who drew them). The way the lines run is so intelligent and elegant and inspiring that he lies awake at night thinking about them. It's a privilege to be allowed to work with them.

There is something so innocent about his enthusiasm and honesty that she finds it impossible to know whether he is pulling the wool over her eyes or not.

But she can't help feeling flattered and her annoyance is dispelled when he orders his journeymen (who are clustered in the bedroom door) to fetch tea and the fabrics and a chair. Then he spreads out the designs and the toiles on his cutting table. They bend over the table (she is taller than him) and he asks what she is thinking and she answers and he suggests pale pastel organza, dove-grey tulle, black velveteen. Their mutual respect and intuitive understanding of what the other is proposing brings to mind the dynamic interaction between two jazz musicians. And so she forgives him yet again for having broken his promise to have it ready by today, for it's impossible not to forgive someone who understands things that no one else understands.

*

* *

Perhaps it was the passing of time that solved it, though there is no way she can be sure of that, but every time she smells the odour of mould rising from the clothes she takes from her wardrobe, she is reminded that, in spite of all the compliments, in spite of all the gifts and admiring glances, there was a time when she felt she was concealing *a mound of festering rubbish* behind the *beautiful exterior* that people complimented her on. It was Sar's infectious calm and easy confidence that caused the self-disgust and anxiety she felt, as well as the unnecessary and increasingly problematic lying, to relinquish their hold on her—or if not relinquish it altogether, at least loosen it.

There are still times when she feels that she is not equal to the perceptions people have of her, but instead of drowning in that feeling, instead of becoming incapable of doing anything and sinking lower and lower until days and weeks merge into a fog of apathy and disgust at what she was and what she was not, she is now above that swamp of hopelessness. Not even the confusing uncertainty she feels about her relationship with Sar can upset her in the way it would have done. Instead of crumbling she has taken a grip on herself or, as she sometimes expresses it to herself, she has pulled it all together. She is confident.

The way Sar was.

The way Sar is. But, she thinks, he has become so in a more and more circumscribed way. The *poetic* aspect of him is no longer as apparent as it was before he went to France. His words and the way he says them and puts them together are undoubtedly the same. As is his smile, his overwhelmingly warm and irresistible smile.

But it's as if what lies within can no longer come to the surface, as if he is encased in his new convictions.

It is perhaps my turn to save him this time, Somaly thinks, to save him from himself as he saved me.

*

* *

Even though she has no chips of her own on the table, her eyes are fixed on the little white ivory ball spinning clockwise in the roulette wheel. The ball's journey comes to a halt and it settles into one of the pockets. The croupier calls the result and distributes the winnings and collects the losses. The faces around the table show no emotion, they remain closed in concentration and their hands place new chips quite mechanically.

She presses her wrists discreetly against the ice-filled glass she received a moment ago. Strangely enough the man who sent it over to her has disappeared. Initially she had turned down the cocktail the waiter brought, but she changed her mind once she realized that the sender was one of the destitutes who'd had to hire a pair of shoes from the Chinaman in the side street by the casino in order to be allowed in. Anyone as desperate as that would probably take it to be a good omen if she accepted a drink. And there was something disarming about his face; not that it was attractive per se, but it had a kind of immediacy she found sympathetic. He had not, however, gone so far as to ask her to bring him luck by touching his chips or anything like that. Just twisted his features into an elated or, more accurately, ecstatic smile when she nodded her thanks, after which he disappeared into the motley patchwork of jacketed backs crowded around the tables.

She asks Voisanne about Mei and Nana. They, too, have been swallowed up by the crowd and the smoky darkness of the room that is lit only by the pale light of the globe lamps. Neither the decorations on the walls nor the mouldings on the ceiling can be made out properly. And an odour of sweat and apprehension cuts through the overpowering smell of smoke.

She feels the alcohol spreading its familiar sense of well-being, making her hands slightly numb. From her position halfway up the flight of stairs, she is able to survey the stage below and follow the small dramas and side plots. The roulette table is surrounded mainly by more affluent fortune-seekers of Chinese descent, whereas the people who don't even possess shoes of their own are throwing dice over near one of the long sides of the room. Behind her, lined up along the brass and mahogany bar or sitting in armchairs, there are the Europeans who are taking a rest from their forays out among the other gamblers. The calls of the croupiers cut through the low hum of voices, the rattle of roulette and dice and the shuffling of cards.

She tries to put herself in the position of the poor people at the dice table and to imagine how they experience the evening she is sharing with them. Their modest bets, which are probably equivalent to many days' toil on a cyclo, at the brickworks or with tangled fishing nets at night. Families waiting for them in rundown apartments or hovels on the outskirts of the city. It's a viewpoint that Sar frequently urges her to see things from and she is glad to do so: she has always felt a particular warmth for people who own nothing. She is in complete agreement with him that they deserve something different. But she has never been given a good explanation of why that should simultaneously have an impact on her own welfare. However desirable it might be, where in the whole world does a society like that exist? She was amazed when Sar wrote from Paris that the people sweeping the streets were white people. Her amazement was then replaced by the insight—both depressing and uplifting—that not even a country as rich and grand as France was capable of caring for everyone.

But actually, as Somaly herself realizes, her feelings of empathy with the worst-off men here, with those who will never be saved from poverty by the dice, is a result of her own father's protracted downward journey, which ended with him being one of them.

Voisanne interrupts her train of thought by asking (at last) about the previous evening. She knows that her girlfriends have been expecting her to say something, which is why she has refrained from doing so. Now she shrugs her shoulders and says it was nothing more and nothing less than *un petit caprice*. The expectant expression that shows around Voisanne's eyes and mouth does not go away. But, my dear, her friend presses her, how *petit*? The Chinese fellow didn't come back, you know, after accompanying you so demonstratively from the *soirée*.

He didn't, did he? she answers with a level of carelessness that she realizes could be interpreted as being intentional. Which is why she adds the truth, that he had escorted her to the car and not a centimetre further.

Voisanne asks, *but why* and Somaly shrugs her shoulders and smiles rather stupidly (as she supposes).

Her friend duly smiles a smile of resignation, like someone who has hoped against her better judgement and, consequently, has no problem in accepting that her hope is dashed. She understands Voisanne. There is no doubting that her friend would like to see her depart from the straight and narrow, but her unambiguous denial puts a stop to the quiet but titillating speculations that have run from one end to the other of her friends' telephone wires. She is in no doubt at all that they will continue to gossip in her absence, but there won't be the same enthusiasm now that the facts are known.

Mei and Nana appear. For a moment they seem to her to be creatures from another world in their beautiful, expensive dresses, the energy inherent in their beauty manifesting itself in every movement, their *self-assurance*. Mei slim and dazzlingly pale. Nana rather more robust but beautiful from every side. Both of them looking superior to anyone else present.

Nana's cigarette is hanging from the corner of her mouth which, Somaly thinks, makes an impression that is rather more than coquettishly decadent. But thanks to the drinks they have taken they have already dropped the cool attitude they are usually at pains to convey. Instead of being distant and unattainable they are now superior but emancipated.

There is no sign of the Monsieur de Cornet who was Nana's escort and their excuse for coming to the casino. Nana had met him for the first time the evening before and doesn't know him any better than that. He is more than twice Nana's age, but it had been flattering to receive such an immediate and unconditional invitation to an evening at the casino from a man who was so obviously affluent and respected, as well as being of noble descent. He did not, however, show more than a fleeting, if polite, interest in them which, between themselves, they acidly ascribed to impotence or homosexuality. So it wasn't any great disappointment to them when he quickly found more agreeable company. They were, in any case, drinking on his account.

Nana seems to her to be even more high-spirited than she usually is. Perhaps to compensate for her disappointment about Monsieur de Cornet? Or perhaps just relief at having escaped him?

Somaly herself feels more and more strongly that the evening needs to take a different turn. Coming to the casino was unexpected in a predictable kind of way, but now they feel locked into something that really is just a repetition of things they are all too familiar with. So she suggests a dance bar, not because she has any great desire to go to such an unsophisticated establishment but because they will create a bigger stir there than anywhere else.

The others are drunk enough to be enthusiastic and they are in the habit of going along with Somaly's ideas anyway. (Thinking about it on her own during an ordinary afternoon, she finds their complaisance and lack of initiative irritating. But now, wrapped as she is in the sweet and warm *now* of alcohol, she thinks it is absolutely self-evident she should be the one to lead them.)

She shares a cyclo with Mei. The warm damp night air is wonderfully clean after the fog of smoke in the casino. All the odours suddenly separate, become individual and verge on the intrusive. They have taken their drinks with them and they carry on a shouted conversation with

297

Nana and Voisanne in the other cyclo. The city around them is silent and closed, the avenue empty. She puts her head back and looks up through the branches of the trees at the glittering stars passing slowly overhead. Is it not strange, she thinks (her thoughts floating like feathers), that she is never happier than when on the move from one place to another?

They draw up in front of the entrance to a bar called the Diamond Elephant. The street stretches empty in both directions before disappearing into the darkness. Outside the bar stands a double row of bicycles, guarded by a lanky shadow leaning against a tree.

Through the tall iron palings of the fence they can see symmetrically laid out tables, their white marble tops reflecting the harsh blue-white light of the strip lighting.

The clientele consists mainly of men of their own age. All of them are neatly dressed, wearing coloured shirts with ties that seem to have been picked at random. Their lack of elegance, she thinks, never fails to be *astounding*. They are well turned out, well washed, hair slicked back with water, but no more than that.

Three musicians are standing on a low stage, each of them wearing a sea-green blazer of a different cut and in a different shade. Waiting in silence, smoking. Beyond them there are a couple of tables occupied by girls who used to be in the Royal Ballet. They are ready to dance with anyone prepared to pay.

As expected, every head in the place turns to look at them as they enter. A slovenly waiter shows them to a table close to the stage and, as she follows the waiter with consciously languid steps, Somaly loses all her sophistication for an instant and revels in being the centre of everyone's attention. As if in a dream she is both present in herself at the same time as observing herself from outside. She and her friends, their gleaming foreign sheath dresses, their pale skin and perfectly applied make-up, have clearly descended from realms that the clientele in a place like this have only read about in *Réalités Cambodgiennes*.

They are served cheap beer in tall glasses filled with ice and she finds the vulgarity of it all wonderful.

The owners of the restaurant—they, too, are Chinese—are sitting at the next table entering figures in various columns. Their backs are turned to the customers. There is a small gong on the table with the accounts and when one of the Chinese strikes it with a pencil, the small orchestra gets ready. The musicians scan the tables with a bored and indifferent look and, encouraged by his companions, a plump young man approaches the guitarist. They come to an agreement and the young man steps up to the solitary microphone in the middle of the stage.

There is scattered applause from his friends and he smiles nervously but strangely self-confidently at her table. The guitarist plays a few introductory phrases (the subtlety of their emotional quality contrasting with the *tristesse* signalled by his shrunken figure). The young man is a good singer and she feels a wave of goodwill wash over her. The quality of his full brown baritone is such that she feels she is hearing Tino Rossi's *Au pays de l'amour* in a new way, whereas usually the memory of Rossi's original cuts mercilessly through every thin tenor who tries to imitate the master.

Au pays de l'amour / Venez, venez, venez / le ciel est bleu / on est heureux la vie est belle.

She thinks her taste has changed, that love songs have started to describe how things really are.

When he sings of the heart as a powder keg, he turns towards her table in a theatrical way to the accompaniment of whistles and roars of laughter from his friends.

His audacity brings a flush to her cheeks and a flash of indignation runs through her veins. If she had been sober she would have been able to regain the advantage by giving *a dazzling smile*. But the distance between one emotion and another is too small at present. Instead, she turns back to her girlfriends, turning her back on the stage. (But the gesture is far too demonstrative and is consequently one more small but frustrating defeat.)

The discoloured marble tabletop, the beer bottles, the glasses in which the ice has melted. The ugly light from the strip lighting. She tries without any success to fall in with her friends' frivolous mood and to shrug off her low spirits.

Nana says, without lowering her (now intoxicated) voice, don't you get the urge to seduce that sort of jumped-up twerp? Just because it would be *so utterly unthinkable*.

Nana has unintentionally touched on a topic Somaly has frequently thought about and even written about. She has considered, for instance, the extremely proper cashier at the bank, the garbage collector with the evil eyes, the self-righteous foreman on *Maman*'s plantation. And if anyone were to ask her whether she included Sary in that category she wouldn't have been able to give an immediate answer. That he doesn't belong in that category *now* is absolutely certain, but what about the first time she saw him? A married man, sixteen years older than her, with five children and notorious for his womanizing? She is glad that she is not alone in recognizing that attraction can arise when the odious coincides with the forbidden. But she overcomes the impulse to agree with Nana's little *confession*. To admit to quite such a prejudicial desire would be to bare her soul and she is not in the mood for that sort of intimacy. Nor do the others let themselves be drawn, so Nana is left sitting with a fixed smile on her face in the heavy silence that follows.

Mon amour, mon amour / Ces deux mots sont très courts / On les dit et redit tous les jours / J'ai deux mots dans mon coeur.

Some of the guests have hired dancing partners. They are not dancing *à l'occidentale* but in the traditional style, a few steps away from one another and with graceful hand movements. The women with the expressionless faces they learnt at the ballet, their partners drunk and leering, commenting shamelessly on the bodies in front of them.

It is tediously provincial.

She tries again to regain her earlier carefree mood, but now that she is in the grip of low spirits she is afflicted by the old feeling that she is wasting her life in the wrong part of the world. Week after week, *soirée* after *soirée*, all peopled by the same mediocrities and in the company of the same ridiculous little entourage of old school friends.

With people who are prepared to put up with it.

And what is *she* doing here?

She suddenly feels a wave of nausea, which turns into a shivering fit that makes the skin on her arms break out in gooseflesh. Fortunately, it passes. But she is left with the uncertainty of whether that was the end of it or just a presentiment.

Voisanne says, let's get out of here, Nana can stay with her fatty if she wants to.

Yes, Nana says, in the same loud voice as before. To *Florida*!

The nightclub is owned by one of *Maman*'s cousins and his French wife, who refuses to speak her mother tongue these days. If the whole business hadn't become so childish she would have considered going with them. But her alcoholic elation has turned sour now and the thought of more beer at a shady dance hall disgusts her.

If only she knew where Sary was she could go there.

An idea which, on reflection, she drops. This is not the time, and nor is she in a condition, to seek him out.

So what is left of the evening?

She stands up and has the dizzy sensation of the floor rising to meet her. But then everything stays still. And she walks towards the exit through a narrow tunnel of voices, music and dazzling strip lights.

SUNDAY, 18 SEPTEMBER 1955

The shutters are already open when she wakes. The scent of lilies is overpowering. She thinks that Kunthea is going to have to burn that disgusting bouquet.

Her night's sleep was brought to an end by a different smell, one that arose from the drains in the street after torrential rain. It had forced her to breathe through her mouth. At first she had been surprised that a smell could wake her, then she had become more and more desperate. And as always when the underground pipes flooded, cockroaches came up in their dozens through the sinks and drains.

She lay there in the pitch-dark breathing the sickening smell, listening to cockroaches scuttling blindly round the room.

Now she neither wants to get up nor to stay in bed. No longer is it the sickness of the night, now it's the sickness of the last few mornings closing ever more insistently around her.

And in spite of sleeping so soundly for much of the night, the weight of her weariness is overpowering.

It occurs to her that it's almost two weeks since that trip to the casino at Kep-sur-Mer. She wonders: how can time seem so long and yet so short?

The restaurant of Le Club Nautique had been closed but she'd still been able to walk out along the shrunken boards of the long wooden pier. Faded pennants twisted in the wind. Where the pier ended the sky and the sea seemed the same size. Pale grey. Milk white.

Through the foliage she had caught a glimpse of lawns and of more houses in the same light modern colours. Private swimming pools, an empty tennis court.

He had gone by the time she woke. That hadn't bothered her. She spent the morning at the deserted clubhouse, which was built on stout pillars high above the water. When the first rain of the day began to fall, she sat at one of the tables and watched the world around her dissolve in the cloudburst.

She thought she made far too few trips to the coast. She had the same thought whenever she saw the sea.

Then she had sat on the pier, thinking of them lying in silence in the darkness afterwards. The way every sound had seemed magnified and distinct. As if the sounds were only there for them. The surge of the waves, the insects, the frogs.

The moonlight through the window had been so bright that it formed a silver square on the floor. Beside it lay a silver wedge of light falling through the half-open door. They had stayed close to one another in spite of the heat. Forehead to forehead.

The hardness of the underlying bone, the sweat on the thin layer of skin there. His closed eyes. A moment of rapture, outside time. No more than a little blood and a layer of bone separating our thoughts just then. But it didn't help, of course: it was impossible to know what he was thinking. It always is. He could have been somewhere else entirely, and with someone quite different. He could have been betraying her utterly while lying just a centimetre away from her thoughts. And such thoughts, blissful thoughts.

Kunthea knocks, enters, asks if she can clean the room now.

She says she can.

Her eyes move from the girl and her palm-leaf broom and come to rest again on the small, thin-skinned, almost transparent lizards up on the ceiling. She thinks that it's a month since she last saw Sar. He feels very far away. Further than just a month. The time since he came home seems unreal, almost as if it is something she has invented. She remembers something Monsieur Hanin told her on some now forgotten occasion. He said that in his homeland stories always began with "Once there was, once there wasn't". That seems to her so much more beautiful and so much more comforting than the absolute nature of the French opening, "Once upon a time there was". She thinks that once there was, once there wasn't a fiancé who came back from a far country. And then what will be will be.

*

*   *

Only the rich can afford to marry for love. That is another of Sar's statements that has *lodged* in her mind, against her will. The words are meaningful in a self-righteous kind of way, their import stays the same however much they are moved around. She finds it irritating, not least because it was Sar (in the days when he often talked about things other than politics) who pointed out that most of what she says or thinks consists of words and phrases she has heard or read. Whatever she thinks, she ends up using other people's ready-made structures. It is not that she has any ambition to revolutionize human thinking, it's just that there is something joyless about that particular insight. Like wearing faded second-hand clothes.

Only when drunk does she feel any release from this intellectual straitjacket. It seems that there needs to be an endless row of champagne cocktails lined up in front of her and for her to fill the table with empty glasses before she can tear herself free from the linguistic stranglehold and express her innermost thoughts without restriction.

And, she asks herself, isn't passionate love, as described by *Maman*'s friends after the film they watched together, rather similar? A structure that locks you into a pattern.

To be permitted to marry for love has long been a goal, a battle she has fought, but what, she now thinks, what would actually be the point? Wouldn't it imply capitulation, self-destruction? And what would be left of her and her ambitions then? Even if she can, so to speak, afford it, can she really afford to subordinate herself to love?

Because it's a structure that even champagne would be hard put to make any impression on.

*

* *

Mother's voice through the rooms. A question that isn't a question. Somaly studies the face she has created in the mirror, shouts that she is coming at once. Immediately. At once. Her starting point had been Vivien Leigh's Egyptian princess, but it has turned into something else. Exaggerated. That's what always happens when she doesn't have a particular purpose in mind.

She washes her face in the basin. Wipes everything off and starts again. She must keep it simple. The lines of her eyes and mouth. And then go and satisfy *Maman*'s desire for company. It will be a welcome interruption and one that rarely involves more than just being in the same room. And the post should have brought her magazines by now.

Through the open windows of the dining room she can see Kunthea out on the covered veranda slowly folding the washing that has been hanging there since morning. Out beyond Kunthea the afternoon light is turning to the gold that precedes darkness. She enquires about the papers and is told brusquely that they are where they always are.

The rest of the day's deliveries are on the table by the front door, between two armchairs of dark polished wood. As expected, there are red roses accompanied by a card in Sar's handwriting. She doesn't read it, picking up a square package instead. Wrapped in violet paper with a beautiful golden pattern on it. In the small attached envelope is a greeting signed by the Chinese man from last Friday's *soirée*. The paper encloses a simple metal box containing China tea. Judging by the seal it is exclusive tea. What a bizarre present, she thinks. She looks through the other flowers in an absent-minded way. She doesn't know the people who sent them. Nothing original, just everyday congratulatory phrases and the usual unimaginative praise of *her unique beauty*. Everything seems to have been written in the secret and unnerving hope that she will reply. One young man—young to all appearances, anyway—has even enclosed a small photographic portrait. A touch of the film star. Dark suit and a wave of glossy hair. He has been taken in half-profile, smiling, his mouth closed (probably to conceal bad teeth, she thinks). She drops the photograph and picks up a twig of temple flowers with yellowish white petals that shade over to reddish violet at the centre. No wrapping, nothing but the solitary twig. An Indian custom, perhaps, she thinks, seeing the name Klein, the cultural attaché, on the card. He writes that he *insists on a rendezvous as a matter of urgency* since there are *important issues* involved.

Klein's insistence certainly raises the spirits anyway, she thinks.

Through the doorway she can see the new housekeeper preparing dinner. Watches her bony hands gripping the slippery pale body of a squid, sees the knife slicing through the flesh. The sight makes her feel sick. She picks up one of the presents, a box of candied fruit that also fills her with nausea, and asks whether the housekeeper would like it. For her children? She does have children? The woman smiles, nods, thanks her *most humbly*.

The papers are on the counter. She takes the package addressed to her and moves on into the drawing room.

She sits at the table, gently smoothing out the cover of the magazine with the woman in the bright yellow sundress and thinking if only I could be as pale as the foreigners. She hasn't gone beyond the first page yet. It has become a monthly ritual, which she usually manages to stick to, to wait until evening before abandoning herself to all the beautiful pictures of beautiful people in beautiful clothes.

Brigitte Bardot is on the cover (*SI ELLE LIT ELLE LIT ELLE*) again. On closer inspection the yellow dress has white spots. The photograph was taken looking diagonally down, with Bardot sitting on a red floor and leaning on a grey wall. The dress is spread out and her petticoat is visible, as are her shoes and naked calves. The context seems to Somaly to be an essentially private one, unlike the photograph of the actress in an evening dress on last November's cover. Bardot is cuddling a grey tabby cat and her eyes meet Somaly's.

They are almost the same age and she wonders whether they could be friends. They might perhaps meet in Paris and get to know one another. That is, if Bardot would have anything to do with *natives*.

The theme of the number is relaxation, which she finds disappointing since she knows everything there is to know about tedium.

To spin things out a little longer she lights a cigarette. Takes a sip of the sweet red wine her mother has poured for her. An advertisement for cherry pralines takes up the back page of the magazine. *Mon chéri*. She smiles at the wordplay and thinks I ought to send some of them to someone at some point.

Her mother is sitting curled up on the velvet sofa with a small limp-covered book in her hand.

A car can be heard approaching outside. To judge by the sound of the engine, it slows down as it passes and then speeds up again as it departs.

It's a starless night. The rain is holding off.

She has tried to follow her mother's example and read novels, but she finds it hard to keep her interest going for the whole of a long book. And she can't remember the plot afterwards anyway. Film is obviously much more her medium, though certain passages or episodes in novels do stick in her mind. Like the one where a man and a woman have an extramarital affair. The unfaithfulness, if it can be called that, is limited to the two of them deciding what underwear the other should wear when they meet to share innocent meals at restaurants. No kisses, no embraces, just the knowledge that each has decided what the other will be wearing next to their body. She finds something peculiarly sensual in this curious behaviour. But the rest of the novel has been completely wiped from her memory.

She has a sudden urge to share this little story, hoping perhaps to understand better why she remembers it and has forgotten the rest. She hesitates several times before interrupting her mother's reading.

Her mother's expression changes from distant to amused. Which novel is she referring to? She confesses that she doesn't know and regrets having broached the topic. Her mother says she would like to read it and Somaly can't decide whether she is being ironic or not. Her mother goes on: I really think you would like what I'm reading at the moment. It was written by a French girl who is only nineteen but has an impressive ear for psychological subtleties. Its sales run into the hundreds of thousands.

She asks (with a touch of envy) what a woman that young could write that Mother of all people would find enlightening?

They top up their glasses and Mother nods in the direction of the cover of the magazine. *Even Brigitte Bardot reads novels.* Somaly looks at the photograph again and notices now that Bardot's left hand is resting on a book she has perched on her knee. And on the floor there is a small stack of volumes of various sizes. A half-empty glass is sitting on top of the pile. She feels annoyed to have been caught out, even though her mother can't know that she hadn't noticed all the books on the cover.

Her mother sits down again and, with her eyes on her book, says that the main character is supposed to be spending the summer studying for her matriculation exam. Maybe it would be a good idea for Somaly to pick up her studies again?

She doesn't know what to answer. Once her mother has decided something, that something happens. For lack of any other way of delaying her mother's mind from moving towards such an unwanted decision, she says in an acid tone that she would have been only too happy to do that five years ago when she was still going to school: she wasn't the one who had wanted to stop. Her mother carries on reading for a moment before answering in a preoccupied way that it had been a matter of money, as she well knows. Their finances at that point were not what they had been. Their circumstances are different now.

So her attacking move is unsuccessful. She decides on honesty instead and says in a conciliatory tone that it's too late now. She has other plans. Her mother raises her head at that point and says, *I see?*

She takes a breath, looks out of the window instead of at her mother and reminds her what Miss World, Miss Riviera and Miss Elegance said to her. Then she talks about her thoughts of France and about the invitations she has had and those that will undoubtedly come. About Paris and the possibility that one day there could be a fashion house bearing the family name.

She looks back at her mother who, in her turn, is studying her. There is a long, almost unbearable pause and then her mother makes a quick movement with her mouth before returning to her novel.

*

* *

She has just heard the car slow down as it passed. Again. It's pointless: all the lights are out, she is already in bed, hidden from view. Whoever it is at the wheel will have to drive on disappointed.

She is tired, too tired to read but still unable to get to sleep. Her thoughts will simply not be at rest; they tug at their chains, stamp restlessly, anxiously. The night outside is silent again, apart from the insects and the old gecko up in the roof lining.

It's very annoying, because she has already become accustomed to this new sort of sleep that washes over her the moment she puts her head on the pillow. That fills her head with convincing colourful dreams. It would also give her some relief from this vague nagging ache which has settled in just below her navel.

The darkness in the room is complete and it seems it might last for ever.

The thought of Sar comes into her mind. The difference in him when he returned from France. He wasn't a new person, for the most part he was just as before, but still. There was a new self-assurance about him, a kind of distance that came at the expense of the vulnerable, almost childlike quality she used to find so attractive. And the part of him that had earlier been tentative and seeking had ossified into certainty. His objection to injustice—a seemingly natural part of his character—had turned into an obsession with justice that…

Indeed, how best to put it?

… that seemed more important than every other consideration? It has become a rule that allows no exception?

She doesn't know why she finds it so maddening. To some degree frightening even, in fact. It only deals in absolutes, and there is an iron-bound answer to every objection.

His earlier attitude (permissive, questioning) has disappeared almost completely.

Instead of filling her with enthusiasm, as it almost certainly would have done a few years ago, it merely increases her desire to tear it down. To destroy it utterly. To erase that self-sufficient smile from his complacent face.

But why?

Is it because he left her and when he came back he was someone else? Or is it because of her inability to share his vision wholeheartedly, to become part of a community that she finds intolerable because of its rigidity and because of its insistence that she should be the one to adapt on point after point after point? Or are all these things merely excuses to cover the fact that she herself has changed?

If you cannot even be sure about your own inner world (which, after all, is in a state of perpetual movement, so that what seemed to be a guiding star can easily turn out to be no more than a will-o'-the-wisp leading you astray), how is it possible to be so *confident* about how the external world with its countless unpredictable inhabitants and circumstances should be organized?

But without all that, what is there left apart from loneliness?

MONDAY, 19 SEPTEMBER 1955

More roses from Sar and she wonders where his imagination, his finesse, has gone? Does he believe that if he just keeps sending more bouquets the whole business will be resolved (as if the problem is one of too few roses)?

Red roses. Always the same dark shade and probably, she thinks, from the same florist in the Old Market. She strokes the silky half-open buds and wonders whether deep, deep down in the capillaries of the petals the flower knows it has been cut. Red, firm, they spring back when she squeezes them. Almost animal. A slightly musty, earthy smell.

She recalls that it was Monsieur Joly, her French tutor, who first pointed out to her that all the flowers in beautiful arrangements are dead. At that time, almost ten years ago, she had been horrified, finding it both sad and macabre. Now, however, she feels it enhances their beauty. She rarely thinks of him these days, the jovial professor with the paunch whose job it was to educate her and her brother in all things French. He was different from the teachers at school who demanded that their pupils could repeat the sentences on the blackboard word-perfect. Monsieur Joly encouraged them instead to reason their way to a solution of the problems he laid before them. But he also considered it appropriate to extend his mandate to include the more philosophical aspects of biology. Particularly when she was alone with him, when her brother was occupied studying other things. Initially, Monsieur Joly restricted himself to ad hoc comments, such as the one about the dead roses which everyone thought of as being alive. But without departing from his elegant academic didacticism the professor then moved on to human anatomy, more specifically to that of the male, and even more specifically to that of the male organ (his own). One afternoon, when instruction included *ocular inspection*, it all got too much even for a thirteen-year-old who was well disposed to Monsieur Joly. And that was the end of his employment.

She had found it difficult to understand at that stage. But with a decade's experience behind her she knows that men who say they want to show her their amazing collection of art, or a unique but unfamiliar beauty spot, or—as in the case of Monsieur Joly—*the dubious relationship between man and nature*, or—as another Frenchman put it—*his immortal soul*, actually only want to show her their erections.

She suddenly remembers that when Monsieur Joly came to tutor them at home in the evening, he used to stay to dinner in order to discuss the latest French literature with *Maman*. She finds it vexing that she will never be able to bring herself to ask her mother whether she and Monsieur Joly stuck to the subject on those occasions.

*

*   *

She brings the tips of her fingers to her nose. A hint of eau-de-cologne and something else. Sweat? She presses them gently to her lips, which still feel warm and swollen.

She carries on smoking the cigarette he gave her and looking out at the streets, the frontages, the few people being picked out by the pale white light of the headlamps as they pass.

The driver drives steadily, carefully. His broad dark shoulders above the seat back.

She suggested to Sary that she should leave the hotel first, him perhaps a quarter of an hour later. Or that he should wait for an extra half hour in order to forestall any suspicions. He dismissed her concerns with amusement, moving restlessly around the room while tying his tie. As if the hour they had spent together had supercharged him.

She thought that he looked happy there. Their eyes had met while he was straightening his jacket in the mirror. With a playful glint.

So they left at the same time, handed in the key to the night porter together, stepped out onto the street arm in arm. And, she thinks, she can't get enough of this frivolousness. This madness. She does, of course, recognize that they are being foolhardy, but it feels as if it's impossible for anything bad to happen to him. Or to her when she is with him.

The station building, its lights off, was on the left when they came out. The railway park stretched away for a kilometre on the right.

The half moon layered the darkness in various degrees of dark. The odd shadowy figure showed up on the pavement, sitting outside closed shops, squinting out over the station square.

Then a cyclo crossed in front of them. For a moment she thought she could pick out the driver's face in the gently swaying light of the paraffin lamp. The man had met her eyes without any expression in his. Then he had crossed the boulevard and continued along the park (which had once been a canal and was the place her parents had met). His unbuttoned light shirt receded like a ghost before being swallowed by the night.

She had stood there, pulse racing, watching the image of his broad nose and thin lips shrink in the distance. It was the same man, wasn't it, whom she had seen before, on several occasions? Was she being stalked? By whom? She very nearly said something to Sary, but he hadn't noticed anything. He was still in a state of carefree sensuality. She let him lead her impatiently to the car that was parked discreetly round the corner. He told her the driver would take her home and he would walk. She had tried to refuse. It's not right for one of the most powerful men in the kingdom to be out on foot in the city at night. Nor is it safe. But she was still feeling uneasy about the cyclo man. Perhaps she was imagining it all and it was just chance? But she was reluctant to take a cyclo, which would take a good while to get her home, and so she accepted the offer of the car without any further objections. Sary said to the driver pick me up afterwards, gave him an address and shut the door behind her.

Half-lying on the back seat she allows herself to sink back into the afterglow of alcohol and the hotel bed. (And of that momentary sensation of a piece of ice running through her body from the soles of her feet to the crown of her head.) In a half trance and from the safety of the car, she can watch the world outside the windows. The flickering of the treetops against the starry sky.

She thinks that he too is on the move, albeit in a different direction, and she wishes she had left the mark of a bite somewhere on his body. Or let her nails scratch his skin until it bled. There would have been consequences, but he would no longer have been able to deny her. Not to Em and, above all, not to himself.

In this unstructured flow of thought, tomorrow begins to emerge. She tries to remember what it contains. Is it a special Tuesday? Is there something she has agreed to do? She doesn't have an answer. The day opens out on the far side of the night and is pleasantly without shape. She feels, though, that she wants to see Sary again: at a fashionable cocktail reception together, followed by a late visit to a restaurant, and then the hotel again. The hotel yet again. But she remembers she has agreed to have dinner with Voisanne, Nana and the others. He will probably be busy anyway. If not, she can always meet him when she has finished with her friends.

He isn't her first lover. She had a number of lovers during the years Sar was away. But they were always casual affairs and never with men who live in the city. Why did she break her promise to Sar, whom she loved so devotedly? The answer is the simplest imaginable: just in order to break it.

However much she had wanted to hold to their agreement, the temptation of the forbidden was stronger. The emotional experience of breaking her promise was so much more intense than sticking to what was expected of her, sticking to uncomplicated *chastity*.

And once she had given in to it, new and unknown experiences were revealed and had to be tested.

Take the odour of skin, for instance. How different her men have smelt behind their soap and aftershave. There was the young French adventurer who was visiting the country with his even younger wife in order to hunt tiger. When she got close to him she was overpowered by the strong spicy odour he gave off. It bordered on the repellent, was as pungent as that of an animal, but it had nothing to do with a lack of hygiene. It was his natural scent. Which was why she absolutely had to have him. The first and second times it was amazingly exciting, but after their third encounter she threw away the clothes she had been wearing because the smell had begun to disgust her. She thinks of Sar's smell, which is dry and pleasant. It reminds her of dried petals. And Sary's? For want of a better description, his is *distinctive*, like cinnamon. And Somaly thinks that someone else might react to it as she did to the Frenchman's smell. But she thinks it would be impossible to grow tired of it.

She asks the driver for another cigarette. He passes her a packet of Red Club without taking his eyes off the road. She then asks him, without really thinking about it, what kind of place is the address Sary gave him. The driver laughs and says it's not his place to say anything about it. If she wants information of that sort, Miss will have to ask His Excellency herself.

If she had been in a different frame of mind his answer would have annoyed her, but now she doesn't let it worry her. She thinks that if she is ever in a position to employ a driver of her own, she wouldn't be pleased either if he answered a question of that sort.

That thought leads her to start fleshing out the future she envisages for herself. In a few months' time she may be sitting in a French taxi on her way through a city pulsing with nightlife and flashing neon signs. Alone, or perhaps sitting beside new friends? When that time comes, how will she remember tonight's journey through sleeping streets with no street lights and just the stars above? She will feel nothing but joy at leaving most of this behind. A joy bordering on contempt. But she also thinks that now, as things are just now, she is in fact utterly content. However hopelessly tangled everything is at present, she may well find herself hankering after this moment.

The car slows down, turns right and drives along the long straight street that leads to her house. All that is left is one more left turn and then a couple of blocks. She opens her handbag to check in her mirror that she is presentable. Her cigarette case is there, too, along with the money from Sary, the notes new and smooth. When she opens the cigarette case she sees it is half empty. But the driver's cheap cigarettes add to the special feeling of the moment, and she asks for one more and leans over the seat back to get a light.

A sudden impulse causes her—against her will—to turn her head and look out of the rear window. There is no cyclo in sight, just darkness. And the road unrolling behind them in the weak red glow of the rear lights.

TUESDAY, 20 SEPTEMBER 1955

With the tip of the nail of her index finger she traces the narrow black line around the photographs on the cover of the magazine. She looks down into them, seeing smoky crowded bars in which young women and men are leaning forward and gesticulating as they talk. She sees the bare brick of a low vaulted cellar in which a sweating band is playing, the sharp outline of their own shadows on the wall behind. She sees dancing couples frozen in strange poses with ecstatic expressions on their faces.

Brigitte Bardot is standing outside a restaurant, smiling together with someone called Albert Camus (as she discovers from the text).

Her own outside consists of dazzling white light and deserted afternoon streets. The humid heat is pressing down on the city, squeezing all life out of it. The soft rumble of distant thunder. In the photographs in front of her, however, it always seems to be night or a sort of greyish dusk. The next picture: a wide boulevard dissolves into darkness and mist, the weak globe lights of the street lamps resembling a lonely line of abandoned lighthouses.

She hates the powerful longing that these pictures awaken in her, the way their emotional magnetism sucks out infinite quantities of energy while giving her nothing but emptiness in return. She wants to be part of that world that both Sar and Sary learnt to know thanks to their royal scholarships. Neither of them, however, was clever enough to take advantage of the possibilities: Sar says he prioritized *political meetings*, Sary *his studies*. As if it isn't just as easy to devote yourself to politics and books here, she thinks.

Her wardrobe with all her beautiful clothes, all the small jars on her dressing table, all the eyes on her at *soirées*. Spending your time on things like that makes existence bearable. But the photographs in the magazines reveal something very different from polite conversations about familiar and harmless things, from the constantly repeated appearance of the same faces, from the oh-so-familiar social structures. And now even political change seems to be off the agenda, so everything will continue as before.

Nana was talking recently about a dinner with her parents and her father's business acquaintances. For no reason at all the wife of one of the guests told them about a miscarriage she had suffered and what a distressing time it had been afterwards. Nana pulled a disapproving face as she recounted the story. So utterly unsuitable, Nana insisted, *it completely spoilt the atmosphere.*

That's just it, she thinks, nothing of any significance can be discussed. Only what is safe and inoffensive is permissible.

And while that is happening here, the café tables in the cellar over there witness heated discussions on the very nature of existence, while one band follows another onto the stage! Long night after long night the fashion studios teem with models, with genius and with champagne. A world that she cannot be sure of gaining entry to, but one which is irresistibly desirable and where she will find—she searches for the right term—*the real thing.*

That, she thinks, that is the place where what happens happens.

At the same time, however, she recognizes that her image of Parisian life has more to do with the photographs in the illustrated monthly magazines than with reality. Just as the clientele in the dance restaurants of her home city do not have access to the beautiful venues she is at home in, she knows that the majority of Parisians live their lives without ever coming into contact with the nocturnal universe she perceives as being *the real thing*. But the distinction is this: the division here is on the basis of birth and wealth, there it is a matter of talent. And she thinks, in spite of her uncertainty as to whether she is up to it, that if she were ever to find herself sitting alone in the Café de Flore, some young man with a pale brow and a riot of brown curls would immediately invite her to a *vernissage* or to a wild masked ball or to a nightclub *réservé aux membres*. Once there she would be introduced to new and fascinating acquaintances and would quickly become part of a small and intimate group of girlfriends, who accompany each other through the unpredictable adventures of night. The difference between them and her current companions being that all the new ones would be enviably talented.

She looks over at her mother who has fallen asleep in her armchair. In relaxation her face looks older. Ink stains on her fingers like an accountant. There was a time when she used to wonder how her mother put up with these petty circumstances. One way of dealing with them is no doubt provided by all the novels and the various forms of escapism they have to offer. But she has come to recognize that her mother, in spite of her intelligence and her offhand attitude, is firmly ensconced in her milieu. That any break with the narrow boundaries drawn around life here would probably be neither welcome nor possible for her. This is where *Maman* belongs. To *seem* to be destined for something different is actually what Mother is destined for. Or at least chooses to be.

*

* *

The neon sign flashes out the restaurant's name in red French, green Chinese and pale-blue Khmer. Large clay pots with plants poking out of them form a small avenue running up to the entrance. A couple of cyclo drivers are squatting on their haunches by the door, engrossed in a low-voiced conversation with the uniformed doorman.

It is a clear dry evening and the gravel crunches under her heels as she walks to the door. One of the men nods to draw the doorman's attention to her arrival, and the doorman smiles obligingly, says welcome and opens the door.

For some reason that is the picture that will stay in her mind most clearly afterwards, much more so than what happens later.

*

* *

They are sitting at the one big round table in the restaurant. She is late, she is always late. And they all turn towards her as she arrives. They are Nana and Mei, Voisanne and Mari. Voisanne's brother Phirun and Cédric, his French friend. Pale pastel dresses, high collars and black or gold trimmings. A dark brown suit and an even darker blue one. Welcoming smiles. A light-hearted expectancy in the voices.

There is an element of *making an entrance* about her arrival, she thinks. The way she is suddenly there in front of them, all eyes on her. The way they allow themselves to be interrupted.

There are seven tall glasses of Kir Royale already standing on the table, dishes with thick-sliced sausage, pistachio nuts, fried grasshoppers, potato crisps, green olives.

She sits down and remembers that on the way there she had continued her afternoon train of thought: that her friends lack sophistication. That they willingly put up with circumstances (such as the present ones) that are so far removed from those of the truly metropolitan cities of the world. That they are incapable of stepping beyond the bounds of convention and, indeed, they have no wish to do so. And that now, by allowing herself to be drawn unresisting into their carefree pleasures, she no longer considers that particular thought to be burdensome. They are here now, she is here now and there is no need for anything to be much more significant than that.

Cédric, Phirun's French friend, tells them that he recently experienced something quite improbable. He holds some position at the bottom of the hierarchy in the French Embassy, but they have known him for a long time, from the Lycée Sisowath. She finds him very ordinary, but these days he has that paradoxical mixture of the gravitas that pertains to a diplomatic post and the insubstantiality that arises from inexperience and a juvenile appearance. At first, with his new suits and his topics of conversation, he seemed to her to be playing a stage role, but he becomes more and more of a stranger as he grows into the role. A different person is taking shape, a person who might make a reliable and solid impression on people meeting him for the first time, whereas she, from certain angles anyway, continues to see the schoolboy in him.

Cédric says that he spent last weekend by the sea, at Kep-sur-Mer. He says he was there with acquaintances from various embassies and that he and the daughter of the new Yugoslav ambassador went swimming together. How old she is? Eighteen, perhaps nineteen. Is she pretty? Cut all that. She was wearing a little ivory figure around her neck on a leather thong and she told him she had found it washed up on a beach in Africa. It didn't look much to the world at large but she valued it very highly, saying it brought good luck. Where in Africa? Not clear. Just listen now. As they were swimming she suddenly shouted that she had dropped the amulet. She was absolutely desperate. Absolutely. He says that he fetched his diving mask even though it was completely hopeless. He had no idea where she had been when the leather came undone and the open sea starts there, after all. But, just to be nice, he dived pretty much at random. You couldn't see more than half a metre or so—in other words, the situation was *doubly hopeless*—and once he thought he had done everything that could be expected of a gentleman, he turned towards the shore. But he made one last dive, for its own sake, so to speak, and there it was, half buried in the sand at a depth of a couple of metres! Yes, honestly! Well, he says, as you can imagine, I was nervous and I had to surface first to get some air before I could swim down and dig it up. All it would have taken was the slightest current and I would have been in the wrong place and never found it again. Diplomatic relations between Paris and Belgrade have never been as good as they are now! Phirun says that sounds like a story his uncle the sea captain could have told and, as an example, he tells of his uncle's encounter with a whirlwind. In the Pacific. Or it might have been the Indian Ocean. Well, the crew sighted the whirlwind on the horizon and tried to steer away from it. Too late! The storm struck one side of the vessel and when they went and looked afterwards, all the paint had been stripped from that half of the ship. Polished steel! Whether it's true? *Mais alors.*

She drinks her drink, picks at the dishes. The alcohol is already making her thoughts light, translucent. She wonders vaguely what was so special about the amulet. And what colour the ship was painted afterwards.

Voisanne touches the back of her hand. She feels the touch of cool damp fingers on her skin before she follows her friend's eyes to the entrance.

Immediate recognition, the blood rushes from her head.

It's Sar.

The familiar silhouette, in his usual black suit, his hair impeccably combed. Not striking, but still handsome. She sees his eyes searching and, before his gaze fixes on her and he pushes his way through the tables towards them with a cold hard face, she has time to think that

far from being the hunter, there is actually something of the hunted
about him.

WEDNESDAY, 21 SEPTEMBER 1955

The tennis courts are immediately below the balustrade and through
the pink frame of the bougainvillea, she sees a couple of Europeans
with rackets in their hands. A dozen or so sparkling white balls in
irregular formation on either side of the net. She listens to the sound
of soft thuds alternating with the crump of taut strings and the short
exchanges between the players. In the background there is the laughter
of children at the swimming pool on the other side of the building.
The sky is greyish white and the air stifling. She feels hot and very
listless. Her stomach is troubling her again. She wonders whether she
is coming down with something?

It feels uncomfortable to have people looking nosily in her direction,
even though she knows that outwardly she looks *every bit as radiant as
she always does*. Perhaps she ought to make an appointment with Dr
Siebold? But then she would have to talk to *Maman* first. That's easily
done, of course, but she has no desire to be met with the usual absence
of care and concern. (*Maman* tends to receive news of a temperature/
headache/rash/sore throat with the same mixture of uninterested-
ness and irritation as when some item of domestic equipment or the
plantation lorry needs repairing.)

Now and again she reminds herself that her situation changed
radically the evening before. But it hasn't really sunk in. She thinks:
what exactly is it that's changed? Is it really a lasting change or is it
still merely parenthetical?

To be in the zone of the undecided has become a habit. A habit
that clearly cannot be broken so easily. So she constantly finds herself

falling back into the frame of mind she had been in before, with the same vague recognition that there was something to be decided, something to be settled.

An older French couple is sitting at the next table. The woman is eating soup, the man carefully picking at an omelette. They haven't said a word to each other since they sat down. At first she wondered whether they had just had a quarrel. But there is no tension between them and she becomes more and more convinced that they no longer have anything to say to one another. She thinks that she will never live in the kind of relationship in which all topics of conversation have run out. Her marriage will be an unbroken exchange of thoughts, *a perpetual voyage of discovery into the world of her partner*.

She is not used to sitting waiting like this. But he will come. And until he does she is free to leave whenever she wants to. If only she felt really well, but it will probably pass, soon.

She notices the way her eyes are skimming through the items on the menu. She is hungry, but every item makes her feel slightly nauseous.

The waiter had a message for her when she arrived. Things had come up, he would be anything up to an hour late. But he hoped she would be patient.

With nothing to do, the waiter is now standing by the balustrade looking out over the almost empty car park. It's not like the beauty contest when every car importer in the country had been invited to show off the latest models. And all the guests had arrived by car. That, she thinks, was possibly the first traffic jam this kingdom had experienced. And she remembers that ridiculous part of the contest when each contestant was paired with a man dressed as an animal. "*La Belle et la Bête*". She had been partnered by one of the car importers, a garrulous man of her own age dressed as a turtle. *Trop bête quoi*.

She wonders whether they serve turtle soup? That would be a suitable choice, wouldn't it? She beckons the waiter over and, with a smile, he regrets that they don't. He asks whether she would like anything else and she orders at random a glass of wine and a *Croque monsieur à l'ancienne* as a sort of gesture of defiance to her delicate stomach. And regrets her choice the moment the waiter disappears down the stairs.

The Turtle had invited her out for a drive in his dark-green Mercedes. That year's model. He pointed it out to her. He had needed to, it being so low-slung that it was scarcely possible to pick it out among all the ordinary hulking black models. Its hood was down and its lines made it look as if it were in motion even when it was standing still. To her delight he had offered to let her drive it, with himself as instructor. And carried away by all the cocktails, by being right at the heart of the pageant, by all the beautiful things around her, she had answered with a euphoric yes.

By the following day, however, she had recognized her mistake and avoided answering his suggestions as to when would be a suitable day for their excursion. His telephone calls and postcards ceased after a while, as they always do. Sooner or later everyone's patience runs out.

But her discomfort at the thought of bumping into him at one event or another stayed with her.

Which is why that morning's invitation to inaugurate the new winter collection of *prêt-à-porter* at Petit Paris surprises her. She is sure that the Turtle boasted that he was on the board of the department store. So should this invitation be seen as a renewed approach on his part, or has the whole business of her ignoring his suggestions already been forgotten?

So be it. Modelling at a department store is hardly a grand offer but it is nevertheless a first confirmation of what she herself is convinced of. Still half asleep and feeling distinctly sick she said she would get back to them. (Just getting out of bed felt like an insuperable task.) Now, a couple of hours later, she thinks she will accept the offer. Any career is bound to involve less showy jobs. Especially in the early stages.

The crowning of Miss Cambodia may have been exactly that kind of routine and less attractive task for Miss World, Miss Riviera and Miss Elegance, when they were actually dreaming of rather more sumptuous galas in Hollywood. Every stage in life ought to have its heartfelt desires that contrast with the occasional pettiness of everyday existence. Isn't that so?

She hears the jangling bell of the telephone on the ground floor. She takes the mirror out of her handbag, raises her sunglasses and looks into her own eyes. Unchanged, brown. No visible sign of yesterday evening. Everything is where it should be, everything is as it should be.

She holds the gaze in the mirror, recalling the incomprehensibly contradictory emotions she felt when Sar suddenly appeared in the foyer of the restaurant. A bubble of childish joy at seeing him again at the same time as being paralysed by ice-cold terror. She had wanted to flee, and she had wanted to embrace him. It had been impossible to separate the two impulses. And then she had been unable to understand what he was saying, finding herself transfixed instead by suddenly recognizing the buttons of his suit, the composition of his face, the sight of his pale, slim, beautiful hands that she is so fond of holding. And how strongly she had sympathized with him because of the rage, or was it hatred, or perhaps sorrow, that was in his eyes where love used to be. Confused by the way everything seemed to be happening simultaneously, she had been overwhelmed by the presence of something uncontrollable she had never seen in him before, something that had lain hidden behind his usual friendly dignity. After that everything had gone into slow motion as, in reality, can only happen on film: her friends were rising to their feet and telling him to leave, while he continued to repeat whatever it was he was saying to her. And the intensity, she thinks, did not lie in his words or in the rough way they took hold of his jacket and bundled him out when they thought he was going too slowly, it lay in the way she just sat still and said nothing in spite of all the things she could have said and done. It could all have been prevented, she could have run after him, but she did nothing. The intensity and overpowering nature of her passivity proved insuperable, and she finds it quite impossible now to give a reason why.

The waiter returns with her order. The sight of the toasted bread, melted cheese and glass of red wine makes her feel sick. She needs something light. Something light as air.

For want of a better idea she asks for a glass of champagne and, she adds, a bottle of Vichy water. When the waiter brings that order she realizes that it, too, was a mistake.

She lights a cigarette instead, asks the French couple for the time.

Perhaps she should go to Petit Paris instead and tell them what she has decided? The money from last Monday is still in her handbag and there will doubtless be something she wants once she sees it. And in view of what she is going to tell them, she may be offered a reduction or shown some special item they have been keeping back.

She beckons the waiter over again and says that her delayed companion will take care of the bill when he arrives. And tell him that she can be reached at the department store, or the Café de la Poste, or on the telephone in the evening. He gives a professional nod and says, *but of course, Mademoiselle.*

She asks the doorman at the entrance to get her a cyclo. He, in turn, yells at a boy of school age to get hold of what she has asked for.

She stands in the shade looking at the trees and the green grass of the garden. The scent of damp foliage, the chattering of birds and a passing moped. The sweating tennis players are sitting on the other side of the court and, with an attentive smile, a different waiter is taking their order.

What she would like most is to go home and sleep away this weariness that ordinary sleep seems incapable of remedying.

The boy returns with a well-maintained cyclo, its frame painted red and with a white leather saddle. The driver is an older man in short trousers. He has an unusually stern face. At first he seems almost frightening, but when he asks politely where she wants to go his voice is very deep and has a gentle dark tone.

She settles in her seat, senses the driver's muscles overcoming the inertia of the vehicle and slowly getting it moving. They turn onto Avenue Daun Penh and the soft crunch of sand is replaced by the quiet hum of rubber tyres on asphalt.

epilogue (retake)

The car's headlamps cast a beam of soft yellow light. Fleetingly they pick out the white flash of collar and cuffs and capture the tight arc of an empty cigarette packet curving towards the gutter.

In the silence left by the car his footsteps echo from peeling walls and closed shutters, from hoardings with faded posters for toothpaste, tobacco, tyres.

Behind him a restaurant, its name pulsing in three languages, three colours.

In the lamplight at the corner a parked cluster of cyclos. Brakes on and drivers sleeping, curled in the passenger seats.

He moves on.

A departure that cannot be other than a departure. To turn, to go back—that is not his nature.

And her. She seems to be listening to the words being said, her eyes on the speaker. Lost in thought she takes a fried cricket from the plate, bites into it, careful of the smooth pink surface of her lipstick. A leg breaks from the insect's body and drops unnoticed.

She looks over her shoulder for a moment. Her neck, her high red collar. Her skin seems to glisten when she turns her head. Their respective movements, and her painted eyelashes which blink once and then twice before smiling at the others round the table. Spiralling wreaths of cigarette smoke. The insect's leg in her lap.

postlude

Sar later called himself Pol Pot and led the 1975 Khmer Rouge revolution in which 1.7 million people lost their lives. He died in 1998, still fleeing justice.

Sary fell out of favour in 1958 and joined the opposition to Prince Sihanouk. He was assassinated in exile in 1962.

Somaly had a daughter by Sary in 1956 and was then (along with another pregnant lover) installed in his home as his concubine. She later emigrated to the United States, where she still lives.

Author's Thanks

A novel is rarely the work of one individual and the present one is no exception. I should particularly like to thank (for conversations, reading support, words and deeds):

Pernilla Ahlsén, David Chandler, Nina Eidem, Richard Herold, Ulf Krook, Ida Linde, Zabbar Neang, Milton Osborne, Nhek Sarin, Steve Sem-Sandberg, Philip Short, Alexander Skantze, Kim Son, Sara Stridsberg, Jenny Teng and Emma Warg.

I have also, both intentionally and unintentionally, gathered inspiration (and the odd word here and there) from other works of literature. I am grateful to the authors.

PUSHKIN PRESS

Pushkin Press was founded in 1997, and publishes novels, essays, memoirs, children's books—everything from timeless classics to the urgent and contemporary.

Our books represent exciting, high-quality writing from around the world: we publish some of the twentieth century's most widely acclaimed, brilliant authors such as Stefan Zweig, Marcel Aymé, Antal Szerb, Paul Morand and Yasushi Inoue, as well as compelling and award-winning contemporary writers, including Andrés Neuman, Edith Pearlman and Ryu Murakami.

Pushkin Press publishes the world's best stories, to be read and read again. Here are just some of the titles from our long and varied list. For more amazing stories, visit www.pushkinpress.com.

———

THE SPECTRE OF ALEXANDER WOLF

GAITO GAZDANOV

'A mesmerising work of literature' Antony Beevor

BINOCULAR VISION

EDITH PEARLMAN

'A genius of the short story' Mark Lawson, *Guardian*

TRAVELLER OF THE CENTURY

ANDRÉS NEUMAN

'A beautiful, accomplished novel: as ambitious as it is generous, as moving as it is smart' Juan Gabriel Vásquez, *Guardian*

BEWARE OF PITY

STEFAN ZWEIG

'Zweig's fictional masterpiece' *Guardian*

THE WORLD OF YESTERDAY
STEFAN ZWEIG

'*The World of Yesterday* is one of the greatest memoirs of the twentieth century, as perfect in its evocation of the world Zweig loved, as it
is in its portrayal of how that world was destroyed' David Hare

JOURNEY BY MOONLIGHT
ANTAL SZERB

'Just divine… makes you imagine the author has had private access to your own soul' Nicholas Lezard, *Guardian*

BONITA AVENUE
PETER BUWALDA

'One wild ride: a swirling helix of a family saga… a new writer as toe-curling as
early Roth, as roomy as Franzen and as caustic as Houellebecq' *Sunday Telegraph*

THE PARROTS
FILIPPO BOLOGNA

'A five-star satire on literary vanity… a wonderful, surprising novel' *Metro*

I WAS JACK MORTIMER
ALEXANDER LERNET-HOLENIA

'Terrific… a truly clever, rather wonderful book that both plays
with and defies genre' Eileen Battersby, *Irish Times*

SONG FOR AN APPROACHING STORM
PETER FRÖBERG IDLING

'Beautifully evocative… a must-read novel' *Daily Mail*

THE RABBIT BACK LITERATURE SOCIETY
PASI ILMARI JÄÄSKELÄINEN

'Wonderfully knotty… a very grown-up fantasy masquerading as
quirky fable. Unexpected, thrilling and absurd' *Sunday Telegraph*

RED LOVE: THE STORY OF AN EAST GERMAN FAMILY
MAXIM LEO

'Beautiful and supremely touching… an unbearably poignant
description of a world that no longer exists' *Sunday Telegraph*

COIN LOCKER BABIES

RYU MURAKAMI

'A fascinating peek into the weirdness of contemporary Japan' Oliver Stone

TALKING TO OURSELVES

ANDRÉS NEUMAN

'This is writing of a quality rarely encountered… when you read Neuman's beautiful novel, you realise a very high bar has been set' *Guardian*

CLOSE TO THE MACHINE

ELLEN ULLMAN

'Astonishing… impossible to put down' *San Francisco Chronicle*

MARCEL

ERWIN MORTIER

'Aspiring novelists will be hard pressed to achieve this quality' *Time Out*

JOURNEY INTO THE PAST

STEFAN ZWEIG

'Lucid, tender, powerful and compelling' *Independent*

POPULAR HITS OF THE SHOWA ERA

RYU MURAKAMI

'One of the funniest and strangest gang wars in recent literature' *Booklist*

LETTER FROM AN UNKNOWN WOMAN AND OTHER STORIES

STEFAN ZWEIG

'Zweig's time of oblivion is over for good… it's good to have him back' Salman Rushdie

ONE NIGHT, MARKOVITCH

AYELET GUNDAR-GOSHEN

'A remarkable first novel, trenchant and full of love, highly impressive in its maturity and wisdom' Eshkol Nevo

MY FELLOW SKIN

ERWIN MORTIER

'A Bildungsroman which is related to much European literature from Proust and Mann onwards… peculiarly unforgettable' AS Byatt, *Guardian*